Waves of Desire

Secrets of the Seas
Book 1

Lauren Everly

ARE YOU SIGNED UP FOR DRAGONBLADE'S BLOG?

You'll get the latest news and information on exclusive giveaways, exclusive excerpts, coming releases, sales, free books, cover reveals and more.

Check out our complete list of authors, too!

No spam, no junk. That's a promise!

Sign Up Here

www.dragonbladepublishing.com

Dearest Reader;

Thank you for your support of a small press. At Dragonblade Publishing, we strive to bring you the highest quality Historical Romance from some of the best authors in the business. Without your support, there is no 'us', so we sincerely hope you adore these stories and find some new favorite authors along the way.

Happy Reading!

CEO, Dragonblade Publishing

Dedication

For Mom, who has never stopped loving me, never stopped believing in me. Every word of this book is yours as much as it is mine.

Acknowledgments

My sincere thanks to Kathryn Le Veque and Dragonblade for offering a home to the *Secrets of the Seas* series. To Audrey Salo, my editor for this book, thank you for your excitement and enthusiasm for this story. Natalie Sowa and the incredible Dragonblade design team, thank you for creating the most breathtaking cover I could have ever imagined. I still get goosebumps every time I look at it.

To my brilliant and fearless agent, Christina Miller at Nancy Yost Literary Agency: I truly don't have enough words to express my gratitude. You have championed my work and my characters with such fierce loyalty that it gave me courage and motivation to keep going. You've read these pages more times than either of us will admit, and helped me make this book the very best version of itself. The unwavering love you hold for Samantha and Christian has meant the world to me.

To my dear friend and fellow romance author, Livy Hart—thank you for being my anchor and my comic relief all at once. You read my messy drafts, cheered me on when I couldn't see the finish line, and loved my characters as fiercely as your own. Your humor, wisdom, and perfectly timed sarcasm carried me through the hard days and made the good ones even brighter. I couldn't have done this without you. My writing group, the Llamasquad, thank you for helping me navigate the wild world of publishing and for being my people—y'all know who you are! To my best friend, Brooke, your unfailing support has never gone unnoticed. I'm so grateful to have you in my corner. And to my AMM mentee, Michelle Asmara, thank you for celebrating every book milestone with such infectious joy.

Most importantly, to my family—you are the heart of everything I do. To my handsome husband, David, you're my real-life hero and the blueprint for every brave and passionate gentleman I write. Thank you for sweeping me off my feet time and again (and for your patience as I stared off into space plotting my next scene instead of answering your questions.) To my kids, for putting up with "Mom's writing time," thank you for your unconditional love.

To my parents, especially Mom—my biggest cheerleader and the heart behind everything I've written—thank you for believing in me from the very beginning. You've celebrated every milestone and bit of good news with the same joy and pride as if it were your own dream coming true. You're the reason I fell in love with historical romance (thanks to those Johanna Lindsey novels I secretly "borrowed" as a teen) so in a way, this story is all your fault.

To my sisters—Chelse, Nicole, and Kandace—and my lovely cousin Amy, for filling our group texts with love, laughter, and constant encouragement. Chelse, in particular, who reads romance with a passion that rivals my own—thank you for your sharp insight and spot-on suggestions.

To my enthusiastically proud grandparents, who share my news with every stranger they meet (Grammie, please skip the steamy parts!), and to my in-laws, whose home in Savannah inspired this book during a quiet morning walk along the river. I also want to mention Mrs. Rook, my high school creative writing teacher, whose prediction that I'd one day be published inspired me to keep writing.

Of course, to all my readers, whose excitement, messages, and love for this story make it all worthwhile—thank you from the bottom of my heart.

And above all, I give thanks to God, who is my constant source of strength, grace, and peace. His hand has guided my path and sustained me through every season of this journey. I am endlessly blessed by His faithfulness, His timing, and the way He weaves purpose into every step I take.

Chapter One

June 11th, 1803
Somewhere on the Atlantic coast of Florida

SAMANTHA'S FINGERTIPS SKIMMED across the jagged edge of a worn shell and a piece crumbled beneath her thumb. With lips pulled tight, she tossed her find back into the surf.

Not quite right.

The screech of a seagull echoed in the distance and Samantha tucked a stray copper curl under her wide-brimmed hat. She scanned the glistening sand where the waves broke.

There.

Her bare toes curled into soft sand. The tines of a sizable shell jutted into view as crystal-blue water pulled back from the beach. A wave crashed toward her and she strode into the sea. When she bent to pluck her prize from its hiding spot, foam swirled around her knees, soaking her breeches, but her fingers continued their search.

A laugh bubbled forth when her palm brushed a rigid mass. She pried the shell loose, shaking sand away in the rushing water before lifting it into view. Twice the size of her hand, the conch's pink interior reflected the bright glare of the sun. A perfect specimen.

Yes. It would do.

Samantha's pulse beat a happy tune when she slipped the shell into the leather bag tied at her belt. She stayed in place, letting her feet sink deep into the cool sand. Another wave swept in and she stared out at the horizon. A subtle urge to dive into the temperate water tugged at her while the sparkle of sunlight dancing across the water called to her soul.

"Captain?"

The voice snapped her from the ocean's trance and she turned toward the shore. Griff, her first mate, gestured at the sun. "She'll start setting soon. Best be on our way."

She nodded and trudged to dry ground to join her men. They hiked together to the single longboat resting on the beach. Beyond it, the *Siren's* silhouette loomed from where she anchored offshore and Samantha's heart swelled with pride at the fine figure the brigantine cut on the water. Two masts thrust into the sky with canvas sails hanging slack. A crisp line of white paint ran below the main deck to hide a dozen cannon hatches.

Her ship.

Well, for this trip at least.

Her gaze slid back to Griff as he heaved the boat into the surf. His grey beard was trimmed short and weathered wrinkles spread from the corners of his eyes. Most days, the *Siren* was his ship.

She splashed into the water and vaulted into the small boat. The men picked up their oars and they glided into the calm waters of the bay.

Once Samantha's feet landed on the solid planks of the *Siren's* deck, she strode to the stairs of the quarterdeck. Griff followed her up to the helm. Puffy white clouds had sprung from the horizon to their south and she grinned.

"Looks like the winds will be in our favor tonight."

He followed her gaze and nodded. Though the weight of the shell at her belt begged to be added to her collection, she brushed aside the need. She needed to make a good impression. Her little jaunt to shore had wasted precious time and risen more than a few brows. Time to prove to the men—at least the new ones who hadn't spent the last decade with her underfoot—she wasn't just a wealthy brat indulging in a passing whim.

Though she'd graced the decks of her uncle's fleet since she could walk, no one on the crew would have expected her to be allowed to sail in command. No matter how many times she'd voiced her wish to, they'd always laughed it off. Women didn't sail—not as a profession—and they definitely did not captain ships.

This trip might be her one chance to show she deserved a spot captaining in the fleet. So far, everything had gone as planned. Even better? A decent chance they would arrive back in Savannah early. A good impression, indeed. Her lips tugged up.

A few quick steps and she stood at the ship's wheel. Her hand settled on one of the worn spokes. "Ready the sails and raise the anchor."

Her command spurred the crew into action. The sails unfurled almost instantaneously and she bit back a wry smile. Griff's crew—her crew—worked like a well-oiled machine, ready to be on the move at a moment's notice. They had already prepared the ship to sail while she'd been ashore. Not a coincidence. They'd been trained to be the best, and that meant one thing.

Never be caught unawares.

When the anchor lifted from the sea bed, her fingers vibrated with the gentle thrum of freedom running through the ship's hull. A tepid breeze flitted around her face as the sails caught the wind and pushed them out to sea. Soon, she had to press her hat to her head while the *Siren* sliced through the water.

Each subtle movement of her hand brought the ship under her control and she closed her eyes, taking in each groan from beneath her feet, each slap of rigging against the sails above. The ship sang to her, and little by little, Samantha gave herself over to the song. Until she and the ship were one.

Her smile broke free. This was what she was made for.

The minutes stretched into the better part of an hour as she stood still, content to listen. Once they were well on course, she turned to Griff. "You take her until supper." It was still such a foreign thing to speak down to him. He'd been "Captain" to her for as long as she could remember.

He took the wheel, his hands sliding into grooves worn by a thousand hours beneath his calloused fingers and a twinge of guilt pricked at her as he stared out over the rolling sea. Though he had accepted his temporary demotion with grace, part of him must be rankled. Who wouldn't be? With a heavy swallow, she walked away.

In her cabin, Samantha stepped over a pile of dirty laundry and went straight to the bookcase built into the wall. An eclectic collection of shells lined one railed shelf. She hefted the conch from her pouch and set it in the middle of the others.

Perfect.

She turned to her desk and slid open a drawer. Nimble fingers lifted the false bottom out, and she pulled a worn scrap of parchment free. Her fingers traced the faded lines of ink before she folded it and returned to the shelf. She flipped the conch over and slid the folded paper into the smooth pink of its spiral. A lump of pliable wax lay inside the drawer and she pressed it to the shell's opening.

When all the gaps were covered, she gave the conch a good shake. The map remained secure.

Safe.

Just as her uncle had instructed when he gave it to her before this voyage.

Samantha sank into the chair at her desk and pushed aside a stack of papers. Her ledger laid open and she pulled it in front of her. She frowned. Where was her quill? Another flurry of papers, and she pulled it free. Her hair stuck to her neck in the still air and she sighed. Though she yearned to go back above and let the breeze cool her, there were numbers to be run.

Her uncle expected an accurate account of the cargo they'd picked up in Nassau. A mostly legal run, so nothing too exciting. Her quill tapped the page. Barrels of rum, bolts of cotton, and most importantly, sugar. Those crates held heavy bars of gold nestled among the fine white crystals.

A smile tugged the corners of her lips.

Uncle Henry owned one of the biggest shipping companies in the country. His merchant ships ran up and down the coast, ferrying in goods from the West Indies and storing them in his multitudes of warehouses.

All a cover.

Behind the shield of his shipping empire, her uncle ran another operation. One in which he was known as Captain Remington, a notorious gentleman pirate. Beneath the benign facade of merchant ships, his fleet hid extra guns, men trained in combat, and always an empty cargo hold to stash smuggled—or stolen—goods.

Shouts above chased the smile from Samantha's face and she jumped to her feet. Boots. Where were the blasted things? With a curse, she dug through the piles on the floor. She should have worn them on her excursion instead of going barefoot.

After wasting a full minute, she found them and tugged them on before racing up to the deck.

"Ship ahoy!"

Samantha's eyes narrowed. This far off the trade route, there should be no other traffic. When she climbed up to the quarterdeck, Griff's stony face confirmed her fears.

"Who is it?"

He handed her the spyglass and she whipped it to her eye. When she focused on the approaching frigate's flag, a chill ran up her spine. The fifteen stars of the American flag flapped in the wind, but below it, a small flag bearing the Georgian seal garnered her full attention. None of the governor's ships would stray this far off their route.

Unless they were pirate hunters.

"Damn," she muttered.

"What are your orders, Captain?"

Griff emphasized her title, a clear message for her to choose wisely. The rest of the crew gathered near and fixed expectant gazes on her. The wise choice would be to stand down and fabricate a story to explain their location. Samantha turned back to the sea and took another look. Her fingers clenched around the spyglass when she zeroed in on the figure standing on the forecastle of the approaching ship.

Tall and handsome in his blue uniform.

And very familiar. She didn't need to look at the nameplate at the bow to know the ship's name. The *USS Falcon*.

"It's Lieutenant Thompson."

Griff yanked the glass and stared through it for a long moment. His lips drew into a thin line. "Insufferable cur."

Samantha had to agree. Christian Thompson had recently arrived in Savannah with the lofty ambition of wiping out the pirate trade. And damn him if he wasn't doing a good job at it. In less than three months, the young lieutenant had captured four ships. Every vessel that sailed in and out of the harbor now passed by the crow-picked skeletons hanging on Cockspur Island.

A clear—if not crude—warning by the lieutenant himself. Go pirating and meet the noose.

"Captain?"

Griff shifted his position to stand between her and the fast-approaching ship. The protective moment was not lost on her. Just as she'd inspected their visitors, the lieutenant would have his own spyglass trained on them. Her uncle's number one rule at sea? Do not be recognized.

Ever.

Thompson had been a constant irritation the last few months. Late-night runs had to be cancelled, cargos better hidden—which took time and money, and one of their best partners had pulled out of Savannah because of the added risk. Not to mention the men who had been hanged. None of their own men, of course, but comrades in the trade nonetheless.

Samantha squared her shoulders. Griff and his crew were among her uncle's finest. Today, Thompson was merely an annoyance. One that could be dealt with. If she returned to shore with a win over Thompson, Uncle Henry couldn't say she wasn't fit to captain. After all, how could one top besting a US Navy ship?

She faced her crew. "I think it's time Lieutenant Thompson got a taste of his own medicine."

A gleam flashed through Griff's eyes even as he pressed his lips together in a disapproving line. "Aye, Captain." He lowered his voice and leaned close. "Your uncle would not approve. Are you sure you want to do this?"

Samantha gave a curt nod while a burst of adrenaline coursed through her veins.

Her first fight as a pirate.

"I hope you understand I'll be stepping back to my position."

Her shoulders dropped. Not her fight after all. Her uncle had made it clear, if there were trouble, Griff would be back in charge. Though a retort formed on her lips, the *Falcon* had gotten close enough for Samantha to hear the wind whistling through her sails. No time to argue.

She bit her tongue and dipped her head. "Of course, Captain."

With those words, the leadership seamlessly transferred over.

Griff turned. "Alright, men. Shall we show the lieutenant what happens when he stirs up a hornet's nest—or should I say, pirate's nest?"

A soft cheer rose from the crew.

"You know the drill."

A flurry of activity followed and Samantha's heart filled with pride. Under the scrutiny of the approaching ship, the preparations would seem benign. Ropes were fastened and coiled while conveniently placed crates of weapons were unlocked. The men who would fight pulled out leather half masks. They turned their backs to the *Falcon* and secured the masks tightly.

Griff always said there was something about being locked in battle with another man that had a way of etching an opponent's face into one's mind. Inconvenient for a pirate wanting to stay anonymous. Every crew member was issued a mask the day he signed into her uncle's service and risked punishment if he were ever found without it on his person. The thin leather didn't impede vision or movement while disguising the upper facial features enough to escape identity.

Griff was the only one who kept his face clear. A risk. But one he would need to take the lieutenant by surprise. It just meant he'd have to lay low and avoid town for a while. He coughed and gave Samantha a pointed look. "Best get below. And stay down there until it's over."

No.

She opened her mouth to say so and he shook his head. "That's an order, Miss Warstein."

With a scowl, Samantha jumped down to the deck. Before she approached the door to her cabin, she caught a glimpse of the lieutenant—and the frown on his face as he steered his ship close.

She dashed inside and locked the door behind her before heading to a window. With a flick of her fingers, she unlatched it and pushed it open a crack. The lieutenant's baritone voice floated over her.

"Ho there. State your business."

"Just passing through after picking up cargo," Griff answered without missing a beat.

"And why have you ventured so far off the trade route?"

"I could ask the same of you."

Silence fell save for the slap of waves trapped between the two ships. Samantha bit back a laugh as she imagined the look on the lieutenant's face.

"We patrol these waters on behalf of the governor."

"Yet you fly the Georgian seal. Curious, as last I checked, we are off the coast of Florida." A mocking tone had entered Griff's voice.

"I assure you, we have every right to be here. You, on the other hand . . ." The lieutenant's voice trailed off. "I trust you understand we will need to board your ship and conduct an inspection. If all is in order, you'll be free to go."

More silence. And then Griff's voice. "I'm afraid that won't be possible."

Lieutenant Thompson cleared his throat. "Excuse me?"

Samantha held her breath, waiting for the command.

"Now!"

The men above her exploded into action, and shouts came from both decks. Muffled thumps confirmed her crew had begun to swing to the offending ship. The clank of steel followed and Samantha craned her neck to catch a glimpse of the action.

A view of wood planks covered with a fine mist of sea spray greeted her. She couldn't see a damn thing.

"Drat."

Her gaze flitted between the window and her closed door while her fists clenched at her side. To hell with Griff's orders. If she stayed below, she would miss the whole thing. She grabbed her mask from the corner of her desk and ran her fingertips over the supple black leather. She'd never had to use it before. Never thought she'd have the chance to. It would cover her from forehead to nose, enough to shield her identity.

The shouts outside intensified and her pulse quickened. Just a quick peek. No one would know.

She tied the mask on and scooped up a handful of hairpins. With practiced fingers, she twisted her hair atop her head and stabbed the pins in. On her way out, she snatched her rapier—the one thing she never misplaced—from its rack on the wall. Once on deck, she pressed her hat low and edged around the mainmast.

Her heart caught.

Even with the element of surprise on their side, her crew struggled. A flash of blue caught her eye as the lieutenant sent one of her men careening to the deck. Her stomach clenched into a hard knot when the man didn't move. Griff turned with a snarl and rushed forward.

As the two men fought, Samantha's throat seized. Though Griff was one of her uncle's most talented fighters, the young lieutenant possessed more stamina and strength. When the fight turned in Thompson's favor, she dragged her eyes away.

Panic clawed at her gut. If the lieutenant overtook Griff, the battle would be lost. And they would all face the noose.

Her hand tightened on the hilt of her rapier. Not if she could help it. Her uncle hadn't hired the best swordsmen in America to teach her for nothing.

She dashed from her hiding place and grabbed a rope hanging from the main yard. Twisting the oiled cords in her hands, she leaped from the railing and the thrill of weightlessness grabbed at her stomach.

Her boots hit the *Falcon's* deck with a thump and she dropped the rope, yanking her rapier free. The battle raged around her with groups of men locked in combat. Samantha twisted around the fighting pairs and launched over a prone body. She found the lieutenant's blue coat near the helm and sprinted that way. *Please don't be too late.*

She took the stairs two at a time and burst onto the quarter-deck where Lieutenant Thompson's sword gleamed in the sunlight. Griff stood doubled over, clutching his blood-soaked side, sword hanging to the ground. With no time to prepare herself, Samantha flew between the men with her own blade raised.

Clang!

The blow reverberated up her arm in a thousand shards of hot pain, and she jumped out of reach before the lieutenant could strike again.

His eyes narrowed on her and he barked out a laugh. "Sent in a boy to do a man's work did they?"

She held her stance. Sweat dripped down the Lieutenant's forehead and his broad shoulders heaved with each breath.

Good.

He lunged and she darted to the side. When he cut, she parried. Their feet began to glide across the deck in a deadly dance.

Keep him moving.

Don't let him regain his breath.

Her instructor's words rang loud and clear in her ears.

She pressed forward and met his blade in a bold thrust. Dark green eyes widened a fraction before he swung back at her.

Though exhausted, he still made a formidable opponent. But what Samantha lacked in strength, she made up for in speed.

The lieutenant grunted when she advanced, deflecting her cuts as they came.

Right. Left. Back.

She read his eyes to determine his next move, given away by a quick glance before his blade followed.

And he scowled.

He wasn't used to losing.

"Too ugly to show your face, boy?"

She ignored the taunt and sidestepped the heavy blow that came with it.

Don't engage.

The clanging and shouting around her faded while she focused on her opponent. Perspiration dampened her brow as she fought to maintain her position. Good God, he was good. His footwork rivaled her own as they circled each other.

"Enough," he growled. He moved to place the setting sun in her eyes and rained several blows on her in quick succession. Each step she took back brought her closer to the stairs—and her defeat. The blows came so fast, she had no choice but to maintain defense.

He stopped a cut mid-air and somehow turned it into a vicious thrust at her belly. She leaped back as the blade whistled a hair's breadth from her torso. The wild movement sent her hat flying and her hair tumbled free, pins scattering on the deck. The lieutenant's eyes went wide and he sucked in a breath.

React!

She dove forward in his moment of confusion and met his blade. As her steel slid toward his body, he recovered and twisted his sword to stop her advance.

So close.

Before she could pull away, he used his height to his advantage and bore down on her. Samantha gritted her teeth and pushed back. Her arm began to shake. *No . . . focus!*

"So, wench, you've chosen to align yourself with filth?" He murmured the words from above her while a dark glint flashed through his eyes.

Do. Not. Engage.

Heat spread through her veins and her vision wavered. *Use your anger.*

With a guttural cry, she used up her wildcard. A move her instructor had aptly named *"Last Chance."* She grabbed her hilt with her free hand and threw all her strength into twisting the blade in a sharp motion. Before he could compensate, she jerked the lieutenant's sword free from his compromised grasp.

It clattered to the deck and she whipped the tip of her rapier to his neck.

"That's Captain to you." She pressed the sharp steel into the space below his Adam's apple. "Now call off your men."

Chapter Two

S AMANTHA'S LUNGS BURNED and her arm threatened to give out. But she held her blade steady until the lieutenant shouted the order to stand down. One by one, swords dropped to the deck and her men gathered the defeated crew together.

The young lieutenant kept his gaze locked on her through it all. Chestnut curls had come loose from his tie and clung to his face while gold-flecked green eyes bore into her.

If looks could kill . . .

She swallowed and broke the eye contact when two of her men tied his hands behind his back. Sheathing her sword, she surveyed the main deck. Her gaze landed on a dead man on the main deck and she pivoted away. But two more bodies lay within her sight and bile burned a path up her throat.

Griff limped over to her. "Your orders, Captain?" His eyes gleamed with an emotion she couldn't place. And he'd accentuated the title *captain* as if it were an insult. Was he angry?

She drew in a breath. "Bring the wounded back to the ship. That includes you. The rest of you, take anything of value from our new friends."

Bending, she retrieved her hat and ignored the weight of the lieutenant's eyes on her back. Some of her crew descended into the ship to scout out what they could, while others gathered the weapons laying scattered across the *Falcon's* deck. When the last of the crates and barrels were shuttled over to the *Siren*, she raised her face to the sails, glowing with the orange hues of sunset.

"Bring them down."

A few men scurried up the masts, daggers clutched between their teeth. Each slash of ropes and canvas made her flinch. It could easily have been her ship receiving this treatment. She could order their spare sails dumped into the sea. But that would truly cripple the *Falcon*, and she wasn't heartless. It would take them half a day to refit the sails and her crew would be nearly back to Savannah by then.

One of her men approached her. "The lieutenant's quarters are locked, Capt'n."

She swiveled to face Lieutenant Thompson, who still glared at her. His gaze slid down to her feet and back to her face. A prickle of unease swept through her. It was as if he could see right through her mask. She swallowed. Nonsense.

"Search his pockets." Her voice cracked and she straightened her spine when his gaze sharpened.

When a key was produced, she arched a brow. "Lead the way, Lieutenant."

He growled his dissent in the back of his throat, but one of her men pressed a dagger between his shoulders and he lurched into motion. They descended the stairs to the main deck and came to a stop in front of an ornately carved door below the quarterdeck. She nodded to the sailor with the key. He slid it into the lock and the door swung open.

Samantha waved the lieutenant through. "After you."

Her eyes roamed his quarters and she blinked. Not a single item out of place.

"Secure him to the chair." She pointed toward his desk, immaculate and polished to a sheen, and her men dragged him over.

When he was bound, she strolled around the room. Her fingertips drifted across the spines of nautical books and charts housed in his bookshelf. Crisp sheets, folded in perfect creases, draped his bed. She opened his wardrobe and a row of neatly starched uniforms greeted her. Her hand lingered on a pair of soft white breeches and heat blossomed on her cheeks at the thought of how this very fabric would stretch tight over his muscles.

She yanked the hand back. "I must say, Lieutenant, I'm dismayed to find little of value here."

He pressed his lips together and Samantha drifted to his desk. She slid a drawer open and riffled through a stack of parchment. A dagger with a ruby embedded in the hilt lay beneath the papers and she flipped it through her fingers.

"Is this where you slit my throat with my own blade?"

Her head fell back and she laughed, the sound echoing through the chamber. She pocketed the dagger and closed the space between them. "My dear lieutenant, what a vivid imagination you possess."

Her hand lifted to his face and she stroked his jawline, rough stubble grazing her palm and sending a prickling heat up her arm. "I'm sorry to disappoint you, but we are much less barbaric than that."

He jerked from her touch and she glanced down at the desk. A wrinkle marred the map laid out on it, prompting her to reach out and smooth it. When her fingers brushed the heft of a compass, his eyes darkened.

Something of value.

She lifted it and examined the tarnished brass with a frown. Quite plain for a commanding lieutenant. With a toss, it sailed into the air and the corded muscles in his forearms bunched. Definitely valuable to him, though.

A worn inscription scrawled across the back:

E.L. Thompson
1701

An antique.

"Leave it. It's worthless to you."

She clenched her fingers around it. "I rather like it."

With a smug smile, she pivoted and walked away. The chair rattled as he fought his bonds.

"You'll pay for this, wench." Disgust dripped from his words.

Her teeth clenched at the insult, and she turned back to him.

With a smirk, she waved the compass in front of her. "On the contrary. It looks like you're the one who's paid, Lieutenant."

With a quick nod from her, the man closest to Lieutenant Thompson slammed the hilt of his sword against the Lieutenant's temple. He slumped forward and she left the room.

Activity had ceased on the main deck and most of her men were back aboard the *Siren*, preparing her to sail. Griff had not returned and stood near the group of men tied up on the *Falcon's* deck. One man wore a nicer uniform than the rest. The first officer.

He was young, with dark sandy blonde hair tied in a messy queue. Not as tall, or muscular, as the lieutenant. Not that that mattered. She shook her head and approached him.

"Did you kill him?" He blurted the words out when she came to a stop in front of him. His blue eyes shone bright, and he shifted from foot to foot.

"Though he expected me to slit his throat, I'm sorry to have disappointed him."

His face softened while his shoulders slumped. "Thank you."

She shrugged and her knee dropped to the deck as she reached for his boot. When her fingers brushed his calf, he stiffened. The hilt of a dagger poked above the opening of his boot and she plucked it free.

"You should do a better job hiding your weapon." Color rose to his cheeks while she twirled the blade. "Now, promise you'll be good and won't try to do anything heroic?"

His brows pressed together and she pressed the blade to the ropes binding him. When they fell away, he stood still. She flipped the blade around and handed it to him. By the time he released half his men, her ship would be well out of cannon range.

She gave a little curtsy. "Please forgive me for saying this, but I hope we never meet again."

He didn't answer and she turned to follow Griff to the railing.

"Captain?"

She swiveled back with a raised brow.

"You do know, he'll make you wish you'd killed him?"

She laughed. "I look forward to it."

Once Samantha's boots landed on the *Siren*, her shoulders curved inward. Being on the *Falcon*, facing the lieutenant had taken more out of her than she could have ever expected. She fought to take normal breaths as Griff gave the order to sail and took his place at the helm. Once the wind filled the sails, she approached him.

He stared out to sea. "You disobeyed a direct order."

"What was I supposed to do? Let him kill you?" Her nails bit into the tender skin of her palms.

"If it came down to it, yes."

"Griff, if I hadn't stepped in when I did, you'd be dead, and the rest of us would be prisoners."

He swung to face her. "What is the penalty for not heeding a captain's orders?"

Samantha's throat went dry. "Twenty lashes." Griff stared down at her and she pushed the toe of her boot against the deck. "If that's what this is about, I will gladly take them."

She'd never been allowed to witness the infrequent but brutal punishments. But by God, if that's what it took to earn respect, she would take a hundred.

"Your uncle would have my skin if I harmed you. Whenever you've sailed under me, I've never shown you any special favor. How do you think this looks to the other men? This little game of yours is over, Miss Warstein. For the rest of this trip, you will address me as your captain."

Coldness laced his words and she took a step back. "I did what I had to. Don't you dare tell me you wouldn't have done the same."

A muscle ticked in his jaw and he pointed to the main deck, where two bodies lay draped in spare sails.

Samantha blanched.

Those men had died because of her choice.

"The sea is no place for a woman. No matter what your uncle thinks. I was foolish to agree to go along with his request."

Samantha dragged her eyes from the felled men and faced Griff. "I take responsibility for their deaths and will make sure their families are taken care of. They won't want for a thing."

His fingers tightened on the wheel and he pressed his eyes closed. "The responsibility is mine alone. I allowed the raid and they died under my command."

Her gaze dropped to where his bloodied shirt stuck to the gash in his side. "You need to bandage that, Captain."

"'Tis but a scratch." He let out a long sigh. "While I appreciate your heroics today, it was a reckless decision. That very well could be your body lying there."

It was as close to a thank you as she would get. She pulled her shoulders back. "It was the right choice."

"We will let your uncle make that call. You are dismissed."

Samantha wanted to keep arguing, but several of the men had drawn near with ears conveniently turned their way. She swallowed her pride. "Yes, sir."

Head held high, she retreated to her cabin. The door slammed behind her with a loud bang and she stalked to the window. Reckless indeed.

She'd turned the tide to win the fight and Griff responded by demoting her. A growl rumbled in the back of her throat and she kicked at a rumpled blanket at her feet. She'd bested Lieutenant Thompson. A feared and hated pirate hunter. No one else could say the same.

Even when she did everything right, it wasn't good enough.

The sea is no place for a woman.

How many times had she heard those words? They made her skin crawl. Made her want to throw things.

Just because she'd been born the fairer sex, everyone had been loath to give her the chance to prove herself. Even though she'd worked as hard as the other sailors. She'd fought tooth and nail to get her uncle to allow her this practice run. It had taken years of pleading her case, of proving herself capable on the decks, before he took her seriously. Griff called it a game. This was her life.

She strode to the open window with a scowl. Surely, the great lieutenant hadn't had trouble getting his foot in the door. Everyone worshiped the ground he walked on. One of the youngest lieutenants, they'd entrusted him with a coveted frigate—a ship usually reserved for seasoned officers. With the navy's real captains off fighting the war in Tripoli, the governor had seen fit to hand the ship to a wealthy Yankee who had yet to earn such status.

Now she really wanted to throw something. She could probably command his ship as well as he could. Maybe even better. But she was a woman. So, no one would let her see that potential.

Her fingers gripped the smooth wood on the windowsill and her vision wavered. Would she ever gain respect? Even if she got her own ship, her own crew, people would still scoff at her. Never mind there had been great female pirates a century before. Had the legendary Caribbean pirate Anne Bonny faced the same disillusionment as she had?

Leaning into the warm night air, she closed her eyes. She'd thought she had it all figured out. Do a good job, gain her uncle's approval, captain her own ship. Take control of her destiny. Earlier, it had seemed so close. Now, impossibly far away. She'd lost her course. Like a ship with no sails adrift at sea, waiting for help that would never come.

Her eyes jerked open. Being melodramatic wouldn't solve anything. Still, a heavy weight pressed on her shoulders. On shore, she had no one she could relate to. Even her best friend, Abigail, had no inkling of Samantha's dreams. On the ship, her crew followed her directions, but she was the boss's niece. They didn't have a choice.

God, was she being naive? Did she have any chance at all? Would she ever captain her own ship?

She took a deep breath. No need to get worked up about it.

Not until she spoke with her uncle.

Besides, she had a bigger problem.

Arms crossed, she stared out at the silhouette of the *Falcon* as it grew smaller on the horizon. Her hand dipped into her pocket to touch the warm brass there. With a grimace, she pulled the compass free and set it next to her prize conch. It had been a foolish move, to take something of sentimental value from the lieutenant. In the silence of the cabin, her gut twisted as his first officer's words echoed in her mind.

He'll make you wish you'd killed him.

Caught up in the thrill of victory, she'd made a grave misstep. Stepping back, she closed the window and leaned her head against it. She'd broken an important rule: Never goad your enemy.

Chapter Three

"I SHOULD GROUND you."

The words hit Samantha like a punch to the gut.

"Uncle—"

He wagged a finger at her. "You'd cause a lot less damage if I forced you to stay ashore."

With him gone on a pirating run up north, she'd had a week after returning to Savannah to formulate her argument. Still, she hadn't expected Uncle Henry to call her into his study immediately after his return. So much for her hopes Griff wouldn't tell him everything. Samantha opened her mouth. Yet words failed her.

"What were you thinking?"

Taking a deep breath, she recited one of her memorized lines. "I did what was best. If I hadn't joined the fight, we'd all be locked up in prison, or worse."

She winced as his chair screeched back. He stood. "And whose fault is it that there was a fight in the first place? You should have known better and stood down. The ledgers were in order, they would have let you go."

"Don't tell me you're not happy we trounced Lieutenant Thompson. Besides, the men were itching for a fight after so many cargo runs."

Uncle Henry smoothed his grey mustache. "A good captain doesn't let his crew's emotions dictate his choices."

An icy barb pierced Samantha's heart and she lowered her head.

"Accept that you made an error and don't make it again. If

sailing is truly what you desire, you have much to learn."

"I'm sorry, Uncle."

"For now, you will do your part onshore. If I'm not mistaken, we have a ball to attend tonight."

Samantha groaned. "I'm not going."

His brows raised. "As mistress of this house, you will go. You've missed too many events lately and we don't need people talking."

She bit her tongue and he shook his head. "Trust me, Samantha, this is not news I wished to come home to today. One of my best captains injured and two men dead. But worse? By beating him, you've made the lieutenant more zealous in his quest to take down piracy. Word has it that in the week since you got back, he's garnered the governor's support for more ships. My men will be in much more danger each time they sail."

Samantha's heart dropped. She hadn't considered the ripple effect of her actions.

"I'm . . . I didn't think—"

Uncle Henry strode forward and placed an arm around her shoulders. "You're young, Samantha, only twenty-four. So many of these things must be learned through experience."

His face softened and some of the tension drained from her.

"Do we have to go tonight?"

He chuckled. "It will do you well to show your face in society. And I have an important meeting." He stayed by her side until they reached her bedroom door.

Inside her room, Samantha kicked off her slippers and crossed the plush Turkish rug to flop onto her bed. Sunlight reflected off pale blue walls, bathing her in mottled warmth. A humid gust blew through the open window to shift her curls against her damp face.

She wiped her forehead with the back of her hand and lifted a silent thanks that her uncle hadn't grounded her. Being ashore during the hot summer months would be the worst kind of punishment. She already missed the cool sea breezes and the wind in her hair. A week after coming ashore, she still couldn't sleep well without the gentle rock of a ship upon the waves.

Samantha stared at the ceiling and replayed her uncle's harsh remarks about a good captain not making choices based on his crew's emotions. In truth, the decision had not been made on behalf of her crew, but on her own excitement to finally witness a real battle. After years of hearing stories of the adventures her uncle's men partook in, how could anyone fault her for wanting a taste of the life that had always been dangled just beyond her reach?

Her throat burned anew. This adventure had cost two men their lives. It turned out a battle was not all glory. It was filled with sweat, blood, and despair. They'd won. But at what cost?

A soft knock on the door jostled her from her spiraling thoughts. Anna, her maid, entered, dwarfed by a monstrous heap of silk and lace. Samantha's ball gown. With a groan, she sat up.

Under the maid's skillful hands, Samantha's breeches and blouse were stripped off to be replaced with a chemise and horrendous stays followed by her petticoats and gown. The lace edging on her puffed sleeves clung to sweaty skin and Samantha forced herself to take a steadying breath. If she wasn't careful, she'd have a heat stroke before they even left.

Anna twisted and pinned Samantha's hair into a pretty mass atop her head and teased a few long curls out to cascade down her shoulders. The pale blue muslin of her gown bore a striking resemblance to her walls, gathered at her waist and flowing gracefully to the floor.

After clasping a long pearl necklace around Samantha's throat, Anna dusted powder across her cheeks and nose in a vain attempt to hide her freckles. Samantha ran a finger across her skin. The stubborn spots returned with a vengeance each time she sailed.

Anna stepped back and clapped her hands together. "Such an improvement!"

Samantha rolled her eyes. Her maid was forever trying to get her to dress "normally." It had become a common occurrence for her breeches to go missing on wash day. But Samantha could not be deterred and would continue to buy new pairs. Someday, Anna would give up. Until then, Samantha would continue to fund the discreet tailor who kept her legs free of restrictive skirts.

Samantha descended the curved staircase to meet her uncle in the great foyer. The soles of her satin shoes clicked across the gleaming marble floor while he guided her to the door and they made their way to the waiting carriage.

"You look enchanting, Samantha."

She nodded her thanks and let a footman help her up. After several minutes of arranging her skirts, she was finally able to sit. She folded gloved hands in her lap and stared out the window.

Great oak trees with moss-covered branches lined the road to the Hermitage Plantation. The great estate rose from its perch on a hill overlooking the river. Soon, they joined a line of carriages snaking up the palm-lined drive. Lanterns flickered from curved lampposts, chasing dusk's shadows away. When a footman opened the door to help her down, she couldn't help the burst of awe in her chest. Twice the size of the impressive Warstein Manor, the home could be likened to an ornate fortress.

Huge Grecian columns flanked the steps to the double front doors, and each upper room sported its own balcony. Bright light streamed from the windows and when they entered, thousands of candles twinkled from chandeliers and sconces. A crush of guests awaited in the ballroom, where a string band played. Every party Frenchman John Montelet and his beautiful young wife threw had the city socialites clamoring for invitations. If one wanted to rise among the ranks of the elite, Hermitage was the place to start.

Servants scuttled about carrying trays crowded with cham-pagne flutes. One turned her way and Samantha frowned. Not servants. Slaves. She pushed back the hot wave of anger that rushed through her. No surprise there. Her uncle remained one of only a few refusing to take part in the abhorrent practice in coastal Georgia.

"Samantha! Thank goodness you're here."

She turned to find Abigail Ross, her best friend, striding her way.

"Where have you been? I haven't heard from you in a fortnight."

Samantha smiled. "My uncle let me sail with his crew on a cargo run to the Bahamas." The lie flowed easily; after all, it was mostly true. Still, a heavy pit formed at the center of her gut.

Abigail shared everything with Samantha. Keeping secrets from her friend hurt. No matter how small the lie, it ate away at her. But who could she tell? Abigail hated the water, so she would never understand Samantha's passion. And if anyone found out her uncle's identity, they could lose everything.

Abigail shuddered. "How can you stand being on a boat that long? I get green just thinking of it. And think of the danger. What if you came across pirates?"

Samantha choked back a laugh. "Nonsense. You read too many stories."

Land folk always thought the worst of pirates. Never mind only a quarter century before, thousands of privateers had been lauded as they took out British supply ships and hurt the enemy's bottom line. Revolutionary War heroes, they were. These days, no one would care that her uncle only preyed on Spanish and French merchant ships or occasionally, rival pirates.

They would only care about one thing: the label "pirate."

Her friend took her arm and steered her to the wall. "It's not nonsense. Just yesterday, Lieutenant Thompson captured a pirate ship right outside the mouth of the river. There's to be a hanging in a few days."

Samantha's stomach clenched. Damn the man. Should have slit his throat after all. She shuddered. No.

Most pirates weren't so bad. At least not bad enough to deserve facing the noose. Most were too inept to do any real damage and stuck to smuggling goods up the river. Their little sloops and schooners were no match for massive merchantmen and brigantines loaded with valuable goods. Even with her uncle's well-armed fleet, blood was rarely spilled.

At the reminder of lives lost, she curled her fingers into a fist and forced a smile across her lips. "Well then, I have nothing to worry about with such a brave man patrolling the seas."

Abigail missed her sarcasm and let out a girlish sigh. "Brave *and* handsome. He's a perfect man. All that wealth he inherited, and yet he still chooses to serve his country." She pushed up on her tiptoes to look across the sea of people. "I do hope he comes tonight."

Samantha stiffened. He had better not. "I'm sure he has more important things to do."

A sad smile flitted across Abigail's face. "You're probably right. Saving the world is a busy job."

Samantha turned so her friend wouldn't see her scrunched nose. He'd served in the Quasi-War with France as an officer, and after returning, had been promoted to lieutenant. Governor Milledge had commissioned the *Falcon* and convinced Thompson to leave his estate in New York. *He shouldn't have come.* But he had, and no wonder. The chance to command a frigate at his age and rank would be a powerful draw for any man. If he succeeded, it could set him on a swift course to captaincy.

They stood in the shadows while the lovely notes of a violin drifted across the ballroom. Abigail used the time to point out which eligible gentlemen were in attendance and speculate if they would ask her to dance. Samantha let her gaze wander over the crowd, but none of the dandily dressed men caught her eye. They never did.

She let out a sigh and her friend leaned in. "Looking for someone in particular?"

"Very funny. You know how I feel about—"

"Yes, yes. I know. You can't picture yourself with any of them. Same as always. Come now, when you close your eyes and think of the perfect man, what do you see?"

Samantha groaned. "Why do you keep asking me that? The answer's never going to change."

Abigail grinned. "But you're wrong. One day, you'll see someone. And I'm going to keep asking until you do. Close your eyes and try."

Samantha turned. How could she tell her friend how hurtful her words were? Because every time she went along with the little game and closed her eyes, there was nothing. Just an endless stretch of black emptiness. But she wanted there to be something. Some indication her heart wasn't doomed to remain lifeless. That she wasn't meant to be alone.

Was something wrong with her? Growing up with Abigail, she'd gotten to listen to every far-fetched romantic fantasy her friend cooked up. Gotten to see the longing glances across ballroom floors. The yearning in Abigail's voice.

Samantha had never yearned. Not even a little.

Another sigh. Abigail would never understand. Better to just close her eyes and go along with it. She braced herself for the blank nothingness about to greet her. *Please, just for once let there be somebody. Anybody.* And like an answer to her desperate plea, an image appeared.

Lieutenant Thompson, standing at the forecastle in his blue uniform.

Her heart clenched and she recoiled as if someone had slapped her. No. Anybody but him.

Abigail blinked. "Well, that's certainly not the reaction I expected. Who in the world was it?"

Traitorous mind. Samantha breathed out. They had just spoken of him. Plus, she'd been in close contact with him last week. A perfect explanation for why he, of all people, would show up. Definitely not because of his piercing green eyes, or the well-muscled thighs hidden beneath his breeches.

She choked. "No one."

"Liar! There was too someone." Abigail clasped her hands together. "This is wonderful progress."

Samantha shook her head and found Uncle Henry in the crowd. She hadn't missed the inflection of the word "meeting" earlier. He often used society events as a cover for exchanging information with other gentleman pirates. When a footman approached him, she almost missed the covert handoff of a note.

"If you don't stop being a wallflower, using all your time to pester me about potential suitors, no one is going to dance with you." She gave Abigail a little push. "Go make yourself seen so one of your gentlemen can ask you. I'm going to catch a breath of fresh air."

Her uncle had already left the room without so much as a backward glance and Samantha pressed through the throngs of people to catch up. She made it to a long hallway leading into the east wing of the manor just as a door at the far end clicked shut. Kicking her shoes off, she retrieved them and padded softly across the tiled floor. Holding her breath, she edged to the door and pressed an ear to it.

"We have a problem."

Uncle Henry's voice.

"I have confirmation Captain Thorne has returned from the Caribbean."

Hushed murmurs reached her ear and her pulse jumped. Her uncle may be the most notorious pirate in America, but Thorne? His notoriety stretched the globe. While her uncle was known for his cunning skill in capturing ships and keeping his identity hidden, Thorne was feared for his sheer brutality. Sailors dared not even speak the name of the feared pirate's ship, the *Reckoning*, lest they tempt fate and summon its captain. A fitting name indeed, for if Thorne captured your vessel, the last thing they said you'd hear was his cruel laugh as he sent you to a watery grave. A shudder ran through her.

Another man's voice reached her. "Why would he come north? He's made it clear the Caribbean is his domain."

Silence fell and she had to cup her hand around her ear to make out her uncle's soft words.

"He's come for me."

She blanched, pushing down the fear coiled in her belly.

"Or rather, he's come for something I own."

Another round of murmurs, more frenzied this time.

"Fifteen years ago, my brother and his wife died while searching for a fabled treasure. Unfortunately, they weren't the only pirates interested in those particular riches. They were killed for that map. A map my brother entrusted to me in the days before he left on that fated trip."

Samantha jerked her head from the door and staggered a step away, her hand clutched over her mouth to hold back a cry. The shadows in the hallway spun around her. *Don't faint.*

She'd grown up believing her parents died in a shipwreck. Believed her father to have been an honest merchant sailor.

That map. Her heart gave a little stutter. The one her uncle gave to her last week. She was sure of it.

Heartbeat slamming, she pressed her ear to the door again.

Her uncle continued in a gruff voice. "The map is safe for now—"

The clip of footsteps echoing in the corridor interrupted her spying. Samantha spun around. No place to hide. And then her heart stopped beating.

Lieutenant Thompson strode around the corner, headed straight her way.

In the space of a breath, she backed against the door and rapped her stockinged heel against it.

Once.

Twice.

Three times.

"You there, what are you doing?"

Samantha swiveled to face the approaching lieutenant with wide eyes. Her throat went dry and she took a steadying breath. *Don't let him recognize you.* A pirate must always be a master of disguise. Even when dressed in an extravagant ballgown and facing the man who had sworn to make her pay.

Especially then.

She let a hand rise to her throat. "You startled me, Lieutenant."

He ground to a halt in front of her. And damn her pulse for quickening. His blue uniform cut a fine figure with a crisp cravat and his glossy curls were tied back to frame chiseled features. No powdered wig like most of the stuck-up men out in the ballroom. He went still, staring at her. She breathed in as his masculine scent washed over her. Something spicy. She sniffed again. Sandalwood and cloves.

"What are you doing here, Miss . . ."

"Warstein. Samantha Warstein." She sunk into a curtsy and his eyes narrowed.

"What's behind your back?"

Oh, God. Her shoes. She'd forgotten she still clutched them. Heat flooded her cheeks and she slowly brought them forward.

"I—I . . ." she stammered, and the perfect disguise came to her. She would play the simpering wallflower. Easy enough as it was a role she played so often at these society events. "My shoes were too tight and I just wanted a break. I—I didn't think anyone would find me back here." She hung her head, staring at his polished boots—a stark contrast to the pink stockinged toes peeking from beneath her lace hem.

"Never fear. I was not seeking you." Good. He bought it. So why did her heart sink a little at the words?

"Excuse me." He reached past her and flung the door open.

An empty room greeted them.

Lieutenant Thompson's lips pressed together and he stepped inside. Alarm coursed through her. If Uncle Henry and his men were still in there, hiding. . .

"Oh dear." Samantha poked her head in and she faked a gasp. "Oh my. Did I interrupt a—a rendezvous?" She used her shoes to fan herself and the lieutenant spun to face her.

"Of course not."

Another gasp, and she backed away from the door. "If anyone

should see us here . . . alone . . ."

That did the trick. When in doubt, the age-old threat of losing one's bachelorhood over being caught in a compromising situation could be counted on to spur a man to action. With one last look around the dark room, Lieutenant Thompson joined her in the hallway.

"Put your shoes back on."

She blinked at his sharp command but obeyed.

He held out his arm and after a pause, she set her hand at his elbow. Her fingers burned at the touch and she stared at the spot. Only a week before, she had battled this man. She nearly laughed at the irony.

The lieutenant gave a little cough and she jerked her gaze away. "Now, back to the ballroom with you, before your absence is noted."

When they passed through the arched doorway into the crowded room, she let out her breath and released his arm.

"Thank you, Lieutenant," she murmured before twisting toward the wall. Abigail stood there with a slack jaw. Wonderful. She'd never hear the end of this. She took a step forward.

"Not so fast, Miss Warstein."

Chapter Four

CHRISTIAN WAITED, NOTING how Miss Warstein's body went stiff before she turned to face him.

"Yes, Lieutenant?"

Her face had paled, but he couldn't drag his eyes from her hair. The candlelight from a chandelier overhead reflected off the fiery curls draped over her shoulder. When he first caught her in the hallway, all he could think of was that infuriating vixen who had called herself "Captain." Such a rare color. And to see it twice in the same week? Fate liked to taunt him.

He let his eyes slide over Miss Warstein, who stared at his boots. Taller than most women, her body stretched long and lithe beneath her gown. She chewed on her lip, pretty and pink, and he couldn't help sweeping his gaze to where her neckline plunged low, baring the rounded flesh of her breasts. Desire slammed through him, heavy and hot, and he took a small step back.

Goodness, what was wrong with him?

It was because she reminded him of *her*.

All week he'd tried to picture what she must look like behind her mask. If only he had ripped it free when he'd had the chance.

Miss Warstein wrung her hands together under his scrutiny and he cleared his throat before extending a hand. "Would you like to dance?"

The poor girl looked at his hand as if he'd offered her a dead fish. After a succession of rapid blinks, she met his gaze. In the light, her eyes shone like the azure waters of the sea.

"I don't dance."

He caught his snort of disbelief before it emerged. Surely, men tripped over themselves to claim dances with this enchanting woman.

"Nonsense. I promise I don't bite."

Long lashes shielded her eyes as she gave a longing glance toward the wall where another young lady watched them with rapt attention. With an unladylike sigh, she settled her fingers into his outstretched hand.

He guided her onto the dance floor and she set her other hand on his shoulder, her touch light as a feather. "For a moment there, Miss Warstein, I thought you would turn me down before all of Savannah. I'm not sure my pride could have withstood the blow."

She stiffened and he frowned. He rarely had a hard time charming the ladies, but she seemed immune to his flirting.

The music started and her feet moved in unison with his, and he knew her claim to be false. She danced like a master. A tight-lipped master who stared at his chest as if he were a wall.

Shy, then. Too bad.

"So, Miss Warstein . . ." He trailed off. What did one converse about with a shy wallflower?

"I heard you captured a pirate ship." She spoke to his buttons.

"Yes. One less crew of criminals to plague the waters."

She shivered and he fought the urge to pull her closer. "It must be so frightening to fight them."

He guided her through a turn. "Not at all, Miss Warstein. You see, pirates are cowards."

The hand at his shoulder tightened its grip and she missed a step. She glanced up at him then, her eyes swirling with the colors of the sea.

"Surely you jest."

A smattering of faint freckles lined her nose. He shook his head.

"It's the truth."

She returned her gaze to his buttons. "I shall endeavor to

remember that if I'm ever unfortunate enough to cross paths with one."

They reached the center of the dance floor and he used the central location to scan the crowd around them. Would she melt into hysterics if he told her that somewhere in this very room, pirates lurked?

Her uncle stood with a group of men and noticed them with raised brows. Henry Warstein owned the biggest shipping company south of New York. Christian tried to remember how the mogul had come to raise his niece. Something about a shipping accident that had claimed her parents' lives when she was young.

When he finished his perusal of the room, he maneuvered them toward the open doors to the terrace. No unfamiliar faces anywhere. The music drew to a stop and Miss Warstein pulled from his grasp and curtsied.

He offered his elbow and nodded to the door at their side. "Care for a stroll onto the terrace?"

After a moment's hesitation, she took it and they left the stuffy air of the ballroom behind. At the railing, she took a deep breath and closed her eyes. He let her loose and looked out over the river twisting below them. A half-moon glistened over the water, where lights twinkled from ships anchored in the bay. One of which was the *Falcon*.

He'd petitioned President Jefferson for more ships. And Georgia's governor had recently added his voice to the request. Soon, no more pirates would sail the seas or even walk this land.

When he turned back to Miss Warstein, she was examining him. With a start, she jerked her gaze away. Even in the pale moonlight, the color on her cheeks was visible.

She looked off into the distance. "Thank you for bringing me out here."

He nodded. "I could tell you were not enjoying yourself inside."

Her shoulders sagged. "Was it so obvious?"

He shrugged. "To others, probably not. To myself, yes. I'm very good at reading people. I have to be, to excel at what I do."

Her gaze snapped back to meet his. "And what else about me have you read?"

Finally, some spunk. He grinned. Being demure did not suit her.

"Quite a bit. For instance, you've received some of the best training to be had in dancing, so I would expect you excel at most every activity you partake in. Also, I know this image you portray is fake."

She swallowed and glanced around them as he continued. "I think you're afraid to let the world see the real you. So, you hide behind the convenient mask of a wallflower." He paused to look her up and down. "Would I be wrong to bet that you're a completely different person at home?"

She opened her mouth, but he lifted a finger to her lips. "Don't answer." God, her lips were soft. He fought the wild urge to claim them with his own. Instead, he pressed on. "I think you've been hurt."

Her eyes widened.

"No, not by a lover. By your parents' loss. And that hurt lingers. It dictates your choices. You try to bottle up how it makes you feel, and in turn, bottle up who you are."

Something in her eyes went hard and he clamped his mouth shut. He hadn't meant to dig so deep.

"Don't presume to know me so well, Lieutenant." Ice crept into her words. She stepped back. "Now, if you'll excuse me, I have a wall to grace."

Her hands bunched into fists at her side, and she spun away.

When she disappeared into the ballroom, he sighed and leaned over the railing. Familiar footsteps approached.

"Not like you to let a beautiful woman hamper a mission." Isaac, his best friend and first officer, appeared from the shadows.

Christian ran a hand through his hair. "The mission was aborted before I set eyes on Miss Warstein. With her in the hallway, the bloody criminals would have never chanced their meeting."

His blood simmered.

So close.

So damn close to putting a face to the elusive Captain Remington. Intelligence had hinted the pirate would be in attendance. And when the meeting place had been leaked by a well-paid footman, it had all but sealed the crook's fate. Only to have a pretty redhead unhinge the whole plot with her aching feet.

Pretty redheads in general had become a new source of trouble.

He sent a silent curse out against ridiculous women's fashion and pounded his fist against the railing. "How did we miss him? Who knows when we'll get another chance like that?"

His friend drew nearer. "Don't worry. We'll get him in due time. Plenty of other fish to catch. For now, how about we head to the tavern? I think a few rounds of ale along with a warm, willing body would do you good."

Christian's finger rose to the tiny scab on his neck. "I'm going home." A vision of flaming hair billowing in the wind flashed before his eyes.

Other fish indeed.

"FIND HER." CHRISTIAN slammed his dagger into the map on his desk. His new dagger, since a certain wench now had his government-issued one. "I don't care how you do it."

His officers nodded and filed from the room, but Isaac stayed behind.

"Are you sure it's wise to expend so many resources on one pirate?"

Christian turned from his friend and paced in front of the

desk. "I'm willing to do whatever it takes. Hell, I'll fund the mission myself if I have to."

"All because you were bested by a woman?"

Muscles tensed, Christian stopped and stared at the painting above the fireplace. *Bested by a woman.* He'd heard the whispers among his men since that day. His teeth ground together. He would never live it down.

"No," he growled and pointed to the portrait.

His mother.

"Because of her. Because she was taken hostage and God knows what she suffered at their hands before she died."

Isaac remained silent for a long moment while Christian stewed before pressing his fingers together. "Chris, I know you don't want to hear this, but you tread a fine line between duty and following your father's footsteps."

Christian blew out his breath. "Don't you dare bring him into this."

Isaac cleared his throat. "The real question is, are you really willing to send a woman to the noose?"

"Women have hanged for far lesser crimes."

"At your order?"

Isaac's soft words broke Christian's fragile hold on his control.

He spun around. "What exactly are you suggesting? That I let her go? That I ignore her crimes because she's female? If that's the stance you're going to take, I swear, I will relieve you of your duties right here and now. You can go back to Washington. Find yourself a new mission."

Isaac raised both his hands. "You know I'll follow your orders."

"Then help me find her."

Christian pressed his fingers to his brow. Isaac had been his friend since they were boys. He'd been the brother Christian had always wished for. They'd gone to boarding school together and later attended Columbia. It hardly surprised anyone when they enlisted in the navy after graduating.

"Put out a reward. Someone around here has to have heard of her."

Isaac bowed his head and left Christian alone in the room. His gaze flitted to the empty spot on his desk. Where his compass should be. Hands clenched, he sat down. His great grandfather had received it when he served in the Royal Navy and the instrument had been passed down to each generation.

His father had given it to him the day he'd sailed away to take revenge on the pirates responsible for his wife's death, never to return. Told him to keep it safe.

Now, a blasted pirate had it.

He hadn't been jesting earlier. If the governor told him to back off, he would hire privateers to hunt her.

She could run. She could hide.

But he would find her.

He stared at the map and the little red "X" he'd marked off the coast of Florida. If she tried to sail that route again, one of his men would see her. Jerking the knife free, he traced the point up and down the coast. The question was, which way from that mark did her lair lie?

North would be best. He'd sent men to investigate well-known hideouts from Brunswick all the way up to Charleston. But he'd visited many of those cities himself in the last few months. Surely, he would have noticed a saucy flame-haired wench.

Another fiery-haired beauty crossed his mind and he cursed.

He'd offended Miss Warstein last night. And keeping on her uncle's good side was vital. The merchant had more ships out on the water than anyone else, and making an enemy of him would upset the governor. Dropping his blade, Christian pressed his fingers together.

Time to pay a well past due social call.

Outside, the sun beat down on him while he waited for his horse to be tacked. Once mounted, he kicked the bay gelding into a trot. The Warstein estate lay less than a mile from his manor and he frowned. He should have called on Henry Warstein months ago, when he'd first moved to Savannah. Gaining the merchant's eyes and ears would be a huge asset to his mission.

When he rode up the drive, he nodded his appreciation for the well-maintained grounds. Large oak trees leaned over him and the stately white manor commanded one's attention. A footman rushed forward before Christian pulled his horse to a stop. His boots crunched into the dirt and he tugged at his cravat as sweat dampened his skin. The buzz of cicadas filled the air and he yearned for the slap of waves against a hull.

The butler opened the door at his first knock. A responsive and alert staff. Which reminded him, about time to hire on his own butler. Being at sea so much over the last few months had pushed it to the back of his to-do list.

"Lieutenant Thompson, calling on Mr. Warstein."

With a nod, the butler turned. "Of course. Right this way."

The oppressive heat followed them inside and Christian scowled. No sense staying ashore in this weather. He'd make sure to be back on a ship before the week's end. His boots clicked against marble and he glanced up the sweeping mahogany staircase before following the butler into the drawing room.

"If you take a seat, Mr. Warstein will join you momentarily."

Christian bypassed the settee and came to a stop in front of the fireplace. He ran his thumb across the mantle. Not a speck of dust. A bookshelf sat in the corner and he drifted over. An eclectic mix of tomes stretched across the shelves. In one handspan, he found a bible, a collection of astronomical charts, and a book on dry land farming.

A slight breeze found its way in through the open double windows and he strolled to them. From here, the glimmer of the river could be seen between the trees.

"A poor substitute for a man of the sea."

Christian turned at the deep voice and Mr. Warstein joined him. "On days like this, I'd almost rather not be able to see the water. A sorry tease it is."

The merchant extended his hand. Tan skin and calluses betrayed his well-manicured nails and starched shirt. A firm grip spoke of a man still in his prime. Christian rose a brow. So, Warstein didn't sit behind a desk all day, content to rake in his profits. This man worked. And hard from the looks of it.

"Lieutenant, what can I do for you?"

Christian released Henry's hand. "We've been neighbors for several months now, and I thought it high time we met."

Warstein chuckled. "Nonsense, Lieutenant. A man like you doesn't pay a visit unless he wants something." Grey eyes sharpened as they swept over Christian's profile. "After all, I hear you're a busy man these days."

Christian turned back to the window. "If I'm to be honest, I wanted to hear your thoughts on the pirate trade you've encountered. I'm sure you've heard the governor's plan to make these waters safer for all."

"An ambitious plan it is. Though it's well known you're doing a fine job on your own. What insight could I possibly give that you don't already know?"

Christian stared hard at the water. "I've heard it said you've never suffered a loss to pirates. An amazing feat for having such a large fleet."

"Lieutenant, it's no secret my ships travel heavily armed. Any vessel foolish enough to pick a fight with one of my captains will find itself resting on the seabed, far below the waves."

"A bold statement."

Warstein took a step to close the space between them. "When you've spent your whole life at sea, you learn the only way to survive is to be bold."

"Word is, a dangerous captain has moved into these waters." Christian turned to face Henry, whose fingers twitched on the windowsill.

He met Christian's gaze. "Captain Thorne."

Christian nodded. "He's a pirate who kills for—"

"He kills for sport." Warstein's eyes darkened. "You have my full support in your endeavor to take him down."

There was more to Warstein's dislike of the infamous pirate, Christian would bet his life on it. He fought back the urge to command more information from the merchant. From what he'd perceived thus far, Henry Warstein was not a man who would take well to being ordered about.

"I'm glad to hear. If you receive any intelligence on his whereabouts, let me know. He's made quite the name for himself and the president wants the threat he poses eliminated before he becomes too comfortable in American waters."

Warstein peered at him. "I've already put out some feelers of my own. Perhaps my men can find something of use to you."

He pivoted and Christian followed him from the room. Before they made their way toward the foyer, Christian paused. A white brow lifted when Henry looked back.

"Was there something else you needed?"

Christian scratched his chin. "I wondered if I might have a word with your niece."

The merchant stopped and his gaze raked over Christian. His body had gone rigid. Interesting.

"Samantha?"

"I believe I may have offended her last night and I'd like to make amends."

Some of the tension eased from the other man's shoulders. He gave a little laugh. "My niece, offended? You must have said something very foolish indeed."

After a pause, he turned and led Christian back down the hallway. They walked out onto the veranda and Warstein pointed down the steps.

"You'll find her in the garden somewhere. My guess would be under the big oak tree."

No chaperone? Perhaps the merchant wasn't as sharp as he came off. Christian started down the steps.

"I will warn you, Lieutenant, she's in a mood today. If you're the reason, I wouldn't want to be in your shoes."

Chapter Five

SAMANTHA NIBBLED ON her lower lip while she stared at the canvas in front of her.

Angry blue lines clashed together, an appropriate representation of the turmoil raging within her. Why had her uncle lied to her about her parents' deaths all these years?

Killed by pirates. How foolish she'd been to believe otherwise. They hadn't been traveling on shipping business. They'd been treasure hunting.

Pirates. The word quickened her pulse. No wonder she loved the sea so much. It was in her blood.

Her uncle should have told her. All her life she'd felt so out of place on shore. If she'd known her legacy, she could have embraced it more fully. Could have used the information to convince her uncle to let her sail with his crews sooner.

She smashed her brush into a pot of grey paint and swept it across the canvas with a scowl. After she perfected the curve of a towering wave, she stared down the hillside. The trees had been clear cut here and the vista offered an unfettered view of the river below. Her lifeline to the ocean.

On the horizon, sails unfurled upon ships headed out to sea. Somewhere out there, the *Siren* was anchored. She scrunched her nose. No longer the *Siren*. By now, the brigantine would have a new name and a new figurehead. Re-christened to ward off bad luck. Any time one of her uncle's ships engaged in a skirmish, it received a thorough transformation. It was one of the main reasons none of their ships had ever been caught by authorities.

"It seems I was right about you after all."

The brush slipped from Samantha's fingers and she spun to face the lieutenant, her heart in her throat. He stood a few paces away. How did he sneak up on her? Blast.

Her mouth went dry. His cocked hat perched atop dark curls, but his usual impeccable appearance ended there. He'd untied his cravat and it draped loosely around his neck. The top two buttons of his shirt hung open and a few wisps of hair graced the swatch of tanned skin there. Her eyes traveled down the lean lines of his stomach and when they lingered where his trousers stretched across his thighs, heat crept up to her ears.

She jerked her gaze away.

"I thought young ladies painted landscapes."

She focused on the painting. "It is a landscape."

"I'll rephrase that. Young ladies don't paint hurricanes."

Samantha pulled her lips between her teeth. Young ladies also didn't sail the seas with a bunch of so-called criminals. Or sword fight handsome lieutenants. She stared at the scene in front of her, a black sky with cresting waves heaving into the air, and shrugged.

"I was upset."

The lieutenant stepped forward. "I hope it's not on my account."

A cricket chirped from the nearby grass and the breeze picked up, shifting the branches above. Dappled light slid across the lieutenant and she almost laughed at the concerned look on his face.

"Do not fret, Lieutenant. It's not on your account."

He smiled, his teeth even and straight. "Good, I'm not sure my pride could withstand the blow of knowing I'd caused a beautiful young lady to paint a raging storm."

She stilled and he looked away, rubbing his neck. Good God. He was flirting with her. Best change the subject.

A faint scar twisted across the back of his hand and she pointed to it. "Where did you get your scar?"

"This one? Fighting pirates, of course."

Of course.

"Have you ever lost a fight with a pirate?"

His eyes went dark and the smile faded. "I've lost several."

"Tell me about them."

His gaze snapped to hers. "Miss Warstein, those stories are not fit for a lady's ears. I promise you don't want to know."

Samantha huffed. More likely, he didn't want to admit he'd been beaten by a woman. Now would be the appropriate time to agree and end this conversation, but something in his eyes tugged at her, and lord help her, she didn't want it to end.

She stood and smoothed out the pale yellow skirts of her day dress. Thank goodness she'd given in to Anna and forgone her usual breeches.

"Do you think I could fight a pirate?"

"Don't ever suggest such a thing." Alarm filled his eyes, and she blinked at the intensity in the words.

He grabbed her by the shoulders and she bit back a gasp at the forward behavior even as her pulse jumped. "Miss Warstein, if you ever found yourself among pirates . . ." He trailed off and dropped his hands. "May God help you."

Samantha bit her tongue. *If only he knew.* Still, the solemnness lacing his voice sent a chill through her.

He waved a hand down the path. "Walk with me?"

She fell into step with him and adjusted her straw hat when they left the shadows of the tree.

"Enough talk of pirates. Tell me what has made you upset. Perhaps I can help."

He flashed her a roguish smile that made her stomach flop. No wonder every woman in town fawned over him. She pulled her shoulders back. This was her enemy. Two of her men had died at the hands of his crew. And countless others had hanged— or would yet hang—because of his mission. He had no right to come here and charm her. She should leave. But first, she would firmly make sure he never put two and two together.

"I'm afraid the two go hand in hand, Lieutenant." She quickened her pace and angled toward the house. "You see, last night, I found out I was lied to about my parents' deaths."

He frowned. "I heard they died in a shipwreck."

A rush of heat slid through her veins. "So did I. But we both heard wrong." Her hand trembled and she clenched her fingers into a fist. "They were killed by pirates."

The lieutenant came to a stop. "So, this is why you've been asking so many questions."

She stood silent and his forest-hued eyes widened a fraction. "Miss Warstein, I hope you do not harbor any foolish notions of revenge."

"I thought you said they were all a bunch of cowards."

"That they are. But I've learned that cowards can be the cruelest of them all." His eyes softened. "Trust me, Miss Warstein, I promise your uncle hid the truth from you to soften the blow. What young girl would want to hear her parents died that way?"

"I would have." Her words came in a rush.

"It's easy to say that now. But if you had known, what could you have done, other than be angry?"

Her spine went straight. "I don't like being lied to."

He pulled his hat off and passed it between his hands. "Nobody does. But sometimes, I wish I hadn't been told." She frowned and he continued. "You see, Miss Warstein, my own mother died at the hands of pirates when I was a boy."

Her hand flew to cover her mouth. "I'm so sorry, Lieutenant. How selfish you must think I am."

He shook his head. "Never. But you can rest assured I will do everything in my power to make it so that other children will not have to endure what we have."

SAMANTHA EXAMINED THE cargo being brought aboard, checking each item off on her ledger. Griff stood next to her.

"You're lucky to have a second chance."

She let out a huff. "Shuttling crates of goods to The Bahamas is hardly a second chance."

No matter how hard she focused on the sheet of parchment in her hands, her eyes kept sneaking a peek at the ship anchored on the other side of the river.

The *Falcon*.

And each time she did, her traitorous thoughts brought her back to the garden the other day. She scowled. Not only was her enemy the bloody most handsome man in Georgia, but he had also devoted his entire life to avenging his mother's death.

How could she blame him?

"The numbers match up." She pushed the ledger into Griff's hands and strode to her cabin.

Inside, she went straight to her shelf and grabbed the big conch and peeled the wax back. Once the map slid out, she unfolded it and stared at the lines. This was what her parents died for. An emptiness gnawed at her insides. Killed over a piece of parchment.

She swiped at the dampness gathering at the corners of her eyes. She may not be able to get revenge, but she could do one thing.

She could make sure they hadn't died in vain.

Clenching the map in her hand, she charged from the room.

"Griff!" Her shout drew curious looks from the crew.

He handed the ledger to another man and approached her.

"Tell me what you know about this." She waved the map in front of his face and his eyes widened.

He snatched it from her. "Where did you get this?"

"Uncle Henry told me to keep it safe. Little did I know, it's the reason my parents are dead." She spat out the last word.

He quickly folded it and glanced around. "Let's go inside."

When they entered her cabin, he shut the door behind them.

"So, you did overhear our conversation the other night."

"Don't you dare lecture me on eavesdropping. If I hadn't warned you, Lieutenant Thompson would have walked in on your little meeting."

He stared hard at her for a long moment before his shoulders dropped. "I'm sorry you had to learn that way."

"What happened?"

A sadness filled his eyes. "We don't know. They didn't return from a voyage and we went searching. Never found a trace of the ship or any survivors. Your father had been worried before they left and told your uncle someone was after the map. It's why he left it behind."

"Why did Uncle Henry keep it from me?" Her stomach clenched. "Why hide that they were pirates?"

Griff sighed and looked out the wall of windows. "I think he wanted to make sure that you decided your future on your own, without the influence of their legacy."

Tears stung the corners of her eyes. "He had no right to make that decision."

"Perhaps not, but he did it out of love." Griff unfolded the map and laid it on her desk. "Don't ever let anyone know you have this."

She stepped forward and slid it until it rested in front of her. "Why not?"

Griff pushed his lips together. "This is one half of the map to Read's Revenge. There are men out there who would kill for it—have killed for it."

Samantha blinked. "I thought that was just a myth." Legend said that the one who found Read's cache would be the richest person alive. Supposedly stashed away a hundred years before in a time when pirates ruled the sea without opposition, amassing their fortunes from the Spanish fleet, there'd never been evidence it existed.

Until now.

Mary Read.

One of the greatest female pirates to have sailed the seas.

Every pirate or smuggler who was worth anything knew the story. The famous trio, Calico Jack, Anne Bonny, and Mary Read had amassed a fortune during their plundering. Read had known pirate hunters were after them so she gathered the group's riches and hid them away. When they were captured, the government raided their known homes and hideouts but found nothing. And Read took her secrets to the grave with her.

Samantha sank into her chair and studied the parchment once again. She twisted it so the coastline ran parallel to the edge of the desk. The map had been torn diagonally so that the entire coastline was on her half. The line snaking inland was cut off.

"Your parents had determined the location to be here." He pushed the parchment aside to point to the big map on her desk and his finger came to rest on the southern coast of Florida. "They spent years combing the mangrove swamps and forests ashore, but without the other half, they had no idea how far inland to go, or in which direction."

Her pulse quickened. How many times had she sailed past that very spot?

"And where is the other half?"

He shrugged. "Never even heard a whisper of it. But if Thorne is wanting your half, you can bet he knows where it is— or already has it."

She jumped to her feet. "If he has it, we could—"

"Never. Only a fool would cross him. A dead fool." He turned toward the door. "Wherever you hide it, don't tell a soul. Not even me."

The door clicked shut and Samantha drummed her fingers against the map. There had to be a way. But how? With a sigh, she returned the parchment to its hiding place. Plenty of time to brainstorm on this trip. For now, she needed to get the newly named *Hurricane* ready to sail.

After setting the shell back on the shelf, she headed below decks. In the kitchen, Francis, the cook, stashed a crate of eggs beneath a counter.

"Looking fetching as always, Captain."

Samantha smiled. The kindly old man could always bolster her spirits. "Thank you. What else do we need for our voyage?"

He patted a barrel. "Fully stocked, Captain. Can't fit nary a thing more."

A bell clanged above.

"Good, because we don't have much time."

She slipped out the door and bumped into Tommy, the cabin boy.

"Apologies, Capt'n." He straightened with a grin. "Say, did ya hear that no-good lieutenant put a reward out for information on your whereabouts?"

Samantha went still.

"You sure did make him mad, beating him the way you did."

She regained her composure. "How much is this reward?"

The boy's eyes lit up. "One hundred dollars."

Half a year's pay for a deckhand. She chewed her lip. Would her crew remain true?

Tommy read her mind. "Don't you worry. Ain't one of us that would snitch."

Not now. But what if he upped his price? Lieutenant Thompson was quickly becoming a thorn in her side. She would have to find a way to convince him to back off. But how? The damn man would probably die before giving up his chase.

Tommy shifted on his feet while she looked him up and down. He frowned. "You alright, Capt'n?"

Her lips curved up. "How would you like to collect that reward, Tommy?"

Chapter Six

T HE THRILL OF the hunt never grew old.

Wind tugged at Christian's hat, threatening to send it into the waves below. The *Falcon* cut through the swells with grace as she closed in on the vessel ahead of them. He raised his spyglass once more, squinting at the ship. A brigantine. Same type as the one the fire-haired wench captained, but there was no way to know for sure it was her. Not until they got closer.

"Are you certain you want to do this?" Isaac came to a stop next to him and Christian shot him a scowl.

"Don't start that again."

Isaac shrugged. "And what if it's a trap?"

Christian thought of the exchange he'd had with the scraggly boy one week earlier. At first, he'd scoffed at the whelp's insistence that he knew where she would be. The reward had brought forth all manners of unprovable claims. Christian had ordered him tossed back out onto the street, unwilling to listen. Until the boy had pulled out a black leather mask.

The child refused to tell how he'd come across the info and, when Christian gave him his reward, had run like the hounds of hell were after him. Christian's men had followed the boy to no avail and the brat lost them among the warehouses lining the docks.

Christian tugged his hat down. "We've got at least a dozen guns on that ship."

Isaac gave him a sideways glance. "That didn't stop her last time."

Christian growled and shoved the spyglass at Isaac. He stalked to the wheel.

"Ready the cannons." A flurry of activity filled the deck as his men followed the order. "And set extra sails. She's not getting away this time."

Isaac chuckled from the railing and lowered the spyglass. "No need. Looks like your prey is going to meet us."

Christian narrowed his eyes and strode to where his friend stood. He yanked the glass back. Sure enough, the brigantine had done an about-turn and pointed straight their way. His pulse jumped. It was her.

It had to be.

He stood there as the distance closed between the ships. And when he raised the spyglass once more, his breath caught. Hair streaming behind her in the wind, she stood at the forecastle. A jolt of awareness surged through him. Her spyglass was trained directly on him. She lowered it and gave a jaunty wave.

"Damnation," he muttered, spinning to Isaac. "She knew we were coming."

Isaac shot him a knowing look. "What are your orders?"

"Load the guns. If she tries anything, we take her out."

He turned his attention back to the approaching ship. The wench had disappeared and he crossed his arms. If she meant to hide from him, he would tear the vessel apart until he found her. He'd have his justice if it was the last thing he did.

The ship neared enough for him to assess the threat. Three dozen men above decks. No cannons visible. He frowned. No weapons at all.

The men's faces were disguised with leather masks, same as before, and he remembered the frightening speed at which they'd breached his defenses last time. He wouldn't be caught unawares again.

"Heave to," he ordered. By the time the sails were lowered, the pirate ship had already done the same and crept toward them at a crawl. Her crew had them beat with their efficiency.

Christian rapped his fingers against the hilt of his sword. What would he do with her? His scalp prickled, and he pushed his unease away. He'd worry about that once she was safely locked away in the brig.

Silence fell over both crews as the ships drew alongside each other. The older man who had presented himself as captain last time stood at the wheel, his face like stone.

Christian left the quarterdeck and strode toward the bow. "Surrender now and the charges you face might allow you to escape the noose."

The man didn't move, other than to clench his fists at his side. Christian lifted a brow. The pirate was livid. Before he could ponder why, Isaac's shout rose from the quarterdeck.

"Behind you!"

The sing of a rope through the air preceded a thump on the deck and he drew his sword as he spun to face his attacker.

"What the . . ." His breath hissed out. Where the hell had she been hiding?

Her eyes glinted from behind the black mask hiding her face and his gaze raked over her. The shock of seeing a woman in breeches had not lessened and his throat suddenly went dry. They clung to shapely legs and left nothing to the imagination. The top three buttons of her blouse were unbuttoned, leaving a scandalous "V" of skin bared on her chest that her jacket did little to hide.

Desire shot through him, hard and hot. He swallowed as a wave of heat coursed through his veins. God above, he was attracted to her. His lips settled into a scowl. Unacceptable.

It had to be the breeches.

What red-blooded man wouldn't react like this to those legs? That shapely bottom on display for all to see? With a cough, he raised his gaze. She'd tied her hair into a haphazard braid and a black hat pressed low over the coppery locks. A single red feather jutted from it.

She shifted on her feet and gave a pointed look at his blade. He blinked at her empty hands and his gaze flew to her belt. No sword.

"What's the meaning of this?" he growled.

The wench had the audacity to laugh. "In my experience, men who make such a blatant show of force are compensating for something else entirely."

One of his men snickered. Surely she wasn't insinuating . . .

He stared at her and she gestured over her shoulder to the dozen muskets pointed their way.

"Lower your damn rifles." Isaac's voice snapped the men from their shock and a smug grin crossed her lips.

"I have a proposal for you." She slid her gaze down to his feet and back. "That is, unless you'd prefer to run me through."

He lowered his sword. "You're in no position to offer me anything."

Her laugh came again, echoing from the sails above. "I beg to differ."

She nodded toward her ship and he let out a curse. While his idiot men had been staring at the scene she caused, her crew had not wasted the opportunity. Muskets had materialized out of thin air and hatches on the lower deck now hung open to reveal a row of gleaming cannons.

Impressive.

He grunted. "We have twice as many guns as you. There's no way you would win."

And thank heavens the men at his cannons hadn't lost their minds like the others. They stood rigid at their posts, staring down the length of their iron barrels. One word from him and they would rain destruction.

"Maybe not. But we would certainly get a good bit of damage of our own in before you claimed victory." She grinned. "Are you willing to risk it?"

He should call her bluff. But instead, Christian watched the rise and fall of her chest for the space of a few breaths, then inclined his head. "What is it you want?"

She hooked her thumbs in her belt and met his gaze. "One match. You and me."

He stiffened. "A foolish proposal. And what, may I ask, is your price?"

"Immunity."

He recoiled. "You cannot imagine I'd offer that."

She shrugged, but the tightness in her shoulders gave away her nervousness. If he refused, she and her crew would be his prisoners in a matter of minutes. He took a step toward her and she lifted her chin a notch.

He leaned in to deny her once more.

A mistake.

She smelled of lemons and rosemary.

Her breath hitched, and the tiny sound sent awareness coursing through him. And then, he made a bigger mistake.

"I accept."

Her shoulders loosened. "And your terms?"

Christian took a step back. "I want my compass back."

She laughed again, the rich sound caressing him. "Come now, Lieutenant, surely my immunity is worth more than a measly old compass." Her head tilted to the side as she regarded him with an intense look. "What do you really want? Is there nothing else you wish to take from me?"

Your freedom. You and your crew, prisoners of the US government.

He should say it. It's what he wanted, wasn't it? Because no matter how the match ended, it would culminate with her locked up. He wasn't playing any games. As a lieutenant, he would do his duty. Isaac's warning played at the edges of his mind. If he captured her . . . *when* he captured her, she would face the noose. A vision of a rope around her slender neck hit him like a brick to the gut and an acrid taste filled his mouth.

The wind shifted, sending an errant strand of hair dancing across her cheek and her citrusy scent washed over him again. He rocked back on his heels and met her gaze.

"You're right. There is something else I want."

Copper brows arched from behind her mask. "Go on then."

He let his lips turn up in a roguish grin. "A night with you."

She sucked in a breath and her eyes flashed—a ripple of blue and green escaping the shadows so effortlessly hiding her face. Chuckles came from his men.

"Captain."

The gruff warning came from her ship and the older man strode to the railing. His face had gone red. Christian's gaze flicked between the two of them and his stomach twisted. Were they lovers?

The way the man looked ready to commit murder certainly suggested it. Christian couldn't help the scowl that pushed forth. No. That man must be three times her age. Her father, then?

She kept her eyes on Christian, ignoring the distraction. "A night with me? Impossible."

He lifted a shoulder. "Those are my terms. Take them or leave them."

She turned into the sun and something else entered her eyes.

Fear.

The first vulnerability she'd shown thus far.

Good God, what had overcome him? A night with her? A pirate? He nearly laughed. A navy man on assignment, he had no business sleeping with the enemy. He opened his mouth to take it back, but her soft words cut him off.

"Very well."

An awed murmur swept through her crew. They hadn't expected her to agree.

She spun back to him. "Let's get this over with."

His men cleared the deck and she turned to her ship where the older man held her rapier.

"Bring it over," she commanded.

He stood still, staring at the blade. "And if I don't?"

She brought her hands to her hips. "You should know better. Twenty lashes."

He lifted his head and Christian almost felt pity for the fool and the look of agony on his face. Almost.

"I would take them." The man's voice was quiet.

With a huff, she threw her hands in the air and turned her back to him. "Then I'll borrow a blade from one of the lieutenant's men."

The pirate cursed and grabbed a rope, landing on the *Falcon's* deck a moment later. When she turned to face him, he shoved the slender sword at her. She took it and he grabbed her shoulder.

"You better win, or there will be hell to pay." His fingers flexed and she winced.

A stab of anger shot through Christian. He closed the distance between them and pushed the old man away. "Touch her again, and I'll finish the job I started last time we met."

The man lifted his lips in a snarl but backed away. Christian nodded to two of his men who immediately flanked the pirate. His focus was drawn back to . . . he pressed his lips together, not sure what to call her.

She did not notice his attention and ran her fingers up and down her blade with reverent affection. For a split second, he imagined those fingers stroking him the same way. He hardened at the erotic picture. With a shake of his head, he cleared his throat. No distractions.

"What's your name?"

She went stiff. "It's not for you to know."

"Then what shall I call you?"

"You may call me Captain."

He shook his head. "You may play at captain, but you can't fool me."

Behind her mask, her eyes widened a fraction. Enough for him to know he was right. He'd wager a large amount that the man his crew held at the railing only feet away was the true captain. So, what did that make her?

His daughter, indulging in a whim? Did pirates even care about their children? Clearly not, if this was any indication. The whole situation made no sense. Why let her fight him? What would the old man gain? Certainly, any of the men on board the ship stood a greater chance at beating him than she would.

Isaac approached and drew Christian aside. "I've got a bad feeling about this."

"Weren't you the one to suggest a warm body might do me good?"

"I certainly didn't mean this." The officer kept his voice low. "Just say the word. If we take their captain," he nodded toward the glowering old man, "we can force their surrender."

Christian gave his friend an approving glance. Isaac was smarter than most of his crew combined. He should follow his officer's advice and end this game before it started. With a swallow, he turned back to her.

She bent to inspect the laces on her boot and her breeches stretched tight across her supple bottom. His men stared openly, and Christian narrowed his eyes.

"No." He stripped his jacket off and tossed it to Isaac. "I'll play her silly game."

It was high time this wench learned a lesson. He strode out to meet her and she stood. She stared at him for a moment, then unbuttoned her own jacket. She threw it to Isaac and Christian struggled to find his breath.

In the sun, the flimsy fabric of her shirt left little to the imagination. His eyes followed the soft curve of her side up to the swell of her breasts.

God help him.

Her blouse stretched taut across her chest, exposing a generous amount of cleavage above the linen and his mouth went dry. He shouldn't want her. But his body betrayed him. He wanted to drag her from the circle and take her straight to his cabin—away from the prying eyes of his men—where he could peel those ridiculous clothes off.

"En garde." She lifted her rapier and settled into a fighting stance.

He copied the movement. "I think I'll call you Red." His voice came out gravelly and her teeth flashed in a smile.

"How original."

In a burst of speed, she feigned right before thrusting to his left. His weak side. He parried the blow and the fight began.

Christian came at her, using his height and strength to his advantage, but her feet moved in a blur and she evaded his thrusts. As they circled each other, he couldn't help but appreciate her skill. Each step he took, each move he made, she reacted with precision. And she was fast.

Her blade snaked out and he twisted away. A soft tear reached his ears and he glanced down at his arm. His shirt flapped open from where she'd cut it.

How?

With a shake of his head, he circled once more.

Time to find her weakness.

But she hid whatever disadvantage she might have. Her footwork kept him moving. No faults there. Her eyes stayed on his face, not his sword. Smart.

She held her blade in her right hand, so her left side would be her weak side. A good place to start chipping away at her defenses.

He grunted and jumped forward in an attack, cutting his blade down. With a movement too fast for him to catch, her rapier changed hands. She caught his blow and deflected it in one smooth motion.

Christian's jaw went slack. He'd never seen anything like it.

"Who taught you?"

She grinned at the awe in his voice and came at him. He wasn't used to facing a left-handed opponent and his first few blocks came awkwardly.

"Why, Lieutenant? Are you in need of lessons?" She switched hands again and dealt an impressive cut for her size.

He'd thought she'd won on a fluke last time. Not a fluke. She was a worthy opponent. She could win this.

But she wouldn't.

Last time, he'd been exhausted from the battle before she showed up. This time, he would outlast her. No matter her skill, she didn't have his muscle.

She would tire.

And he would claim victory.

Minutes dragged on and with each thrust he made, he sapped her of precious strength. Soon, her shoulders heaved and sweat dripped down her chest into the valley between her breasts. *Don't look.*

Too late.

She sensed his distraction and switched her tactic, pressing forward with a thrust from down low. He slid to the side and her blade narrowly missed his thigh. She kept moving, forcing him to turn into the sun.

He squinted at where she had settled into a crouch near the mainmast. Her blade wavered for a split second and she stretched her arm. He grinned.

It wouldn't be long now.

"Give it up, Red. You know how this ends."

His men laughed. "Finish the wench off," one of them shouted.

With a shake of her head, she tossed her braid over her shoulder and faced him. She wouldn't give up. Respect flared as she tightened her grip on the hilt. She was going to rush him.

Valiant, but it would be her doom.

He would end this now.

Muscles coiled, he waited for her to move first. When she launched forward, he leaped to meet her. His fingers tightened around his hilt as he took in the determination in her eyes, the way her muscles bunched beneath the leather of her breeches. She flew at him like a warrior goddess.

He kept his sword tucked close to his side, ready to flick it out and capture hers. One of his favorite moves. She kept her blade aimed straight at his heart as she approached. Confident determination shone across her face.

Just before they met, he pushed off the deck with his left foot and extended his arm to disarm her.

But his boot slipped. And with no way to stop his momentum, he pitched forward.

Time slowed to a crawl as he tried and failed to catch himself. Somewhere, in the back of his mind, he heard Isaac's panicked shout, but Christian could only think one thing: He was going to die.

Red's eyes went wide and he braced himself for the bite of steel while her blade continued its deadly plunge.

The bite never came.

Instead, she let out a strangled cry and did the impossible. In less time than he could blink, she twisted her wrist and released her grip—sending the sword flying.

With a clatter, the rapier bounced harmlessly at his side and she slammed into his chest. The impact sent them both reeling backward. She tried to pivot away, but he was already reacting.

His arm closed around her chest and he yanked her back to him. Before she could struggle, he jerked his sword up and pressed the blade to her neck.

Chapter Seven

S AMANTHA WENT UTTERLY still, her pulse reverberating in rapid beats against the cool edge of the lieutenant's blade. She blanched. What had happened?

She'd nearly killed him.

One second, she'd been ready to relinquish her rapier and pull the dagger from its sheath in her boot. Before he could recover, she would have spun behind him and had the deadly blade at his neck.

But the blasted man had slipped.

She dropped her gaze to the deck where a highly polished plank gleamed beneath them. Damn these navy men and their obsession with appearance.

Now, she'd lost.

Tears pricked her eyes as the cheers of the Lieutenant's men roared in her ears.

No.

Her throat constricted while her mouth opened and closed with no effect. She couldn't breathe. An ungodly fire burned inside her lungs, and Samantha's knees buckled. She sagged against the solid form behind her as her vision spun and blessedly, the heavy pressure of the arm beneath her breasts lessened a degree. She sucked in a breath as the lieutenant leaned in and set his lips at her ear.

"If I had known you were so eager to throw yourself into my arms, I would have forgone the fight altogether." The low words rumbled against her skin and she jerked her face away while he sheathed his sword.

His free hand came up and toyed with the laces of her mask. "I think it's time for you to stop hiding your face."

Her blood went cold.

Never.

She thrashed to the side and jerked her head up, smashing it into his chin.

With a growl, he yanked her back. "Hiding something?"

Something? More like everything. Tears threatened to spill when he lifted his hand again. Before he could touch the laces again, she pressed the back of her head into his chest. If he couldn't reach the ties . . .

"I could just rip it off." His fingertips brushed over the bottom of the leather.

"Not here, Lieutenant." She injected as much authority as she could into her voice, but it still cracked.

He paused. Pulled her flush to him.

"Later then?"

She gritted her teeth. "My mask stays on."

He let out a soft chuckle. "As if you're in any position to make demands on this ship."

His chest heaved against her back, and she was suddenly aware of each hard ridge of him pressing into her, especially the one jutting into the small of her back. With an outraged gasp, she attempted to angle her body away from him. He held tight.

"Release me."

"I rather like this position."

Heat flooded her cheeks. "Please."

"My, my, suddenly so polite." He shifted his grip. "You promise not to do anything reckless?"

Reckless.

There was that word again. She might have laughed if she were not still plastered against him. What could possibly be more reckless than this?

His fingers slid up and down her side and an odd warmth

spread from where he gripped her. She squirmed and his breath hitched.

"Careful, Red, or you'll make me do something indecent in front of my men." She stilled. "Now, do I have your word?"

Samantha managed a curt nod, and his arm slipped away. As soon as she was free, she jumped from him. His men had crowded close with lecherous gazes pinned to her. She glanced down and groaned. She may as well be naked for how much her shirt revealed.

With a grimace, she brought one arm up to cover herself and stared at the deck. A pair of boots came into view as a discreet cough sounded. She swallowed and lifted her head a fraction. The first officer stood there and held her jacket out to her. Thank God.

She snatched it from his grasp and shrugged into it. When she'd buttoned it, she met his amused gaze. "I'm glad to find that at least one person on this ship has some decency."

He flashed her a grin and gave a mock bow. "Someone here has to keep their wits about them, and it seems I've been thrust into the role." He gave Lieutenant Thompson a pointed look.

The lieutenant stared at where her hands had paused on the last button at her neck. He took his jacket from the officer and slung it over one arm. "I believe Red and I have an appointment in my cabin."

He took a step toward her and Samantha's heart thumped an erratic beat. A predatory gleam flashed in his eyes and she couldn't help shrinking back. He noticed and raised a brow.

"Or are you going to back out of our deal? Shall we go down to the brig instead?"

She bristled. "Of course not. I am a woman of my word."

He laughed then and she blinked at the rich sound. For a moment, the stern expression on his face disappeared and he was the same man that had flirted with her in the garden. He pulled his hat off, sending tousled locks cascading around his cheeks and her heart gave an erratic thump.

His smile faded. "A pirate, keeping their word? Forgive me if I'm not convinced."

A few more steps and he closed the distance between them. Standing a mere foot away, he seemed so much bigger. Perspiration still glimmered on his brow, but his breathing had returned to normal. Hers, on the other hand . . . she fought to calm her racing nerves.

Breathe.

He extended his hand and she stared at it. "Shall we, then?"

Her eyes widened. "Now?"

"Oh, I'm sorry. Isaac, bring me my schedule so Red and I can find a mutually acceptable time. Perhaps next week after church?" Sarcasm dripped from each word, and she frowned.

"I meant . . . I thought I would . . ."

He tilted his head. "Yes?"

Heat crept up her cheeks. "I would like to go change."

A snort escaped him. "How daft do you think I am, Red? You think I'm going to let you out of my sight for even a minute?"

Her chest seized. She couldn't do this. Not right now.

"I—I . . ." There had to be something.

"You what, Red?" He stepped closer and her mind went blank. His hand rose and he stroked her cheek with the backs of his fingers. "I see no reason to put off our meeting. Besides, you won't be needing your clothes."

"Your compass," she blurted out.

"Excuse me?"

She straightened, pulling from his touch. "I need to go retrieve your compass."

"I'm sure one of your men would be happy to."

She shook her head. "It's in a—a private spot."

He stared at her for several tense moments then shrugged. "Very well. Isaac, restrain our visitor." He pointed to Griff. "You have fifteen minutes, Red. If you don't come back, we'll have a little execution of our own over here."

She frowned as his officer directed two men to tie Griff up.

"You wouldn't."

"Try me, Red. The governor has granted me the power to make these decisions at will." He pulled out a pocket watch and flipped it open. "Fourteen minutes."

Samantha's pulse jumped and she shot him a glare as she twisted to the rope Griff had tied to the railing. She wrapped her hands around the rough cords and prepared to jump.

"Don't do this. Take the ship and leave me."

She stiffened at Griff's whispered words and gave a subtle shake of her head. How dare he think she would desert him. *Of all the cowardly things . . .* Before he could appeal again, she pushed off the railing and sailed to the *Hurricane*.

The crew gathered on deck stood still, unsure what to do. She gave one of the men a pointed look and nodded toward her cabin. He jumped into action and met her at the door. Aware of the eyes on her, she made her instructions quick.

"Make sure we are ready to sail at a moment's notice." She glanced at the setting sun. "I'll wait until dark."

When he nodded, she unlatched the door and slipped inside. As soon as it clicked shut behind her, she crumpled against it. What had she gotten herself into?

The compass still laid on the shelf with her shells and she forced her body into motion. No time to waste bemoaning what was about to happen. She plucked the instrument from its spot and clenched her fingers around it. Somehow, the sheer panic she'd been waiting to overtake her hadn't come. Yet.

In fact, each time she thought of Lieutenant Thompson, her stomach gave a little quiver. If she had to choose any man she'd ever met to be her first, she couldn't think of a single other man she'd rather have. The lieutenant's muscles, his glorious hair, the way his eyes burned into her . . .

Stop it. He's your enemy.

But her traitorous mind couldn't banish the memory of his body pressed against hers, of his hand at her side. What would it be like for that hand to touch bare skin? A flush spread over her and she turned to her wardrobe.

Breathe.

She unbuttoned her blouse and raised her fingers to the spot beneath her ear still tingling with the brush of his phantom breath.

After all, if she wanted to be a captain, she couldn't remain an innocent lass forever.

A thrill ran through her. He would touch her. In the most intimate of ways. And she would touch him. Have full access to him for however long they remained in his cabin.

Her toes curled as her lips curved.

Yanking out a new pair of breeches and a clean shirt, she tossed everything onto her bed. How many minutes had she wasted daydreaming?

Samantha slipped from her dampened clothing. With quick fingers, she unwound the strip of linen she'd used to keep her breasts bound during the fight. She shook a deep, unrestricted breath and rushed to her wash table. A basin filled with clean seawater perched on it and she tossed a bar of soap in. She grabbed a sponge and dipped it into the water. With hurried movements, the worst of the day's sweat washed from her skin.

With no time to do anything with her hair, she left it in the messy braid she'd twisted while hiding in the rigging earlier, doing her best to tuck stray strands back in place. Her breeches stuck to her wet legs, but she forced them up. For a moment, she considered sheathing her dagger at her calf but shook her head. No time.

Samantha buttoned the white shirt and tucked it into the waistband of her breeches. After slipping into her jacket, she left her boots lying next to the bed and crossed over to her desk. Inside the hidden compartment, she pulled a small box forward. It contained six tiny vials, and she plucked two free.

No.

Only one. Two would kill him and bring the entire US Navy after her.

A grim smile played across her lips when she held a single bottle to a ray of golden light. She wasn't naive enough to think the lieutenant had any intentions of letting them go. The clear liquid sloshed as her hand trembled. Henbane extract mixed with opium. Just a few drops of the potent concoction could lull a man into a deep slumber. But how to get the lieutenant to ingest it? With a sigh, she slid the vial into her pocket. She'd figure something out.

Her gaze settled on the satchels of dried herbs tucked next to the box. Tansey, pennyroyal, and Queen Anne's lace. A tea she hadn't thought she'd ever have to use. One of her crew mate's wives was a midwife and had gifted the contraceptive tea to her months ago.

A commotion came from the deck and she grabbed the compass and tightened her mask before flinging the door open. The lieutenant strode toward her and she ignored the flutter in her stomach when he came to a stop a pace away.

"I see patience is not one of your virtues."

He caught her arm and leaned in. "You'll find that I'm a very impatient man when I want something. And you, my little warrior, I find myself wanting quite badly."

Despite her nerves, the words sent a thrill through her. For a long moment, she stood still and stared up at him. He'd washed up as well, his wet hair combed back into a neat queue. Without his uniform hat or jacket, he almost looked as if he belonged among her crew. Almost. With a shake of her shoulder, she freed herself and held out his compass.

"As promised."

A chestnut brow lifted and he took it from her. "Would you look at that? A pirate that actually kept their word. Whatever is the world coming to?"

Samantha rolled her eyes and walked to the railing, where several thick ropes tethered the two ships together. A long coil of rigging line lay discarded at her feet. She slung it over her shoulder and looked up. With a hop, she caught the ratline and a few moments later swung up onto the main yard.

"Where the hell do you think you're going?"

She peered down at the lieutenant and planted a hand on her hip. "Last I checked, Lieutenant, your ship sits several feet higher than mine. Unless you've found a way to defy gravity, I suggest getting a higher start."

He made a grab for her ankle, but she reached into the ropes and climbed to the top yard. A curse floated up her way and she grinned.

"For a gentleman, you sure do have the mouth of a pirate."

The breeze pushed against her and she slowly made her way away from the mast. Her bare toes curled around the smooth wood and she raised her gaze to the horizon, making sure to sway with the swells.

The lieutenant swore again. "You'll break your neck."

She paused and looked down at him. "Worried for my safety, are you? Be careful, Lieutenant, or I may begin to believe you've a heart."

Adrenaline coursed through her veins as she let go of the rigging and edged out further. One strong gust of wind and she'd tumble headfirst to the deck below. She carefully lowered herself into a crouch and made quick work of tying one end of the rope in a knot around the top yard.

Satisfied with her work, she let the line fall and dropped onto it. The muscles in her tired arms screamed in protest. She shimmied down to the main yard and gave the rope a solid tug.

"Are you coming, Lieutenant? I thought we had an appointment."

"There are easier ways to board a ship, Red." He pointed to where his crew extended a gangplank over the water. With a solid thunk, it landed on the *Hurricane's* railing.

She laughed. "Where's the fun in that?"

"Come down here."

"You'll have to come and get me."

He glowered up at her and she held her grin even as her heart threatened to beat free of her chest. She'd never flirted with a man like this before. It felt good. Empowering.

Before she could blink, he'd jumped into the ratline and began to climb with ease. When he lifted himself onto the main yard, she took an involuntary step toward him. With one hand tangled in the rigging, he reached for her. She edged back, just out of reach.

"Red . . ." His voice rang with warning while she slid her foot backward. "Don't think about it."

"Too late."

Samantha pivoted and raced to the end of the main yard. Her hands tightened around the rope as she launched into the air. For a moment, she hung weightless. And then her weight carried her down, swinging in a wide arc over the water. She landed on the *Falcon's* main deck and stumbled to her knees. Not as graceful an entry as last time.

Pushing to her feet, she strode to the railing and tossed the rope back. The lieutenant caught it and narrowed his eyes. She opened her mouth to taunt him, but a voice at her side stopped her.

"Careful, my lady pirate, I dare say you've pushed him to his limits." The first officer, Isaac, joined her.

After a tense moment of silence, the lieutenant took the leap. Samantha's heart caught at the sight. The muscles of his arms corded and the wind plastered his shirt against his body. With his knees drawn together, he flew through the air toward them. And his gaze did not leave her face.

He released the rope at the perfect moment and dropped to the deck next to her. She stepped back, but he was quicker, catching her around the waist and pulling her to him. A chorus of hoots and cheers came from his crew, drawing a blush across her cheeks.

"To my cabin." He tugged her in the direction of the door beneath the helm.

Breathless, she began to follow him before her jumbled

thoughts could catch up. Someone cleared their throat. Griff. She dug her heels into the deck and the lieutenant turned to her.

"Now what?"

She pulled her shoulders back and stood as straight as she could. "I request that my first mate be released."

"No."

His grip tightened and she resisted his attempt to move them along. "Lieutenant, the agreement was for one night with me and did not include any of my crew. I will hold you to it."

"I assure you, he'll be safe."

She shook her head. "I don't trust you."

He shot a dark glare between her and Griff. "You're deeply mistaken if you think he can rescue you."

With a huff, she twisted back to the lieutenant. "You've made it very clear that you outgun us. I assure you, my men will not make any foolish choices while I am aboard the *Falcon*." She lowered her voice. "I forbid them to risk their lives for me."

Something in the lieutenant's gaze softened and after a tense moment of silence, he nodded to the man standing guard next to Griff. "Untie the blasted man."

When his bonds fell away, Griff strode toward Samantha. Isaac stepped between them and held his hand up.

Griff let out a growl and fixed his gaze over the officer's shoulder on the lieutenant. "If you hurt her—"

"That's enough. Return to the ship and wait there." Samantha turned from him before he could say anything else and flashed the lieutenant a cold smile. "I have business to conduct."

Moments later, the lieutenant clicked the door shut behind them. He released his hold on her and she retreated to the middle of the cabin, pulse beating at her temple while she chanced a quick look away from the lieutenant to scan the room. Exactly as she remembered, save for an extra chair pushed up to his desk.

A soft click echoed through the space as the lock slid in place. Trapped. The stark emptiness of the cabin closed in on her and she took a shaky breath when the lieutenant turned to face her.

In slow, deliberate footsteps, he approached and she fought the urge to dart away. Nowhere to hide. One hand extended her way and she flinched. With a raised brow, he slid behind her and his hands closed on her shoulders. When she stiffened, he rubbed his thumbs in half circles of pressure.

"Relax, Red. I'm not going to hurt you."

His hands moved up and down her shoulders, continuing to apply the pleasant pressure. She couldn't help dropping her head when his fingers swept across the bare skin at the nape of her neck.

After a few moments passed, he dropped his hands and stepped in front of her.

He held one palm out. "Your coat."

Tension flooded back through her quick as a wave crashing against the shore.

You can do this. Samantha's fingers shook as she began to unbutton the garment. Each time a button slid free, her heart rate increased a little more. Finally, there were no more buttons and she had no choice but to slip from the garment. She handed it to him and he ran his fingers along it in a quick but obvious perusal. When he finished, he tossed it across the back of a chair.

"I hope you won't object, but I'm going to search you for weapons."

"I . . ." She fell silent and hung her head. She would do the same thing.

His hands went to her shoulders and slowly ran down the length of her sides. Without missing a beat, he slid them over her breeches. She shifted just enough for his palm to miss the vial hidden in her pocket. His fingers continued their search, skimming down to her ankles and then back up along her inner thighs. Gooseflesh spread along her skin and a subtle warmth pooled in her belly.

Mortification washed over her and she stared at the floor. How was she supposed to lie with him? She hadn't an idea of what to do. Her eyes pressed closed. She was a pirate. He would expect her to be knowledgeable about the act.

She had tread out of her depth. How could she fake experience without any inkling of the act itself? If only she'd spent more time listening to her crew's bawdy talk of women and whores. She sighed and opened her eyes.

Her gaze settled on his lips and a little shiver went down her spine. Would he kiss her? She found herself hoping he would. She couldn't bear the thought that he might take his pleasure quickly. Then again, perhaps it might be best. Get it over with and get out.

He waved his hand at a chair. "Sit."

Sliding him a wary glance, she lowered herself into it.

She forced herself to take several steadying breaths while he retrieved a bottle and two tin cups from a cabinet in the wall. He lit two candles and sank into the other chair.

"You're nervous."

Samantha blinked at him and he nodded toward her lap. "Fists clenched, erratic breathing." He slid his gaze to her face. "And you keep biting your lip in the most delightful way."

She relaxed her hands. The damn man noticed everything.

"If you forgive me, it's not every day that I conduct my business this way." The confidence she attempted to inject into her voice fell flat.

He poured two glasses of wine and held one out to her. She reached for it and he paused.

"Take off your mask."

Chapter Eight

SAMANTHA FROZE, HER fingers dangling over the cup. "No."

"You lost, little warrior. Now you get to play by my rules."

Setting the cup down, he reached for her face. She jumped to her feet and clutched a hand over the soft leather. If she took off her mask, it would all be over.

"I cannot."

He tilted his head. "Is there a scar? A disfiguration? Is that why you didn't want to me to remove it earlier?"

"You wouldn't understand. Please don't make me . . ." Her voice trembled and she took a step back. "It wasn't part of your terms."

Her last words came out in a strangled whisper and he stared hard at her. Silence curled around them and she began to take another step back.

He dropped his hand. "Alright. No need to flee."

Samantha blew out a slow breath and sat back down, taking the glass of wine. She tilted it back and took a small sip. The smooth blend filled her mouth with a velvety fruitiness that lingered on the tongue. When she took another sip, her hand drifted to her pocket and she rolled the vial between her fingers.

Could she get it out and pour it without him noticing? Doubtful. It may be her only chance, though. One of her uncle's sailors had shown her a trick when she was young. He'd closed a coin in his hand, and when he spread his fingers, the coin had disappeared. She'd begged him to show her how to perform the illusion. Luckily for her, he gave in to her pleas.

With a slight movement, she slipped the little bottle free and popped the cork out. Lowering her cup to her lap, she forced herself to keep her eyes on the lieutenant's face as she remembered the old seaman's advice. *Never look down at your mark. It'll give you away.*

One shot. If the lieutenant caught her . . .

"What's wrong, Red?" He held her gaze and she passed her hand over her wine, flipping the vial at just the right moment before she lifted the cup to the table.

She set it directly next to his. He caught her hand before she could draw back and flipped it over. The smooth glass of the vial pressed into her other palm and she sent up a silent prayer of thanks that the transfer had worked.

"Why have you chosen this life?" The lieutenant studied her hand and his lips pulled into a soft frown. "Or were you not given a choice?"

"It's none of your business, Lieutenant."

His thumb stroked down her open palm. "Contrary. It's very much my business tonight."

She pulled her hand away, trying to shake away the curious prickle of warmth his touch had sent through her. Quickly, she grabbed a cup of wine. His cup.

After another swallow, she dropped her gaze to the table. "You wouldn't understand."

"You keep saying that. Red, I'd very much like to understand."

The words prodded at a deep part of her. The part that yearned to be able to share her dreams. The part she'd grown very good at keeping locked up. His gaze remained earnest and she sighed.

"I think it would be in your best interest if you stopped trying to understand me, Lieutenant. It's the life I chose. Let's keep it at that."

He picked up the other cup and drank deeply. When he set it

down, she couldn't help but sneak a quick peek. Half empty. Her heart sank. Not enough.

He sprawled back into his chair and gave her a quiet perusal. "Why did you do it?"

Her eyes snapped to his. "Do what?"

"You know what I'm talking about. You could have killed me and avoided this. You would have won." His eyes shone in the candlelight and she pushed to her feet in the silence.

"Come here." He gestured with one finger, and like a moth to a flame, she closed the distance. When she came to a stop, he reached for her wrist, his fingers stroking the exposed skin beneath her sleeve cuff.

"Why?"

She sucked in a breath at the whispered word, trying to ignore the burst of heat his touch caused. "It would have been the move of a coward."

His eyes narrowed briefly at her soft retort and she cringed. She should not have used the very wording he'd used with her at the ball. Too risky.

He moved his thumb in a lazy circle and pressed his lips together.

"I'm not a man to offer favors, but I owe you, Red. I've never forced a woman into my bed before, and I'm not about to start. I release you from your end of the agreement. Call us even."

She stared at where he continued to grasp her. This was her chance. Somehow, by some miracle, she was being offered a way out of this mess.

Say yes.

When Samantha lifted her gaze, the lieutenant cocked his head. His hair fell forward over his forehead and she swallowed. God help her, she wanted this.

Reckless.

The word echoed in her head while she reached forward and pushed his hair back in place in a gentle sweep of fingers. He caught his breath and the sound emboldened her.

"I'd prefer to save your favor for another day, Lieutenant. Tonight, I come freely."

He made a soft sound in the back of his throat and pulled her to him. When her bottom landed on his lap, she let out a little gasp at the contact. His hand caught her neck and angled her face toward him.

"Red."

He murmured the name against her and a moment later, crushed his lips to hers. Samantha gasped and the warm heat of his tongue pressed into her mouth. She'd been kissed before, but nothing compared to this. A little moan formed in the back of her throat.

His fingers twisted in her hair, pulling her closer. She met his tongue with a timid stroke of her own and he deepened the kiss. Soon, she gasped for breath, unable to pull her mouth away as the kiss built in intensity.

Samantha let out a startled cry when he tightened his grip and stood. With no choice, she wrapped her arms around his neck and clung to him as he carried her to the bed. He sat and set her on the floor in front of him.

"Undress."

When she didn't move, he pulled his shirt off in one motion and flung it aside.

"You don't have to be shy with me, Red."

"I'm not."

Still, she stood paralyzed.

He frowned. "We don't have to do this. I meant what I said earlier, I will not force you."

She couldn't pull her eyes from the bulge in his pants. Never had she wanted something so badly before. Time to be bold.

Do it.

Her hand settled on the hard ridge and the lieutenant's eyes widened. He pressed into her touch and she trailed her fingers up and down his rigid length. A hiss of breath escaped him and he caught her hand in his.

"Careful, Red. Or this night will be over before it starts."

Her brows scrunched together, but she had no time to ponder the meaning of his words before he hooked his legs behind hers. He dropped her hand and tugged her shirt free of her breeches. Bending forward, he pressed his mouth to her side, nipping through the linen fabric. The rough contact sent a little shiver through her.

And then his hands were beneath the shirt, skimming along her bare skin. He stopped just below her breasts and she let out a shaky sigh. A wicked grin spread across his face and his thumbs flicked up over both nipples at the same time.

"Oh!" She had to grab his shoulders to steady herself.

The lieutenant chuckled and withdrew his hands, bringing them to her top button. A few fluid motions later and her shirt gaped open. He leaned into her, the hot caress of his breath at her navel sending a wave of fire straight to her core.

Samantha shuddered when he began to kiss a trail upwards. His hands skimmed up her sides and hooked under her shirt. In a feather-light motion, the garment slipped from her shoulders, leaving her bared to him.

A growl rumbled from beneath one breast and a moment later, his mouth closed around a pert nipple. Samantha's fingernails dug into his shoulders.

"Lieutenant," she gasped.

"Call me Christian."

"Christian." The name flowed from her mouth before she could stop it and he groaned his approval.

His tongue flicked out to stroke her and she let her eyes drift shut at the delicious waves of pleasure radiating from the scandalous contact. When he pulled away, his breath came in ragged gasps against her.

One of his hands slid down her belly and slipped beneath her waistband. When he brushed his fingers through the soft curls there, her eyes snapped open. As his fingers traveled down to her most private spot, a throbbing pressure built deep within her belly. Lower.

He paused, and she whimpered. The throbbing increased tenfold and her knees began to shake. The cage he'd made around her with his legs slackened and he tugged her onto the mattress next to him. He unfastened her breeches and peeled them down.

With a soft thud, they landed in a heap on the floor and Samantha covered herself with one hand. Her cheeks flamed while Christian gave her an appreciative look.

"You're beautiful, Red."

His hand closed around one slender calf and he slid it up to her thigh. When his fingers came to rest over hers, she stared at him, mesmerized by the candlelight flickering across his chest. With a gentle tug, he pulled her hand away and cupped her. One finger slipped between her folds and she sucked in a breath.

This was . . . Samantha couldn't form a coherent thought. She wanted . . . she wanted him to touch her.

"Please," she gasped.

And he obeyed, his finger pressing into the throbbing heat.

Christian let out a soft groan. "You're so wet for me, Red."

His fingers stroked up and down the slick cleft of her, sending frenzied bursts of pleasure shooting through her.

He leaned his lips to her ear and nibbled on her earlobe. At the same time, his finger pressed against her core. She moaned as it slid inside her a fraction. He rubbed it in a gentle swirl and her next moan came out more like a cry.

"Mmm . . ." His breath brushed hot against her neck. "Do your lovers make you cry out like this?"

Lovers?

Samantha jerked her head back and stared at him. "I don't have any lovers."

He chuckled and pressed deeper into her, causing her to gasp. "Don't lie, Red. A woman like you must have an admirer in every port."

"Oh." Of course she would. If she were a pirate captain. Samantha squirmed in Christian's grasp, trying to free herself, but he held her tight. "Those lovers. Yes."

His gaze bore into her for a long moment, then he plunged his finger deep inside her.

The feeling was too much.

Samantha fell back against the mattress and arched her back toward him as his finger thrust in and out. Christian leaned over and caught one of her nipples with his mouth. He sucked and she writhed beneath him.

He withdrew his finger and she began to protest, but stilled when his thumb found the sensitive spot nestled within her curls. The contact sent a jolt of fire through her core and the pressure became unbearable.

"Open for me, Red." His words came rough against her chest and helpless to resist, she parted her legs farther.

Another finger joined the first one and he pushed into her once more, stretching her in the most fulfilling way. And then his thumb rubbed a quick circle.

"Christian!" She gasped his name as bolts of raw energy flew from the spot. Her breaths came out in ragged little pants.

The pressure began to spiral out of control and Samantha twisted her fingers in the sheets, trying to find a way out of the exquisite torture. Was this supposed to happen? Alarm weaved itself into each shocking burst of feeling.

She teetered on the edge of a precipice, one she didn't know how to navigate. One that was about to swallow her whole.

"I—I feel like . . ." The words stuck in her throat as he increased his rhythm.

"It's alright, Red. Jump. I'll catch you." His free hand slid beneath her and splayed open across her lower back as if to prove his point.

Samantha closed her eyes as her body trembled. Christian's lips brushed against her nipple.

And the world splintered around her.

The pressure burst free, shooting wave upon wave of white-hot pleasure through her. Muscles she didn't know existed clamped together and drew all her energy to her core as she tumbled over the edge.

Christian shifted and caught her wild cries with his mouth, holding her tight until she collapsed against the bed in a boneless heap. When he slipped his fingers from her and stood, Samantha's eyes fluttered open.

In one motion, Christian stripped from his breeches and the part she had so boldly touched earlier sprang free. Her mouth went dry. *That was supposed to fit in her?* He cleared his throat and her eyes darted to his face and the amused expression there.

Before she could move, he dropped back onto the bed to cover her body with his. Her apprehension melted away when he lowered his mouth to her neck and nibbled the spot below her ear. Suddenly, the throbbing ache between her legs returned, and Samantha wrapped her arms around Christian's back.

She let her hands explore. Every inch of him was muscle and strength. As her fingertips drifted further down, the hard length of him jutted into her belly and he nudged her thighs apart.

Being open below him sent a wicked thrill through Samantha, and she pressed her hips against his. He growled at her ear and slipped his hand between them. The heavy weight at her stomach disappeared, only to reappear further down, pressing against her swollen heat.

Christian rubbed the smooth tip of him up and down her cleft until her slick wetness covered him. The feeling sent Samantha spiraling upward once more and she tugged at his hips. She needed more.

He lifted his head and stared at her with shining eyes.

"Red."

In one deep thrust, he entered her. The sudden stretch sent a sharp bite of pain lancing through her, and Samantha cried out.

Christian went completely still. After a shuddering breath, he gave one more slight thrust forward and she let out another cry. His expression darkened. "Damn it, Red."

He began to pull out and she locked her legs around him. She would die if he stopped. Already the pain dulled into a pleasant throb.

"Please . . ." She didn't know how to ask him for more, but tilted her hips toward him, forcing him to slide back in a bit.

Christian let out a soft curse and lowered his face to hers. "We are going to have a long talk after this." With a groan, he sank all the way into her once more.

Samantha's head fell back at the intimate fullness and he brought his lips to her neck. He kissed her in soft, feathery brushes against her skin. As he worked his way up, he began a slow rhythm, pumping in and out of her with deliberate gentleness. The movement wrenched a moan from her and he caught her mouth with his. Pleasure radiated from where they joined and she started to move her hips in time with his, making each contact press a little deeper.

Christian growled, the sound rumbling against her tongue, and quickened his pace. Each thrust pulled a little cry from her and the stinging pain disappeared altogether. Her fingers tangled in his hair and he suddenly stiffened, pressing deep within her. He jerked his head back and closed his eyes as a loud groan tore from him. Samantha froze, transfixed at the sight of him attaining his pleasure.

After a long moment, Christian opened his eyes and bent to place a soft kiss on her forehead. The gesture sent a bust of tenderness through her and she couldn't help tilting her face to catch his lips with hers. This time, he kissed her slowly, his tongue lingering against hers in a languid dance.

He pulled from her and she let out a muffled cry of dismay at the loss of contact. His lips curved against hers. "You're full of surprises, Red."

After one last kiss, Christian lowered himself to the bed next to her and propped himself up on one elbow. Samantha's skin burned beneath his intense gaze and she started when his fingers brushed her cheek.

He traced the outline of her mask in a lazy motion. "We need to talk. You have some explaining to do. If I had known, I wouldn't have . . ."

No. They most definitely did not need to talk about her virginity. She pulled her bottom lip between her teeth and shook her head.

"Not yet." She started to sit, but he pressed a firm hand to her belly.

"Stay here."

Samantha's jaw went slack when he swung his feet to the floor and crossed over to the table. Candlelight glimmered off the chiseled muscles of his back, and her gaze darted down to his perfectly formed buttocks. The man looked as though he'd been carved from stone.

He picked up his cup and downed the rest of the wine. Thank God. Heat flushed her cheeks when he looked over his shoulder and she jerked her gaze away.

A moment later, he returned with a wet rag. When he reached toward the juncture of her thighs, she snapped them shut.

"Let me clean you, Red."

The cool cloth slipped past her curls and she gasped when he made contact with the searing heat of her core. He gave her a wicked grin and flicked one finger against the still-sensitive nub there.

Samantha's breath hissed out and she scootched back, away from the torturous touch. A moment later, Christian tossed the rag to the floor. She reached for her shirt but before her fingers could reach the fabric, he grabbed it and pulled it away.

"Not so fast, Red. You agreed to a whole night."

Samantha blinked at his implication. "You mean . . ." Her blush crept across her chest. "Again?"

He sat next to her and she averted her eyes from where he had already gone hard again. Damn her pulse for jumping.

Christian leaned back and patted the space next to him. She

hesitated, and he hooked an arm around her waist and pulled her down to his side. Her head came to rest on his shoulder while he caught one of her legs with his. Soon, every inch of her body burned with his heat.

When he tucked a strand of hair behind her ear, she caught his hand and pressed her cheek into his palm. Oh, how she wanted this moment to last. She pressed her eyes closed, trying to memorize the feel of his calloused skin against hers, the way his fingers curved to cup her jaw.

"Red . . ." He murmured the moniker against her cheek before yawning. "Whatever those pirates hold over you, it can't be worth staying with them. Let me save you."

She opened her eyes and stared at the flickering light on the ceiling.

His thumb slid along her jawline. "Come with me, Red. I can make sure they never bother you again. You'll be safe with me."

Who was this man? The more time she spent with him, the less he felt like an enemy. Her jaw clenched beneath his touch. She couldn't fall for him. At the end of the day, they remained opponents in this war. She'd best remember that.

Still, the genuine concern in his voice tugged at something deep inside her. Reminded her she was destined to be alone. That she couldn't have what he offered.

Silence fell over them and he nuzzled into her hair. Samantha took a shaky breath and pulled his hand from her face. He twined his fingers through hers and she stared at their combined fist. Tears pricked at the corners of her eyes.

"You can't save me." She whispered the words into his shoulder but kept the second half of her statement silent. *Not without taking away my identity.*

Christian dropped her hand and embraced her, pulling her tight against his chest. "Let me try, Red. Let me . . ." His voice trailed off and his breathing deepened.

The henbane had worked. Samantha laid next to the lieutenant's still body for several long minutes, until the gentle whoosh of his breathing threatened to lull her to sleep herself. She carefully lifted his arm and slid from the bed, ignoring her body's protest at leaving his comfortable warmth behind.

After dressing, Samantha started toward the window. Halfway across the room, she paused and allowed herself one last look at him. Sleep had softened his features and she swallowed past the lump in her throat. She would remember this night for the rest of her life, every moment seared into her memory.

"Damn you, Lieutenant."

With a shake of her head, she turned toward the closest window. Time to go. With nimble fingers, she unlatched it and carefully swung it open. A cool breeze brushed across her face and salty air filled her lungs. Lifting a foot to the ledge beneath the window, she began to lift herself up.

Wait.

She jumped back to the floor and rushed over to his desk. Slipping her mask off, she laid it next to the compass. The brass reflected the flame from a nearby candle.

Leave it.

But she couldn't. The urge to take something as a reminder of tonight became overwhelming. And before she could talk herself out of it, she snatched the compass up and shoved it into her waistband. A moment later she stood on the ledge.

Holding her breath, she leaned out. No one stood at the railing above. Good. With a leap, she dove into the dark waves below. She slid deep below the surface and for a moment let the heavy weight of the water hold her still. A thousand bubbles roiled around her and as they dissipated, she kicked toward the *Hurricane.*

When she could hold her breath no longer, she surfaced near the hull. Several strong kicks later, she reached it and maneuvered to the other side of the ship. In the pale moonlight, a rope ladder dangled from the main deck. She grinned and pulled herself from the water.

A few moments later, her bare feet slapped against the cool

deck, drawing a startled exclamation from the man closest to her. Griff jumped up from where he sat against the main mast and strode toward her with concern on his face.

Samantha lifted a hand at his advance. "Time to make our escape."

Chapter Nine

WITH A HEAVY sigh, Samantha leaned against her balcony railing and stared at the river glistening through the trees. She ignored the glint of sunlight reflecting from the compass sitting next to her hand. Since she'd returned, the house had been quiet. Dead quiet. Which meant Griff had told Uncle Henry everything.

It would be a miracle if he didn't march over and murder Lieutenant Thompson outright. Her gaze drifted to the east, where Christian's property lay. Only a few pastures and groves of trees separated them. At the thought of his name, her stomach did a little flip.

How long?

How long would she react like this? Her hand rose to her face and she let her fingertips linger on her lips. Every time she closed her eyes, she saw Christian. Christian with his mouth against hers. Christian as he took her to heights she hadn't known existed. And Christian when he held her close.

Held her like she mattered.

"Samantha?"

She jerked away from the warm stone and spun to face her maid.

"Are you alright? You've been standing there for hours."

Samantha nodded and Anna tsked. "Come inside before you get a sunburn."

"The sun is setting. I think we are well past the risk."

The maid crossed her arms. "No matter. Mr. Warstein has

asked you to join him for dinner."

Samantha's heart constricted. "I'd rather not."

Anna looked at her for a long moment and Samantha nibbled on her lip. Had the servants heard what had happened already? Heat pricked along her cheeks.

"He said you might say that." Anna crossed the room and opened the wardrobe. After pulling a pale blue dress out, she held it up. "He told me to tell you that if you won't come down, he'll take dinner in here."

Of course he would. Captain Remington never failed to get his way. Samantha grabbed the compass and ducked into the shadowed room. She set it on the mantel and went to her vanity. In a few short minutes, Anna had her stripped of her day dress and began dressing her.

While the maid pinned her hair up, Samantha stared at her reflection in stoic silence. Her heart pounded an erratic beat in her chest. How was she supposed to face Uncle Henry? Beads of perspiration already dotted her forehead and she wiped the back of her hand across the damp skin there.

Anna took out one of Samantha's mother's old necklaces and clasped it around Samantha's throat. She lifted her hand and gripped the cameo. *You can do this.*

"Thank you." Biting her lip, she pushed her chair back and left the room.

At the top of the staircase, she took a shaky breath. What was the worst he could do? It wasn't like he'd turn her out in the street. She started down.

What if he revealed her identity to the lieutenant? He could demand they marry. Her next step faltered and she had to catch herself on the railing. He wouldn't. It would be too risky for his own cover.

When her feet settled onto the marble floor, Samantha hesitated once more. The double doors to the dining room stood between her and her judgment. She cast a longing look over her shoulder at the open doors leading to the veranda. If she ran, she could be hidden in the garden before anyone knew she was missing.

She pulled her shoulders back. What a ridiculous thought. If she escaped the conversation tonight, he would find her tomorrow. And would be even more upset. She couldn't avoid him forever.

So she strode forward and pushed the doors open.

Uncle Henry sat at the head of the table, studying a chart. He didn't look up when she entered. A place had been set two seats away from him and she clenched her teeth together. Why so close?

With slow steps, she made her way to him. A footman materialized to pull out her chair and she sat. Still, her uncle did not look up.

She folded her hands on her lap and studied the gilded edge of her plate. The heavy silence hanging over them gnawed at the ragged edges of her anxiety. When her uncle flipped the parchment, the crisp sound echoed through the room. Swallowing, Samantha lifted her head. He stared right at her.

Still, he remained silent.

He was waiting for her.

Samantha's fingers twisted together and every rehearsed excuse she had thought of left her mind.

"I'm sorry," she finally whispered. "I made a terrible mistake."

His eyes had gone an icy blue. "No. I made the mistake."

He leaned back as her skin went clammy at the ominous tone in his voice. "I made a mistake in thinking I was doing a favor by letting you sail. I thought I was giving you choices. I was wrong."

Tears gathered in the corners of her eyes and she shook her head.

"The sea is no place for a woman." She pressed her eyes shut as he repeated the very thing Griff had told her. "No good can ever come of it. And I was a fool for not realizing it."

He shifted in his seat. "Your father indulged your mother and she paid for it with her life."

She sucked in a breath at the harsh words.

"If he hadn't allowed it, she would still be here with you. You wouldn't have grown up motherless."

A drop of wetness landed on her forearm.

"And if I hadn't allowed you to do the same thing, you wouldn't be sitting here ruined."

An ache crept up the back of her throat as she searched for and failed to find words.

"You're grounded, Samantha. For good."

Her eyes snapped open. "Please, anything but that."

"You'll begin to act like a proper young lady. No more swordsmanship. No more visits to the docks. No more breeches."

A crushing weight pressed on her chest and she struggled to take a breath.

"I could say I'm angry. Hurt. Ashamed. And all would be correct. But most of all, I'm disappointed. You betrayed the trust I gave you, Samantha. And by doing so, you'll learn the hardest lesson of them all. Once a captain cannot be trusted, he will never be able to lead again."

Tears began to stream down her face in earnest, leaving hot trails in their wake. "Uncle—"

"My mind is made up. Do not try to sway my decision." He pushed his chair back and stood. "You're dismissed."

And just like that, all her hopes, all her dreams—everything Samantha had ever wanted in life—were crushed like a brittle shell beneath the heel. Choking back a sob, she stumbled to her feet and fled the room.

She passed the stairs and burst onto the veranda. Without slowing, she stumbled down the steps and raced across the gardens. Under the big oak tree, she collapsed to the ground and let her grief overtake her.

The minutes stretched by and soon dark shadows cloaked her as the sun slipped from view. Samantha pulled herself from the damp ground and brushed bits of twigs and grass from her dress.

She drew her knees to her chest and stared out toward the river, where the pale sails of a ship stood out against the darkness.

Lights from town twinkled over the water. If only she could tell Abigail what had happened. But she couldn't. Abigail couldn't know. Nobody could. She was alone in her despair.

A vast ache settled in her heart and she gave a bitter sniff. So many *if onlys*.

If only she hadn't come up with her mad scheme to get the lieutenant off her back. If only she hadn't accepted his terms. If only she hadn't . . . no. Another fat tear plopped to the ground and she curled her fingers into fists. She would not regret that part. No matter what.

Her legs began to go numb and she stood. A dull pressure built behind her temple and she pressed her fingers to the sensitive spot. When a mosquito landed on her arm, she swatted it away. Soon the little beasts would be out in full force.

With a sigh, she headed back toward the house. No need to stay outside and get eaten alive. The servants had lit lanterns along the veranda and when she got a good view of her rumpled skirts, a chagrined smile tugged at her lips. Anna would have a fit.

Inside, candlelight flickered from the sconces on the walls. Samantha crept up the stairs, careful to skip the ones that creaked, and padded down the hallway. Slipping inside her room, she crossed to the mantel and grabbed the compass. Once her hand curled around the cool weight of it, she sat on the bed.

The inscription glowed in the light of the single candle Anna had left lit on the nightstand and Samantha ran a fingertip over the etched words. Who had it belonged to? She knew very little about Lieutenant Thompson's past other than what he'd revealed about his mother. Perhaps a great-great-grandfather had served in the Royal Navy and passed the relic down through the genera-tions. Christian's father likely gave it to him. A gift when he joined the navy?

A prick of guilt pressed through her heart and she touched the cameo at her neck. What if it had been something of her mother's or father's that had been taken? She'd be devastated.

Standing, she crossed to the door of her balcony and stared out into the darkness. Mottled light cut through the shadows from the full moon above. The weight in her hand seemed to grow heavier by the moment. She needed to return it.

A soft knock sounded at her door and Anna peeked in. "Do you need help getting ready for bed?"

Samantha tensed at the intrusion and turned back to the night. "I'll be fine."

The door clicked shut and she blew out a breath. Her grip around the compass tightened. Tonight. She would return the blasted thing tonight.

Mind made up, she strode to her wardrobe and yanked open her breeches drawer. Empty. With a curse she opened the rest of her drawers and rocked back on her heels. Every bit of masculine clothing she owned was gone. Her boots had been replaced with dainty shoes and pale gloves and stockings had replaced her buttoned shirts.

Her uncle was serious.

The thought sobered her and she stood. Somehow, she would have to convince him he'd made an error. She would work hard to prove to him she'd learned her lesson. But how long would it take?

Her eyes narrowed. How dare they try to rein her in? She wasn't cut out to be a demure lady, to sit at a window and embroider while her husband was at sea. Striding to her balcony, she flung the door open and peered down. She'd made the climb in breeches, but could she do it in a dress?

Pulling her skirt up she unfastened her bulky petticoat and stepped out of it. Better. With no pockets, she shoved the compass into her bodice. Swinging a leg over the railing, she maneuvered onto the ledge running the length of the manor. Barely the width of her foot, it offered little comfort.

Samantha pressed her body against the smooth siding and edged away from the balcony. As she approached the big oak tree across from the room next to hers, her skirt tangled between her legs and she teetered for an agonizing moment.

"Damn it," she muttered, carefully reaching down to pull the offending material away.

If she fell and broke her neck, it would be on Anna's head. Traitorous maid. Did they not think she'd go right back to her tailor? Even if they convinced him to turn her business away, she'd just find someone else.

A few more steps and she wrapped her fingers around a sturdy branch. Bunching her skirt up, she climbed into the tree and made her way to the trunk. Two branches down and she swung herself to the ground. Brushing her hands together, she grinned. Not so bad.

A bush rustled in the garden and she froze, staring into the inky darkness. The hairs on the back of her neck lifted and she reached down on instinct. She scowled. No boot meant no dagger. But the garden remained silent, and she gave a shake of her shoulders. Probably a hungry racoon.

Samantha turned and hurried around the house and up the drive. Though taking the field would ensure she stayed out of sight, the road would be much quicker. Plus her slippers probably wouldn't survive a trek through grass and mud.

A chorus of crickets echoed through the night, nearly deafening in their volume, and she had to keep her pace brisk to keep the mosquitoes at bay. The humid heat of the night curled around her and stray tendrils of hair clung to her face. Summer was in full swing.

She hummed a little seaman's tune to pass the time and soon came to a stop at the end of Lieutenant Thompson's drive. A cloud covered the moon and shrouded the property in darkness. Several windows downstairs twinkled with light. Samantha wrapped her arms around herself as her heart began to race.

Pulling the compass out, she stared at it, then at the house. Somewhere in there, Christian was doing . . . whatever lieutenants did in their free time. Was he sitting in his library, reading a book by a lantern? Or maybe he sat at his desk, going over his estate finances. Her eyes drifted to the darkened upper windows. He could be sinking into a deep tub of hot water, running a bar of sandalwood-scented soap along . . .

Samantha jerked her head back at the picture the thought conjured and her cheeks burned. Good Lord. What was wrong with her? A pleasant warmth coiled in her belly and she pressed a hand over her heart. She would never be able to be in the same room as the lieutenant again.

Hell, she wasn't even sure she could be on the same property as he was. She clutched the compass and looked back down the road. Perhaps it would be better to have a courier deliver it.

She shook her head and harrumphed. "You're a pirate. Start acting like one."

Still, she stood frozen in place, unable to take the first step. Every instinct told her to turn and flee, to put as much space between him and her as she could. She closed her eyes and weighed her options. Get it over with, or retreat.

The rumble of hooves made the decision for her. Jerking into motion, she rushed toward the house. Crouching near a whitewashed fountain, she waited for the carriage to pass. Her pulse pounded so hard in her head, it drowned out the sounds of the night. The lieutenant's door loomed at the top of a half-dozen stone steps.

She could do this.

Now.

With a deep breath, she jumped to her feet and darted up the steps. She set the compass down and pounded on the door, the sound echoing through the courtyard like a musket shot.

Run.

Hiking her skirt up, she flew down to the drive and cut across the lawn to a neat hedgerow. With an ungraceful leap, she dove behind it, landing on the ground with a muffled thump. Pulling herself up, she swiveled and pulled the branches aside until she had a clear view of the door.

Her chest went tight as it cracked open and a line of light cut into the night. A moment later, the door opened fully to reveal Christian. He wore dark breeches and his shirt hung untucked. And unbuttoned. Unbound, his hair fell in waves over his shoulders.

"What the . . ." He'd noticed the compass.

After a glance around him, he bent to retrieve it. Straightening, he stared out into the night.

"Red, if you're out there . . ." He trailed off. "I meant what I said."

Samantha swallowed past the lump in her throat. He still wanted to save her. She edged away from the hedge. Time to leave.

A twig snapped.

Before she could turn, a heavy hand closed over her mouth and the bite of a blade pressed between her shoulders.

Eyes wide, a scream built in her throat.

"Don't make a sound."

And then, the blow came. It cracked against her head, sending a blinding light behind her eyes, and everything went dark.

Chapter Ten

D AWN'S SOFT LIGHT slanted through the window while Christian sank into the chair at his desk with a groan. His head pounded like the devil. And it should.

After a fruitless search of his property last night, he'd come inside and downed half a bottle of whiskey. What else was he supposed to do when all he could think about was a fearless little redhead who'd marched into his cabin and given him her virtue? His cock stirred. More than that. She'd given him the best damn night of his life.

And then, she'd drugged him and vanished without a trace.

He pulled the black mask from a drawer and ran his fingers over the smooth leather. The sail back to Savannah had been pure torture. Her presence lingered in his cabin, the soft scent of lemon hitting him whenever he least expected it. He'd bunked with the rest of his crew, unable to even look at his bed without glorious visions of her naked body writhing beneath him.

He'd spent the days pondering what the hell she'd been up to. Who the hell she was. And what the hell he was going to do about her.

A virgin pirate.

Nothing about her added up. His gut told him there was more to the story than she had let on. And his gut was seldom wrong.

Speaking of said gut, a hard knot twisted there. In all his years, he'd never taken anyone's virtue. Sure, he enjoyed women plenty, but he preferred them seasoned and experienced. No chance of hurting any feelings.

Damn it.

Any other woman, and he'd be hunting her down and marrying her to take responsibility for what he did. But Red was no ordinary woman. She was a pirate.

Another wave of pain pulsed through his head and he stared at his compass. What did she gain by returning it? Had she followed him to Savannah? How long would she be around?

He'd already sent orders for his men to search all ships on the river and to keep an eye out on the streets. What he needed to do was get some sleep and go out searching himself. He would find her. And then . . .

Hell if he knew. He raked his hand through his hair for the thousandth time.

He could offer her honest work. Hire her on as a maid. His lips curved. To be able to have access to her whenever he wanted . . . *no*.

No.

It would be taking advantage of her.

Mistress.

The word flitted across his mind.

A pounding at his front door saved him from spiraling with his thoughts and he jumped to his feet. This early, it could only be one of his men with news. They must have found her. A slow smile spread across his lips as tension drained from his shoulders.

He swung open the door and frowned. A footman stood there. Not one of his.

"Lieutenant?" The man's eyes searched Christian's face. Of course, he'd expected a butler to answer. Christian sighed. Definitely time to put out an advertisement. Though he'd grown up in a household overflowing with servants, the last few years in the navy had taught him to be more independent. To take care of affairs himself.

He nodded and the footman straightened. "I have an urgent message for you."

Christian's brow furrowed, but he held out his hand.

The footman shook his head. "No time for a written message, sir. Your presence is requested immediately at the Warstein manor."

The headache began to return. Christian rubbed his neck. "I'll have to get ready. And I'm in the midst of a crisis of my own right now. Whatever it is, it can wait until this afternoon."

The color drained from the footman's face as Christian turned away. "No!"

Christian jerked to a stop and looked down where the man grasped his arm. "I thought I made it clear. I have business of my own to tend to. Warstein will have to wait."

He tugged his arm free and shut the door. Except the blasted man shoved his foot in.

"You don't understand . . ." the man started.

"The only thing I understand right now is that Warstein needs better judgment in hiring his servants. I could have you arrested for trespassing."

Instead of subduing the footman, his words incited an intense struggle and the man managed to push his head through. Christian's fingers curled into a fist. If the man wanted a fight, by God, he'd give him one.

He pulled his arm back.

"Miss Warstein has been kidnapped."

Christian blinked and dropped his hand. "What?"

The door swung open as he released it and the man stumbled inside. "It's Captain Thorne. He took her this morning."

Captain Thorne.

A ringing sound buzzed in his ears and he reached for the wall for support. *Kidnapped.* If the blackguard had Warstein's niece, one thing was certain: She wouldn't last long.

"Fuck."

The footman drew back at his curse and Christian shot him a look. "Stay here. I'll be back in a few moments."

He didn't bother waiting for the man's response and rushed

back into his study. After penning a quick note to Isaac to make ready to sail, he swept up his compass and shrugged into his uniform jacket. As he turned to leave, he jerked his gaze to the portrait above the mantel.

His throat went tight.

"I'll find her. And I'll make that bloody pirate pay."

His words echoed through the empty room and he pressed his eyes shut. He'd been so young the night his mother had been taken. All he could remember were her screams. By the time he'd made it to her room, she was gone. Five-year-old him blamed himself. *If I'd only gotten there faster.*

"They would have taken you too. Or worse, killed you," his father had said.

Then, while the entire household went searching, Christian had been locked in his closet to keep him from following. Hours and hours had passed in wretched darkness. Silence. He'd nearly gone mad.

Christian shivered, pushing the memory away.

But he remembered the hatred. So much hatred. It burned through his gut in the dark hours of the night. Kept him going after his father left to seek his revenge. Turned to an aching grief when he never came back.

His housekeeper rapped on the doorframe and he startled. Damn it. He'd wasted precious minutes. He strode to the front door and she followed.

"Have someone bring my things to the ship. I've no idea how long I'll be gone."

When she hurried up the stairs, he tossed the note to the footman. "Bring this to the *USS Falcon* and make sure my first officer receives it."

Striding outside into the early morning sun, he came to a stop when he saw two horses saddled in the drive. The footman hurried down the steps next to him a moment later. "Warstein sent a horse for you, sir. There's no time to lose."

Smart. And efficient. By sending a horse with the footman,

Warstein shaved at least a quarter hour off his response time.

Christian swung into the saddle and kicked the grey into a gallop. He turned toward the Warstein manor while the footman spurred his mount in the direction of the river. A few minutes later, he pounded down his neighbor's drive. Sliding to the ground, he tossed the reins to a waiting groom and hurried up the steps.

The butler opened the door. "I'm so glad you came, Lieutenant. Follow me."

Inside, a weeping maid stood next to a matronly housekeeper who wrung her hands together. All of these servants cared deeply about their mistress, which spoke volumes about her character. Though shy, she was clearly someone these people respected.

Someone who didn't deserve to be at the mercy of a bunch of hardened criminals.

The door to Warstein's study hung open and the butler led Christian in. The merchant stood at the window, looking out over the river. When he turned to face Christian, a glint of something flashed through his eyes. Anger? But why? The man should be relieved to have help arrive.

Obviously, his emotions were heightened by the disappearance of his niece. The man's hands flexed at his sides before dropping limp and Christian shrugged the cool reception aside.

"Tell me what happened."

Henry strode to his desk and sat. "Samantha's maid told me she was missing an hour ago, but we didn't think much of it."

Christian's brow rose. "You didn't think it was odd your niece wasn't in her room at the break of dawn?"

"We had an argument last night. She was quite upset." Warstein tapped his fingers on his desk. "Samantha is an early riser, so we thought she'd taken a morning walk to clear her mind."

"When did you notice something was amiss? And how do you know—"

Warstein slid a folded piece of parchment forward. "This was delivered not half an hour ago."

Christian lifted it and a single lock of copper hair fell into his hand. He unfolded the note into a ray of sunlight streaming into the room and read the short lines.

Bring the map to Tortuga. If it is delivered without incident, your niece will live.

The ransom note was signed with an elegant "T."

Tortuga. The lair of pirates past. With the recent return of piracy in the Caribbean, there was no surprise in Thorne choosing a location steeped in pirate history.

"What map?"

Warstein leaned back in his chair. "A treasure map."

Christian set the note down and fingered the soft lock of hair between his thumb and forefinger. "What is a merchant like you doing with a treasure map?"

"It belonged to my brother, Samantha's father."

"I'll need it."

Henry shook his head. "I don't have it. I gave it to Samantha. I had no use for it."

Christian frowned. "Search her—"

"I've had servants going through her room since the note arrived. No one has found a trace of it."

"Why would Thorne want this map?"

"I don't know." Warstein's voice came out in a growl and his left eye ticked. A lie.

Crossing his arms, Christian leaned forward. "If I'm going to go after the most dangerous man on these seas, I need to make sure I know what I'm up against. If you withhold any information, it could very well be the difference between your niece's life or death."

That should do it.

But Warstein sat in stony silence, his knuckles white from how hard he gripped the edge of his desk. Finally, he pushed his chair back and stood.

"Are you going to rescue my niece, or should I send messages to my own crews?"

As if his merchant captains could take on Thorne. Sending them after her would be a death sentence. Christian pulled his shoulders back.

"My ship will be ready to sail in half an hour. With luck, we'll catch the pirate before he reaches Tortuga. I'll have your niece back before the end of the week if all goes well."

Warstein bowed his head. "I'm in your debt, Lieutenant."

"First, I'd like to see her room."

The merchant stiffened but waved a hand toward the door and followed Christian from the study. He led them up the stairs and stopped at the second door on the right.

"This is her room."

Christian's gaze raked the space. Minimalistic in design, the pretty blue walls and white tapestries immediately reminded him of a clear day at sea. Exotic shells lined a shelf on the wall and several books lay in a heap next to a rocking chair. Her desk drawers had been pulled open as well as the doors of the big wardrobe in one corner. He ignored them and crossed to the bed, pushing aside gauzy mosquito netting.

Leaning in, he ran a hand over the smooth cotton and frowned when a faint whiff of lemon drifted up. *Could it be?* He sniffed again, but the scent was gone. The maid who had been crying downstairs earlier stood to one side of him and he turned to her. "When did you last see Miss Warstein?"

Her red-rimmed eyes blinked and she furrowed her brow. "I came in to ask if she needed help getting ready for bed and she said no. It must have been right around nine o'clock, the sun was setting."

Right about the time Red had visited him.

Christian turned toward Warstein. "Your niece was kidnapped last night."

The man's brows lifted. "How do you know?"

"Her bed was not slept in."

Christian scanned the room once more and the hairs on his neck lifted. No sign of a struggle. Striding to the balcony, he looked over. No clear way up—or down. A tiny ledge ran to a tree a good dozen feet away, but there was no way one could carry an incapacitated body that far.

His eyes narrowed. It was almost as if she had gone willingly. But what—or who—could have convinced her to go? Was Red part of this? Did the lemon scent belong to her? Or had he imagined it?

He twisted at the cuff of his jacket. Too much of a coincidence she'd been at his property around the same time Miss Warstein went missing. And he didn't believe in coincidences. His gut twisted. It could only mean one thing.

She sailed in league with Thorne.

He swore and clenched his hand into a fist.

With a pivot, he strode back inside and brushed past Warstein. "I've seen all that I need to. Thorne has a half-day lead on us. I'm going straight to the docks and we will sail immediately."

Unease thrummed through him as he descended the stairs and exited the house. What part did Red play in all this? And why was Warstein hiding information from him? As he climbed onto the horse, his headache returned in full force.

He pushed the poor beast past its limits and by the time he reached the docks a quarter hour later, foam frothed from the grey's mouth and dark sweat lined its flanks. Christian vaulted to the ground and jogged up the gangplank to the *Falcon*.

Thank God she was nearly ready to sail. Men hung in the rigging unfurling the main sails and dock hands scurried up and down the gangplank with crates of goods.

"What the hell is going on?" Isaac strode down from the forecastle. "Don't tell me this has to do with that fire-haired vixen you've had us up all night over."

"Yes. No." Christian raked a hand through his hair. "I don't know. Miss Warstein has been kidnapped by Captain Thorne."

"My God. The bastard has finally decided to show his face." Isaac cocked his head. "Why would this have anything to do with Red?"

Christian ground his teeth together. "It doesn't look like Miss Warstein was taken against her will. And Red was at my place at the same time she went missing. It cannot be coincidence."

"You think your lady pirate has something to do with Miss Warstein's kidnapping?"

"Don't call her a lady. If she's working with Thorne, she belongs in the noose."

Isaac blinked but his eyes didn't meet Christian's. "That's a rather abrupt change of heart."

Christian spun to face the river. "It's one thing to pirate on her own. But to align herself with a man who's killed hundreds of innocents . . ."

"I wouldn't jump to conclusions just yet." Isaac touched Christian's elbow.

He jerked his arm away and strode to the helm, blinking away the vision of red hair spread across his sheets beneath him. His toes curled in his boots. He shouldn't have taken her to his cabin. An ache pressed against his chest. That particular lapse of judgment might cost Miss Warstein her life if his hunch was correct.

His hand curled into a fist around one spoke of the wheel. He should have taken the whole lot prisoner and let the law determine their fates. Instead, he'd let his lust control him.

Isaac came to a stop next to him. "How soon do we sail?"

"Now."

Chapter Eleven

A GENTLE ROCKING woke Samantha. She rolled to her side with a groan, taking a deep breath. The scent of stagnant water and mildew hung heavy in the damp air and her eyes watered. Darkness cloaked her and she blinked, trying to get her bearings.

The faint light from a lantern swinging in the corner of the small room reflected off the bars of a cell. She pushed to a sitting position. Good God, she was in a brig. Sucking in another breath, she choked on the pungent air.

She pulled herself up and shook the door. Locked. Her fingers trembled around the cold iron. Whose ship was she on?

Stumbling back, she looked around the cramped cell. Nothing but an empty bucket in the corner. Another cell connected to hers. Her chest constricted and she pressed her eyes shut. *Don't panic.*

Exhaling slowly, she let the vibrations speak to her. The ship cut through the waves with heavy confidence. Each swell rolled straight up through her feet. A subtle groan came from deep within the hull and she reckoned all the sails were set. They were moving fast, and this was a big ship. Perhaps a frigate.

Her brow furrowed. Who else had frigates other than the navy? Had Christian's men captured her? Perhaps he had guards on his property. But why take her to sea? It didn't make sense.

And the man who had grabbed her, his voice had been coarse, thick with a West Indies accent. Doubtful the lieutenant would even be allowed to hire on foreign nationals with his government position.

Samantha skimmed her fingers over the side of her head and winced at the tender bump there. Whoever had her, they were not friends. Which meant she needed to get out. Her fingers continued into her hair and she frowned. They'd taken her hair pins. So much for picking the lock.

The thud of footsteps came from overhead and a trapdoor above a ladder swung open. Samantha swallowed and backed away from the bars, her heart slamming in her chest. A boot came into view, followed by a giant of a man.

"You're awake." His deep voice shook her.

She stared. How could she not? His head nearly hit the ceiling. And he was shirtless. The lantern light shone off the deeply bronzed skin covering one of the most heavily muscled torsos she'd ever seen.

When her gaze made it to his face, a gasp lodged itself in her throat. Pitch black lines snaked in heavy swirls over his cheek and forehead. The tattoo continued down his shoulder and ended wrapped around one huge bicep. A gold hoop shimmered from one ear.

"Capt'n wants to speak with you."

Samantha's throat had gone dry and she couldn't form any words. The man shrugged and pulled out a ring with two keys. She shrank against the wall while he unlocked her door.

He swung it open and raised a black brow as she stood frozen in place. "I don't mind throwing you over my shoulder if I must."

His laugh boomed through the room and Samantha forced her feet into motion.

"Who is your captain?" Her voice didn't waver and she drew strength from that. She was a pirate. Whatever this captain wanted with her, she could negotiate.

The man laughed again. "You'll find out soon enough."

She narrowed her eyes. "And what about you? What's your name?"

His eyes darkened. "I have no name."

"Surely—"

Without letting her finish, the giant turned and climbed the ladder. "This way."

Samantha followed him through a narrow corridor past a kitchen and bunk quarters. Another ladder brought them to the cannon deck and this time, she couldn't help her gasp when the men shining the great cast iron guns turned her way.

Each one sported similar tattoos and gold jewelry. Each one flexed great muscles. And each one scowled at her, white teeth flashing in the sunlight streaming through the open hatches.

Here was a crew that would strike fear into the heart of any man.

When they climbed onto the main deck, and she received the same reception, her blood began to go cold. She spun around, taking in the lay of the ship, and her eyes settled on a huge black flag whipping from the mainmast. Only one man would be bold enough to fly a pirate flag in the open. Her breath caught, sharp and shallow. She didn't need to see the nameplate to know which ship she sailed on.

The *Reckoning*.

Her skirts billowed around her and she slid her stance a little wider to keep her balance. She'd never felt a ship move so fast. Extra sails sang in the wind, the high-pitched whine buzzing in her ears. The sun rose on their left and she pressed her lips together. South. They sailed away from the United States.

Boot heels clicked on the deck behind her and Samantha swiveled. She blinked and whatever preconceived picture of the dreaded captain she had imagined vanished. He stood with his arms crossed and she took in his height, impressive, but nothing compared to the giant at her side. A cocked hat perched atop dark brown hair shot through with silver.

"Captain Thorne." She inclined her head, forcing herself to take even breaths. Losing her composure wouldn't help her.

"I see my reputation precedes me." He grinned, and for a moment, his face was transformed into that of a handsome rogue.

If one didn't look into his eyes. A stark emptiness filled them and her skin went clammy. No emotion. Some said he'd sold his soul to the devil. Her throat went dry. They very well may be right. He turned his face into the sun for a moment and a flash of recognition fluttered through her, there and gone again in an instant.

Best get straight to the point. "Why am I here?"

Not that she needed to ask. She'd heard enough outside her uncle's meeting. Thorne wanted the map. Her map.

"Tell me, Miss Warstein, how much does your uncle value your life?"

Right now? Probably not very much. But he didn't need to know that. "I'm his only niece, and he raised me as a daughter." She shrugged. "Do you have children, Captain?"

His eyes went a shade darker. *Interesting*. Of course, with looks like his, he probably had a brat in every port.

Samantha let a smile play across her lips. "Then I'll let you be the judge of how much my life is worth."

He took a step closer. "You'll find quite quickly, Miss Warstein, that life is of little value to me."

His words rang with sincerity, and Samantha fought back a little shiver. Time to figure out his plan. "So then, what is it you want? I assume you took me for ransom."

The captain walked a slow circle around her and she forced herself to remain still.

"Your uncle has something I require. I do believe he will bring it. When he does, I will kill him, and you." He reached out and grazed his knuckles against her hair. "Too bad, really. I do hate wasting such beauty."

Samantha reeled back. The man was mad.

"You don't want to beg for your release?" He regarded her for another long moment. "It is, after all, more along the lines of what I'm used to. Perhaps you'd wish to bargain."

Those dark eyes became predatory and she took a step back. No way she'd ever stoop that low.

"I will never beg."

A dark brow rose. "Never say never. I will take great pleasure in proving you wrong."

Samantha stiffened. *Stop goading him.* She turned and found his crew had gathered close.

"I will say, Miss Warstein, you've got your mother's pride."

She spun back to him as ice shot through her veins. "What did you say?"

But he didn't need to repeat himself. The open deck around her suddenly seemed to close in and the wind became a roar in her ears.

Captain Thorne's eyes gleamed. "She refused to cower to me, even in the end. You have her looks, you know."

And then everything went silent, save for the heavy thump of her heartbeat.

He killed her parents.

For the map.

"You bastard," she snarled, launching herself at him. Never mind she had no weapon. Her fingers curled, ready to swipe the smirk off his face.

But a huge hand clamped around one arm and yanked her back.

The captain barked out a hollow laugh. "Take Miss Warstein back to her quarters. I do believe she's outstayed her welcome."

The giant yanked her back toward the hatch and she twisted to face the captain. "He'll never give it to you."

He laughed again. "Oh, I think he will."

SAMANTHA STARED AT the uneven boards above her head and wiped her eyes. When she swallowed, a harsh burning filled her throat. Though she'd grown accustomed to the stench, the rancid air was taking a toll on her. She turned to the flickering lantern and sighed.

There was no good way to keep track of time down here with no view outside, but to the best of her knowledge, two days had passed. They could be as far as The Bahamas by now.

How much farther would they go? And what would her uncle do? He knew better than to believe Thorne would let her go if he turned the map over. Not that he even could. The map still lay curled in her conch, aboard the *Hurricane*. And no one knew.

The hatch lifted with a groan and she jumped to her feet. When the small boots of the cabin boy came into view, she breathed out. Most of the time he was the one who came to bring her meals. She preferred him to the giant, who checked on her periodically.

The boy jumped to the floor and held up a tray. "Brought yer dinner."

He slid it under the bars and she pulled up her nose at the stale hunk of bread and dried fish. The exact same thing she'd been given for every meal.

She picked it up and asked him the same question she asked each time. "Where are we sailing?"

As always, he ignored her. After a moment, he pointed to the bucket in the corner. "I'm to grab yer piss bucket too."

Thank God. She gingerly picked it up and brought it over. The boy pulled a key from his pocket and slipped it into the lock. When the door swung open, just wide enough to pass the bucket through, her muscles coiled.

She could overpower this whelp. About the same height as her, he was all gangly limbs. Her shoulders slumped. But then what? Escaping her cell while at open sea served her no good.

He narrowed his eyes. "Don't try nothin'."

Samantha flashed him a weak smile and he grabbed the bucket from her. The clank of the lock a moment later reverberated in her head and she forced the smile to stay. *Get him to talk.*

When he turned to the stairs, she cleared her throat. He paused and looked back. How could she get the young teen to open up? *Play to his pride.* Of course.

"What's it like being cabin boy to such a notorious pirate?"

It worked.

The boy gave her a crooked grin. "It's real swell. He says I'm the only one good enough to keep his schedule. Get to do all his laundry and bring him his meals." He gave a pointed look at the tray she'd set down. "He eats a lot finer than that."

"I'm sure he does," she said dryly. But this was good info. "A pirate that keeps a tight schedule?"

"Yep. He eats at seven-o-clock on the dot every night no matter what."

She nodded at the keys still in one hand. "He must trust you an awful lot to let you hold the keys to the brig."

His dirty fingers clenched around the metal ring and his chest puffed out. "There's only one set of keys on this whole boat. Capt'n keeps them on him at all times, 'cept when we check on ye."

"Only one set? That seems risky. What if he falls in battle?"

The boy looked at her as if she'd sprouted horns. "That wouldn't ever happen."

She lifted a shoulder. "I meant hypothetically." He blinked at the word and she revised. "What if someone stole them from him?"

"I dunno. Guess ye'd rot then. Ain't no one getting the keys from him though. He's got more pockets than one would have time to search."

In other words, little chance of her getting the keys, unless she swiped them from the boy.

She flashed him a smile. "Well then, I hope, for my sake, he doesn't come to any misfortune."

He cocked his head. "If someone was going to kill me, I'd wish for something bad to happen to him."

Cool iron pressed into her forehead when she leaned against the bars. "What's your name?"

"Skip." His eyes dropped to his boots. "But most hands just call me 'boy.'"

"I think Skip is a lovely name."

His cheeks reddened and he scrunched his nose. "Ye stink."

"Oh." She gave a little sniff. "Well, I'd be grateful for a bucket of clean water and soap if you could spare it."

"Won't make a difference. Smell's like a bull's arse down here."

Samantha let out a chuckle. He wasn't wrong. "If you can't tell me where we're going, can you tell me how much longer we'll be at sea?"

He shrugged. "Guess it don't hurt. We're just less'n two days from port."

Four days of travel. After the first day spent sailing at break-neck speed, they had slowed. After some quick calculations, the answer seemed obvious.

"Tortuga," she whispered.

Skip jumped back with wide eyes. "How'd you do that?"

But she didn't have time to answer. The faint ringing of a bell reached them and the cabin boy's eyes lit up. "Ship ahoy!" He turned and scurried up the ladder.

"Wait!"

The hatch slammed shut.

At least she had gotten the kid to talk. She replayed their conversation, trying to pick out anything of use. After a few minutes, the ship shifted and she leaned with it.

They were turning.

She backed against the wall and splayed her fingers against the damp wood. When they finished the turn, the frigate slowed. Vibrations and thumps came from the deck above and her pulse jumped. Cannons being readied.

The infamous Captain Thorne was about to attack a ship.

God help them.

Samantha closed her eyes and concentrated. Not much longer till they engaged. The thrum of activity above came across muffled. She breathed out. The brig lay below the water line. No need to worry about getting blown apart in a cannon blast.

Her hands tingled against the wall, the ship's energy pulsing through her. They had come to a near stop. Soon. Very soon.

A muffled shout came from above.

And hell broke loose.

The explosion of a dozen cannons going off in sync rocked the ship. A strange quietness followed in the seconds after, and her shoulders went tight.

Crack!

The impact was followed by another. And another. The ship trembled at the onslaught and Samantha slid down the wall to the floor. Her back vibrated with the explosions of another round of cannon fire from above and tears pricked her eyes.

Several more impacts rocked the hull, but the frigate rested steady in the sea. No critical damage had been done. She strained her ears, and the faint echoes of shouts came from above. For the first time ever, the thought of battle made her go numb. Whoever was on that ship was going to die.

The minutes began to stretch by, and Samantha pulled her knees to her chest. She flinched when the cannons above her sounded again. The battle had been won. A silent prayer caught in her throat for the lives lost. Those last shots from the guns would have been aimed below the waterline and it wouldn't take long for the captured ship to sink.

A cheer rose from the upper deck.

And then silence.

Samantha leaned her head back and closed her eyes. Her heart beat a dull thump in her chest. She wasn't naive. The chances of her escaping this alive were slim to none. Heavy on the none.

She was going to die.

Alone.

Her eyes pressed against hot tears. Everything she'd worked for, all the long hours learning to sail, training to become the best, all were for naught. She'd wanted to become a pirate. Now, her career was ending before it even started.

Footsteps sounded above her and the hatch flung open. She blinked against the bright stream of light as the giant descended. Samantha scrambled to her feet while two more feet came into view. Dangling feet.

A body dropped down and the giant caught it with a grunt. She pressed back against the wall while the huge man threw the limp form over his shoulder and unlocked the cell next to hers.

When the door swung open, he glanced over at her with a grin. "Brought you some company."

He tossed the body to the floor and slammed the cell door shut. A moment later, the hatch closed and she was alone with the stranger. She swallowed and stepped to the bars separating her from the man lying face down on the dirty floor.

"Sir?" She fell to her knees and reached through the bars to touch his shoulder. "Are you alright?"

The man groaned and rolled over. He flopped onto his back and squinted at her.

Samantha jerked her hand back. No. It couldn't be.

But it was.

The room around her began to spin and she sucked in a breath.

"Lieutenant."

Chapter Twelve

CHRISTIAN PUSHED INTO a sitting position. "Miss Warstein."

Her face had gone pale in the shadows and he frowned. She looked at him as if she'd seen a ghost.

"What's wrong?"

She blinked and her mouth opened. And closed.

"Are you injured?" If Thorne or his men had hurt her . . . he leaned forward and grasped rough iron bars.

Her hand rose toward him before clenching into a fist. She gave a little shake of her head. "I'm not. But you are."

That much was true. He'd taken a beating at the hands of Thorne's crew of giants. He drew in a long breath, trying to determine where he hurt the worst. Though his muscles ached, everything seemed to be in working order. No broken bones.

Something dripped into his eye and he automatically wiped at it. A sticky wetness ran down his forehead and when he pulled his hand away, it glistened red in the dim lantern light.

He swiveled and took in the tiny brig. Their two cells took up most of the space. Without a porthole, the only way out was the ladder. Which led directly onto the gun deck. Putrid air filled his nose and he fought to keep from coughing.

They were alone.

His blood went cold. How many of his men had perished? The sting of bile crept up his throat. Too many. And where were the survivors?

After he'd been knocked down and restrained, the pirates had gathered his remaining crew together. They had begun to be shuttled back onto the *Falcon*, but a voice from the quarterdeck, where the infamous captain observed from the shadows with his hat pulled low, had stopped them. For some reason, Thorne had decided not to send him and his crew down with his ship. Not even after Christian had shouted for him to show his face and fight him like a man.

The bastard had ignored him and disappeared into his cabin.

And left Christian to be dumped into this dark and tiny room. With no way out.

His heart began to pound as he sucked in a steadying breath. He couldn't lose control. Not here.

A soft rent of fabric came from behind him and when he turned, Miss Warstein held up a strip of her chemise. "You've a nasty cut above your eye, Lieutenant." She bent to retrieve a cup of water and motioned him closer.

"Don't bother yourself. I'll be fine." He let his fingers explore the spot and winced at the little burst of fire the touch caused.

"Sir, it's liable to fester in these conditions." She swept her hand around the room. While moments before, he would have put money on her fainting, a look of determination had settled over her.

"Very well." He leaned against the bars and she dipped the bit of cloth into the water.

When she raised her hand to his face, her fingers trembled. The pulse in the lovely dip of her throat beat a wild rhythm. Her other hand gripped the bar between them so tightly her knuckles had gone white.

"Miss Warstein?"

The cloth hovered inches from his forehead and she met his gaze.

"You don't have to do this." He reached for the dripping fabric. "I can clean it myself."

Her lips pressed together. "Nonsense. You can't see what you're doing." She waved his hand away and brushed his hair aside. "This is going to hurt."

If he were a gentleman, he would close his eyes and let her work in privacy. And he was a gentleman. But he couldn't pull his eyes from her as she sucked in her bottom lip and gently touched the cloth to the tender skin below the gash.

He swallowed. Even in her disheveled state, Miss Warstein exuded a quiet beauty. Here was a woman worth pursuing. Distinguished. From a respectable family. Not a criminal. Perhaps when . . . if they got back to Savannah, he could contemplate courting her. He gave a little shake of his head. No. No time for courting.

In a featherlight movement, she washed the edges of the wound. Christian ground his teeth together when she touched raw flesh. His gaze traveled down to where her breasts strained against the pretty blue neckline. She was breathing too fast.

He reached over and touched her still-clenched hand. A little jolt ran up his arm and she jerked her gaze to his.

"Miss Warstein?"

She froze. "Yes?"

In a slow movement, he pried her fingers loose from the bar.

"Take a deep breath."

After she followed his instruction, he pressed her hand between his. "Again."

She gulped in a breath and he pressed a thumb to her wrist. Her pulse still raced.

"It's going to be alright."

Her brows furrowed. "How can you say that?"

He couldn't.

He'd watched his ship sink. Watched bodies of his men thrown into the sea. And now, he was locked in a brig. It was hopeless.

Yet, he couldn't bring himself to admit it.

Not yet.

"I gave your uncle my word that I would—"

Her hand tightened within his. "My uncle sent you?" Disbelief laced her words.

"Who else would he send?"

She stared at him for a long moment. Then she laughed.

Had she lost her mind?

"Miss Warstein, have faith."

Her shoulders shook and she gave him a sad smile. "Lieutenant, you're the greatest pirate hunter on the seas and look where that got you. If you couldn't save me, who else can?"

He began to protest, but she was right. Warstein wasn't coming. No one was. And if they did, they'd suffer the same fate as he did. A worse fate.

Hopeless.

His jaw clenched. No. He'd reached her in time. She was still alive. A tightness formed in his throat. Somehow, he would get her out of here.

One thing was certain. He would die before letting her suffer the same fate as his mother.

She pressed the cloth to him again, this time without the careful gentleness she'd used before. When she finished, she tore another strip of fabric and bunched it up. She pressed it over the cut and his breath hissed out. "Hold this here until the bleeding stops."

Grabbing the bars, she pulled herself to her feet and fluffed out her rumpled skirts. Christian leaned back against the wall and watched her pace. The hairs on the back of his neck lifted as he watched her. For a split second, when he had first opened his eyes, he'd seen Red. Thought his suspicions had been confirmed.

Until his vision had cleared and he'd found the frightened Miss Warstein staring at him instead.

Still, he couldn't shake the feeling Red had a part in all this.

"What happened?"

She stopped. "Excuse me?"

"I saw your room. There was no struggle. How were you abducted?"

Her eyes widened and a blush darkened her cheeks. "You were in my room?"

"Briefly. But that doesn't matter. Start from the beginning. Warstein told me you quarreled. What happened from there?"

"You needn't have searched my room, Lieutenant. I was outside when it happened."

"Your maid said you didn't leave your room after you declined her help."

She met his gaze and flashed him a small smile. "I climbed down the big oak tree."

He raised a brow. "In that dress?"

"I have excellent balance, Lieutenant. I was in the gardens when a man came at me from behind. He held a knife to my back."

"A man? Was there anyone else?"

She cocked her head to the side. "No. Just the man." Her hands tightened into fists and she dropped her eyes to the floor. Lying. His pulse quickened.

"Miss Warstein, I need to know." How could he get the truth from her? "Was there a woman?"

Her head jerked up and she took a step back. "A woman?"

"That night, or here on the ship, have you seen or heard a woman?"

She faced him, blue eyes blazing. "Other than myself, no."

Truth.

His lips pressed together. Perhaps he was wrong about Red after all. Still, he couldn't shake the nagging feeling he was right.

"What was your argument with your uncle about?"

With a shrug, she resumed her pacing. "My family affairs are none of your business."

"Seeing as how we are both locked in Thorne's brig because of your family's affairs, I would beg to differ. Where is the map?"

"It's on—" She snapped her mouth shut and frowned. "It's safe."

He tugged his cravat loose and tossed it to the floor. Miss Warstein was as tight-lipped as her uncle. Silence fell across the brig, save for the tapping of her slippers on the damp wood. His eyes drifted shut as he contemplated his next course of action. If he could get out and free his crew, perhaps they could take Thorne's men by surprise.

A creak of hinges brought him to his feet and the hatch swung open with a groan. The same man who'd thrown him in the cell earlier came down the steps. He dangled a set of keys in front of him.

"Captain Thorne wants a meeting."

Already? Christian crossed his arms. "No."

Miss Warstein glanced over with worried eyes while the big man came to a stop in front of the cell.

"Did I hear you wrong? I could have sworn you said no." The man's voice came out in a low growl.

Thorne could wait. Christian wasn't going to bow to any demands. He may be locked up, but he would show the mangy pirate that some things would happen on his terms.

He met the giant's eyes. "Tell Thorne I'll meet with him after supper."

"You'll meet with him now." A key slid into the lock. So much for prisoners' rights.

When the door swung open, Christian launched himself at the man. He aimed low, throwing a punch right into the groin. No reaction. *What the hell?*

His opponent's hand snaked out and wrapped around Christian's neck. He struggled to pull the vice-tight fingers loose while the man let out a laugh.

"You'll have to try harder than that, boy."

Christian swung again. Higher. But his reach wasn't long enough and the blow missed. His vision swam as the grip at his throat tightened.

"Now are you coming, or not?"

He gritted his teeth. "Not." The word barely came out.

"Have it your way."

With a violent shake, the man dragged Christian forward. Miss Warstein let out a little scream as the thick fingers crushed against his windpipe. Christian wheezed, trying to get air.

"Stop it!" Miss Warstein pleaded. "You'll kill him."

Another laugh. "He'd be better off dead."

Christian aimed a kick at the giant's knee but his energy had waned and it glanced off. The room swam around him as rings of blackness grew larger in his vision. His hands fell from their struggle at his neck and his muscles slackened.

"Lieutenant!" Miss Warstein's voice came from a long distance away, so faint he could barely hear it.

Damn pirates.

THE CLINK OF silverware brought Christian back to the present. His eyelids slit open and he bit back a groan. Fire burned through his throat. He tried to lift a hand but couldn't.

He was bound to a chair.

His fingers flexed against the armrests and he opened his eyes. A man in a crimson jacket sat at a table. Thorne.

The captain faced away from him, cutting a piece of his meal. He lifted his fork to his mouth, then dipped his head.

"You're awake."

Christian didn't answer and swept his gaze around the cabin. Immaculate. The floors shined and the shelves behind the desk were lined with neat rows of books. A captain's bed was set with nary a rumpled sheet. It reminded him . . .

It reminded him of his own cabin.

"I was going to offer you dinner." Thorne waved at an empty plate next to him. "But after hearing about your behavior, I don't believe you deserve it."

Christian pulled his brows together. The man's smooth voice pulled at a memory. One from a long time ago. Too distant to fully remember. The hairs on his neck rose a fraction.

The room went silent, save for the captain's fork and knife.

Each bite was cut with precision and Thorne chewed slowly. Quiet minutes passed and Christian began to test his bonds. If he could get loose . . . but the knots were tied perfectly, without even a bit of give.

Picking up a silver goblet, Thorne drank deeply. Save for his dinner spread, the desk lay empty except for a map and compass. Christian's eyes narrowed. His compass.

"Why am I here, Thorne?" He strained against the ropes at his wrist. "Why didn't you kill me?"

The pirate pulled a napkin from his lap and wiped his mouth. He pushed his chair back and stood. Another minute dragged by. His fingers clenched and unclenched one time, a brief flash of hesitation. He reached out and picked up the compass, rolling it in his hand. And then he turned around.

Christian slammed back into his chair.

"What kind of father kills his only son?"

He was dreaming. This had to be a dream. A sick, twisted nightmare. It was the only explanation.

Other than the greying hair and weathered skin, the man standing in front of him could have walked straight out of his memories.

"You're dead." Christian's words came out hollow, barely able to escape his rapidly tightening chest.

"Oh, I promise you I'm very much alive." In two steps, the captain crossed the space between them.

Christian shook his head. This wasn't happening.

He must have said the words aloud because his father laughed when he crouched down.

"You've grown into quite the man, Christian. Followed my footsteps, I see. I wish I could say I was proud, but alas, we stand on different sides of this war."

He flipped open the compass and ran his thumb over it. "I've missed this. Thanks for bringing it back."

Christian stared at the man who'd disappeared from his life twenty-four years before. He'd been five years old the last time he'd seen his father, drunk and insisting he would avenge his wife's death. The next morning, he'd disappeared.

The stiff muscles in Christian's back began to ache and he fought to relax. But his breaths came in ragged gasps. For an agonizing moment, he was transported back to the day the navy had called off the search for his father. *Manner of death: lost at sea.*

"I waited for you. They told me you were dead." His voice cracked and he cleared his throat. "How? How could you do this?"

"Ashamed to have a pirate for a father?"

"I don't understand. You hate pirates. You said—"

"Trust me, I've killed plenty of pirates. Hunted them down like the scum they were. I still do. But it wasn't enough. It was never enough."

"But to become one?"

"One day, I looked into the mirror and saw a monster." Thorne shrugged. "Grief will do funny things to a man, son. I wouldn't expect you to understand."

The chair rattled as Christian tried to lunge forward and a red-hot burst of heat slid through his veins. "Wouldn't expect? Damn you, I lost my mother and father in the same year. Don't tell me I don't understand grief. It's consumed my entire life. And yet I'm still on the right side of the law."

His father stood, smoothing his coat. "For now."

"I will always stand for what is good and right. That's far more than you can say."

"The problem, my boy, is that everyone's vision of good and evil is different. And sometimes, there is no right or wrong."

"What about all the innocents you've killed? All the ships you've sunk?" Bile burned a path up his throat. His men. His ship.

The smile slipped from his father's face. "No one is innocent."

"What would Mother think?" The words came out in a snarl.

Christian didn't see the hand. But the impact sent his head snapping back. He kept his face twisted away as a sharp metallic taste filled his mouth.

"You will not speak of her."

Christian spat out a mouthful of blood and faced his father. "I'll speak of her whenever I want. How dare you try to justify becoming the very thing that killed her?"

A mottled flush crept above his father's beard. "Perhaps I made a mistake in letting you live."

Speaking of lives . . . "Where are my men?"

"They're safe. For now."

"How many?"

"Such concern for your crew, Lieutenant." A greying brow arched. "It's misplaced. I could turn every one of them against you by the time we anchor in Tortuga."

Christian's lip pulled back. "Never."

His father chuckled. "I'll give you the same advice I gave Miss Warstein: Never say never."

What had she said never to? He tried to imagine her facing off with the feared captain. Poor thing. His pulse steadied. He needed to focus on getting her out of here. "What are you going to do with her?"

"I'll wait until her uncle shows his face. I've got special plans for him."

Christian remembered the elusive answers Warstein had given him. "What's the history between you two?"

His father's eyes darkened. "I think it's time for you to leave." He strode to the door and opened it. The giant entered immediately and crossed over to Christian.

Once his bonds were free, he jumped to his feet. "What about my crew? What is their fate?"

"For your sake, I will spare their lives. Think of it as a reuniting gift. I'll sell them in Tortuga."

"Slaves? You mean to make them slaves? They are members of the United States Navy."

"Which means they will bring me a high price. Would you rather I killed them?"

Christian ground his teeth together. *Choose your battles.* "And me?"

His father leveled his gaze at him. "I've yet to decide." He turned to his table and sank into the seat. "Take him away."

The giant grabbed Christian's shoulder and pulled him from the room. Before the door shut behind them, he twisted and faced his father's back.

"I'll tell you what Mother would think. She would hate you."

Chapter Thirteen

S AMANTHA GLANCED AT Christian. When he'd come back last night, he'd paced his cell for hours. She'd sat in silence, waiting for him to calm down enough to speak. But she'd fallen asleep before then.

He leaned against the wall, his eyes closed. Was he sleeping? The ribbon tying his queue had come loose and a wave of hair obscured his cheek. A dark scab covered the cut above his brow. As if alerted to her thoughts, his eyes opened and she jerked upright.

He watched her for a long minute before stretching. "What are you thinking?'

How handsome you are.

She swallowed. "That we only have a day and a half at the most before we reach Tortuga."

"You'll be safe. He thinks your uncle is bringing the map. He won't risk harming you."

"For how long? Eventually, he'll realize no one is coming."

Christian stared at her with those all-seeing eyes and her scalp prickled.

Would he recognize her? Her hand lifted to push a mess of curls over her shoulder. If only she could braid it. But she couldn't risk it. Not with how perceptive he was. With a sigh, she wiped at her sweat-dampened neck.

"For a timid wallflower, you're handling this all quite well."

The term sent a barb of heat through her. "Just because I choose not to socialize doesn't mean I'm incapable of surviving a crisis."

He blinked at her sharp retort and flashed her a rueful smile. "Clearly I've been searching for competent partners in all the wrong places."

She rolled her eyes. Flirting? In a filthy brig. How romantic. Her blue dress had gone grey in places and the wrinkles made her skirts stick to her legs in the most unsightly way. Still, she couldn't help holding his intense gaze.

"Surely you have more women to choose from than you could ever know what to do with."

His lips curved. "I suppose."

Something cold flashed through Samantha's belly and she blinked. *Jealousy?* She nearly laughed. She had no right to be jealous.

"Even with my. . . hordes of women, I can't stand most of them."

This conversation was entirely inappropriate. But she couldn't help asking.

"Why? Don't you want to marry?"

He shrugged. "They want the idea of me. The brave lieutenant. But they don't want the reality. The fact that I spend more time at sea than at home would drive them away eventually. Why would I want that?"

"What if you found a woman who wanted to make her home at sea with you?" She flushed and dropped her gaze to the floor.

Christian snorted. "Good luck finding a woman like that. Besides, even if she existed, the navy wouldn't allow it."

The navy. What was she doing? Even if he said yes, she would never be a consideration. At the end of the day, Christian remained her enemy, and she'd do well to remember it.

"What about you, Miss Warstein? Why aren't you married? Don't tell me a woman as beautiful as you hasn't had offers."

"Believe it or not, Lieutenant, not every young woman dreams of leaping into the arms of the first man who asks for her hand."

"What about the second or third?"

She winced. He would never understand. Besides, what could she tell him? *Because I want to be a pirate, to sail the seas with a ship under my command, and no man would accept that.* She bit back a laugh. Imagined his reaction. Any man's reaction. No, marriage was not for her.

But deep inside, a dull ache started. The same one she got when Abigail tried her silly close-your-eyes trick. She wrapped her arms around her legs. He'd shown her what it could be like between two people. For one brief, glorious, hour she'd experienced passion. And now she wanted more.

Damn him.

She searched for a generic answer. "I haven't found the right man."

"Ah. Say no more." The words dripped with male knowledge.

"What's that supposed to mean?"

"You're one of those girls who believe in true love. You're waiting for a knight in shining armor to come sweep you off your feet."

She choked. She couldn't help it. While her shoulders heaved, she bent, gasping for breath. When she finally regained her composure, she straightened. Christian stared at her with wide eyes.

"Oh, Lieutenant. I'm afraid I don't harbor such fanciful notions. Love is for fools." He blinked and she cleared her throat. "I meant, I haven't found a man willing to give me freedom. One who won't keep me under his thumb."

His head tilted to the side. "You're looking for a spineless fool then? One who will bow to your every whim and never stand up to you."

"Yes. No." She frowned. Why did he make it sound so unappealing?

He looked her up and down with a sad smile. "No wonder you're not married."

She bristled. The nerve. "You, sir, are incredibly rude."

He winked. "I never claimed otherwise."

A flush spread over her cheeks. Christian was teasing her.

"We need to get out of here." He pushed to his feet with a grunt and examined the lock. "Do you have any hairpins?"

Did it look like she did? She pushed the unruly locks out of her face for the hundredth time. "They took them all."

Christian turned a slow circle around the brig and stopped when he faced her. "Your bucket."

Her eyes went wide.

"Mine doesn't have a handle, but yours does. Bring it here."

He was right. How had she not noticed the bent half-circle of wire? She scrambled over to the bucket and gingerly began working on it. No way she was handing him her unmentionables.

The tip of the wire bit into her finger and she let out a little cry.

"Miss Warstein, for goodness' sake, bring it here."

"No." The word came out strangled.

"Are you embarrassed?"

"Of course I am!"

His chuckle sent a wave of mortification through her. "You should try living on a ship full time. Without the basic necessities you enjoy onshore, we learn very quickly not to be shy about bodily functions."

Heat rose all the way to her ears. Clearly, his sailors behaved differently than her own. Mayhap her pirates could teach him a thing or two.

She stiffened. "I'll do it."

Throwing her hair over her shoulder, she bent above the bucket and worked her finger beneath the wire once more. Each end threaded several times around two holes drilled in the sides of the bucket. After carefully working one end of the wire through its hole to loosen it, the rest of it unwound with less trouble. She repeated the steps on the other side.

"Got it!" She waved it in the air. Though she could pick the lock herself, the lieutenant would never expect her to know how to, so she passed the wire over to him.

He bent it and slid one end into the keyhole. His face settled into hard lines of concentration and she had to bite her lip as he twisted the wire the wrong way. She could have had the lock picked by now. Instead of saying something, she focused on the way his clenched teeth squared his jawline.

When a clink echoed through the room, she let out the appropriate ego-inflating gasp. He grinned up at her and swung the cell door open. A moment later, he worked on hers. This time, he picked the lock correctly and moments later it clicked open.

Christian met her gaze. "See? All hope is not lost."

He tugged her door open and she couldn't help her smile. After nearly three days of being locked up, her heart gave a little skip as she stepped past the threshold. Still . . . she reached out and touched Christian's shoulder as he turned away.

"What's the plan? It's midday, surely you don't expect to get out of here unnoticed?" Even if they did, with a full day of sailing before Tortuga, there would be nowhere to go. And plenty of sharks.

Christian grabbed hold of the ladder. "If I can free my men, we can take the ship."

Samantha's stomach churned. "That's a terrible plan."

He twisted and peered down at her. "Our best bet is to take them by surprise when they least expect it."

She swallowed and crossed to the ladder while he climbed. "Have you seen his crew? I'm not sure they are capable of being taken by surprise."

"No one is invincible. Now, be quiet and get ready to follow me."

Samantha wrung her hands together as the lieutenant set his palms against the hatch. This wouldn't end well. The muscles in his arms bunched and he pressed up.

Nothing happened.

He frowned and tried again. It moved up a fraction and a

chain jingled. A soft curse came from above her and Christian dropped his arms. "It's locked."

Thank God.

She began to take a step back as Christian slid to the floor. Before she could make room for him, he bumped into her. Her foot slid out to correct her balance but tangled in her skirt. With a little gasp, she tumbled backward.

For a moment, the dark room spun around her. And then, with a jerk, everything went still. Christian's hands clamped around her shoulders, sending a million jolts of energy through her. All she could do was blink up at him in mute silence as she hung suspended between him and the floor. She couldn't move if her life depended on it. Fingers of heat spread from where they touched and gathered in her core. He frowned. Could he feel it?

"My apologies, Miss Warstein."

He pulled her upright and she stood on wooden legs. Her heart threatened to beat free of her chest as he held her gaze. *Back away.* But she couldn't. The ship rolled down a swell and with her momentary loss of coordination, she pitched straight into him.

"Oof!" His chest muffled her exclamation. But the sudden full-body contact did nothing to draw her from her stupor. In fact, her entire body burned like a pile of driftwood lit aflame.

When she tilted her face up, his forest eyes blazed back at her. Was it desire? Or the lantern light? Either way, she stood paralyzed.

"Miss Warstein?" His hands loosened their grip but remained in place.

She didn't—couldn't—answer and his fingers splayed behind her back. Surely he could feel the pounding of her heart? Her entire body reverberated with the frantic thumps.

"Are you alright?"

Speak. Her mouth opened. But nothing came out. His gaze dropped and she licked her lips. The fire in his eyes burned brighter. If only she could read his thoughts. They rode through another swell, and his muscles tensed against her.

And then his face lowered. If he kissed her . . . her mind began to race. She needed to remove herself from this situation. Forming an attachment with the lieutenant as the shy Miss Warstein was the absolute worst thing that could happen. She needed to keep him away from her secrets, not closer.

His lips brushed hers in the softest of caresses.

And she ceased thinking at all.

He pulled away a fraction, hovering an agonizing hairsbreadth away. She held her breath as everything about him consumed her. The light pressure of his fingers on her back. The smooth hardness of his thigh pressed against hers. His breath coming in gentle puffs beneath her chin.

No woman could resist this.

So, she didn't.

A tiny sound came from the back of her throat and she lifted her hands to his chest. They skimmed up to his shoulders. To his neck. His breathing hitched. And she pulled him back to her.

With a groan, the hand at her back crushed her to him. His other hand tangled in her hair, trapping her mouth to his as he pressed into the kiss. Samantha's lips parted and he took control, darting his tongue into her mouth. The silky brush of it against her own undid her.

Her knees went weak and she sagged in his grip as the fire at her core became an inferno. How? How could he make her feel this way? Her fingertips dug into the back of his neck. He responded by catching her lower lip between his teeth and pivoting them so her back rested against the ladder.

"Miss Warstein—"

No. No talking. She mimicked him, pulling away and biting at his lip. The muscles of his arms bunched around her and he ran his tongue along hers. The room swayed around her. *Breathe.* She'd been holding her breath all this time.

With a gasp, she tore her mouth away and sucked in a gulp of air. Christian slid his lips along her jawline, leaving a trail of fire until he reached the tender spot beneath her ear. The burst of raw desire that shot through her when he grazed his teeth there nearly brought her to her knees.

She twisted his hair between her fingers. But it wasn't enough. She needed more. More of him. More of this.

She dropped her hands to his chest once more and fumbled with his top button. Undone. And then the next one. One more, and his shirt gaped open enough for her to slide a hand inside. The heat of his bare skin seared into her, and crisp wisps of hair pressed against her palm. Christian went still beneath her touch.

He untangled his fingers from her hair and caught her chin, angling her mouth to his. His kiss was frenzied, his tongue moving with an intensity she could not match. Her nails scraped across his skin and he growled, the sound vibrating through her mouth.

His other hand moved up her side, coming to rest directly over her breast. Her head fell back as he massaged it, the pressure almost unbearable. He followed her movement, his lips refusing to relinquish hers.

"Red."

The barely whispered word hit her like a bucket of cold water.

Samantha yanked free of his embrace and staggered back a step, her breaths coming in ragged pants.

"What did you say?"

He stared at her with a horrified expression. "Oh, God. I—I'm sorry." He stepped forward and reached for her but she ducked away. "I got caught up in the moment. You . . . you reminded me of someone."

Heat slamming in her chest, she twisted from him and stumbled back to her cell. What had she done? For a brief moment, he had recognized her. She'd crossed the line and nearly paid for it. She needed to deflect. Now.

"A paramour?" Somehow, her voice worked enough to choke it out.

"Miss Warstein, please . . ."

She shook her head. The shy, proper Miss Warstein needed to come back. "I don't know what came over me. I apologize for my forward behavior. It won't happen again."

He stepped closer. "What if I want it to?"

Heat pulsed between her legs. Traitorous body. She pressed her thighs together, but the throbbing only intensified.

"Miss Warstein, look at me."

No. She couldn't. She stared at the floor. Was it too much to wish for the boards to part and dump her into the sea?

The rustle of the chain above saved her. Christian leaped into his cell and pressed the door shut as she scrambled into hers.

"Quickly, close yours."

She swung it closed and it bounced back a bit. "What now?"

If the pirates discovered the cells unlocked, who knew how they would react?

"Lean against it."

She turned her back to the bars.

"Wait. Here." He tossed the bent piece of wire to her.

"Hide it," he whispered when she stared at it.

With wide eyes, she shoved it beneath her skirts and tucked it into her drawers.

The hatch swung open and she dropped to the floor and pushed the cell door fully closed. Christian stood by his, one hand on the cell door, the other on the bars next to it.

Skip climbed down a moment later with two trays. More footfalls came from above him. Heavy ones. The giant. She slid a glance over to Christian, who eyed the boy with an opportunistic gleam in his gaze. He had better not try something. She gave a little cough and he looked at her. With a shake of her head, she nodded toward the hatch.

The cabin boy slid the trays beneath the doors and pinched his nose. "Lucky for you, we made good time. We'll be anchoring off Inagua Island tonight and will make it to port in the morning. Hopefully, Capt'n will give you all a good dunk in the sea."

Christian's eyes narrowed. "Leave us be."

Skip's chin jutted up. "Not yet. Bring me your piss buckets."

Samantha stiffened.

"They aren't full." Christian leaned against the bars and stared the boy down.

Skip wavered. The job had to be his least favorite. With any luck, he would listen to Christian. But the kid pulled his scrawny shoulders back. "Orders are orders."

He pulled out the keys and slid one into Samantha's door. She tensed. No click. But he didn't react. Her breath whooshed out and she crawled forward to grab the bucket. He didn't notice the lock. But would he notice the missing handle?

He didn't. Oh, to be young and oblivious. He set the bucket down and locked her door with a loud clank. When he moved to unlock Christian's door, the lieutenant did a better job of masking the unlocked state. He shook the door while Skip turned the key.

The boy frowned. "Don't you try nothing. My friend up there will beat you to a pulp if you do."

Christian didn't say anything and handed the boy his bucket. His hands clenched around the bars so tightly his knuckles had gone white. If he did something foolish . . . Samantha glared at him. But he didn't move.

Skip quickly took the bucket and pushed the door shut. The lock clicked into place a moment later and he yanked the key free and jumped back. He handed the buckets up and scrambled up after the man above took them. The hatch slammed shut and Samantha leaned her head back against the bars.

"I could have taken him out."

"And then what? What about the man waiting there?"

"I could have taken him too."

Samantha jerked her gaze to him. "Lieutenant, that man nearly killed you last night."

"I was tired, weakened from fighting. Today would have been different."

"Hmph." She turned away.

"Give me the wire."

She ignored him.

"Miss Warstein—"

The stubborn man was going to get them killed.

"No."

"No?"

She crossed her arms. "There's no reason to risk our lives like that again. You heard the boy. We'll be anchoring off an island tonight. It would make far more sense to try again then."

"Miss Warstein, with all due respect, you have no experience in these sorts of things."

Ha. She had far more than he could know. Her nose scrunched. Although, she had never been captured by an enemy before. Still, she wasn't going to give him a chance to rush headfirst into certain death. If they were going to escape, she needed him hale and whole.

"I would appreciate it if you considered my wishes. I do not feel comfortable trying another escape right now. I would prefer to wait until dark, where this monstrosity," she pointed to her dress, "won't stick out like a sore thumb."

"It's not a monstrosity."

"First thing I'm going to do if I get out of here is burn it."

He chuckled, and some of her tension drained. "Though I want to disagree with your plan, I will concede. A night escape will be easier with fewer men on the decks."

She fought the urge to look at him. Perhaps not as stubborn as she'd first thought.

"Miss Warstein?"

What now? She swiveled to face him.

He'd crossed to the bars separating them and her gaze dropped to where his shirt still gaped open. Her pulse jumped and her throat went dry.

He ran a hand through his hair. "About earlier. I'm sorry. I shouldn't have kissed you."

No. No, no, no. She was not going to think about it. Not the kiss. Not the way his skin felt beneath her hand. Definitely not his hand over her breast.

Her cheeks flamed. "Can we please not talk about it?"

"I don't want you to feel uncomfortable."

Too late.

"Talking about it makes me uncomfortable."

He shifted on his feet. "I wasn't trying to . . . trying to take advantage of you. I usually have much better self-control."

Was that supposed to make her feel better? She stared at him with wide eyes.

"I'm not saying I didn't enjoy it. In fact, I very much would like—"

She groaned. "Look, Lieutenant, it was a nice kiss, but—"

"Just nice?" His eyes sparkled in the dim light.

She couldn't help her grin. "Fine. A very nice kiss. But it can't happen again."

The ship groaned beneath them. A heavy rudder adjustment. Christian noticed it as well and the teasing glint left his eyes. "We're slowing."

Silence fell around them and Samantha spread her fingers on the floor. It wasn't long until a series of vibrations ran up her arms. Her smile widened. "Anchor's dropped."

Christian peered at her as the ship jerked to a stop. "How did you know?"

"A stroke of genius, clearly," she muttered beneath her breath. She really needed to keep her mouth shut. Time to change the subject. "So what's the grand plan?"

His eyes narrowed for a split second before he sat. "We'll wait to make our move until later tonight when the boy brings back the buckets."

But Skip didn't come back. No one did.

Chapter Fourteen

*B*ANG!

Samantha jumped when Christian's fist slammed into a thick wooden plank. The damp wood absorbed most of the sound. Still, she couldn't help glancing at the deck above.

"I should have made my move when I had the chance."

She slumped against the bars and her throat constricted. How was she to have known no one would come back with the buckets? The uncomfortable pressure in her bladder flared at the thought and she squirmed in place. Had they been forgotten?

"We could have had control of the ship and been on our way back to Savannah by now."

Her toes curled inside her slippers. "Or we could be dead."

"Well, we won't ever know now, will we?"

Tears pricked her eyes. "Maybe they will still come."

They wouldn't. It must be past midnight by now. Christian hadn't looked her way for quite some time. She'd ruined their only real chance of getting out.

And now the lieutenant hated her.

She should be happy. Surely, he would stay away from her now. No chances of discovering her secret.

So why did she feel so awful? She kept formulating apologies, but each time she opened her mouth to speak, she snapped it shut at the last moment. She couldn't bring herself to speak to the rigid form standing at the wall across from her.

Look at me. If she could see those dark eyes, she could gauge how angry he really was. Could say the right thing. Make things better.

She gave a little shake of her head. Nonsense.

Whisper-quiet footfalls came from above and she froze. Not the quick steps of Skip or the heavy ones of the giant. The chain rustled and she jumped to her feet.

"Lieutenant."

He turned and jumped over to his cell's door. "Thank God. Quickly, the wire."

She began to hitch up her skirt, but the hatch opened. Silently. Her hand froze short of the wire as a boot appeared. Too late.

Christian held out his hand to stay her. "I'll make my move when they return the buckets. Be ready," he whispered.

Her brows pulled together while a hooded figure dropped down the staircase. Too big to be Skip. Too small to be one of the captain's giants. The hairs on the back of her neck pricked as she eased the wire free.

With his head down, the man approached her cell and she took a step back. A lock pick appeared in his hand and she let out a little gasp.

"Who are you?" Christian's voice broke the silence.

"Hush, lest the brutes above hear."

Samantha's eyes widened and her hand lifted to her throat. She'd recognize that voice anywhere.

"Griff!"

"You know him?" Christian crossed to the bars separating them as her door swung open.

"Quickly." Griff beckoned her forward and turned back to the ladder.

Heart pounding, Samantha rushed forward. If Christian recognized Griff, he would know the truth instantly. Still, she couldn't leave him.

"Wait." She turned to the lieutenant's cell.

"No. He doesn't come with."

"I'm not leaving him." She reached toward his lock with the wire.

"What the hell is going on?" Christian's eyes darted between her and Griff. "You there, show yourself."

She jerked her head around as Griff stepped onto the first rung of the ladder. The old man's eyes gleamed in the lantern light. He wouldn't.

He did.

"So be it." With a flick of his wrist, the hood slid from his head.

Samantha's hands clenched.

"You." Christian staggered back as he stared at Griff. "I know you."

This wasn't happening. Her chest constricted and she grabbed hold of one of the bars to keep herself from sliding to the ground. *Breathe.*

Christian snapped his gaze to her and his eyes narrowed.

He knew.

Her blood went cold.

Griff tossed her something and she caught it out of reflex. She unfolded the black leather. One of her masks.

"You'll be needing that, Captain."

Christian's lips lifted into a snarl.

Her hands began to shake and she tried, and failed, to slide the wire into his lock. "I can explain."

"Get. Away." He pushed the words through clenched teeth.

"You'll die!"

"I'd rather face death than align myself with the likes of you."

"You don't mean that."

Tears burned the corners of her eyes and she tried to pick his lock again. His hand swept out and he ripped the wire from her grasp and threw it across the room.

"I mean it."

She shook her head as he pointed to the ladder. "Go. And hope to God our paths never cross again."

The air rushed from her lungs.

"Captain? We need to leave. Now." Griff disappeared

through the hatch.

"Christian—"

"Don't ever say my name again." He turned away.

Damn it.

She slid the mask on and started up the ladder. Before climbing through the hatch, she looked back. She couldn't help it. But the lieutenant kept his back to her.

"I'm sorry," she whispered.

Griff grabbed her arm and yanked her up. He lifted a finger to his lips and pointed into the darkness. They pressed against the wall and slowly made their way to a hatch leading to the main deck. Griff went up first and, after a tense moment of silence, beckoned her up.

As soon as she climbed through, boots sounded on the quarterdeck above. Griff took her arm and tugged her behind a stack of crates. Two giants came down the steps and walked the main deck. Samantha held her breath as they passed by. It would be a miracle if they didn't notice her pale blue skirts.

"Did you see that?" one said.

Her heart slammed, but they walked to the railing opposite them.

"I swear I saw a light."

Griff breathed out and picked up a coiled rope. He rushed to the railing and tied one end to it. Samantha followed him, keeping one eye on the two pirates as they stared into the darkness.

"I say your mind's playing tricks on you."

Griff motioned Samantha down and she clambered over the railing. The giants continued their patrol. Any moment, they would turn toward Griff and her. She grasped the rope and dropped. The rough cords burned her palms as she jerked to a stop, and she bit her cheek to keep from crying out.

A tiny rowboat floated below her and, one hand after another, she lowered herself to it. Griff followed a few seconds later and untied the boat. He unfolded a piece of dark canvas and threw it over her.

"Stay down."

She wrapped the oiled cloth around her and peeked her head out. Griff maneuvered the boat along the ship's hull until they reached the stern. Captain Thorne's balcony jutted out above them and she shuddered. The clouds broke and moonlight shimmered off the waves.

A dark form rose from the water a few hundred yards away. The island. But how would they make it that far without being spotted? She rubbed the raw skin on one palm and pulled her knees to her chest. Water seeped through her skirt as the little boat rocked on a swell.

Griff lifted a lantern.

"What are you doing? Someone will see."

He grinned. "Precisely."

A spark fizzled from a flint and a flame flared to life on the wick. Samantha fought the urge to knock the lantern into the water as he lifted it above his head and waved it back and forth.

Her jaw dropped as a light onshore blinked in reply. Griff grunted and extinguished the flame. He sat down and slid two oars into place. Two broad strokes and they glided away from the ship.

"Griff!"

He nodded forward. "Watch."

She turned just as a blazing ball of fire erupted in the distance. It blossomed into a tall column of angry orange and moments later, a loud report boomed across the water. Shouts came from the deck above and Griff began rowing with all his might.

The rowboat slid through the waves away from the frigate and soon shadows surrounded them. Samantha couldn't drag her eyes from the horizon, where the ball of flames had turned into a dark smudge of smoke.

"What was that?"

"Gunpowder. Several kegs of it." Griff let out a chuckle. "I've always wanted to do that."

The hull scraped against sand and Griff jumped into the surf. Samantha followed and a wave crashed around her, billowing her skirts around her legs.

"Quickly." Griff took off at a run across the beach and into the scrub. Samantha's skirts dragged in the sand and stuck to twigs as she tried to keep up. Forget burning the blasted things, she was ready to rip them off and run in her drawers.

Clouds covered the moon again and she stumbled through the brush. A sharp pain bit into her side. "Griff, wait."

He stopped and she closed the distance between them. As she drew near, he let out a bark of laughter. "You look like a blue pufferfish."

She scowled. "How much farther?"

"We're halfway there. I'm sorry, but we need to press ourselves. With luck, we can get out of here before Thorne decides to sail around the island. You'll have plenty of time to rest on the ship."

Samantha pressed her hand into her side and forced herself back into a run. The humid heat of the night pressed around her. Minutes dragged past as sweat ran down her face and chest. When they crested a hill and the glimmer of water reached her eyes, she came to a stop and hunched over.

Griff made his way down to the beach and joined two men next to a longboat. Samantha's gaze flew out to the water and her heart soared. The ship rested offshore, a dark beacon of hope. She stumbled down the hillside and the two sailors gaped at her.

"What happened to you?" one asked.

The other jabbed him with his elbow. "Never mind him. Did you see our diversion?"

She grinned. "It was spectacular."

"We had to blow up one of our longboats, but it was worth it."

Griff grabbed the edge of the boat and started to drag it toward the water. "Stop gabbing and get us to the ship. We can celebrate later. If we do indeed escape."

The sailors sobered and helped him. Once the little vessel left the beach, they all clambered in. With three sets of oars, they pressed through the breaking surf and set off.

Samantha watched the dark brush on the island, half expecting a hoard of giants to break onto the beach at any moment.

"Don't watch the shore."

She jerked around to face Griff and he nodded to the west side of the island. "He'll come by sea."

For now, the horizon remained clear of any sails. Silence fell around them, save for the slap of oars as they dipped into the water, and she turned.

"Griff?"

He grunted.

"Why did you show yourself to the lieutenant?"

A grey brow rose in the pale moonlight. "Why do you care?"

"Because he still didn't know who I was. Now, who knows what he'll do?"

"Miss Warstein, it doesn't matter."

"Don't Miss Warstein me. Why ever doesn't it matter? What if he comes after me?" A little shiver ran up her spine at the thought of those angry green eyes bearing down on her. *You better hope . . .* His last words rang in her head.

"It doesn't matter . . ." Griff stared ahead, over her shoulder, as he rowed. "Because Thorne will never let him live."

Her throat went dry and a heavy weight settled in her stomach.

"So you left him to die?"

He ignored her.

Samantha grabbed one of his oars. "Look at me!" She waited for him to swivel his steely gaze to her. "We have never willingly let innocent people die before."

He jerked the oar free and began rowing again. "The lieutenant is far from innocent."

"Griff—"

"Look. He's too smart for his own good. Even if I hadn't

shown myself, he still would have figured it out. It was too big of a risk to take. Plus, you were about to waste precious more time trying to free him."

Samantha crossed her arms.

"Don't try to lecture me. You're the one who got us into this mess in the first place. You have no one to blame but yourself. You want experience and lessons? Here's one: Sometimes a captain needs to choose between two wrong choices."

Something uncomfortable pricked along the back of her throat.

Of course, he was right. She dropped her eyes to the dark water sloshing against the small boat's hull and twisted her dirty skirt between her fingers. Why did it feel so wrong, then?

The clouds chose that moment to cover the moon and shadows swept across the bay. Despite the sticky air, Samantha shivered.

Yes, the lieutenant was their enemy. Yes, he would make her life hell. But did he deserve to die?

They pulled up alongside the brigantine and rope ladders were lowered. Yet another nameplate had been affixed to the ship's prow since she'd last been aboard. *Raven*.

Once they safely secured the longboat on the main deck, the crew exploded into action. The anchor chain clinked and she smiled at the efficiency. They must have started raising it as soon as she and Griff had emerged onto the beach. With loud flaps, black oiled sails were lowered. Samantha stared up at the inky canvas. She'd never seen a ship rigged with dark sails before— only heard the crews tell stories—but her lips tugged up for a brief moment. They certainly fit with the new name.

Even the jib sails had been set to give them all the extra speed they could muster. The topgallant caught the wind and the planks beneath her feet vibrated. Samantha lifted a hand and set it onto the mainmast. Her eyes drifted shut as the ship began to cut through the waves.

Boots echoed from the deck behind her and she turned to find

Griff standing there.

"You really love her, don't you?"

She lowered her hand. "What do you mean?"

"The ship. You hum her song. I've never seen anyone do that before."

Heat crept up her cheeks. Had she been humming aloud?

"How about you captain her for the rest of this voyage?"

Her limbs tingled. Did he mean it?

"The rest of the voyage?"

He nodded.

"You swear?"

"Blasted woman. Yes." He shook his head and pointed to the quarterdeck. "Take us home."

Samantha took a deep breath. "No."

"No?"

She strode to the railing and stared at the little crescent of the island as it faded from view. "We sail to Tortuga."

Chapter Fifteen

THE SAILORS NEAR them stopped what they were doing and stared.

Griff's face had gone a shade darker in the shadows. "We're not going to Tortuga."

"You swore."

"Well, I take it back. I'll lock you in the damn brig if I have to. We are going back to Savannah."

Samantha backed up as he advanced toward her.

"You'd get us all killed, just to rescue the lieutenant? Have you lost your mind?"

Maybe. "No. Not for him. For the other half of the map to Read's Revenge."

A hushed murmur ran through the crew and she took advantage of their shock to race up the steps of the quarterdeck.

Griff followed at her heels. "How do you know he has it?"

"He has it. I would bet my life on it. Why else kidnap me for my half?"

Another murmur, louder, and the crew pressed closer. Griff pressed a hand to his forehead.

"I told you not to let anyone know you had it."

"I trust my crew." She spoke the words loudly and faced the men below her. "This is our only chance at getting the treasure. If we run back to Georgia, Thorne is only going to follow, and try again. He won't stop until he has the map. And I'm guessing his next attempt to get it will be a lot bloodier."

The wrinkles at the corners of Griff's eyes deepened. "So we go to Tortuga? It'll be like walking into a den of snakes."

She smiled. "That's why it will work. He'll never expect us to go there. He'll be caught off guard."

"It's too dangerous. Remington would never approve."

"We're pirates, Griff. We're always in danger."

"Not like this kind of danger."

She whipped to face him. "My parents died trying to find this treasure. They were so close. I want to do this for them."

Before he could answer, she swallowed and turned back to her crew. If she could win them over, Griff would have a harder time getting them to agree with him. "Think of what you all could do with your share of the spoils. This won't be like taking a cargo ship of goods. Read's treasure will make every one of you rich. Rich enough to buy your own ships." Money spoke. It always did. "The treasure will be evenly split between each of us."

Eyes bulged below and Griff's breath hissed out behind her. Her uncle always took fifty percent of the haul and split the rest into shares for his crew. An even split was unheard of. But she didn't care.

She didn't need the money. She needed her crew to back her. And if this was how she won them, so be it.

"If we go back, Thorne is going to hunt us down. And he'll likely kill most of us. But if we can get that map and find the treasure before him, he won't be able to do anything." That was stretching things. He would probably still try to get his revenge, but they would cross that bridge when they got there.

"What do you say, men? Do we choose the bold path and take our chances at a reward far greater than any of us could imagine? Or do we return to port like dogs with tails between legs?"

The energy running through her crew filled the deck and it didn't take long before fists and hats were thrown into the air. Not a single man shouted *Nay*. Warmth radiated through her body and she turned to Griff.

"What say you?"

"I say you're making a big mistake."

"Come on, Griff, don't tell me you wouldn't be happy to find the treasure."

"Not with Thorne breathing down our necks. Happiness is a moot point if one is dead."

"I can do this."

He shrugged. "You've convinced the men, so I will not stop you. I've no wish for a mutiny. But when it all comes crashing down around you, remember that this is the moment you had the choice to take the safe route."

The safe route. All her life she'd been forced to take the safe route. It was time to take control.

"I'd rather live my life with purpose than hide beneath supposed safety. Besides, what is truly safe? We could shipwreck in a storm just as easily as succumb to Thorne's brutes."

He waved a hand at the wheel. "Go ahead. Sail us into your destiny, whatever it may be."

She set her hands on the spokes and steered the ship south. "Make sure all the lanterns are out and we sail in silence. Let's go to Tortuga."

Her words spurred the crew back into action and they scrambled to work. The darkness hugged around them like a cloak as the *Raven* rolled over the swells. Each sail billowed above like dark storm clouds and she adjusted their course to set the ship in line with the wind. Soon, the rhythm of the waves became steady, and the creaks and groans of the yards dissipated.

Griff set a hand over hers. "Go chart our course. Tortuga is only a few hours' sailing from here. And change out of that wretched dress."

She squeezed his fingers. "I won't let you down."

He raised his face to the sky. "I hope you have a plan."

A plan.

All she had to do was get on Thorne's ship and sneak past several dozen giants. And then steal the captain's most prized possession. A walk in the park.

"I'll figure something out."

But the heaviness in her chest returned in full force as she descended to the main deck and opened the door to the captain's quarters. With a groan, she pushed it shut behind her and stopped at the bookshelf. Griff had left all her shells there.

With numb fingers, she quietly rearranged them and flipped the conch over. The map was safe. Setting it down, she opened the wardrobe and pulled a pair of breeches out. Thank God her uncle hadn't had time to remove her things from the ship. She clutched them to her chest and debated calling for a tub of seawater.

No time.

Tugging the dress and her undergarments off, she opened a window and flung them out. The damp skirts fell into the frothy wake and moments later disappeared from view.

"Good riddance."

She used a rag to give herself a quick sponge bath and, after pulling the breeches and her boots on, selected a blouse. Running her fingers through her tangled hair, she frowned at the knots. They would take ages to comb out. For now, she did her best to part her locks evenly and twist them into a braid.

With a sigh, she flopped at the desk and flipped through the maps until she found the one she needed. Her fingers traced a path from the little island to Tortuga as she memorized their bearings. Griff was right. They would sail into the harbor before sunrise.

A pressure had begun to build behind her temple and she pressed down on the tender spot. Not the time to get a headache. She ignored the pain and studied the outline of Tortuga.

They would never be able to take Thorne's ship by force. Even if by some stroke of luck they could overcome the giants, the other pirates in the harbor would take the attack as an affront to their freedom and join the fight. So it came down to stealing the map from under Thorne's nose.

Simple.

She sighed and drummed her fingers on the map. There had to be a way. Opening her drawer, she pulled her dagger free and slid it into the soft sheath inside her boot. As she closed the drawer, she paused. The little box of glass vials lay in the open.

Flipping the lid open, she brushed a fingertip across one. Rendering the dreaded captain unconscious would surely help. But how to get him to drink it? She plucked the vial free and rolled it between her thumb and index finger. Skip had said the captain kept a strict schedule.

And then she knew what to do.

She tucked two vials into her pocket and grabbed her hat from a hook on the wall. Outside, she strode to the helm and took the wheel from Griff.

"Have the men switch the sails. We don't need anyone talking about the ship that arrived with black sails."

She took his compass and checked it, making a slight adjustment to the wheel. "Also, I need an inventory of our supplies. We need to sell or trade as much as we can, make it look like we're just a ship in need of funds passing through."

After he gave the orders, she called for Tommy. He ran up the steps and grinned. "Good to see you, Capt'n."

She returned his smile. "You as well. I have a favor to ask."

"He's not among them."

Samantha shifted in the bushes and took the spyglass from Griff. She focused on the group of prisoners being led down the dock and let out a soft curse. He was right. Christian was nowhere to be found. Her shoulders curved inward as her stomach roiled. Had Thorne already disposed of him?

The thought sent bile up her throat.

"It's for the best." Griff's soft reassurance was anything but.

Samantha jerked the spyglass down and took a shaky breath. She needed to focus. Pulling out a pocket watch, she checked the time. Not that she needed to. The sun had begun to dip below the horizon. Which meant it was almost half-past six.

Time to get moving.

After waiting most of the day and beginning to worry that Thorne had decided against making port in Tortuga after all, Samantha had nearly given up and agreed to return to Savannah. But the tall masts of the *Reckoning* had appeared a few hours ago and once anchored, wasted no time offloading cargo. Nearly half of the hulking crew were ashore.

It made her plan only slightly less dangerous.

Getting onto the boat would be the hardest part. At least, that was what she kept telling herself.

They made their way to the docks where two other crew members waited for them. One of the men cocked his head at her disguise and laughed.

"Just make sure no one sees you from behind, lass, ain't no way they'll think you're a boy if they see that view."

Her ears burned but she ignored him. Men saw what they wanted, and those giants would be no different. Roughly the same size and build as Skip, she should be able to pull off the ruse in the dusk.

Should.

She climbed into the longboat and Griff threw a tarp over her. The little boat rocked when the sailors climbed in, the sounds of water slapping the hull amplified beneath the canvas.

Samantha huddled in the darkness, cringing with each stroke of the oars. This was madness. Pure madness. *Turn back.* She wanted to scream it aloud, but her chest constricted to the point where even taking a breath took effort.

"Ho there!" Griff shouted the greeting and every muscle of hers went rigid. Her stomach churned and she took several short breaths. If she vomited, she'd blow their cover.

The little boat slowed and she pressed against the frame,

willing herself to be as small as possible. Preparing herself for what came next.

Still, she flinched when the booming voice of one of the giants answered. "State yer business."

Now, it was up to her crew to put on the performance of their lives. The longboat wobbled as someone stood up. Griff.

"We hail from the Golden Lantern." A rowdy tavern they'd scoped out earlier. "A round of drinks has been purchased for your crew."

She stilled, waiting for the man's answer. It was true. Griff had sold a barrel of whiskey to the proprietor for a handsome discount, with the stipulation that Thorne's crew got free drinks tonight. The man had barked out a laugh and agreed. Without haggling.

A frown pulled her lips down and her pulse sped up.

"We don't drink."

Silence fell around them and she closed her eyes. Of course. No wonder the barkeep had been so quick to make the deal.

To his credit, Griff improvised fast. "I'm sure the amount could be applied toward other activities. The ladies would be happy to oblige."

The giant snorted. "We've no need for women to warm our beds."

Griff nudged her with his toe. Her signal to get ready. But if they continued to approach with no good reason, they risked drawing the pirate's ire.

Griff didn't miss a beat. "Surely, there must be something? Don't tell me you don't eat as well?"

One of her crewmates sniggered. And then the gentle bump of wood against wood. Time to move.

Samantha pulled the canvas back just enough to slip over the edge of the longboat. Warm water enveloped her, soaking through her breeches and shirt, and she pressed against the ship. Here, the curve of the hull obscured her from view.

She kicked her feet and edged along the waterline, away from

Griff and her crew who negotiated free meals with Thorne's crew. The anchor cable rose from the water off the bow and she swam to it with strong strokes. Lifting herself into the air with waterlogged clothes proved harder than she'd thought. Hand over hand, she ascended, wrapping her feet around the massive rope for more leverage.

When she reached the hull, she swung her feet over to the figurehead, a busty mermaid with an angry scowl upon her face. Chest heaving, Samantha edged toward the railing as Griff and her crewmates rowed away. Shadows began to cast across the bay and she flexed and unflexed her fingers. Not much time left.

Moments later, her feet landed on the deck of the forecastle. She checked that her hair remained pinned in place under Tommy's hat and glanced down at her soaked clothing. Thank goodness she'd had the sense to bind her breasts.

"What the hell are you doing up here, boy?"

She stiffened before turning to face the giant. As a cabin boy, the forecastle would be off-limits to Skip.

Backing toward the stairs, she dropped her gaze to the deck and tugged her hat lower. "Wanted to get a better view of the visitors." She jutted a thumb toward the retreating longboat.

"Why are you wet?"

"I fell in."

He approached and she gulped. "Why didn't you call for help?"

She stepped down onto the first step. "I didn't want anyone to know."

Silence.

She took another step.

"Why are you above deck in the first place? What time is it?"

Her gaze jerked out to the darkening sky and her surprise was not an act. She may already be too late. "I gotta go!"

Samantha turned and sprinted for the hatch, ready to dive out of the way. But the giant didn't chase her. She dropped to the gun deck and ran without stopping to the next hatch. Once in the darkness of the hallway below, she reached out to the wall to steady herself. Her entire body trembled and she took a deep breath before staggering down the hallway toward the galley.

She tested each door she passed until one opened into a small storage closet. Perfect. In one corner, a broken mop leaned against the wall. Even better. Leaving the door ajar, she peeked into the galley, where a large man bent over a steaming cauldron. A platter of food and a wine goblet sat on a table near the door and she nearly doubled over in her relief. Not too late.

So where was Skip? Her gaze continued down the hallway and stopped at the open hatch on the floor. The brig. With a tight throat, she dragged her eyes away. No distractions. Not right now.

But a movement there made her suck in a breath. Skip climbed through the hatch and slammed it shut. When he bent to lock it, her heart leaped back to life. It could only mean one thing.

Christian was alive.

While Skip locked the chain, Samantha backed into the closet. Her fingers wrapped around the smooth wood of the broom handle. Before the cabin boy could enter the galley she leaned out.

"Hello, Skip."

He skidded to a stop with wide eyes. "Who're you?"

She grinned. "Your replacement."

His face fell and for a split second, she almost felt sorry for him. He didn't even see her swing the mop handle. The blow took him by surprise and he crumpled to the floor.

"Skip, is that you?" The cook. She grabbed the cabin boy under the arms and dragged him into the tiny closet.

Dropping him, she took out a vial. "Sorry about this." She emptied the liquid into his mouth and he coughed and sputtered as it went down.

"Skip, you're going to be late."

The cook's voice jerked her into action. She tugged the boy's shirt off and ripped her wet one free. No time to change anything else. Pulling the dry garment over her head, she sent up a silent thanks it fit well and checked her hat once more before darting into the kitchen.

The big man didn't even turn from his pot. "You'll be getting a whipping if you don't hurry."

She grabbed the tray and goblet. If her timing was right, there were only minutes to spare. Once back in the hallways, she balanced the goblet on the tray and emptied the other vial in it.

None of the crew seemed to give her more than a passing glance as she made her way back up to the main deck. Still, her heart slammed against her ribs and the tray trembled in her hands. A moment later, she stood in front of Thorne's cabin. Too late to back out now. She took a deep breath. Knocked. Opened the door.

He sat at a desk, his back to her. His quarters were clean and tidy and she blinked in the darkness. Thank goodness he only had a few candles lit at his table. Still, she'd expected . . . More. He was a notorious pirate. There should be treasure adorning every nook and cranny.

The plate clattered on the tray as she shut the door behind her.

Click.

"You're late."

He snapped a pocket watch closed and swiveled to face her with raised brows. Right. His dinner.

She rushed forward and set it on the table, clearing her throat to lower her voice. "There you are."

As soon as she released the tray, she pivoted and headed back toward the door. But she only made it a few steps before Thorne cleared his throat.

"Aren't you forgetting something?" She turned to stare at his outstretched hand and her stomach dropped.

"The keys, Skip."

The keys. The ones still on Skip's belt.

Thump.

Thump.

Her heart slammed inside her chest.

"I—I . . ." His eyes narrowed and she backed away another step.

"I left them in the kitchen." Her words came out in a strangled whisper. "I got distracted. I swear, I didn't mean to. I'll go get them right away."

"What could possibly distract you from the most important job on this ship?"

She swallowed and wracked her brain for a worthy excuse. "The prisoner."

Thorne's gaze zeroed in on her. "What about him?"

"He said something. It was nothing, really. Doesn't matter," she mumbled. *Stop blabbering and get out.* She took another step toward the door.

The captain drew a dagger from his boot and studied the pointed blade. "Tell me."

She said the first thing that came to mind. "He threatened my family." She winced when her voice cracked and coughed to cover the higher tone.

"You don't have family."

Blast.

She straightened her back. "I know. That's why it doesn't matter."

He studied her for a moment and she leaned into the shadows along the wall. That piercing gaze cut into her and her stomach sank. She dropped her eyes to the ornate rug on the floor. No way she was getting out of this.

The knife clattered to the table and she flinched.

"Go and get the keys. I'll mete out your punishment when you return."

She jerked her head up. He held the wine goblet in his hand and swirled it before taking a drink. With a wave of his hand, he dismissed her.

Tears sprang to her eyes as she dashed out. When the door

shut, she slumped against it. Too close. Too damn close. Darkness had fallen and she spread her hands against the wood, letting her feet absorb the almost indecipherable rocking on the gentle waves while her pulse pounded in her temple.

Blowing out a long breath, she steadied herself and ducked behind a barrel. Kneeling so that if anyone passed it would look like she was lacing her boot, she waited. And waited.

The trill of tropical frogs drifted through the air and Samantha's heartbeat slowed. She leaned her head against the barrel and counted out the minutes as they stretched by.

A soft thud came from the other side of the wall and she jumped to her feet.

Finally.

With a quick glance around, she opened the door and slipped inside. Thorne lay on the floor, the goblet upended at his side. A small puddle of crimson glimmered in the candlelight. Now, to find the map.

She turned a slow circle around the room and stopped when she faced the desk. Moments later, she had all the drawers open.

Nothing.

No false-bottomed drawers.

Wait. There was one false bottom after all. She found the latch and wiggled the compartment open.

And blinked.

"What the . . .?"

She reached out and picked up Christian's compass. Why in the world would Thorne have taken the worthless thing? And even more confusing, why stash it in a hidden compartment?

Her hand tightened around the instrument and she turned back to Thorne's prone body. The map was his most prized possession. So he must keep it close.

Her eyes widened.

Of course.

Dropping to her knees, she let her hands hover above his chest. *More pockets than one would have time to search,* Skip had said.

She ran her fingertips over the fabric, up and down, until she found a stiff rectangle sewn into his upper sleeve. Yanking her dagger free, she made a slit until a corner of waxed parchment popped free. Sliding it out, she held it to the light. Her lips tugged into a grin.

The map.

Thorne's chest rose and fell in even breaths and she glanced at the blade in her hand. If she killed him, she could end it all. Make sure he never bothered her family again.

Samantha pressed the sharp steel above his heart. One quick thrust and it would be over. Her hand began to shake.

You can do this.

She increased her pressure and the blade cut through the pirate's shirt. Pierced his skin. A few drops of blood blossomed crimson on the white fabric.

Bile burned her throat.

A frustrated growl rumbled in her chest as she tried and failed to push deeper. Her hand wouldn't cooperate. If she killed him, unarmed like this, it would be murder. She would be trading one evil for another. Tears blurred her vision.

The dagger clattered to the floor.

Chapter Sixteen

CHRISTIAN BANGED HIS head against the cell door.

His eyes scanned the floor in the dark corner for the hundredth time. Somewhere over there lay the wire. His chance of getting free. That he had thrown away.

He'd made a right mess of things. The scrawny little brat was smarter than he seemed and had refused to give Christian his bucket back. And made sure to push his meals just within reach instead of below the door. Not to mention that even if Christian did get a chance to overpower the boy, one of his father's giants always stood guard at the top of the hatch.

He glared at the plate still lying outside the cell. Damn the brat. Damn his father.

And damn Red.

His teeth ground together at the thought of her. He still couldn't believe it. Shy Miss Warstein. A pirate.

All this time, she'd played him for a fool. His hand curled into a fist, but he refrained from smashing it into the bars. He ran a thumb across his bloodied knuckles. He'd done enough of that.

So many questions crowded for attention in his head.

Did her uncle know? No, he would never allow such a thing.

But most importantly, how? All along Red and Miss Warstein had been one and the same. All the clues had been right in front of his face the entire time. How had he missed them? Her hair. Her lemon scent. Finding her outside a pirate meeting at the ball. The way she'd fucking kissed him yesterday before the old man had shown up and whisked her away.

His traitorous cock twitched and he fought the urge to slap it. No more self-harm.

A bitter laugh broke free. He'd been right after all. No coincidences.

Perhaps somewhere far back in his mind he had wondered all along. Knew that something wasn't quite right. But he'd let the perfectly cultivated image of Miss Warstein cloud his reasoning. In his mind, a high-bred young lady couldn't possibly be connected to pirates—to Thorne—so he refused to give even a moment's entertainment to the thought.

A fucking mistake.

He couldn't help the fleeting vision of taking his full pleasure with her that first night—assuming she was an experienced lover—and raked both hands through his hair. "Fuck." The word echoed through the cell as the seriousness of her inexperience hit him like a cannon ball.

He began to pace. One thing was certain. There would be hell to pay when he got out of here and caught up with her.

If he got out.

The thought sobered him and he sagged against the iron bars. Prisoner of his own father.

Captain Thorne.

If the navy found out . . . his blood chilled. He could be dismissed just for being related to the notorious pirate.

How ironic.

The chain above rustled and Christian snapped to attention. No reason anyone would be coming back so soon. It couldn't have been more than a quarter-hour since the boy left.

But small boots and slender legs came into view.

Christian leaned into the bars. Damned if he was letting the brat stay out of reach this time.

"Forget some . . ." Christian trailed off as the boy descended.

Not the same boy.

His eyes narrowed at the rounded bottom on display.

Not a boy at all.

Had he summoned her with his thoughts?

"Red."

She jerked around, losing her grip on the ladder, and said bottom landed on the floor with a thump. He stood perfectly still as she jumped to her feet. After a hesitant step his way, she came to a stop and adjusted her cap.

"How'd you know?"

Something hot blazed through his veins and his fists began to tremble where he gripped the bars.

"Why are you here?" The words came out soft. Deadly soft.

With a shaky smile, she approached. "To get you out of here."

She said it so matter-of-factly. Like it was a perfectly normal thing for her to be here. He frowned when she unclipped the keys from her belt. How the hell had she gotten them?

She inserted the key into the lock and turned it.

Click.

Before she could move, he flung the door open, knocking her back. Jumping out, he grabbed her arm and tugged her his way. The rough movement made her stumble and her bottom brushed against his thighs. He sucked in a breath at the contact and shoved her into the cell.

Ripping the keys from her hand, he slammed the door shut. His pulse pounded in his ears as she turned and stared at him with wide eyes.

Wide eyes filled with betrayal.

"Christian, what—"

"Don't call me that." He forced his gaze from her face.

"Lieutenant, have you lost your mind?"

Perhaps he had. His mind raced. This turn of events may work in his favor. "I could trade you to Thorne for the release of my crew."

Her hand settled over his and he yanked away from the contact.

"Your crew are no longer on board."

He met her earnest gaze. She wasn't lying. Damn it.

"Lieutenant, I know you're upset . . ."

He snorted. Upset didn't even begin to cover it.

"But we need to move quickly." She pushed on the cell door, but he didn't budge.

She pulled her bottom lip between her teeth.

Son of a . . . he raked his free hand through his hair. He couldn't leave her.

"You can shout at me later, do whatever you want to me later. But we need to get off this ship."

A whole other type of heat slid through him. Whatever he wanted. Even disguised as a boy, he wanted to throw her down and—good God. He needed to get far away from her. That was what he needed.

He released his hold on the door and she pushed past him. "Follow me."

Before he could protest, she scrambled up the ladder and disappeared. If this was another trap . . . He climbed slowly and peered through the hatch. No one but her, and she stood with her hand extended.

He brushed it away. "I'm fi—"

She shushed him and pressed a finger to her lips. Right. Escape.

Senses heightened, he started down the hallway after her. A clatter came from a room ahead and she jumped past the open door and motioned for him to follow. He slid against the wall and breathed out when he cleared it with no one the wiser.

She started up the ladder to the gun deck and he couldn't help letting his eyes wander over her bottom, inches from his face. No man could resist that.

"It's clear," she whispered. He climbed onto the shadowed gun deck. Only a few lanterns had been lit and he followed Red to a dark space between two cannons.

"Now what?"

She lifted her finger to her lips again and pointed to a group of pirates sitting on crates farther down the deck. Directly beneath the hatch to the main deck. If Red distracted them and he could get a weapon from one, there was a chance he could take them. He turned to tell her his plan. And found himself staring into empty space.

A creak came from his side. She'd unlatched one of the port hatches and pointed out. His brows rose. No way he was fitting through there.

He shook his head, but she reached out and grabbed his hand. Her fingers were cold and trembled over his. And then she was touching his shoulders.

He stepped forward, pinning her between him and the hull, and lowered his mouth to her ear. Her breath caught and his pulse jumped in response.

"That opening is half the size of me." He whispered the words and her hands tightened on his shoulders.

She turned her face into his and her lips brushed his cheek. "Try."

Now, his pulse roared in his ears.

They stood still for a moment until Red started and pulled away. She gave him a little push toward the hatch. Christian stuck his head out into the night and took a deep breath, clearing his mind. He ran his hands over the wood frame and pressed his lips together. If he turned sideways, it might work.

But first . . . He stepped back and pulled his shirt over his head. "Hold this."

Red took it with wide eyes and he bit back a smile at her discomfort. Served her right. Stepping through, he dropped his feet to the little ledge beneath the hatch. Now the hard part.

He twisted his shoulders together and began to wiggle. Half-way through, he had to stop. He couldn't move any farther. The sensation of being stuck half in one place, and half in another squeezed around him and his breaths came fast. Too fast. His vision swam as darkness closed around him. If he couldn't get through . . .

He jerked against the frame until his shoulders burned. Red appeared above him, her cool fingers cupping his cheeks. She rubbed her thumbs in slow circles and stared into his eyes until he stopped his struggle.

"Let me help," she whispered.

He nodded and she slipped a hand down to one shoulder, pressing and pulling back at the same time. Her other hand pushed against his bottom shoulder and a moment later, he popped out.

Thank God.

He swallowed and looked down. About twice his height down to the water. Not far. Still, his muscles refused to move, his pulse still roaring in his ears from his near slide into panic. He took a deep breath. It had been years since he'd had an episode like that. Avoiding small, dark places was key. Jaw clamped, he forced his foot forward a smidge. No time for this. Before he could jump, Red's feet connected with his back and he tumbled forward. He hit the water with a hard smack and sank into the darkness.

As he swam toward the surface, another splash and Red's body slid past him. He thrust his head up into the air and sucked in a breath before she surfaced next to him.

"You almost landed on me."

She grinned. "Sorry. You were moving too slowly."

He shook his head and kicked away from the ship, but she grabbed him and dragged him against the hull.

"What now?"

She pointed up and sure enough, a voice floated down. "Did you hear that?"

Red motioned with her head and they eased along the ship toward the bow. Once they bobbed beneath the figurehead, she glanced over at him. "How far can you swim underwater?"

"Far enough."

She nodded and disappeared.

Taking a deep breath, he dipped beneath the waves and

kicked for shore. Without his shirt, he glided with ease. The cool water and pressing quiet eased the frantic beat of his heart, tension draining with each powerful sweep of his arms.

Soon enough, his lungs burned. But he forced himself to keep going. One kick. Two. Three . . . all the way to ten. His breath whooshed out in a cloud of bubbles and he surfaced.

Gasping for air, he turned to wait for Red. She was nowhere to be found. He treaded water, scanning the dark surface of the bay. What if she'd gotten a cramp? Were there sharks in these waters? Surely she hadn't . . .

Water splashed.

He turned back toward the island and there she was, several yards past him. She waved and continued toward shore.

Show-off.

Shaking his head, he started after her. His broad strokes helped him catch up and when they reached the beach, they staggered up onto the sand together. While he shook the water from his hair, something hit him in the stomach.

His shirt. Christian wrung it out and pulled it over his head. Red set off down the beach as he jabbed his arms into the sleeves. He jogged after her and grabbed her shoulder. No way he was following her.

Turning, he started toward the brush, ignoring her attempts to resist. He half dragged her into the trees and started up the hillside toward town. When they reached a clearing, she dug her feet in.

"Where are we going?"

He ground to a stop and let out a growl. "I don't know. The governor. A mayor. Somebody with authority."

She gave a soft laugh and reached up, brushing a trail of water from her cheek. "This is Tortuga."

He wanted to shake her. Or worse, kiss her. Instead, he turned away. "We aren't living in the 1600s. This isn't a lawless island anymore."

She tugged her arm free and rubbed where he'd been gripping her. "But there is sympathy for the pirates here. Why do you think Thorne chose this spot?"

"I'll find someone."

"Does the United States hold sway with Tortuga?"

"I don't know. We'll find out." He took hold of her arm again. "Let's go."

"Wait." She pulled free again. "I cannot breathe like this."

Like what? His eyes widened as she lifted her shirt and exposed a long strip of linen tightly wound around her torso. She unwound it and threw it to the ground, taking a deep breath.

"That's better."

His throat went dry. Her wet shirt clung to her chest, molding around her breasts. Each nipple pressed against the thin fabric and his gaze traced the contours of her side to the gentle swell of her belly.

When he jerked his eyes up, a flush had crept across her cheeks. But she didn't shrink away from him.

"You're a reasonable man. Or so I'd like to think."

His nose flared. Anytime a woman started a sentence with that statement, beware.

"Let me take you back to Savannah."

"No."

"Lieutenant. Hear me out."

"No. I will not indebt myself to any pirate."

She gave him a pointed stare and mumbled something beneath her breath.

"What was that?"

"I said, you're already indebted to me."

His fingers twitched. And the wretched girl laughed.

"Is it that bad, Lieutenant? Would you rather still be locked up on Thorne's ship than admit you owe me?"

He growled and turned away, but she followed, stepping in front of him before he could reach the edge of the clearing.

"Come with me, Lieutenant. The quicker you get back to Savannah, the quicker you can put a plan together to take down

Thorne. As much as it may pain you, we are on the same side in this." Her blue eyes flashed with emotion and some of his anger dissipated. She was scared.

He closed his eyes. She was right to be. His father would continue to try to get her family's map. Would kill to get it.

Well, she would have to face Thorne on her own.

"Lieutenant, will you sail with me?"

Before Christian could answer, a twig snapped in the bushes behind him. He spun and nearly impaled himself on a sword.

"Choose your next words wisely, Lieutenant." The old man—Griff she'd called him—held his blade steady.

Two more men materialized next to him. One of them tossed Red her rapier. Christian pushed Griff's sword aside.

"No. Once you leave, Thorne will follow you, leaving me free to rescue my men and find a ship."

Griff nodded and stepped aside. "Very well."

Christian strode past him.

"Wait."

He stiffened, but let the old man approach him.

"You might need this." Griff passed him his blade.

Christian's fingers clamped around the warm hilt. He inclined his head, the closest he could bring himself to saying thank you, and strode into the woods. When Red called his name, he increased his pace.

She would be fine.

If she was smart, she'd pack up and get out of Savannah. Move far away.

He had more pressing things to take care of: finding his crew.

CHRISTIAN SHIFTED ON his heels and tested the weight of the pirate sword.

Four guards.

He could take them.

Finding his men had been far easier than he had thought. A simple question to a drunk on the streets had sent him in the direction of the auction house. Climbing the wall to the big yard had been easy too.

Now, he crouched behind a stack of crates and waited for the right moment. His men's lives depended on him. They sat in a tight group beneath a tall palm with their hands and feet bound. Thirty-six of them.

Less than half his crew.

His lips pulled back even as his chest tightened. Good men had died trying to rescue Miss Warstein.

All for nothing. Worse—for a pirate.

He closed his eyes and took a deep breath. Focus on the task at hand.

Isaac sat in the middle of the group, hunched over. Christian pressed a fist to his chest. Thank God. If he had lost his friend . . . He shook his head and slid his gaze back to the guards, his grip tightening around the sword's hilt.

One of the men stood and began a perimeter walk. Once he made it to the far corner of the yard, Christian made his move. He stayed in the shadows and approached the three remaining men from behind.

They didn't see him until he was upon them and the one closest to him barely got his sword up in time to block Christian's blow. He gritted his teeth as the man recovered and thrust back at him. He'd hoped to take at least one of them out before the fight began.

The other guards drew their weapons and joined in the fight with shouts. Their blades came at him from all sides, and when the fourth man reached them, Christian swore. He'd misjudged. Considerably. These men were well trained.

Sweat trickled down his brow as he put everything he had into the fight. But against four men, he could only stay on the defense, blocking blow after blow. It was only a matter of time.

One of the men got behind Christian, and when he spun to keep the man's sword from piercing his back, another blade twisted against his. And just like that, he was disarmed.

He began to sink to his knees in defeat when a shadow flew in front of him. Another clang of swords and the fight started again. Long copper hair shone in the moonlight as his defender pushed the man back with a series of lightning-fast blows. Her crewmates joined her and engaged the other men, but Christian couldn't drag his eyes from Red.

She'd changed. No longer disguised as a boy, she wore a ruffled blouse with a deep V-cut neckline. Her belt cinched tight around her waist and she sported that ridiculous hat with the red feather.

She kept one step ahead of her opponent at all times. Each move he made, she reacted and countered before he'd even finished. And her feet kept them moving in a dizzying circle. No wonder she danced so well.

From his position as a bystander, he could see the man favored his right leg. But Red had already figured it out and pressed her attack so that he was forced to use it as much as possible. When he came at her with a high cut, she twisted and slid her blade along his, using her momentum to yank the sword free.

She stood there with her rapier pointed at the base of his neck, her shoulders heaving. Like a damn avenging angel. He frowned. How had he ever believed she needed saving? She took control, took charge, of every situation they'd been in. Far from needing to be saved. Hell, she was saving him. Again.

The rest of her crew disarmed the other three guards and silence fell around the yard.

"Sir," Red spoke first. "I apologize for this disturbance."

What?

The man gaped at her as she lowered her sword and moved to Christian's side. She stiffened, then thrust her arm around his waist.

"My husband is known to make reckless mistakes like this."

Christian blinked. What game did she play?

"You see . . ." She swept her other hand through his hair above his ear. "He received a blow to the head years back and has never been the same."

"What's this got to do with me?" The man crossed his arms.

She laughed. Too shaky to be believable. "He was to come here and negotiate a price on these men. We've acquired a new ship and need a crew."

"Then why'd he attack us?"

Her arm tightened around his side. Right. He'd better play along.

He scratched his head and gave the blankest stare he could. "I attacked you?"

Red patted his hand. "It's part of his condition. He has periods where he blacks out and believes he's still in the very battle where he received his injury."

The man stared at him with wide eyes for a long moment before turning back to her. "Then why'd you attack us?"

She shrugged and gave Christian an adoring gaze. "I couldn't be sure you weren't going to kill him. Even though we have our differences, we are very much in love." Christian bit back a snort and she elbowed him before continuing. "I couldn't bear to see him die."

Good God. This story was getting less and less believable. But these fools were eating it up. One of the other guards gave him a look alternating between pity and jealousy. His lips tugged up. Two could play this game.

He turned to her and ran his knuckles along her jaw. Red shivered at the contact and he leaned in and brushed his lips against her forehead. "Yes, very much in love."

Her breath caught and he fought the urge to drag her into his arms and kiss her senseless before all these men. Would he always react to her like this? Before he could ponder the answer, she jerked away from him and rubbed her palms over her breeches.

"Back to the matter at hand. What would you consider a fair price for these men?"

"They aren't for sale."

She flashed a wide smile. "For the right price, everything is for sale."

When she held out her hand, Griff approached and set a bag in her palm. She untied it and pulled out a gold coin, flipping it between her fingers. Torchlight gleamed off it and the man's eyes became hungry.

"How many men are—?"

"Thirty-six." Christian answered before she could finish.

Her smile turned sly. "There are fifty pieces in here. More than enough to cover their cost and leave a bit extra for your troubles tonight."

The man swallowed and she tossed the coin. His grubby fingers snatched it out of the air and he examined it.

"What do you say, sir? We're on a tight schedule."

His eyes gleamed. She'd won him. "Very well. The boss won't be happy we made a deal without him, but he'd be a fool not to take this price."

After she passed over what amounted to a small fortune for his men, she strode toward his crew, some of whom stared at her with confused recognition. "Alright men, I dare say you heard us."

Christian hurried over to her and set a hand on her shoulder, quieting her so he could be the one to address his crew. "You belong to me now. In return for your work, I promise to be a fair master. Do you agree to the terms?"

They responded with a rousing cheer. Too rousing. Still, the guards stood aside and let them file from the yard. Red led the way down the street and Christian walked next to her in silence.

When they turned a corner and were out of sight of the auction house, Griff approached. "We need to go."

She nodded and drew to a stop. "Lieutenant, my offer of passage to Savannah still stands."

"And what of my men?"

She glanced at Griff, who shook his head. "Only you, Lieutenant."

"Then I turn it down."

Isaac cleared his throat and stepped in. "Go."

Christian stared hard at Red as the breeze kicked up and blew a loose strand of her damp hair back. No way he was spending several days alone with her. He'd lose his mind by the time they returned to Georgia.

"We can procure a ship here."

Isaac frowned. "But what if we can't? It could take days. If you go with her, you can return with haste. Thorne must be taken down. The quicker you get back, the better chances you have of capturing him."

Christian blinked at him. Now was not the time to reveal Thorne's real identity. He dragged his fingers through his hair. Christ, the opposing interests were piling up.

Red pulled something from her pocket and held it out to him.

His compass.

"How . . . ?"

"Later. Are you coming or not?" The two other crew members already hurried down the hill toward the water, leaving her and an impatient Griff behind.

He took the compass and flipped it over in his hand, staring at the engraving on the bottom. He was going to regret this.

"I'm coming."

Chapter Seventeen

Samantha helped push the longboat into the water, ignoring the silent form next to her. Definitely ignoring the tanned muscles of his arms exposed by his bunched-up sleeves. Christian hadn't said a single word since agreeing to come with them.

Why had she pressed so hard for him to join them? The question continued to echo in her mind as they climbed into the boat. So that he could go after Thorne sooner. Except, could he really stand up against the pirate? Look at what had happened last time he tried.

But if the governor gave him more men, more ships, he might stand a chance. And Thorne might not come after her. She let her fingers brush her pocket, where the stolen half of Read's map rested and gave the dark ship on the other side of the bay a sidelong glance.

When Thorne woke and discovered his map missing . . . She shivered and grabbed an oar, throwing all her weight into each stroke. Best to get as far away as possible.

True to form, as soon as they climbed onto the deck, the crew had nearly finished preparations to sail. The anchor lifted from the water before the longboat had been secured in place and the ship slid forward. Samantha left Christian on the main deck and sprinted up to the helm.

As her hands closed on the wheel, the sails unfurled. The topsail slapped in the breeze and when her crew tied it down, it filled and the *Raven* eased into motion. Her heart rate eased and she guided the ship from the bay.

The rest of the sails were secured and the ship picked up speed. Samantha took off her hat and tied it to her belt as they began to cut through the swells. Still damp from her swim, her hair whipped back in messy curls. It would be a nightmare to tame later, but for now, she let herself fully enjoy the freedom.

Stars sparkled in the clear night sky and she made a few adjustments to their course by memory. She closed her eyes and stroked her hand across the wheel. *I missed you.* Her lips twisted. If anyone, even Griff, ever found out she spoke to the ship, she'd be a laughingstock. One thing to sing with a ship, quite another to have a conversation with it.

"This isn't a game for you, is it?"

Christian's words jerked her back to reality and she turned to where he stood leaning against the railing.

"Of course not."

He watched her for a long while. "I don't know what to think of you."

She turned back to the wheel. "Think whatever you want. I won't try to sway your opinion of me."

"You're a good liar."

Her hands tightened on the spokes and he sauntered over. "You almost had me believing we were married."

She rolled her eyes. She'd made a terrible fool of herself with that little act and still didn't understand how the guards hadn't called her bluff. "Nonsense."

"You did have one thing right, however. We have our differences."

Of course they did. What did he want her to say?

His face darkened. "You had me fooled. All that time. All one big lie. You must have been laughing at my expense."

She shook her head. "No. It was quite uncomfortable, if you must know."

He leaned over. "You didn't seem uncomfortable when naked beneath me. In fact, you were quite enthusiastic, if I recall."

Thank God for the darkness, because her cheeks flamed. "I—"

"Tell me something, Red. That sob story about your parents, that was a lie as well, wasn't it?"

Her lip trembled as a ringing began in her ears.

"Don't you dare bring my parents into this." She wrenched from the wheel. "Griff!"

Without even waiting to see that he was on his way to take over, she marched down the stairs to the main deck. Her steps led her as far away from the helm as she could go, until she leaned over the bow spirit. Dark waves crashed against the hull below, sending stinging mist into her face.

"Why do you keep saving me?"

He'd followed her.

She twisted with a cry. "Why can't you leave me alone?"

He pushed a wet strand of hair from his eyes. "God help me, Red, I don't know."

She blinked at his honest response.

"Ever since I first laid eyes on you, I haven't been able to get you out of my mind." He stepped closer to her and she swallowed at the intensity of his gaze. "I don't know if I want to arrest you for your crimes . . ." He closed the distance between them and grabbed her shoulders. "Or kiss you senseless."

Everything around them faded away until all she could hear was the roar of her pulse. *Breathe in. Breathe out.* The *Raven* pitched down a swell and a spray of water smacked into them. Still, he stared at her, even as water dripped down his face.

Her throat went dry. And suddenly, she couldn't lie to herself anymore. This was why she'd wanted him to come with them. This was who she wanted. What she wanted. When she closed her eyes, he was who she saw.

He stood still, inches from her, his eyes filled with intensity. His jaw ticked. Could she do it? Should she? In three days, they'd be back in Savannah. Back to being enemies.

All the more reason to.

She let go of the railing and pulled his face down to hers. Several days' worth of dark stubble rubbed against her cheek as he caught her mouth with his. He tasted of salt. Of raw energy.

One of his hands tangled in her hair as his tongue pressed against hers. When he caught her lower lip between his teeth, she let out a little moan and pressed her body against his solid form. His other hand closed around the small of her back and he pushed against her until her back hit the railing.

The heat pouring through her body began to consume her, tearing through her at an alarming pace, and her kiss became frantic. He kept up with her frenzied movements, licking and sucking and biting until she could hardly breathe.

A whistle came from somewhere above in the rigging, piercing through her foggy subconscious, and she jerked her head back. He kept his hands in place, keeping her pressed against him, and his breaths came hot and ragged against her forehead.

She twisted from his grasp. "I—I need to go."

Ducking beneath his arm, she fled past several wide-eyed crewmates. So much for winning their respect. Griff glared at her as she ran across the main deck. How much had he seen? With burning cheeks, she fumbled with the door to her cabin and slammed it shut behind her.

Taking a few deep breaths, she sank into her chair at the desk and leaned back to stare at the ceiling. Not good. All her life, she'd avoided falling for anyone. She'd been able to focus on her sailing. Been able to ignore Abigail's attempts at matching her with random gentlemen.

And now she had feelings for Lieutenant Thompson.

She groaned and dropped her head to the desk. Banged it once. Twice. Of all the people in the entire world, him. And she had kissed him in front of her crew. Her stomach still fluttered from it. Even now, an uncomfortable warmth bloomed in her belly.

Good God. Was this yearning?

She rubbed the smarting spot at her temple. Yearning or not, she had work to do.

Pulling the bit of parchment from her pocket, she gingerly

unfolded the damp wax-coated paper and breathed out a sigh. A few lines of ink had gone blurry, but the coating had preserved the majority of it. Opening a drawer, she lifted a fresh piece of parchment and found her quill and ink.

Time to make a copy.

Whoever had torn the map had done it very strategically. The line on this half snaked back up to the coast, but quite far to the south.

Her parents had never been close.

With a shaky breath, she stood and retrieved the big conch, peeling the wax plug free. Slipping her half of the map out, she unfolded and pressed it to Thorne's half. A little thrill went through her. She was the first to lay eyes on the location of the two-hundred-year-old treasure.

Now, to get it before Thorne caught up to them.

A grim smile settled on her lips as she dipped her quill into the ink. With painstaking movements, she slowly drew the black stained tip across the paper. Each scratch, each dip into the inkwell brought the map into clarity.

After at least an hour had passed, Samantha threw down the pen and stared down at the completed map. Her breath blew out and she lifted it into the lantern light. Not bad. A few shaky lines and a blot of ink here and there, but certainly good enough to guide her to the treasure.

She carefully folded the new map along with her original half and slid them into the conch before pressing the soft wax back into place. Thorne's half went back into her pocket. It didn't feel right to put it with her parents' half. She'd find somewhere else to hide it.

Clearing her desk, she pulled out a few nautical charts and made some calculations. Once they made it past The Bahamas, it would be a straight shot to Savannah. Three days of sailing with the wind in their favor.

Before her hand closed around the handle of her door, she paused and took a deep breath. She needed to focus and sail this ship, and she couldn't afford any more distractions. Hopefully, Christian would be below by now.

He wasn't.

As soon as she opened the door, her sight zeroed in on the tall form leaning against the mainmast. At least she didn't have to walk past him. With a forced swallow, she climbed the stairs to the quarterdeck and took the wheel from Griff.

"Take a rest. I'll sail her until dawn."

ALL NIGHT, SHE ignored Christian. He never did move from his spot against the mainmast, although he did finally sit down at some point.

As the stars tracked their courses through the sky, his dark gaze never left her. At first, it sent goosebumps across her skin. But as the hours crept by, it became a nuisance. When her hair blew in her eyes, she didn't dare sweep it away. When her feet ached and she wanted to shift onto one leg, she held steady.

She would prove to him she was a true captain.

When the soft grey line on the horizon gave way to the pink of sunrise, Griff rejoined her.

He took the wheel and glanced at her. "You look like hell."

"Thank you."

With a nod to where Christian sat, he checked his compass. "Anything to do with that fellow?"

Her shoulders sagged and she fought a yawn. "He hasn't moved."

"Stubborn, then."

She shot him a quizzical look, but he gazed out over the open sea. His spyglass hung from his belt and she snatched it and marched to the stern. In dawn's early light, the water glistened lavender. This was usually her favorite time of day. Most mornings, she would climb up to the crow's nest to watch the sunrise in its entirety.

Maybe not today, however. The sore muscles of her feet and back ached for the soft sheets of her bed. First, she raised the spyglass and scanned the horizon. Her stomach clenched as she swept her gaze back and forth.

Nothing.

Bed, then.

She climbed down to the main deck and shot Christian a glare. "Do you ever sleep?"

He stood and stretched his arms above his head, the movement tugging his shirt up to reveal a swath of his waist, tan and sprinkled with dark hair. "Someone had to keep an eye on you."

With a huff, she dragged her eyes from him. "If you're going to stay up here on the deck, you may as well make yourself useful. I don't abide lazy crew or passengers."

He strode toward her. "What would you have me do, Captain?"

She matched his steps backward until she reached the railing and he came to a stop in front of her.

If he meant to fluster her, it was working.

No. She wouldn't cower to him. Straightening her back, she stood tall and waved a hand toward the deck. "Always plenty of cleaning to do. Ropes to be coiled. Sails to be repaired. I'm sure you know how to do at least one of those things."

He nodded and ran his fingers along the railing. No. Stroked the railing.

When he glanced up, his eyes fairly smoldered. "I meant other things. Surely, you have other needs I can meet."

Samantha's mouth gaped. The nerve of him.

"While I'm sure your offer would have ladies of the land falling head over heels, your insinuations—or intentions—have no place on my ship."

There. She'd said it without stammering. Without an inkling of the warmth that coiled in her belly at his words. Without revealing that yes, she did indeed have needs.

"Ladies of the land?" He snorted. "Very well, Captain."

Still, the knowing look he shot her made her waver. Did he know just how much he affected her?

Arrogant man.

She fidgeted on her feet and turned to the sea to hide the nervous movement. Her fingers itched around the spyglass and she couldn't help raising it again. Before she could put her eye to it, Christian's hand closed over her own, tugging it down.

"Why are you so worried? Thorne has no reason to want to catch up with us. Or does he?" His eyes sharpened when she jerked around and he pulled out his compass. "How did you get this?" When she remained silent, he took a step closer. "While I'm flattered you found it in your heart to free me, I find it odd you paid Thorne a visit as well. Why risk it?"

She swallowed and stared at the compass as he flipped it open.

"What am I missing, Red?"

"I . . ."

His brows rose and he leaned closer. "You what?"

Words formed, then caught in her throat. If she told him . . .

If she told him, what did it matter?

So she straightened and met his emerald gaze. "I may have taken something of his."

He stepped next to her and leaned over the rail. "What did you take, and why do I have a feeling this is going to make me regret coming along?"

She pulled her lip between her teeth as she mulled over the best story to tell him. In the end, she settled for the truth. Best to lay it all out in the open.

"You know that he was after my uncle's map?"

When he turned toward her, his eyes had gone a fraction wider. "Don't tell me . . ."

She hung her head. "I stole his half of the map."

"Christ."

He took a few steps away and pivoted back to her. "What

were you thinking?"

Her hands balled into fists. "He doesn't deserve that treasure."

"Of course he doesn't. That hardly warrants spiting him to ensure he comes after you. Only a fool would steal something like that."

"A fool that has the other half of the map in her possession."

A dark brow rose. Twitched. "You have it? Here?"

She nodded and he cursed, raking a hand through his already mussed locks. "So, you planned to take me on a treasure hunt with you?"

"Of course not. I'm not that foolish. We need to return to Savannah. Restock. Bring extra ships. Extra men." She paused and threw his words back at him. "Only a fool would attempt to retrieve a treasure with Thorne on their trail. May as well hand it to him on a silver platter."

"And where do I fit into your grand plan?" He spoke flatly, staring out to sea.

She crossed her arms. "You're a pirate hunter. Why not take down the biggest name out there? Your notoriety would increase ten-fold. Imagine, *Lieutenant Thompson takes down Captain Thorne.* You'd be famous."

He went still. The sounds of her life—her passion—filled the silence. Boards creaked and sails whistled over the slap of ropes and crashing waves.

His fingers drummed an unknown tune against the polished rail and he turned to face her. "And what of you, Red? What am I to do with you?"

Her throat went dry under his green gaze. "Leave me be."

He laughed then, the sound brittle. "Leave you alone?" His hand left the rail and reached for her. She held her breath, unable to move as he angled toward her face. At the last moment, he halted the movement and let his hand fall aside.

The momentary spell over her broke and she took a step away from him, out of his reach. "I'll promise not to pirate in

American waters. If it helps."

He snorted. "You should know by now I don't put much stock in a pirate's word."

She flashed him a weak smile. "There's a first time for every-thing."

He bridged the distance between them again.

"Why should I trust you? Everything between us has been a lie."

"Not everything." The words slipped out before she could stop them and he stiffened. He knew exactly what she spoke of.

Heat rushed up her cheeks and she stuffed a hand into her pocket. A moment later, she waved Thorne's half of the map in the small space between them. The old parchment fluttered in the wind.

"You can have it. Until we reach Savannah."

He plucked the map from her fingers and unfolded it. "What use do I have for a tattered piece of paper? What does it gain me?"

She gave a harsh sigh. "It's a gesture of goodwill, Lieutenant."

Snatching the map back, she folded it and held out her hand. "Your compass."

His brows drew together, but he handed it over, the metal warm from his grasp.

She lifted the lid and tucked the folded map into the body. When she handed it back to him, a weight lifted from her shoulders. Good riddance. Her hands suddenly burned with the need to lather up with soap and wash all remainders of Thorne away.

Christian stared at the tarnished brass for a long while before sliding his gaze back to her. He didn't say anything, but his emerald eyes flashed in the morning sun. She hadn't missed the sunrise after all.

A shout from above broke his silent scrutiny, and he slipped the compass into his pocket.

"Ship ahoy!"

Something dark flashed in his eyes. "Speak of the devil."

Her stomach lurched as she rose the spyglass once more. Seeing the sails on the horizon sent bile up her throat. It could be anybody. But how many ships that size sailed the Caribbean?

Christian yanked the spyglass from her and took a look. With a growl, he lowered it. "You've got three, maybe four hours until he catches up."

She was already on her way to the helm, panic clawing her gut. They already had every sail set. The masts wouldn't support any more as it was.

"You can't outrun him."

She stiffened at Christian's soft words.

Damn him for being right.

She spun to Griff. "Can we lose them in the outer shoals of The Bahamas?"

His grim face confirmed her doubts. "Nay. We'll be lucky to even reach them by the time he catches up."

A pain pressed against her temples. She should have killed Thorne—or at the very least, given him enough henbane to do the job for her. Her gaze slid to Christian. Or she could have listened to Griff and not wasted time rescuing the lieutenant and his crew.

Even an hour's more of a head start would have given them a fighting chance.

But now? They were sitting ducks.

Chapter Eighteen

S AMANTHA KEPT HER hand steady on the wheel. The only steady thing in the chaos around her. The ship hummed beneath her, pushed to her limit with sails taking more wind than they ever were meant for. Her heart raced, each rapid pump a painful reminder she was alive. For now.

Don't look back.

She didn't have to.

The *Reckoning* was close enough now for her to hear the muffled shouts of Thorne's men.

Shouts filled with bloodlust.

She forced herself to take a breath. Ahead, a smudge of green marred the horizon. The Bahamas. *So close.*

And impossibly far away. She needed hours. They had minutes.

"We need to talk, Captain."

Christian approached, sweat dripping down his brow. He'd been down below the last hour, helping ready the cannons. As much as she hated to admit it, he'd been invaluable. After Thorne's sails were spotted, the lieutenant had burst into action organizing her men. Preparing them for battle.

Now, his mouth settled into grim lines. Griff stood behind him with a similar expression.

"Are you sure you want to do this?"

A sharp pain stabbed through her chest. "What other choice do we have?"

He met her eyes. "Surrender."

Her fingers tightened on the spokes. "I think my crew agrees we'd rather go down fighting. Either way, we all die."

Christian looked between her and Griff. "I have reason to believe he might spare us."

She jerked her head back. "Spare us? Last I checked, mercy wasn't part of Thorne's vocabulary."

He glanced behind her, where the shouts had grown louder. "We are close enough to the islands that if he does sink us, some may survive."

"And what if he takes us prisoner again? I'd rather die than step one foot back on his ship."

"He will probably make haste to Savannah to confront your uncle directly. I doubt he'd try the same tactic twice."

Griff stepped forward. "Under most circumstances, I would agree to fight to the death. But if there's a chance . . ."

Samantha clenched her jaw. Her gaze swept over the deck, where men hastened with last-minute preparations. Tommy stood beneath the mainmast, coiling a length of sheeting, his face pale in the sun.

Her vision blurred.

Most of these men had families onshore. Wives. Children. So many lives would be thrown into upheaval. The pain in her chest bloomed fiercer. A chance. She would take even a thread of hope.

With a tight throat, she turned to Christian and Griff. "What do we do?"

Christian pulled up his nose. At least this was hard for him too. "We stand down."

He jumped down to the main deck and began shouting orders. Guns were rolled back and hatches closed, and the entire crew gathered in the open. Nervous energy thrummed through both ship and man.

"Go join them." Griff stepped next to her. "They can't see you now, but if Thorne gets his eyes on you at the helm, it will be worse for you."

She handed the wheel over. "I'm sorry, Griff. You were right."

"We got much farther than I thought we would." He gave her a half smile. "Now go."

She descended to the deck and came to a stop next to Tommy. His eyes darted to hers and she couldn't help putting a hand on his shoulder.

"Do you think the lieutenant was right?"

With a gentle squeeze, she let herself face the approaching ship. No wonder Tommy's voice quivered. As the *Reckoning* approached, a dozen cannons gleamed from open hatches, and the crew of giants lined the decks, armed with long scimitars. Several huge black flags whipped in the wind from each mast. The vivid white skull and crossbones insignias sent a ripple of coldness through her.

Flying those flags was an invitation to the gallows for most pirates.

Not Thorne.

"We can only hope." Her mouth had gone dry, however.

After a shouted order from their captain, the brutes reefed the sails and the towering frigate floated alongside the *Raven*.

Staring down the barrel of a cannon, Samantha tried and failed to swallow. Numbness crept over her, winding through her limbs and heart until the world around her slipped away. Leaving her and the thud of her pulse.

Would her life flash before her eyes? Should it? She closed them. What was worth remembering? Her parents. She tried to picture their faces. Nothing. Sailing. Wind in hair and one with the ship. Still nothing.

She scowled. Surely there was something she could think of. Something that had given her pleasure.

And then a vision did come: Herself. Tucked against Christian's chest, his fingers cupping her jaw with quiet possessiveness.

Her eyes snapped open and she glared at Christian's back. He had placed himself between her crew and Thorne's men. How gallant. She growled. How dare he occupy her last thoughts?

She made to close her eyes and try again when Thorne's

voice boomed between the ships.

"And here my men were itching for a fight."

"Leave us be, Thorne." Christian took a step toward the railing.

The pirate laughed. He stood at the forecastle, his jacket tails flapping against his thighs.

"After you've stolen something of mine? You must be out of your mind, boy. Give it back, and I shall give you all quick deaths."

Samantha's fingers dug into her palms. She shouldn't have given the map to Christian.

"I don't know what you're talking about."

She blinked. The honest lieutenant, lying?

Thorne's gaze roamed the crew and settled on her. His eyes narrowed and after a long moment of silence, he grinned.

"Search the ship."

His crew began swinging over with ropes and tethered the ships together. A gangplank thunked across the railings and Thorne walked over, his eyes never leaving her.

When he stopped in front of her, he pulled a dagger from his belt. Running his finger over the blade, he leaned close. "There's a special punishment I reserve for those who steal from me."

"Leave her alone, Thorne." Christian's voice rang with warning.

"You're in no place to give me orders." Thorne ran the tip of the dagger along her jawline. Saliva pooled in her mouth and she fought to stay still as his gaze traveled over her attire. "You look better in a dress, Miss Warstein."

Thumps and crashes came from below deck. Her gaze flitted to the lump in Christian's pocket. Would he give it up?

Thorne moved his blade down until it rested above her heart. Right where she'd placed hers the night before. He pressed until a sharp pain pierced her skin.

"Should have killed me when you had the chance." Flipping the dagger, he sheathed it and laughed. "You make a lousy pirate."

He pivoted and began a slow stroll around the deck. He ran his hand along the railing, over sheeting and pulleys. Samantha's hands clenched as he touched her ship so intimately.

One by one, his men reported their news to him. No map.

Her crew stood in tense silence as the minutes dragged by. Christian stood rigid with his hands clasped behind his back and Thorne approached him.

"I know what you're trying to do, but let me tell you something. My patience is wearing thin. You're only delaying the inevitable."

Christian didn't budge.

"So be it." Thorne turned to his men. "Take their weapons and tie them up. Everyone but her."

The giants lashed her crewmates' hands and feet together. Griff and Christian were dragged over to the group and bound as well. Samantha gave a little cry when one of the men yanked her away from the group and toward Thorne.

She dug her heels into the deck and received a harsh shake.

"Thorne." Christian's voice followed them. "Leave her and take me. I can be ransomed. I think you know how much the governor would pay."

Tears pricked her eyes. Ever the hero. Even after all the animosity between them, he hadn't hesitated to offer himself in her place.

The captain ignored him and nodded to the brute gripping her arm. With a kick behind her leg, he shoved her to the deck. Pain lanced up from her knees and she sucked in a sharp breath.

"This is your last chance. Give me the map."

She locked eyes with Christian. His lips pressed together in a tight line and his bound hands reached around his side, grasping at his pocket. She gave a little shake of her head and swiveled to face Thorne.

"What a familiar scene. Where have I seen this before?" He ran his fingers through his beard and flashed her a malicious smile. "Oh yes, your mother died like this. Kneeling before me under the same circumstances. The bitch refused to tell me where the map was as well."

Samantha let out a snarl and lunged forward but the man next to her yanked her back in place.

Thorne laughed and waved another brute over. The man removed something from a leather pouch and handed it to the captain. A tremor ran through her.

A cat-o-nines. The woven leather strands dangled in the breeze, each with a little hook glistening in the sun. They clinked together, the odd jingle ringing in her ears. A gruesome wind chime.

Her vision swam and she splayed her hands against the warm deck. She'd never been allowed to watch a flogging. But she'd tended the bloodied backs of men afterward.

Stay strong.

If she faltered, Christian would give up the map. And there would be nothing left to keep Thorne from executing them all. Now, she understood why he hadn't given it up right away.

The pirate wouldn't kill them until he got his hands on the map.

"Thorne, don't do this." Christian struggled against his bonds. "Thorne!"

She couldn't watch him. The rest of her crew stared on with horror, so she dropped her eyes to the deck. To her trembling fingertips.

Only one thing ran through her mind. Over and over again.

Don't scream.

The crack of the whip shattered the silence and the hooks whistled past her face to bite into the deck not an inch from her hand.

She screamed.

The next blow would come to her back.

Thorne jerked the whip and the hooks yanked free of the wood, clattering against the planks as he coiled the leather around one hand.

Her nails curled into the deck as her heart thrashed in her chest. She couldn't do this. Spots covered her vision and a sob broke free.

"Stop!" Christian's strangled cry broke through the buzzing in her ears. "I'll give you your damned map."

Thorne chuckled. "You're making this too easy. Guess it's true what they say, men will do anything for a pretty lady." He strode to Christian and lifted his chin with the coiled whip. "I should have known you had it."

One of the giants frisked the lieutenant and pulled the compass free. Thorne took it and tapped his fingers against the brass. He flipped it open and slid out the map.

"That's better."

He turned and walked to the gangplank. "Tie her next to him."

Someone grabbed her arms and dragged her next to Christian. When the huge hands released their grip, her legs gave out and she sagged against him. The giant lashed her wrists to the foremast.

One by one, the pirates left the *Raven*. The gangplanks were removed and ropes untied. A group of the giants climbed up into the frigate's rigging.

Once the last line had been cut, Thorne strode to the railing and faced Christian. "Don't look so angry, boy. I'll at least give you the pleasure of something I never had. Dying at your lover's side."

Before she could ponder what he meant, the world exploded. The cannons fired in perfect harmony, blasting through the *Raven's* hull.

"No." Samantha choked the word out as her beloved ship shuddered beneath the onslaught. She struggled to take her next breath and slumped forward while everything spun around her in a blur.

"Red." Christian's voice cut through the haze surrounding her. "Stay with me."

His elbow nudged her side and she leaned into his steady weight. Another round of cannon fire brought splashing crashes below. They were firing below the waterline.

No.

She thrashed against her bonds, rubbing the skin at her wrists raw.

Christian braced his leg against hers, the solid touch bringing her back. Ceasing her struggle, she took a deep breath. And another. The movements of the ship were foreign to her. The *Raven* listed to her port and Samantha imagined the cargo holds filling with water below.

The grind of cannon wheels snapped her attention to Thorne's deck, where a group of giants pushed a gun to the railing. Once in place, they swung the barrel to point at the group of captives. Sweat beaded on Samantha's brow.

Thorne patted one of the men's shoulders. "He's an expert marksman." His gaze narrowed on Christian. "I do say, Lieutenant, I wish we could have met under better circumstances."

He flipped open the compass and strode to the quarterdeck while the man at the cannon grinned at their group. After several tense moments passed, he shrugged and swiveled the barrel toward the mainmast.

Her heart calmed, but only a little. If he took the mainmast down, he could still kill them all. Between the mast itself and the yards, sails, and rigging, it could be as deadly—or worse—as a shot taken directly at them. Christian had gone stiff at her side, angling himself between her and the mast.

As if he could save her from a thousand-pound piece of wood.

Her eyes alternated between the man at the gun and the mast. He took his time, sighting down the iron barrel and making minute corrections to his aim. Without moving, he gave the order to light and the man behind him struck a flint next to the fuse. The giant made one final adjustment and stepped away.

Boom!

A crack accompanied the thunderous blast and Samantha

flinched. The impact traveled up her legs but not as violently as it should have. Her eyes flew to the mast, where a deep scar furrowed its side. It stood.

For now.

The cannonball had gouged itself nearly halfway through the mast. A few inches farther and it would have been brought down. The giant already fiddled with the smoking barrel and her heart clenched. Even if he didn't hit it square on, the next shot would take it down.

Thorne set a hand on the man's shoulder. "No need to waste any more lead. They'll go down quickly. Set the sails."

At his shout, the men up in the yards unfurled sails and the white canvas billowed out. Thorne stared straight ahead as his ship crawled forward, content to let the sea finish his job.

"Coward," she whispered beneath her breath.

As soon as the *Reckoning* turned away from them, Christian began struggling. The *Raven* slanted hard now, and Samantha had to lean far back to stay upright.

"If anyone has a knife hidden on them, now's the time to share." Griff shot her a look and her eyes widened.

Of course.

"I have one."

Christian jerked around to face her and she nodded toward the deck. "In my boot."

She lifted her foot as the ship tilted even further. Balancing on one foot became impossible and she slipped. The ropes around her wrists yanked tight and she cried out at the wrenching pain in her shoulders as the weight of her body threatened to dislocate them.

"Lean on me." Christian extended his leg until she was able to hook an elbow over it. "There you go. Easy now."

He held his leg still as she righted herself inch by inch. The mainmast groaned and rigging slapped against the yards above. She faltered and slid back a bit.

"Ignore it." His words held her steady and a moment later, she stood again.

"Turn to Griff. Use his body as support and see if you can lift your leg toward me."

Griff twisted so she could use his back. Leaning into him, she swallowed and inched her foot toward Christian. He'd gotten his hands to one side and grunted as he strained against his bindings to reach her.

"That's it. A little closer."

Her leg began to shake. Could she even lift it that high? New tears pricked at her eyes as her muscles burned. And then his hand closed around her ankle. Pulled her leg the rest of the way up. A moment later, he released her and the soft slice of rope filled the air.

After he freed himself, he cut her loose. Once her hands were released, she grabbed the ropes binding Griff and worked at the knot. He and Christian began freeing the other men and several crewmates raced to ready the two longboats.

Christian paused mid-slice at another man and glanced at her. "Get in a boat."

She took a step toward it and froze.

The map.

"I'll be right back." She turned and sprinted to her cabin, ignoring his curse. When she passed the mainmast on the way, little cracks filled the air. The strain on it at this angle had to be incredible. They had precious little time left.

Flinging her door open, she let out a sharp gasp.

Water poured into the cabin through broken windows in a dark torrent, frothing against the floor. Her desk, fastened to the boards, hung suspended at an impossible angle. Climbing in over the door frame, she half-slipped half-scrambled toward her shelves. They lay empty. One shell had caught against a rumpled blanket above where the water circled in angry eddies. The rest . . .

Her gaze flew to the water, deepening by the second. They were down there somewhere. Splashing in, she dove under. Opening her eyes, she couldn't see her hand in front of her face.

Blast it.

She surfaced, sucking in a breath, and submerged again, her hands skimming across the tilted floor. At this angle, all items would be against the far wall. She came up once more, next to her floating chair. One more deep breath and she went back down, kicking hard against the rush of water. There. The wall.

She ran her fingers to where it met the floor and across the rubble there. A few of her smaller shells. Her rapier. Clothing and blankets twisted around her arms like seaweed trying to drag her down. Her lungs burned as bubbles escaped her nose. A little further.

Pushing aside something, maybe a drawer, she felt beneath it. Shapeless items. Her lack of oxygen made it too hard to focus on what she touched. She drew her knees under her to push up off the floor. And touched something hard. Something familiar. Her fingers closed around it and she shot to the surface.

"Damn it, Red. What the hell are you doing?" Christian's bellow echoed off the water as she tried to stand upright.

Glancing at the conch in her hand, Samantha grinned and took a step toward him.

She felt it before she heard it.

A little tremble ran through the ship before a massive pop rent the air. The floor shifted beneath her and she grabbed the edge of the desk to steady herself as water swirled around her waist.

Time to get out.

She sloshed toward the door, where Christian frowned at her. "Don't worry, I'm—"

A mighty groan filled the air followed by an earsplitting snap and her eyes widened. Not the—

Christian let out a shout and leaped backward. Something crashed against the door and slammed it shut. The jarring impact sent her reeling backward along with a torrent of wood shards and pain blazed across her back as the ceiling caved in.

The mainmast.

Chapter Nineteen

"R ED!"

Christian heaved himself from the deck, ears ringing, and threw himself against the splintered mainmast crushed against the door.

The ship listed hard to port and he had to grab a hanging line to keep from falling again. Waves began to slosh over the deck as the sea tightened her grip on the floundering brigantine. It wouldn't be long now.

With a snarl, he grabbed the mast once more and leveraged his legs against the door. Nothing. Damn it. Water swirled around his thighs. His waist. Still, he clawed at the wood. But the weight of the mast had pinned the door to its frame. Without an ax and minutes he didn't have, there was no hope of opening it.

"Red!" He shouted her name again.

Silence. His gaze went higher. The mast had also crashed through the decking above her cabin.

"Son of a—"

A huge groan trembled through the ship as she slipped deeper beneath the waves and the frothing waters tangled rigging ropes around Christian's torso and neck.

"Lieutenant."

Griff stood on the mast where it jutted from the water and reached out.

Christian shook his head. "I can't let her drown."

The old man's face twisted with grief but he shook his head. "You'll kill yourself as well if you stay there any longer."

As if on cue, the ship shuddered with one last effort to remain upright. Christian's feet were swept from the deck as a new cascade of water crashed over him.

A hand closed around his arm and dragged him to the surface. He clambered up onto the mast and looked down into the dark water encasing the main deck. His heart lurched in his chest and heat gathered at the corners of his eyes.

"There's nothing you can do." Griff touched his shoulder and pointed to the longboat floating next to the sinking vessel, and as the ship rolled again, they dove into the waves.

The sea washed away his tears and when he surfaced, the *Raven* had gone bottoms up. Her barnacle-covered keel glistened in the sun as she rapidly descended to her watery grave. More hands grabbed at his shoulders and the crew dragged him and Griff into the longboat.

All eyes were glued to the sinking ship. In a matter of seconds, her hull submerged until only the bow jutted from the water. It bobbed. Once. Twice. Then with a quiet whoosh, it slipped beneath the waves.

Thick silence crushed around them as Christian stared at the spot. Huge bubbles broke the surface where ropes, sails, and bits of broken wood drifted in an ever-widening ring. He gripped the roughhewn wood at the edge of the longboat, his breaths coming in irregular, harsh gasps. He should have stopped her.

Damn it. If he had gone after her sooner, he could have kept her from entering that death trap.

Now, she was . . .

His chest splintered with an acute pain.

She was gone.

Every complicated feeling he had for her crashed forth, squeezing the air right out of his lungs. His brave, fierce, exasperating pirate.

Gone.

The cabin boy let out a strangled sob and Christian's eyes burned once more. Clenching his teeth together, he dragged his gaze from the tragic scene to where his father's sails were still visible against the horizon.

Damn the man. Damn him to hell and back again. A growl rumbled in the back of his throat. He would go to Savannah, would petition for more ships. And would take the bastard down. His fingers curled into tight fists.

Thorne would pay.

The boy cried out again and Christian jerked around. One of the men pointed and Christian's heart gave a hopeful little leap. It couldn't be.

It was.

Fiery hair glistened in the sun as she surfaced, coughing and sputtering. The most beautiful sight he'd ever seen.

Before anyone could react, Christian was already in motion. After a sloppy dive that smacked the water against his face, he kicked out to her in broad strokes.

When he reached her side, she continued gasping for air.

"How did you get out?"

"A window. But she pulled me down with her. I almost—" A cough wracked her and her face slipped beneath the water.

Wrapping an arm around her chest, Christian tugged her close to him and started back toward the longboat. He helped push her in and joined her a moment later.

The men had moved to the edges to make room and she lay on her side, chest heaving with each ragged breath she took. She closed her eyes and Christian reached down to make sure she was alright.

Before he could touch her, she raised her hand, white-knuckled around a huge shell. "I got it," she whispered.

The cabin boy stared at her with wide eyes. "You almost drowned yourself for a shell?"

She gave a small smile. "Not just a shell. The map is in here."

Christian grabbed her shoulders and pulled her upright. "Are you hurt?"

She laughed, then winced. "I hurt everywhere."

He ran his hands down her arms, up her sides. No broken bones.

When he finished his perusal, she cocked her head. "Worried, Lieutenant? Be careful, or I might think you care for me."

I do care for you. The words echoed in his mind, unspoken.

Griff wiped at tear-streaked cheeks. "Glad to have you back with us, Captain."

She frowned at him and her shoulders slumped. "I'm no captain."

Her soft statement brought a chorus of nays from the men gathered round and a sad smile tugged at her lips. "Look at where I got us. Shipwrecked and adrift at sea."

Her grip on the shell faltered and it tumbled to her feet.

Griff cleared his throat and pointed north to the sliver of green on the horizon. "Not adrift. Everyone made it off the ship alive. We've strong men aplenty and oars. We'll reach that atoll by dusk."

"And then what? Who knows when the next ship will pass by?" She pressed her eyes shut. "I failed you all. I could have killed him on his ship. Started to. But I couldn't go through with it."

Christian's jaw ticked. She'd nearly killed his father. The man who'd killed her parents.

Griff reached out and touched her shoulder. "Taking a life is not something to be done lightly. No matter how much they might deserve it. Once you've crossed that line, there's no turning back. It changes you—forever."

Christian could still remember the first time he'd killed a man in battle. The retching and violent dreams that had followed. The questions he'd been forced to ask himself. Wondering if it could have been avoided. "He's right. Not killing him doesn't make you a failure. It makes you human."

He reached down and picked up the shell, hefting its weight until sunlight reflected off pale pink tines.

Red stared at him with watery eyes. "You should toss it overboard. That map has brought nothing but misery."

She stared out at the floating wreckage and her face paled.

Funny how a brush with death could change perspectives. She was right. So why didn't he throw it? He tilted the shell until a wax plug became visible. He peeled it back and a corner of parchment became visible.

Such a small, inconsequential thing. A piece of paper. Yet so many lives had been lost over the years for it. His gaze slid back to her. The spunk that had lit her eyes, both as Red and Miss Warstein, had faded. He didn't like it.

The crew stood silent. Waiting. These men had given everything for the promise of what the map represented. Gruff faces, weathered by years of sun and salt, watched him with wary, and weary, eyes.

Something squeezed his heart. Sympathy? For pirates? He shook his head. It had to be the aftershock of the day's events. Still, he couldn't bring himself to throw these men's dreams overboard.

He reached down and picked up Red's limp hand, giving the shell back. The chilled flesh gave him pause. She wasn't staring at the wreckage after all and didn't flinch when he passed his other hand in front of her eyes. Shock.

The cabin boy stood frowning at her back, and Christian turned her. A hiss of pain escaped her lips and he let out a curse. A tear in the white blouse revealed smooth skin, marred by an angry red welt. At the edge of the linen, a small splinter of wood poked out. The wet fabric clung to her, pink around the edges from blood.

Once again, his hands clenched. She'd nearly died.

He stood. "To oars, men."

They jumped into action, splitting into watches that would take turns at the oars. Red sat silently through it all, but at the third change, she took a place at an oar.

Christian set a hand on her shoulder. "No."

She pulled from his touch. "Don't coddle me, Lieutenant."

He made to respond, but Griff met his eyes and gave a shake

of his head.

"Fine," he ground out. "But you're not rowing alone."

He sat on the bench next to her and closed his hands over the rough wood of the oar. He'd rowed through both of the previous watches and his arms burned, but he gritted his teeth and extended the oar.

Minutes slid by and he began pacing his breaths, counting them, willing time to pass by with greater speed. When a warm heat crept up his thigh, he glanced down. Red had shifted and her leg pressed against his. Each pump of the oar increased the pleasant pressure. Suddenly, he didn't care how much longer the watch took.

He could row like this all day.

Griff had been right, and they approached the atoll before the sun began to set. Navigating over the reef took all their effort and concentration, and once the longboats passed the breaking waves, they made quick work of pulling up to the beach.

Someone dragged a large box from under a bench and Red distributed supplies, delegating men to find shelter and food. New watches were organized to post men on each side of the little island for keeping an eye out for any passing vessels. Christian helped gather driftwood and when a decent stack had been piled, he sank onto one of the lightweight blankets procured from the chest.

A rusty glow fell over them as the sun edged toward the horizon. Red walked over and threw down a sack filled with young coconuts near the small fire now burning in the center of all their activity. She barely spared a glance for him.

It shouldn't bother him.

But it did.

The men sat on mats of palm fronds and passed around a tin of hard biscuits. When the notes from a tin whistle floated over them, Christian let out a chuckle. Leave it to a bunch of rough and tumble pirates to be so utterly prepared for such an event.

Red didn't join them. She stood at the edge of the group,

kicking sand around in a little pile. Griff patted the empty spot next to him, but she shook her head.

"I'm going to go for a swim and wash up." She turned and began walking down the beach.

A prickle of unease swept over Christian and he stood. "She shouldn't be alone."

Griff huffed. "We certainly don't have any ladies' maids around, and I'm positive she wouldn't want any of us spying on her."

Christian grabbed the blanket he'd been sitting on. "No. Swimming so soon after being in shock could be dangerous." A vision of her sinking beneath the water thrust itself to the front of his mind.

"Does that chest contain any bandages?" He folded the blanket as Griff rummaged through it and produced a roll of muslin.

By the time he set out after her, she'd disappeared around a bend. He quickened his pace and jogged along the water's edge, wet sand pressing into his bare feet. The chatter from the crew faded away until only the quiet sounds of night surrounded him. The soft lap of waves against the beach. The rustle of palm fronds to his right.

When he rounded the bend, he drew up short as Red strode into the water.

Naked.

Her hair cascaded down her back in unruly curls, hiding the welt he'd meant to wrap. Water splashed around her ankles, up to her knees and his throat went tight. The setting sun silhouetted her body, the curve of her buttocks barely visible.

Shit. He rubbed his hand along the itchy stubble on his jaw. If she turned, she'd see him.

Spying.

She didn't turn. Instead, she dove beneath the swell of a wave. He held his breath until she surfaced. And then his breath left him completely.

She flipped onto her back, floating on the glassy surface.

Water covered her belly, but her breasts thrust into view. His cock went hard so fast, he doubled over. She swept her arms back and kicked out into deeper water.

God, he felt like a green schoolboy peeping on his first nude woman. He should leave. Give her privacy. Her feet disappeared and she bobbed in the water. Over her head. He thought of the after-effects of shock. Dizziness. Shortness of breath. If she fainted . . .

"Red!" He shouted before thinking his plan through.

She spun in the water, her lips forming a perfect O before her eyes slanted. "What are you doing?"

He shoved the blanket and bandages behind his back. No chance he would admit he was concerned. Which left only one thing to do.

He dropped the items onto the beach and pulled his shirt free. When he unbuttoned the fall on his breeches her gasp rang out over the water.

"I decided I need a bath as well."

"You—you . . ." She trailed off and twisted to face the sea. "There are plenty of other places to bathe, Lieutenant."

"You don't have to watch." He peeled his breeches off and threw them to the sand. The water splashed around his legs as he strode toward her. When it closed around his waist, he relaxed his muscles. The perfect temperature.

He bent, submerging his head and running his fingers through his hair. The cool water caressed his scalp and he straightened, shaking his head. A few more steps into deeper water, he lowered his hands and scrubbed at his sides. Dropped one hand farther. Closed it around his cock.

Damn, he was harder than he thought.

A few strokes to clean himself. His eyes darted out to Red's stiff shoulders and he groaned at his palm's rough contact.

"Are you decent?"

He let go of himself and held back a laugh. "Depends on your definition of decent."

She turned. Swam back until she could touch. Took a step toward him. And cried out.

In an instant, he was moving toward her. He crossed the distance between them in a few strides. "You shouldn't be swimming."

She gave him a blank stare, and he cleared his throat as he came to a stop in front of her. With wide eyes, she crossed both arms over her breasts. "Lieutenant, this is far from proper."

A soft chuckle pushed forth. "When have we ever been proper with each other?"

She hopped on one foot as a swell lifted them.

"What's wrong?" A cramp could be lethal in the water.

"I stepped on something."

"Don't get angry with me."

"What do—?"

He swept her into his arms and she let out a shriek. One hand closed around her waist and the other beneath her knees. The slip of her skin against his brought forth a rush of heat. When he took a step toward shore, she threw her arms around his neck.

He forced himself to keep his eyes above the water. See, he could be a gentleman.

Then one of her nipples brushed across his chest.

God help him.

"Let me see your foot."

She stared at his neck and gave a quick shake of her head. He slid his hand down to her calf when she remained silent. The movement made her suck in her breath and she wiggled, slipping lower. Onto his erection. Maybe she wouldn't notice.

She noticed.

Her eyes went round and she tried to wiggle back up.

It made things worse, and her bottom pressed firmly against him.

"Red," he choked out. "I'm not a saint. If you want my help, please let me see your foot."

She swallowed but stilled. "I didn't ask for your help."

"Well, you're getting it."

She glared at his chest and he shifted, lifting her higher. Some of the tension in her shoulders eased and a moment later, her foot bobbed to the surface. He slipped his hand from beneath her legs, causing her to tighten her grip. God, the contact was amazing. He forced himself to ignore the cool press of their flesh together and examined her foot.

When his fingertips slid along her sole, she jerked it back with a snort. His lips curved. Ticklish. He pressed on and found a small shard of shell jutting out.

"Here we go." He pinched it between his fingers and yanked it free.

"Ouch!"

A tiny drop of blood welled from the spot and he pressed his thumb over it. He held her that way for a long moment, savoring her nearness. The last orange sliver of sun dipped below the horizon and shadows wound their way around the two of them. Too soon, she slackened her grip and he released her.

As soon as she got her feet beneath her, Red turned from him. This was when he should return to shore. But he couldn't.

He stood behind her, watching her hair swirl around her shoulders. The soft blanket it created obscured her body and his hands yearned to part it. He clenched them at his side as silence stretched heavy between them.

He took a step closer, tugged forth by an invisible tether, and she angled her face toward him.

"Do you feel it?" she whispered, searching his eyes.

Did he feel it? God, every inch of his body buzzed with feeling. He reached out with his hand and paused inches from her.

"May I?"

She nodded and he swept her hair to the side, over one slender shoulder. And he feasted on the curve of her sides, all the way down to where they blended with the dark water. With deliberate slowness, he set his hands on her shoulders, rubbed his thumbs in circles just above the water.

Her sigh was his undoing.

He dropped his hands, slipping them along slick skin. When he closed them around her waist, she turned to him. Nibbled on her bottom lip.

She'd hunched so that her breasts remained underwater, but he couldn't miss the soft swells. Nor the dark points of her nipples blurred beneath the surface. He groaned and tugged her to him, pressing her belly against his cock. She didn't try to wiggle away this time, just stared at him with parted lips.

He rocked his hips against her. "Feel what you do to me?"

Even in twilight's shadows, he could see the color rise on her cheeks.

He lowered his lips, set them on one cheekbone. "I wonder, do you blush everywhere like this?"

His thumbs swept out, brushing against the curls between her legs, and she made a soft noise in the back of her throat. And then her hands were on his chest, tentatively traveling up. He growled his pleasure and caught her mouth with his.

It was like unlocking Pandora's box. She leaned into him, sweeping her hands up to his neck, tangling in his hair. When he slid his hands around her bottom, she pushed off the seabed and wrapped her legs around his waist. Her tongue met his eager strokes and she made the sweetest little muffled cries.

He pulled his mouth away and she dug her nails into his scalp, trying to pull him back. Ignoring the pain, he lifted her and dropped his face to the valley between her breasts. Her back arched as he closed his lips over one pert nipple, grazing his teeth over the taut skin.

This time, she cried out aloud, grinding her core against him, inches above the throbbing tip of his erection. One hand delved between her thighs, parting the folds there and he grinned. Slick heat surrounded his finger. So wet.

Her hips tilted into his caress and he sank a finger into her. So soft. His breaths came in pants against her skin as he lapped his tongue over the salty drops beaded across her breast. She clung to him, muscles deep inside her velvet softness clenching around his finger.

Need pulsed through him in an ever-stronger crescendo, bordering on pain as every inch of his cock strained to reach her.

He withdrew his finger and she shook her head. "Please, don't stop."

Pressing through her curls, he found the nub of flesh there.

"Oh," she whispered into his hair. "Oh."

His lips trailed up to her collarbone, up the curve of her neck. Nipped at her earlobe. "Do you like that?"

She moaned when he rubbed a quick circle and he sucked at the tender place below her ear.

Mine.

The word thrummed through his mind and he tried to push it away.

Mine.

He let her slip lower. Lower. Until the part of him aching most for her touch bumped against her. The ache intensified.

He moved his hand, guided himself to her entrance. Something sharp dug into his neck. Her teeth. And then she wiggled her bottom.

He slipped inside her a blessed inch and her breath caught. Reining in the very last shred of self-control he had, Christian went still. "Is this . . .?"

She bit him again. "Christian. Please."

"Please, what?" His voice came out hoarse. "What do you want?"

She clamped around him, a tight, hot, glove.

"I want you."

With a guttural growl, he tugged her hips down and sank himself all the way into her.

Bliss. Pure bliss.

The buoyancy of the water gave the movement a whole new feeling as he gripped her hips and moved her in rhythm to his thrusts. Her head fell back and he pivoted so the last remnants of twilight flickered across the front of her.

With eyes closed and mouth slack, her face fairly glowed with passion. Her breasts bounced with each thrust and he groaned at the crash of pleasure the sight sent spiraling through him.

Wound tight as he had been, he'd already climbed to his peak, and he slowed his movements. Not yet. Not so soon.

But she clenched her legs tight and, using his shoulders for leverage, began the movements herself. She slid up and down his shaft, bumping her forehead against his. The determined frown on her face gave way to a satisfied smile as she got the hang of it. She sank onto him and wiggled.

God help him.

He needed to stop her.

"Red."

Everything in his world centered around that one word. Her cries faded into background noise, his own grunts unrecognizable. Until it was just him and her. The slide of their bodies together. Her fingertips digging into his skin. The salty residue still on his tongue.

He looked down, to where their bodies joined in the darkness, her copper curls entwined with his. She let out a gasp and his name slipped past her lips. His cock surged and he groaned. Too late. The urge to finish inside her—to claim her as he had before—consumed him. *No.* The hazy thought pricked the back of his mind. This was different. She wasn't just a pirate. Not anymore.

He began to pull free and she pressed her brows together in protest, clinging to him.

"I can't. Not inside you. Too risky." The words left him in a breathless gasp as he struggled to hold off his climax.

She tightened her grip and bumped her forehead against his. "It's alright. I take special herbs. No risk." Angling her hips, she began to slide down him once more.

Thank God. Because time was up.

Clamping his fingers into the soft flesh above her hips, Christian slammed into her with one more deep thrust. He held her tightly in place, even as she squirmed against the pressure, as wave upon wave of release exploded through him.

He shouted. At least he thought he did. The force of the orgasm left him speechless, struggling for breath.

Chapter Twenty

S AMANTHA'S SHOULDERS HEAVED as Christian panted against her.

She still stretched tight around his manhood. Quivering. Aching.

He didn't move when she pulled her face from his. With his eyes closed, she let her gaze roam across him. The dark stubble along his jaw verged on a beard, and his hair stuck to his cheeks in wet ringlets. Muscles bulged in his upper arms where they wrapped around her. All the disapproving lines had slackened, softening his face.

Power surged through her. She had done this. He'd stopped and it had nearly driven her mad. So she'd taken the reins. Not bad for an inexperienced pirate. Not so inexperienced anymore. A wide smile broke free.

His eyes opened, and her grin faltered at the intensity blazing in the dark green depths. He shifted his grip and his arm brushed across the welt on her back, sending a barb of pain slicing through her. She jerked, sucking in her breath and he released her. A rush of warmth spread between her legs when he pulled out and she grimaced at the strange sensation.

"I'm sorry." His voice rumbled across her, breaking the silence. "Let's get you to the beach."

A hand settled in the small of her back, pressing her forward on wobbly legs. When the waves lapped around her waist, she paused. He wanted to walk all the way to the beach. Naked.

"You know you're beautiful, Red. Don't be shy."

How was it he always read her mind? Still, she didn't move. It didn't matter that darkness cloaked the beach, the pale crescent moon above providing little light. She turned to ask him to turn his back.

And his lips closed on hers in a soft, yet unyielding kiss. She tilted into him, still unsteady on her feet.

He pulled away a fraction. "Plus, you're not the only one unclothed here."

Swatting at him, she stepped back. "But you're . . ."

Perfect.

The word died on her lips and his eyes twinkled like the stars strewn across the sky above them. The cad knew.

Straightening her back, she twisted toward the beach and strode forth.

His chuckle echoed after her and she quickened her pace. Once on shore, she hurried to the pile he'd left on the ground and swept up the blanket, wrapping it around her. She turned in triumph.

And the smirk fell right off her face.

He exited the water in long strides, water sluicing off him in streams. Her gaze flew to his face, definitely not lingering on the very male part of him on full display. Or the flat planes of his stomach. Or the delicious line of dark hair stretching down from his navel.

Her legs turned to jelly as he approached with a sly grin.

She raised her face heavenward. "You, sir, are no gentleman."

He stopped in front of her and ran a finger along the edge of the blanket, just above her breasts. "So you keep reminding me."

A shiver ran through her and he winked. Bending, he retrieved a roll of fabric from his pile of clothes. "Let's get you bandaged."

She shifted, her toes digging into the still-warm sand. "I'm fine."

"I'm sure you are, but I'll feel better if the worst of it is covered."

"I'd feel better if you were covered." She blurted the words out and he laughed.

"You wound my pride, Red. I'm not sure any of my lovers have asked me to cover myself before."

"We're not . . ."

Good God, were they?

Her heart thumped. When she lowered her face, he gave her a knowing smile. But he didn't say anything. Instead, he swept up his breeches and stepped into them. Once he tugged his waistband up, he sank to the ground and patted the sand next to him.

Lovers. She chewed on the word for a minute. What did it mean? And more importantly, for how long?

With a sigh, she sat and Christian slid behind her. His hands were gentle when he pulled down the back of the blanket and began wrapping the muslin around her chest.

At first, she tried to keep the blanket up, but after lots of tangling of arms, she dropped it around her waist and covered herself with her hands. As the bandage got higher, his knuckles grazed hers and her blood pounded. If she dropped her hands, would he touch her again?

Her fingers tightened and she sucked in a little breath at the contact. Of course, she'd touched herself before. In front of the mirror, wondering why men loved bosoms so much. But never had she had a reaction. Not like this.

Was it because his arms were twined around her, tying the bandage off at her side? Perhaps because she imagined him touching her, closing his hands over her?

His hands lingered beneath the bandage, stroking up and down her sides, and gooseflesh spread over her flushed skin.

"I was selfish." His breath slid across her nape before his lips pressed a soft kiss there.

Her mouth went dry. "What do you mean?"

He began to nibble and she squirmed as little bolts of fire shot straight to her core.

"I took my pleasure without giving you yours." His fingers

brushed the top of her thigh and her eyes fluttered at the muted contact through the blanket.

"I assure you . . ." She trailed off as he slid them closer to where she burned, hooking them under the fabric. "It was pleasurable."

"Mmm . . ." He inched closer. "I want you unable to find words for what you feel. Pleasurable should not even touch the surface."

She laughed, the sound throaty and foreign to her. "I don't understand."

Her body still thrummed from their joining in the sea and heat crept up her chest as she gazed over the waves. She'd never be able to look at the water the same again.

Christian spread his legs to either side of her and gave a gentle tug. "Lean back."

She relaxed and a moment later, nestled against his chest. The bandage pressed between them, an unwanted intrusion, and she angled farther, resting the back of her head on his shoulder.

"That's better." He leaned down and kissed her exposed throat.

Her eyes drifted shut. The velvet contact of his lips moving down to her shoulder sent pleasure coiling around her core. When his tongue flicked out, hot and wet, a little moan formed in the back of her mouth.

His hand slipped beneath the blanket and the searing contact of flesh against flesh made her quiver.

"Shh," He kissed back up to her ear. "This is about you, Red. Open for me. Let me give you your release."

The carnal promise in his whispered words slackened her muscles and her thighs parted. Christian made an approving noise and dipped his fingers into her curls.

With expert precision, he used two fingers to spread her open. She gasped at the brush of night air against her most private place.

His other hand slid down and one long finger delved into her heat. He slid it into her and when he pulled free, she blushed at the wet noise.

He closed his teeth over her earlobe and slipped his finger up, stopping on the sensitive nub he'd exposed. She jerked, but he held her in place until she relaxed against him. He stroked and swirled his fingertip across that spot until her legs trembled. A throbbing ache settled beneath his touch and she whimpered, arching away from him. Too much.

He pulled his hands up and she cried out at the loss of contact. Not enough.

His lips curved at her neck and he slid his hands up and out from under the blanket.

"Christian." She panted his name and tilted her face toward him. He caught her mouth, bit her lower lip, and sucked it into his mouth.

"I know, love."

He eased out from behind her and spread the blanket out, lowering her to her back a moment later. All the time, his lips never left hers, his tongue dancing against hers.

She drew her knees up as the breeze rippled across her damp skin and Christian's hand slid back to the inferno blazing between her legs. She pressed up into his touch and he chuckled. "Patience, my dear."

He slipped one finger, then another into her, swallowing her cry. His hand plunged against her, imitating the thrusts he'd given her in the water earlier, and all the little tendrils of pleasure gathering at her core began to spiral up through her.

It was happening again. She was climbing to that dizzying height once more.

His kisses traveled down her neck, leaving a trail of fire behind. Down to her chest, where he grazed his teeth over one nipple. But he didn't linger, and his lips trailed lower and lower. When he dipped past her navel, she squirmed. Surely he didn't mean to . . .

He did.

"Christian!" She tangled her hands in his hair and tugged, trying to deter him.

He ignored her and climbed between her legs, settling so his nose nestled in her curls. His fingers slid free and she stilled, warring with the urge to ask for more and the embarrassment heating her blood.

And then his mouth closed over her.

The shock of it sent her bucking against him. His tongue pressed around her and started to move in quick circles. Samantha flung her face side to side, gasping for breath while her fingers twisted against his scalp.

She teetered on a thin edge of sanity, the pressure building until it became unbearable. One hand disengaged from his hair and dug into the sand as she rocked against him, trying to find her way down. To find release.

"Christian. Please."

"My pleasure." His words came muffled, but he increased the speed of his greedy laps and slid a finger back inside her.

She came unhinged.

White-hot pleasure crashed around her and she cried out into the night, every muscle in her body spasming. Each clench of her core around him sent a burst of blinding sensation flying through her.

When the tremors subsided, she panted, unable to take a proper breath. Her limbs lay useless, unable to move. It was as if her bones had left her.

Christian sat up and stared down at her, his eyes hooded and dark.

"That was . . ." She trailed off with a frown. "That was . . ."

He smiled and laid a hand on her still quivering thigh. "I know."

With a thud, he hit the ground next to her, lying with his shoulder against hers. Several minutes passed in silence, their chests rising and falling in tandem. The soft fall of waves upon the sand began to lull her eyes closed.

Christian's knuckles grazed hers. "Why pirating?"

She stiffened, but he closed his hand over hers.

"I love the sea. I love the feel of a ship shifting below my feet." She turned and met his gaze. "It's part of who I am."

He chuckled, the sound deep and sensual. "You could have sailed for your uncle."

Her breath came out in a sharp huff. "No. No respectable man would sail under a woman. You should know better than most."

"And what makes your crew different than law-abiding men? Why do they sail under you?"

They had no choice. Because her uncle had forced them. Her eyes pressed closed. Though it had felt good, though she had tasted freedom, none of it had been real. The hard truth was none of those men would have voluntarily signed up.

She forced a swallow. "Because pirates follow a different code."

An ache formed in her chest. This was the first time she'd been able to be open with . . . with anyone. The dull pain intensified. Would she ever be able to speak this freely with anyone else? The need to be understood, to have someone care about the things that mattered to her, became almost over-whelming.

After a steadying breath, she faced him again. "If I weren't a pirate . . ."

"If you weren't . . ." He trailed off and tightened his grip on her hand. "God, Red."

The night sky stretched out, vast as the differences that would ultimately keep them apart.

A shooting star sliced across the inky backdrop. Her mother had once told her to make a wish when she saw one. Tears pricked at the corners of her eyes. She wanted . . . she wanted this moment to last forever. Just the two of them on the beach. Away from the realities of life. Away from differences.

A shadow fell across her and she blinked as Christian leaned over. He bent and pressed a single kiss to her forehead.

"We still need to have a talk."

She flew upright, smashing her forehead against his jaw. The blow made him sit up and she rolled from under him and scrambled to her feet.

"Damn it, Red." He glared up at her and she retreated to her pile of clothing. She yanked her breeches on. By the time she got her blouse over her head, Christian stalked toward her. His face was serious. Too serious.

The muscles in her legs twitched and she turned to flee.

He caught her arm. "You can't keep running away whenever I say that."

She tugged on her arm but he held tight, his frown reflecting pale moonlight. "What's wrong, Red?"

"I don't want to talk about that."

"Well, we're going to." He dragged a hand through damp locks. "I've compromised you, Miss Warstein."

She froze. It was the first time he'd used her name since he'd figured out her identity.

"I wanted to be compromised."

She could barely say it. Such an ugly word. *Compromise.* It spoke of ruined lives and dashed dreams. All because society deemed women incapable of making decisions for themselves.

He loosened his grip. "It doesn't work like that."

"Of course it does. I'm a pirate, remember?" This time, when she yanked, he let go.

His eyes bore into her. "But you're not just a pirate."

Heat rippled through her. "What does it matter who I am?"

"It matters because you are Warstein's niece. I assume he doesn't know of your little side endeavor, but nonetheless, these things are not done."

Her eyes narrowed. "And if I wasn't his niece? If I were *just* a pirate? Then what? Would it matter then? Or would your conscience be able to live with it?"

He blinked under her verbal assault. "I didn't know who you

were the first time."

She stilled, pulse pounding in her ears. He was right. He hadn't. *Let me save you.* His words still echoed in her mind, haunted her dreams.

Turning to the water, she wrapped her arms around her chest. "Once we get back to Savannah, I understand this . . ." She waved one hand in a hectic circle. "Whatever this is, is over."

He stood silent behind her.

"Your conscience is spared, Lieutenant."

A wave crashed as it rolled up the beach. Palm fronds rustled in the breeze. The warble of a bird floated over them. And Christian's heavy breathing drowned it all out.

"It doesn't have to be over."

The words went straight to the center of her heart. Twined into her flesh. Tugged at her soul. Then, understanding slammed into her.

She pivoted and speared him with an icy glare. "Yes. It does. Because I will never be anyone's mistress."

Before he could respond, she pushed past him and ran up the beach. When she came around the curve and the dancing flames of her crew's bonfire became visible, she slowed lest the men see her agitation. She was the daughter of pirates, not a coward. *No more running.*

Not from Thorne.

Not from the lieutenant.

Griff saw her first and stood. "We were beginning to worry. Are you alright?" His gaze traveled up and down her.

She brushed some sand from her arms. Heavens knew what she looked like. "I'm fine."

Liar.

Chapter Twenty-One

"SAILS!"

The shout brought Christian scrambling to his feet. He shook the sleep from his eyes and squinted down the beach where a man ran toward them waving his hands. Reflexively, he searched out Red. *Miss Warstein.* A dull ache pounded in his temple.

Sleep had evaded him most of the night. And for good reason. His words had been foolish, because she'd been right. He couldn't offer more to her. A navy lieutenant could never have a future with a pirate. And as tempting as it was to offer her the position of mistress, he'd seen the look in her eyes.

It would break her.

So he would do the honorable thing and leave her alone.

If I weren't a pirate . . .

His fists clenched. If she weren't, so many things would be different.

She'd slept next to Tommy and he frowned at the empty spot next to the boy. As the men around him began to stir, he scanned the beach.

There.

Fiery hair streaming behind her, she sprinted toward the large pile of driftwood they'd built last night. A little trail of smoke followed her and it took him a moment to comprehend she carried a stick from the fire.

He staggered forward and grabbed a bundle of dried dune grass some of the men had gathered before following her.

Dropping to his knees next to her, he ignored the little buzz of energy tugging at him and found a spot to tuck the grass into.

She touched glowing embers to the little nest and leaned forward to blow. The grass twisted and curled, turning black. She blew again, a long slow puff, and lines of concentration furrowed her brow. A sizzle came from the ball and a moment later white smoke billowed up.

Little flames flickered and rose toward the dry wood above. Soon the fire consumed the pile and Christian turned to the crew.

"Find more wood. Bring the palm fronds from the campsite. We need as much smoke as possible."

When he turned back, Red was gone.

Griff ran by with his spyglass and Christian followed him. The old man looked out to sea and pointed. "There."

Reflecting the pink of the rising sun, two fore-and-aft-rigged masts hugged the horizon. A schooner. The smoke from the fire rose in a thin stream. From that far, the ship would never see them.

"We need a bigger fire."

When he spun to help the crew, Griff stopped him with a hand on his shoulder. Christian stopped and Griff nodded toward where Red helped drag a pile of palm fronds toward the fire.

"She's a good girl."

Christian watched her toss her load into the flames. Without hesitating, she ran back to camp.

"Why the hell is she mixed up with your lot?"

Griff pressed his lips together. "That's for her to tell you."

Christian frowned. "She's a pirate. As are you. You know my job." He dragged his gaze from her. "I advise you all to find honorable jobs when we return to Savannah. I'm not going to show any of you special favor if we meet again."

Griff nodded. "Fair enough. I'll only ask you one thing."

Christian met the pirate's steely eyes and raised a brow.

"We'd all hate to see her hurt, Lieutenant. Don't break her heart."

Too late.

With a scowl, he left the man and his spyglass to go help with firewood.

An hour later, sweat blossomed on his face, dripped down his back. The sun had risen high enough for the sticky heat to beat into them. At this point, they'd stoked the fire as high as they could, and white and grey smoke billowed into the air.

The men lined the beach and an uneasy silence settled over them as Griff watched the ship. Minutes dragged by and a few broke out into prayer. Red stood next to Griff, soot streaked across her face.

The distant ship had continued her course so far. Soon, she'd be past the island and any chances of their signal being seen would fade. Christian's pulse raced. Such a slim chance. But one they desperately needed. Once that ship passed, it could be days or weeks before another one did.

Griff lowered his spyglass and faced the men. "She turns our way."

A cheer rose from the group and Red pressed her eyes closed for a measure of seconds, her shoulders rising and falling in one long breath. Upon reopening them, she glanced toward Christian. When she noticed him watching her, she spun away.

While the ship approached, the men took turns in the water to wash and cool off. Even Red dipped in, scrubbing her face and tying her hair back. On the beach, they waited in the shade of the palm trees. By the time the ship was close enough to anchor, the sun hung high in the sky.

Christian twisted his hands together. While the rest of the group showed obvious relief, he knew better. This far off normal trade routes, the chances of the ship being friendly were slim. They could be slavers, or more pirates.

He forced himself to take a deep breath. Anything would be better than being stranded. The men gathered around him were capable. He'd seen them in action. If they needed to, he was sure they could take over this ship.

A longboat was lowered into the water and Christian strode out to where Griff still stood. He didn't have to ask for the spyglass and raised it to his eye when the old man handed it over.

"I think you can stop worrying, Lieutenant."

He squinted at the man in the longboat.

No.

He let out a shout and tossed the spyglass back to Griff before running out into the waves.

Minutes later, Isaac jumped out of the boat and clasped him in a hug. "Good God, am I glad to see you."

Christian leaned back. "How on Earth did you catch up so fast?"

Isaac laughed and they walked up to the beach. "You trained me well, Lieutenant. We went straight to the governor's and he found us a ship. You owe him. Quite a bit. Anyway, we left only hours behind Thorne." He looked at the ragtag group onshore. "What happened?"

"He caught up to us."

They strode from the water and Griff pulled his hat off. "Never thought I'd say it, but you're a sight for sore eyes, Officer."

Isaac surveyed the beach. "Is anyone injured?"

The old pirate shook his head. "Safe and accounted for."

"Our crew will more than double yours. Is there room?" Red approached, her eyes on the schooner.

Isaac lifted a brow. "Good to see you as well, my lady pirate. The ship has an empty cargo hold. It may be a tight squeeze the next two days, but I'm confident she can handle us all."

She nodded and turned to the men on the beach. "You heard him. Pack up and get ready to sail."

Christian set a hand on her shoulder and she stiffened. "Remember who's in charge here. From here on out, you and your crew sail under me."

He raised his voice so everyone on the beach could hear. "I run a tight ship. You'll follow my orders and defer to my men. If anyone disobeys this, you'll find yourself in chains until we reach Savannah, and the local magistrate can decide what to do with you."

Red twisted from his grasp and joined her men, keeping her back to him as the first group began boarding a longboat. He turned to the water. Best to deal with her later.

It took two trips rowing back and forth to get everyone on board. Red stayed on the beach until the last man set foot in the boat. She helped push the vessel into the waves and Christian made his way over to give her a boost in.

She swatted his hand away. "No thank you, Lieutenant. I can take care of myself."

With one jump, she lifted herself from the water and took an open space on a bench. He shook his head and followed suit, making sure to sit behind her. The rigid line of her spine never eased. Not until they reached the schooner and clambered aboard. Men crowded the main deck, and with nowhere to go, she leaned against the railing.

Christian pushed through the sailors and climbed up to the forecastle where Isaac and his other officers stood. "We'll be setting up watches. Griff, your men will stay in the cargo hold until morning."

The sun already hovered near the horizon and he scowled. It would have been nice to get sailing before dark.

"Make it quick so my crew can get this ship ready to sail."

Everyone below sprang into action and he turned to Isaac. "Get the anchor raised and ready the sails."

He moved to the railing and kept watch over the sorting process going on below. Everything went smoothly, until a flash of red hair caught his eye. She moved in unison with her crew, toward the hatch.

"Damn it."

He vaulted to the deck and fought his way to her. Just as she turned to climb below, he reached out and grabbed her shoulder. Her eyes narrowed and she tried to pull away.

"Where are you going?"

"To the cargo hold. With my crew. That's where you told us to go, right?"

"I didn't mean you." The thought of her crammed in the small space, between a bunch of men, with no way to see to her needs, sent a frown over his face. "You'll take the main cabin."

She sniffed. "I don't need special treatment, Lieutenant."

"Stop acting so tough. I'm offering you the cabin. Take it. God knows you could use it."

"What's that supposed to mean?"

He raked a hand through his hair before tugging her up. Blasted woman. They made it halfway across the deck before she dug in her heels.

"No need to drag me around in front of your men. I'll follow you."

When he released her, she pulled her arm away and fell into step behind him. Opening the door, he ushered her inside. A lantern had been lit, sending soft light through the small space.

"It's not much—"

She brushed past him. "It's fine."

Not half the size of his old cabin, this one had barely enough room for the desk and shelves against the wall. A tiny captain's bed took up the other wall, and instead of big windows, three portholes gave the only glimpse outside.

At the desk, she ran her hands over a weathered map.

"Red?"

She stiffened.

"About last night . . ."

"It's alright. I already told you, no need to discuss it further."

He crossed the room in two strides. "Look at me."

Turning, she blinked at him. Wary. He sighed. Couldn't blame her. "I didn't mean it."

Her eyes widened slightly as her brows pulled together. "But you did."

Damn her for being right. He did. Even as every gentlemanly

part of him screamed in denial, he wanted her. Wanted her for himself. Wanted to be able to take her in his arms whenever he desired.

He stepped closer, his body only inches from her. "Nonetheless, I didn't mean to make you uncomfortable."

She swallowed, the movement drawing his gaze down to the pale column of her neck. Farther, to the swell of her breasts beneath the still-damp fabric of her blouse.

Her lips parted.

A tremor ran through the ship, and she took a staggering step back. "Best be going, wind is in the sails and her anchor is up."

He took a step back. God, he'd nearly kissed her. With a tight nod, he turned.

"If you need anything, let me know."

Outside, he blew out a long breath. The next two days would be hell.

Sails sang above, the gentle whoosh countering his raging pulse.

Humid air filled his lungs and he turned toward the forecastle. He crossed to the stairs and set a foot on the first one.

Soft footfalls fell behind him.

"Lieutenant?" Red stood there, twisting her clenched fingers, and he lifted a brow. "There is something I need." She took a breath. "I mean, need to talk to you about. Ask you."

His heart gave a little lurch. *Invite me back to the cabin.* The plea filled his mind for a brief second. He shook his head. Nonsense. Still . . .

Without waiting for him to answer, she continued on, her words tumbling out in a rapid stream. "Without Thorne following us, we could stop for the treasure. It's on the way back, wouldn't waste much time at all. Please. It would mean—"

"No." A roiling heat washed through his gut. "No more pirate nonsense."

"But—"

He crossed his arms. "Enough."

The word rang across the deck and a few of his men looked up. Her shoulders heaved and for a moment, he thought she would continue. But she spun on her heels and stalked away. A tightness spread from his jaw.

Let her be angry.

Someone had to put their foot down on her antics. It was a miracle they'd made it this far. He massaged his temples. Besides, he had enough to worry about. Namely, writing a letter to the governor to explain how he lost one of the navy's most valuable ships.

She stopped at the mainmast and flung her hair over her shoulder before climbing up to the crow's nest. The moon reflected off the supple curve of her bottom and he swallowed as she swung one lithe leg over the railing. A moment later a young sailor jumped out and scrambled down.

He forced himself to look away as she set her elbows on the railing and dropped her chin to her hands. Her hair trailed behind in the brisk wind. A beautiful sentinel. Half his crew stared at her as well and he let out a growl. As soon as she went below, he'd have to have a stern talk with them.

She was off limits.

Isaac waved at him from the helm and moments later he joined his friend and took the wheel. They sailed in silence for a while, the crash of waves against the hull echoing through the night. He twisted his hands around the weathered spokes and closed his eyes.

"I take it Miss Warstein's big reveal didn't go over well?" Isaac said nonchalantly. Too nonchalantly.

Christian turned to him. "You knew who she was?"

Isaac slapped his shoulder. "Anyone with eyes could have put two and two together."

Christian pulled away, his muscles tensing. "For how long?"

Something in his look must have warned Isaac because the teasing glint left his friend's eyes. "I suspected it at the ball. Was surprised you didn't see it. But when she engaged us the second time, I knew it had to be her."

Christian's hands pulled into tight fists. "All that time I wasted, resources I wasted, looking for her and you kept it from me?"

Isaac raised his hands. "Compose yourself. I didn't want you doing anything rash. Going after Warstein's niece would have been tricky business. And then there was your little encounter with her after she almost bested you."

"Little encounter?" With flared nostrils, he grabbed Isaac's shirt and dragged him close. "I deflowered her. And you could have put a stop to it."

Isaac blanched. "I didn't think you'd go through with it. Thought you were trying to scare some sense into her. You'd never done something like that before. And then it was too late. I hoped you'd have come to terms with her by now."

"Terms with her?" What the hell did he mean? "Miss Warstein isn't mistress material, if you haven't noticed." Never mind he'd thought along the same lines the night before.

Footfalls came from behind him and Isaac gave a weak smile. "Splendid. So you'll marry her then?"

Christian recoiled. "Good God, no. She's not marrying material either."

His first officer went a shade paler and stared into the space beyond Christian's shoulder. Every muscle in his body went tense and he knew before he turned who would be there. Still, he hoped he was wrong.

He wasn't.

She stood feet away, her face paler than Isaac's. She'd heard every word. Her chin trembled and she took a step back. Then another.

"Red."

She gave a violent shake of her head and twisted away. Not in time for him to miss the glimmer of tears.

Shit.

Chapter Twenty-Two

T WO DAYS.

Forty eight hours of staring at the closed door of the main cabin. At least that's what it felt like. Christian fought the urge to look again. If she was going to come out, she'd have done so by now. They'd docked in Savannah over an hour ago and though he'd stretched his duties onboard as long as possible, he couldn't stay any longer. With one last glance over his shoulder, he walked down the gangplank. His boots hit the dock with a dull thud and he scowled. A small crowd had already gathered.

The mayor strode to the front of the group. "Is it true? You rescued Miss Warstein?"

Something clenched hard and heavy in Christian's gut. If only it were the truth. But he nodded. "She's safe."

"Thank heavens!" The portly man turned to the crowd. "Our hero has returned successful!"

A cheer rose and Christian cringed. The hairs on the nape of his neck lifted and he glanced up to find Henry Warstein staring at him with a frown. As much as he didn't want to speak with the merchant, he'd best get it out of the way. He mumbled his thanks to the mayor and headed over.

"Is she well?"

"She is." Christian braced for more questions, but they didn't come.

He watched Warstein's face as the pirate crew began to disembark. No flicker of recognition. So he didn't know. Or if he did, he hid it well.

"And Thorne?"

Christian's entire body stiffened. "He gave us a lot of trouble, but he escaped."

The older man stroked his mustache. "I'm in your debt, Lieutenant."

But he wasn't. Christian's stomach twisted. It wasn't honorable, taking credit. But what choice did he have?

Warstein held up a sack. "May I go aboard? I have some things for her to change into."

Christian waved toward the gangplank. As the merchant made his way up, Isaac approached. "How about we head to the tavern? I have a feeling a good drink will do you well."

God. He wanted to.

Drowning his memories of the last week into oblivion would be amazing. Yet . . .

The tavern meant more than drinking away everything that had happened. It meant tavern wenches. Ones who would offer him a hero's welcome. One his men would expect him to take. And not partaking . . .

Well, that meant he'd have to come face to face with feelings he wasn't ready to admit. Feelings he couldn't have.

"Not tonight. I'm exhausted. Going home sounds nice for a change."

Isaac arched one brow, just enough to hint he'd read the lie. But he didn't push the issue.

"Officer?"

His friend straightened.

"Make sure the men keep quiet about the identity of the men on board."

"Of course. And your lady pirate?"

"Stop calling her that."

Isaac squeezed his shoulder. "Don't worry. The crew knows better than to spread any gossip. They won't say anything."

Christian pressed his hand to his temple. They'd better. He tread along a dangerous line of treason by not turning the pirates in. It would only take one man, one slip of speech, to bring discipline down on them all.

He climbed up the bank and found a delivery driver with an empty wagon. "I'll pay you a dollar to take me home."

The man's eyes widened at the exorbitant sum and motioned to the bench next to him with a grin. A few moments later, they turned away from the dock. Christian gave the man his directions and settled into the uncomfortable seat. Each bump of the road intensified the ache behind his temples. Thank God he'd found a place close to the city.

When they pulled up his drive, he ran inside to retrieve the man's fare. His housekeeper met him as soon as he opened the door.

"You have a visitor."

He blinked at her.

She motioned toward his study and lowered her voice. "He's not a friendly sort. Told him you might not be home for days and he barged right in. Said you'd be home shortly. It's been an hour at least."

Christian's gaze flew to the cracked door. "Did he give you a name?"

She shook her head.

A visitor was the last thing he needed right now. He sighed. "Thank you. Bring the gentleman outside a dollar and draw me a bath."

He cracked his knuckles and strode to the study. Whoever it was, they would have to come back another time. Nudging the door, he opened his mouth to say just that.

The man stood with his back to him, broad shoulders rising and falling with each slow breath as he stared at the painting on the wall. He didn't turn.

He didn't have to.

Christian's hand grasped the empty space at his hip. Damnation. He didn't even have a knife on his person.

"What are you doing here?" He ground the words out.

Thorne nodded toward the portrait. "I suggest never falling in love."

"It's a little late for fatherly advice. And forgive me if I'm disinclined to take it."

His father pivoted. "Too late for advice? Or too late to stop you from falling in love?" A smirk twisted across his lips. "I saw the way you and that fiery redhead looked at each other."

Christian ground his teeth together. "I find it hard to believe you risked breaking into my house just to tell me this."

"Love will make you do wild things." Thorne's eyes glazed over. "I would have sailed to the end of the world for her. Have sailed to the end of the world."

Christian's hands curled into fists. "All for what? You've gained nothing."

His father met his gaze and took a step toward him. "You're wrong. Revenge, my boy. I take it when I can. Draw every last bit of it out of a man's soul."

The pounding in Christian's head intensified.

Thorne stepped to the window and picked up a navy issued cocked hat. He ran his hands over the soft felt. "They kidnapped her because of my position in the navy. Used her to get to me."

The captain swiveled to face the portrait once more. "Your mother was rescued."

Christian nearly dropped to his knees. "I was never told anything of the sort."

His father's shoulders went stiff. "She never made it back to shore with her rescuers."

The room spun around Christian and he reached out for the back of a chair for support. "What happened?"

"The men that took her, they did terrible things to her. Things no woman should endure. She couldn't bear to face me afterward." His father's voice cracked. "She threw herself into the sea."

When he turned to Christian, his eyes were rimmed with red. "I wouldn't have cared. I would have stayed by her side while she healed."

Christian's vision blurred.

"I spent years hunting down all the pirates and smugglers I could. With every slit throat, I wondered if I had got the right man, the right crew." His face hardened. "Until I learned she was never taken by pirates in the first place. That I had been deceived in the worst way."

Pain exploded through Christian's palms as his nails bit into soft flesh. "I don't understand."

"You never will." Thorne flipped the hat he still held and set it back. "Unless . . ."

Silence stretched between them.

"Unless you join me. Join me and I will tell you everything."

Gone were the lines of grief. Gone was the moment of vulnerability. Gone was the brief glimpse of the father he once knew.

Heat rushed up the back of Christian's throat to mingle with the aching hurt already there. "How dare you? You tried to kill me less than a week ago and now you come to my home with such a ludicrous proposition?"

A hollow laugh rang across the room. "You're alive, aren't you?"

"No thanks to you." Christian spat the words out and took a long stride toward his father. "Get out. Get out of my house. Out of my life. I swear, if I ever see you again, I will arrest you on the spot."

His father stood still for a long moment before dipping into a mocking bow.

"So be it."

THE CHAIR AT Christian's desk creaked when he sank into it. His housekeeper knocked on the door a few moments later with a tray of coffee. Once she set it down, he waved her out and poured it himself.

Swirling the obsidian liquid, he stared at the invitation in front of him. A party. In his honor. The light in the room began to fade, replaced with the warm colors of the sunset, and he sighed. Well past time to leave. Yet he stayed in place, sipping his coffee.

She would be there.

He'd only seen her twice the rest of the trip back to Savannah. Both mornings, she'd emerged in the soft grey of dawn and climbed up to the crow's nest. She stayed up there until the sunrise washed over her, setting her hair aflame in the warm light. The prettiest damn sight he'd ever seen.

If only he'd worked up the nerve to apologize.

She's not marrying material. Damn his foolish mouth. Because it had been a lie. A lie to himself. She was infinitely marriageable.

If she weren't a pirate. But she was. Which meant he needed to bury those feelings once and for all.

And now, the governor was hosting a ball at Montelet's estate to celebrate his daring rescue of Miss Warstein. He snorted. Daring, indeed. He'd blundered his way through the entire mission.

With a groan, he stood and set his half-empty cup down. He'd never dreaded a party so much. His eyes strayed to his whiskey cabinet, but he forced himself to walk out and to the front door. Showing up foxed to his own celebration could only make things worse.

His gelding pawed at the drive where his groom held him. Christian took the reins and the man backed up with a look of relief. Probably had begun to wonder if he'd ever show up.

Christian ran a steadying hand down his mount's neck. When the bay settled, he lifted a foot into the stirrup and swung into the saddle.

"There now. Let's be on our way."

Carriages lined the drive at Montelet's estate and he groaned again. Even with such short notice, the place was packed. It had been less than a week since they'd returned and he'd half-hoped for a small affair.

He should have known. Nothing was ever small when it came to Governor Milledge. His lips pushed together. Last time he was here, he'd failed his mission. Now, he had to face Red.

He wasn't sure which was worse.

A groomsman in a tidy white and black uniform led Christian's bay away and he started up the steps. When he entered the ballroom, people stared. Men clapped his shoulder and the ladies blushed behind their fans. More than a few met his eyes with slanted looks.

He was a bloody hero.

By the time he reached the governor's group, his cravat itched at his throat. Adjusting his cocked hat, he did his best to keep his eyes down but couldn't help a quick glance at the far wall.

Her hair shimmered in the chandelier light, copper curls cascading down from an elegant bun. The turquoise hue of her dress brought him straight back to the island and the temperate waters they'd—

"She's a beauty for sure."

Governor Milledge moved next to Christian and he jerked his gaze from her and to the flute of champagne the big man offered.

"If I weren't already married, I'd have half a mind to ask her for her hand myself."

Christian's gut hardened as one of the men nearby laughed.

"She'd turn you down. Like she's done every other red-blooded man here." The man's hungry gaze hardened. "Something wrong with that one, there is."

With fists clenched, Christian gave him a level glare. "I found her company pleasant."

Another laugh. "The only place she'd be pleasant is beneath my covers." The man tipped back his glass and gave a hearty laugh after polishing it off.

Christian could knock him out with one punch. It would be wasted on the drunk man. And create a stir. He took a slow breath and took the flute from the governor.

"You're creating quite the name for yourself, Lieutenant."

Christian turned back to the crown and watched a young woman in a pale yellow dress approach Red. *Miss Warstein*. God, he didn't know what to call her anymore.

"Yes, well, Thorne still sails, so don't be too quick to heap praise on me."

"I've more men and ships on the way from Washington. I'm sure you'll do us all proud."

His eyes wandered back to the duo. Miss Warstein's friend looked his way with flushed cheeks before leaning toward her and whispering. Shoulders stiff, she turned and their gazes met. Even across the room, he noticed the flash in her eyes before they narrowed. And then, she turned away. Dismissed him.

He turned to the governor. "I'd like to mobilize my men as soon as possible. There's reason to believe Thorne could be here in Savannah."

He'd posted a group of his men at Warstein's property the night he'd found Thorne in his study. But so far, no sign of the pirate or his giants. It was as if they'd vanished into thin air.

He didn't like it.

"All the more reason to get this party started." Governor Milledge gestured to the band and they wound down their music.

The gathered guests quieted and turned to face them.

"Ladies and gentlemen of the great city of Savannah, it's my pleasure to welcome you to our celebration of your very own local hero, Lieutenant Thompson."

Polite applause rang through the room and the governor pulled out a velvet box.

Oh no.

"With unmatched bravery, he rescued Miss Warstein from the clutches of the most feared pirate on the seas, Captain Thorne. In honor of his valor, I present to him . . ."

The box flipped open and the governor swiveled so everyone gathered could catch a glimpse.

"A badge of merit."

Christian cringed as another round of clapping reverberated through him.

"And . . ."

Goodness, could it get any worse?

It could.

"I'd like to call up the dear Miss Warstein to have the honor of pinning it."

He raised his eyes to the gilded molding. And when he looked down, there she was. Feet away. Glaring at him.

He bowed. "Miss Warstein."

She curtsied. "Lieutenant."

Governor Milledge, oblivious to the tension between them, lifted the fabric heart and handed it to her.

She stared at it. Probably thinking the same thing Christian was. He didn't deserve it. Not even close. Stepping closer, she flashed him a smile so brilliant, he blinked. But the smile didn't quite reach her eyes. God, he wished it were real.

Her hand stretched between them and his pulse quickened. Slight fingers brushed against his jacket and she slipped one hand beneath it. Right over his racing heart.

"I'm honored, Lieutenant. If not for your actions, I wouldn't be here."

A double-sided statement if he'd ever heard one.

She stepped away and left the badge hanging below his collar.

"Splendid." Governor Milledge clapped his hands and a waltz began. "As our guests of honor, please do us the favor of opening the dance floor."

Christian half expected her to shun him in front of everyone. But she was a perfect society lady and took his hand when he proffered it. Her face had gone blank, but her fingers trembled in his.

Warmth spread up his arm as he led her out to the floor. Every minute. Every day. He'd thought of her. Dreamed of her. Couldn't stop rehearsing what he'd say to her. And now, with her in front of him, his throat closed.

When he breathed in, her lemon scent filled his nose. Memory slammed into him. Her in his cabin, touching him so boldly. And in the sea, taking charge of—he shifted and pulled her ever so closer, hoping no one would notice his erection.

Slipping his hand behind her back, he began the dance. She stared at his chest but followed his lead perfectly. Candlelight flickered across her hair, making it shimmer with every movement. Other couples joined them and as they twirled around the room, he noticed the stares. Stares of envy. Jealousy. The women in the room who so often vied for his attention were not happy.

Her friend in the yellow clasped her hands over her heart with a romantic smile on her face and he snorted. She had the wrong impression.

Miss Warstein glanced up at him and he steered them toward the doors to the verandah. She noticed and, in a flash, took the lead from him and expertly turned them away.

He raised a brow and found his voice. "Afraid of being alone with me?"

"Whatever you want to say can be said here."

He chuckled. "So you are afraid." His fingers splayed at her back, and with a tug, he turned and regained the lead. "What if what I want to say is private?"

Color tinged her cheeks and her feet stopped moving. The sudden stop made him stumble. He bent into an awkward bow to make it look intentional.

"If you'll excuse me, I'll take my leave."

Miss Warstein pulled up her skirts and fled out the open door.

Chapter Twenty-Three

THE STICKY AIR outside did little to cool Samantha's cheeks. She weaved between happy couples until she found a secluded spot at the far end of the verandah. Leaning against the railing, she stared out into the darkness.

She'd known it would be hard tonight. But that was when she expected to stay with Abigail at the wall and hide from Christian. When the governor had called her over, she'd nearly lost the contents of her stomach.

She'd had to touch him, had to feel the frantic beat of his heart. And then, she'd had to dance with him. Her blood still pounded in her ears, her hand still clammy from where he'd gripped it.

"Was it hard?"

She spun to find Christian's first officer standing in the shadows. "Was what hard?"

He waved his hand toward the open doors where music spilled into the night. "All of it."

Was it so obvious? If his eyes weren't so understanding, she'd turn away. She crossed her arms over her chest and clenched her jaw.

Yes.

Being near to Christian had brought all the last week's events right back to the surface. And it hurt. Awareness had tingled along her bare arms the moment he'd walked in. She'd kept her back to him, prolonging the inevitable. Until Abigail had pointed out how he was staring at her so unfashionably. So she'd looked.

And lost another little piece of her heart.

Isaac nodded as if she'd answered aloud.

"I've never seen him so wound up. If it makes you feel better, I think he's just as miserable as you."

Her chest tightened as a heavy ache settled between her ribs.

"It's amazing how much one's life can change in the blink of an eye." His lips twisted into a wry smile. "All because of one slip."

"Excuse me?"

He met her gaze. "When you nearly stuck him through with your fancy little rapier."

Her eyes narrowed. "I—"

"You were about to win. I know."

She blinked.

"I saw you loosen your dagger. Knew you were up to something."

"Why didn't you warn him?"

"It would have done him good if you had won." He let out a soft laugh and brushed at something on his sleeve. "The question is, do you wish you had?"

He bowed and walked away.

Tears pricked at her eyes.

If she had won, she'd have gotten her immunity. Christian would be none the wiser to her identity. And her heart would be whole.

Still . . . she lifted her hand and brushed her thumb across her lips. He'd shown her passion. Passion she'd enjoyed every minute of.

"Miss Warstein, a word please."

His voice rumbled across her, and she pressed her eyes closed.

Why?

Maybe if she ignored him, he'd go away.

The rustle of a boot on the smooth stone made her fingers clench together. A moment later, his scent washed over her, the soft sandalwood notes threatening to bring back memories.

"Don't make me talk to your back."

A little burst of warmth rippled across her skin and she spun, nearly bumping into him.

"Or what?" She moved to the side, but he copied the movement to trap her in place.

He stood rigid, hands behind his back and her mouth went dry. The double row of gold buttons on his navy uniform jacket shone in the night. No more stubble and his hair was tied back without a single errant curl peeking from beneath his hat. Every bit the admirable pirate hunter.

"I owe you an apology."

Her gaze snapped to his. In the darkness the muted green depths hid his emotions.

"For what?"

"For what I said on the ship."

She's not marrying material.

God, how often had she heard that said of her? It had never hurt her before. So why had it sliced right through her soul when he said it?

She took a shaky breath and smoothed her skirts. Foolish to be upset. After all, he had been right.

Heat flushed through her. "Lieutenant, I'm no naive girl. I never had, nor do I hold, any aspirations to win your heart. Besides . . ." She forced a thin smile. "We would never suit."

She held his gaze while silence wove around them, muting the sounds from the ballroom.

"Nevertheless, I apologize." He fidgeted with his hat. "I wish things could be different."

So do I.

"Apology accepted. Now, if that's all, I'll take my leave." She took a step forward, but he didn't budge.

"No. That's not all."

Great.

"I need your word that you'll stop pirating."

Her teeth ground together. "You have no authority over me."

He somehow straightened even more, his face all hard angles. "You forget who I am."

His hand slipped to his jacket and he lifted something from his pocket. Metal glinted in the light from the nearest torch.

A key.

"This belongs to a set of shackles." He dropped it back in place. "I could arrest you. Here. Now."

"But you won't." Still, her heart dropped at the stark reminder of his job. Why she needed to stay away from him.

He stared hard at her. "I don't want to. But if you leave me no choice, I will do what my position requires of me."

She shifted on her feet.

"I'm giving you a chance, Red. A chance to turn your life around. To start over."

"No."

His fists bunched at his sides. "I have more men. More ships on the way. This little resurgence piracy has seen is over. I will finish what I started."

Her toes curled in her slippers. He would too. She didn't doubt it. Everything her family had worked toward, all of her dreams. He would crush them.

How dare he?

A bitter taste filled her mouth as the urge to put distance between them tugged at her legs. Tension radiated up her arms and she glanced down to where her hands had curled into tight fists.

"I will give you my word that you'll never see my ships again." It was the best she could offer—after all, it wasn't like she'd be seeking him out. She certainly wasn't going to give him what he wanted.

The frown on his face deepened. "That's not enough."

She shrugged. "So be it."

"Red, this isn't a game."

This time, anger flashed hot and quick. "It never was."

He took a slow breath. "It doesn't have to be this way. Why are you making this harder than it has to be?"

Ha. Only one way to make things easier. Get him away from her. Out of her life for good. So she threw his words back at him. "You forget who I am."

Christian lifted a dark brow and she leaned in, her lips nearly brushing his ear. "Your enemy."

He stiffened and she drew back, took one last breath of clove and sandalwood, and walked away.

Once inside the warm light of the ballroom, Abigail pounced, grabbing her arm.

"Did he kiss you? Tell me he kissed you!"

Samantha jerked her arm free and swallowed against the lump in her throat. "No."

"He stood awfully close."

Good lord, had everyone watched their little encounter?

Abigail sighed. "It's so romantic. Him saving you. And the way he looked at you while you danced, I thought he might start a fire."

Samantha rubbed her arms. "Don't be silly."

Her friend pulled her to their familiar spot by the wall. "What if he's in love with you, Samantha?"

She laughed. It was the only thing she could do. The lieutenant, in love with her? Ha. Definitely not after their little altercation.

"I hate to disappoint you, but no."

Abigail stared at the door with wistful eyes. He must have walked back in. Samantha refused to look.

"What was it like?"

An ache had begun behind her eyes. "What was what like?"

"When he rescued you. Was he terribly brave like everyone is saying?"

Samantha scanned the crowd for her uncle. Surely they could leave, now that the governor's little publicity stunt was over. "Sure."

Abigail let out a huff. "Sure? That's all you can say? The most dashing man in Savannah rescued you and all you can say is 'sure'?"

Something hardened inside Samantha as she spun back to her friend. "I was locked in a brig, in a dirty cell with nothing but a bucket to relieve myself. I didn't witness any of it. There was nothing dashing or brave about it. Men died."

Abigail's eyes widened. "I—I . . ."

Samantha pressed her fingers to her temple. Abigail didn't deserve her frustration.

"I'm sorry. My head hurts something fierce. I need to find my uncle."

She turned and pushed into the throngs of dancers. Uncle Henry stood near the refreshment table and frowned when she approached. "Are you alright, dear?"

Her teeth clenched together as she fought tears. She'd been forced to endure Christian's company, quarreled with her best friend. No. She was not alright.

"Can we go home?"

His frown morphed into a look of concern and he glanced past her to the dance floor. For a moment, his gaze hardened. Then he nodded and offered his arm.

As they made their way toward the door, the music wound down and the governor cleared his throat.

"Ladies and gentlemen, upstanding citizens of Savannah . . ."

She rolled her eyes.

"I've just received some wonderful news. As you know, our beloved Lieutenant Thompson . . ."

Whatever the governor had to say about the *beloved* lieutenant, she had no desire to hear. She tugged her uncle's arm. But he slowed and turned his attention to the front of the room. Blast it.

"Has been instrumental in the national campaign against piracy. I've just received word that ships and extra men have arrived from Washington. President Jefferson has directed the lieutenant to focus all his attention on capturing the two most notorious pirates out there, Captains Thorne and Remington. Soon, the dastardly criminals will meet their fate and the waters will be safe again."

Her uncle stiffened, then pulled her toward the door. Her throat burned as the crowd applauded. All the more reason to stay away from him. For good.

As they swept outside, the hairs on her neck lifted. She balled her hands into fists. No looking back. But she couldn't stop her head, the quick glance behind her.

His eyes glinted in the light. Dangerous. Predatory. For a split second, they were the only two in the room, two adversaries staring each other down. A chill ran up her spine.

Enemies.

"Samantha?" Her uncle's voice broke the spell and she lifted her chin and turned into the night.

Silence filled the carriage the whole way home. Fine with her. She leaned against the window, rubbing her pounding temples.

When they drove up the drive, several footmen raced out to meet them. "Mr. Warstein, come quickly."

Her uncle jumped to the ground and Samantha scrambled out after him, yanking up her skirts to keep up.

The butler met them on the steps, his face drawn tight.

Her uncle frowned. "What's wrong?"

"We've been robbed."

THE MUTED LIGHT of dawn filtered through the window and Samantha rolled over to stare at the empty spot on her desk. She hadn't slept, and her head still pounded. Anna had brought her a pot of tea at some point in the night when it became clear she wouldn't be going to bed. She poured a new cup of lukewarm brew and sipped it.

After Anna had left, she'd added a tansy tea sachet. The earthiness filled her mouth and she scrunched her nose before downing the rest of it. After her encounter with Christian last night, best to make sure there would be no consequences of their night on the beach. No reason to have anything tie her to him. Still, her hand drifted across her belly as a pang sliced through her battered heart.

A commotion came from downstairs and she jumped out of bed. Dropping to her hands and knees, she pulled a bundle from under it. Her blouse and breeches. When she'd returned, she'd washed them herself and stashed them away.

She dressed quickly and braided her hair. Her fingers touched her pocket, pressing into the folded parchment there. Thank goodness she'd separated the maps as well.

When she opened the door, the sound of sobbing reached her, and she raced downstairs. The door to her uncle's study was open and she didn't slow down, bursting inside.

She drew to a halt and blinked.

Tommy hunched on his knees in front of her uncle and Griff. He twisted toward her and burst into fresh sobs when he saw her.

"I'm s—so s—sorry." He let out another wail and she glanced to her uncle.

He gave her a silent perusal, then sighed. "You were right. It was an inside job."

Of course it was. Only her crew knew about the conch. So when it was stolen, she'd told him to question the men.

But, Tommy?

She crossed over and crouched down next to him. "Why?"

The boy let out a hiccup. "H—he said he would kill them."

Her stomach tightened. "What are you talking about?"

"T—Thorne. He t—told me if I didn't tell him where the map was, he'd kill my ma and pa." Tears streamed down his cheeks. "I swear, Capt'n, I didn't want to tell him."

She stood and met her uncle's hard gaze. Deep inside, she'd known Thorne to be behind the break-in. Her heart gave a dull thud in her chest. With both halves of the map, the pirate captain was free to collect his treasure.

Unless she got it first.

She patted Tommy's shoulder. "It's alright. You did the right thing. Thorne would have followed through with his threat and your family is far more important than my half of the map." Extending her hand, she pulled him to his feet. "Besides, I don't need it. I made a copy."

She slid the map from her pocket and unfolded it.

Tommy blinked at her, then grinned. "So we still have a chance?"

Samantha purposely avoided looking at her uncle. "We'd have to move fast. Thorne is a smart man, he'll figure out the location soon." He likely had his crew scouring maps as they spoke. It wouldn't take long for him to figure out which bit of coastline to sail to. "But we know right where it is. There's a chance."

She cringed, waiting for Uncle Henry's disapproval. She'd pleaded with him since the day they got back. He'd steadfastly refused. Said it was too dangerous without knowing where Thorne was. That they would bide their time.

He remained silent.

Griff cleared his throat. "She's right. We could pull it off."

"I'm not letting her sail back out there. Not after what happened before."

Griff took the map from her and traced a finger along the line. "If we move quickly, we could be there by this afternoon. Be in and out in a few hours."

"You two already lost one of my best ships. I don't have anything in the harbor with even half the number of guns the *Raven* had."

"It's a risk." Griff's eyes gleamed and her heart soared. He wanted to go.

"Mother and Father died trying to find that treasure. Thorne killed them over it. If he gets his hands on it . . ." She pulled her bottom lip between her teeth. "It just feels wrong."

Uncle Henry ran a hand through his hair. "That blasted treasure is the only thing your father talked about for years. When he got his hands on the map, I'd never seen him so excited. If it's even half the size he claimed, it'll be the biggest haul we've had."

She twisted her fingers together. *Say yes.*

He frowned. "I have a meeting today with the governor. I don't like the thought of you sailing out for it without me."

She held her breath while he turned to Griff. "In and out?" Griff nodded and her uncle faced her. "Don't make me regret this."

She dashed over and threw her arms around his neck with a little squeal. "I promise!"

"And Griff will be captaining."

It didn't matter. Tommy could captain for all she cared. The chance to find Read's Revenge, to steal it out from under Thorne, was reward enough.

"We're going?" Tommy looked between them all and Griff nodded. With a whoop, the boy threw his fist into the air.

"Go gather the crew. Tell them to meet at the docks. We sail in an hour." Griff turned to her. "Do you have another rapier?"

She scoffed. "Of course." Not as fine as the one she lost during Thorne's attack, but it would do.

"Go get it."

Minutes later, she sat next to him on his wagon. He slapped the reins and glanced over at her. "People may recognize you."

She twisted her braid and tucked it up under her hat. How exhilarating it must have been for Mary Read back in the day. To stroll into town with no disguise. To not care if people recognized her.

"Thorne's men may be watching us as we speak. If he follows us . . ."

"If he follows us, we lead him astray. Post extra men in the crow's nest. We'll need the extra eyes." She stared ahead as they rode through town, refusing to meet the shocked gazes of onlookers as they careened by. "And we'll have to be quick."

He pulled the horses to a stop and gave instructions to a dock hand to take them to one of her uncle's warehouses. Jumping to the ground, Samantha headed toward the great wooden docks and took in the ships there. Her uncle leased the spot at the end, his ships always ready to sail at a moment's notice.

A large sloop floated there today. Similar in size to the brigantine and single-masted with fore and aft sails. She would handle similarly. Only seven guns per side. Didn't matter. Even if outfitted with more cannons, the ship wouldn't stand a chance against the *Reckoning*.

Griff shouted orders and the men aboard jumped into action. Chaos marked the next half hour as crew poured onto the ship. Samantha did a walkabout, checking sheeting and rigging lines, inspecting pulleys, and running her hands across weathered wood. She was an old ship, but sturdy and sound.

Samantha glanced at the navy ships anchored in the river. Three brigantines. Not as flashy as the *Falcon*, but no surprise there. The government hadn't many ships to spare these days. These three were likely commissioned from merchants.

Three ships. At least a hundred men each. Possibly double. Together, they would destroy any pirates they came across. Even Thorne couldn't possibly stand a chance against that fleet. And what of her uncle? Could he continue to keep his anonymity?

She turned away from the scene and took a steadying breath. No use worrying about it right now. He'd spent the last decade evading capture, keeping his identity hidden. He'd have a plan.

He'd better.

Chapter Twenty-Four

S AMANTHA ADJUSTED HER hat, pushing damp tendrils of hair from her forehead. Fair skies and steady winds had brought them to their destination ahead of schedule. She checked her map again and squinted at the shoreline.

"There."

A small inlet. Same as on the map.

No need to track through the underbrush with the whole map in hand. They would go straight to the treasure. Less than a quarter mile from the beach.

Once the anchor dropped, the crew lowered both longboats. If—when—they found the treasure, they would bring it all back in one trip. In and out, just like Griff had said.

A barebones crew of three stayed aboard while the rest of the men piled into the boats. The energy buzzing through them filled the air as they rowed to shore. They dragged the boats high on the beach and Griff set a hand on her shoulder.

"After you."

Her heart pounded. "I wish my parents were here."

He smiled. "They'd be proud of you."

Would they? Her thoughts flitted back to her time spent with the lieutenant, and she sighed. The first officer's words had haunted her all day. *Do you wish you had?* And all day, she still couldn't come up with her answer. Yes. No. Both.

She pulled her shoulders back. Time to find some treasure. Raising the map, she pointed to one side of the inlet. "This way."

They pressed through the underbrush while she counted her

steps and kept an eye on the map. In the mottled light filtering through the leaves above, it would be easy to veer off course. The "X" nestled on one side of a small circle. A cave perhaps.

Almost there.

The heavy canopy above gave way to palm trees and intermittent live oaks as they approached a clearing. Samantha wiped sweat from her brow and kicked at the long grass. No need to get bit by a snake.

Several indentations in the grass caught her attention and her heart lurched.

Griff ducked beneath a palm frond and came to a stop next to her. "I'll be damned."

He frowned at the circular expanse of glistening water in front of them. Almost a perfect circle. Steep limestone rose nearly vertical around most of it except for one side where it had caved in, leaving a precipitous bank to the water's edge.

A sinkhole.

She pressed a finger to her lips and pointed to the disturbed grass. "What do you think?"

He bent on one knee and swept his hand over one indentation. After a long moment, he stood and stepped into the sunlight. She held her breath as he scanned the ground around them.

"No sign of more tracks. Must have been a wild animal, perhaps a boar."

She rubbed the back of her hand across her forehead as he waved the crew forward and peered into the underbrush around the clearing. An odd silence wove through the trees. Heat pricked across her skin. Of course it was quiet. In this oppressive heat, they were the only creatures foolish enough to be out and about.

Samantha walked to the rocky edge of the sinkhole and pulled her lip between her teeth. The light limestone walls showed no sign of caves or even a crevice that could have been used to stash any sort of treasure.

The men filed from the woods and milled around, scratching

jaws and tugging beards. Tommy squinted.

"Where's the treasure?"

She sighed and dropped her eyes to the map, then back to the steep bank. "I don't know, Tommy."

Griff fanned himself with his hat. "Do you think this was filled with water two hundred years ago?"

Sticky heat beat against her dark breeches and she rubbed her hands over them. "Let's hope that's not the case." Still, numbness began to creep through her limbs.

Dark water lapped against the rocks as her throat tightened. If the treasure was underwater, it was lost for good.

She yanked her hat free and threw it aside with a growl. After all these years. After so much had been lost. All for nothing.

Fighting the urge to scream, she scanned the map one more time, willing there to be something she had missed. She traced the fresh inked lines. But the circle didn't lie. The treasure had to be down there. Out of reach.

Griff set a hand on her arm. "Perhaps it's best this way."

Tears pricked her eyes. "How can you say that? My parents died for a treasure they never had a chance of finding. If they had known . . ." she took a shuddering breath. "They might still be alive."

"Fate can be a cruel master." He cleared his throat and turned. "Well, boys, best get back to the ship."

A disappointed murmur ran through the crew and a bitter taste filled her mouth. She'd raised their hopes. Dangled the promise of wealth and an easier life if they only followed her. Her shoulders curved in and she kicked a rock.

It hit the water with a splash and she followed the ripples until they bounced against the stone wall. Her brows pushed together at the damp water marks on the limestone.

Could it be?

Tossing her rapier to the ground, she climbed down the steep incline and dipped a finger in the water. Brought it to her lips.

Brackish.

"It's connected to the sea." She pulled herself back up and retrieved her blade. "How long until low tide?"

Griff glanced at the setting sun. "An hour or so."

Her nerves fairly vibrated. "We wait."

He ran his fingers along his jaw and a slow smile spread. "It's genius."

"If it's true." She sank down cross-legged and stared at the water.

It had to be.

The men found shaded spots beneath the trees, but she stayed put, her eyes glued to the rocky wall across from her. The spot beneath the "X" on the map.

Inch by inch, the water retreated. Mosquitoes buzzed around her face, their incessant whine filling her ears. She batted them away, refusing to look away from the sinkhole.

And then she saw it.

A dark crescent played at the water's edge, shadows stretching deep. She rubbed her eyes in case they played tricks on her, and jumped to her feet. "Griff!"

He strode over and his gaze followed her pointed finger. "I'll be blowed. An underwater cave." He gripped her shoulder. "You did it. You found it."

A tremor ran through her as she took a shaky breath. "Do you really think it's in there?"

He grabbed the map from her and jabbed a finger on the "X" with a grin. "In another half hour or so, we'll find out."

Tommy ran over, and when Samantha pointed to the gap above the water, he let loose a whoop. The crew crowded close and Samantha began to unbuckle her belt.

Before she could slide the leather strap free, a sound she knew well slipped through the excited chatter of her men. The ring of steel blades being loosened. Her hand closed over the hilt of her rapier as she spun toward the trees and pushed two men aside.

"To arms!"

But it was too late. While her crew fumbled for their weapons, a laugh echoed over the sinkhole.

"My thanks for solving the mystery of the treasure's whereabouts."

DOZENS OF THORNE'S brutes materialized out of the shadowy underbrush while Griff and her crew bunched together at the water's edge. Samantha's heart constricted. They were good and trapped.

"I'd put those swords down if I were you." The captain strode into the clearing with a smirk. "Wouldn't want anyone getting . . . hurt."

A few of his men laughed.

Thorne came to a stop in front of Samantha. "We scouted the area earlier, to no avail. I must confess, I almost gave up. Until my runners reported spotting your ship."

Her stomach lurched. They'd been out there all along. Waiting in the trees.

She pulled in a ragged breath. "Where's your ship, then?"

He chuckled. "Just up the coast. Although, by now, she's likely on the way to overtake yours."

Bile burned her throat at the thought of the three men they'd left behind. They wouldn't stand a chance.

Thorne lifted his sword and ran his thumb across the point. "A little birdie told me you're quite skilled with that blade of yours."

She blinked at him as he met and held her gaze.

"We've some time to kill before that cave is accessible. How about a little match? If you win, I wait to kill you until after bringing the treasure up. If I win . . ." His lips pulled into a grin and he ran his blade across his open palm.

Her pulse slammed in her head. Swordfight with the infamous Captain Thorne? Even if she won, what good would it accomplish? The pirate's eyes glimmered with amusement. This was all a sick game to him.

Unless . . . unless she killed him.

Her gaze flitted around the clearing, at the giants and their gleaming scimitars. Would they stand down if she took Thorne out?

Only one way to find out.

Resolve flowed through her. She would cross the line. Not to save herself or her family. To give her crew a chance.

She nodded. "Very well."

The captain's grin widened. "That's the spirit."

Before she could step forward, a rumble of thunder came from the distance. She clamped her teeth together. Not thunder. Cannons. The men around her shifted uneasily.

Silence fell over the group as the faint booms rolled across the clearing one after another. More lives lost. Another ship sent below the waves. All for what? If only Christian had thrown the blasted shell overboard when she told him to.

With a snarl, she loosened her blade and stepped away from her crew. Her fist shook around the hilt as she tightened her grip. Tightness clamped around her chest, dripping with slick heat. She'd never felt the overwhelming urge to kill a man. Until now.

Sunlight gleamed off the tip of her rapier as she pointed at her target, Thorne's heart.

The pirate chuckled and shrugged free of his jacket. "I can see why the lieutenant is attracted to you."

The words sent a fiery barb through her heart. Chances were, she'd never see Christian again. She bit the inside of her cheek. It didn't matter. He was just as much her enemy as Thorne.

"Let's get this over with, Captain."

He gave a mock bow. "As you wish."

The speed in which he engaged her threw her off balance. One second he stood paces away, and the next, his blade met hers. She gave a little cry and jumped into action, trying to circle him.

But he was fast. Faster than she was. Each step she took, he copied with expert prediction and inched closer. His eyes never left her face as he read each of her moves. Her stomach went cold.

Here was an opponent she could not beat.

She clenched her teeth. Nonsense. Everyone had a weakness. She just had to find his.

Her feet moved in a blur as she came in with a thrust to his left side. He met it without hesitation, without a falter in his stride, and dealt her a heavy blow from above. The vibrations ran straight through her bones and she scowled.

He already had found hers.

She twisted away before he could deal another and slashed at his knees. Thorne jumped back and his blade snaked out toward her side, connecting before she could block it.

Her breath hissed out at the sharp sting and she let him come forward, let him think he had the advantage. His thrust came fast and she met it with a sharp twist of her rapier. The guise worked and he nearly dropped his sword.

With a grunt, she met his blade again, before he could fix his grip. The next minutes flew by as they parried, each blow coming faster and harder.

This wouldn't work. He would have her exhausted before she found a way through his defenses. She fell back as sweat dripped into her eyes.

Time to play dirty.

Humid air filled her lungs as she darted in and out, staying just beyond his reach. She settled into a pattern, one jab toward his right, two to his left. And waited for him to make his move. He read her movements and jumped ahead to meet her next thrust to his right.

She hit his sword from the inside, sweeping it out and dove forward, slamming into his chest. At the same time, she twisted her blade behind her, just in time to block his as it whistled toward her back. The clang of steel echoed against her spine and she used the momentum to push him backward. He regained his balance and they jerked to a stop.

"Well, this is new." Thorne took a quick step back, forcing her to follow. "I can't say I mind."

His free arm twisted around her back and tugged her closer as he grappled for her rapier. Hot fingers closed around hers and began to pry them open.

Now.

Samantha brought her knee up into his groin at the same time he jabbed his elbow up and slammed it into her jaw. The impact sent a flash of light through her vision and she stumbled to her knees. She tucked into a ball and rolled to avoid Thorne's blade as it followed her. Struggling to her feet, she took a few steps back and spit a mouthful of blood into the dust at her feet.

He didn't give her a moment's rest and stalked toward her, twirling his sword in a slow circle. Her chest burned almost as much as her arm did and she switched hands as she scrambled to the other edge of the clearing.

"I will say, you're a better fighter than your mother."

Ignore him.

Still, her heart blazed with hatred.

That hatred pushed her forward and she thrust up, changing direction at the last moment. This time, the tip of her blade cut through the fabric beneath his bicep. Thorne swore and rubbed his free hand across the spot. His fingers came away red and his jaw went rigid.

The thirst for more blood rushed through her and she tightened her grip and lunged again. This time, he met her with cold determination. Gone was his amused smirk and his eyes had turned a shade darker. He pushed her back, one heavy blow at a time, and her eyes widened as she struggled to deflect each one.

He'd merely been playing with her before.

This Thorne was the one feared across the seas. The cold-hearted brute whose name inspired terror.

She tried to twist his blade away as it slid dangerously close to her hilt, but his arm stayed steady. The blows came faster and her movements became frantic. Every step she took sent waves of fire up her side and her arms started to tremble.

Something glinted in his eyes and she had to use both hands to bring her rapier up and meet the heavy downward arc of his sword. The blow sent her to one knee and her elbows shook as she strained to keep her rapier in her hands.

He didn't let up and pressed harder. And harder. A guttural cry pushed through her clenched teeth as her strength waned.

He laughed.

And with a simple twist, sent her blade clattering to the ground.

Her shoulders heaved and it was all she could do to keep herself from collapsing against the sharp point he pressed into the hollow of her throat.

"Too bad. I would have relished the look on your face when I retrieved your beloved parents' treasure."

Her breaths came too fast, too heavy, for her to respond, and he laughed again.

"Did you really think you had a chance?"

Her eyes pressed shut and she rested her palms against the rough sand. This was it. The end. The pressure at her throat increased until each wild beat of her pulse thumped against the warm steel.

"Come now. Are you giving up so easily? At least your mother fought until the very end."

Her fingernails dragged through the sand, but she didn't move. "I'm tired of your games. Do as you will."

"Very well."

Time hung still as his boot scraped the dirt. As the blade twisted to a better angle for him. She held her breath.

"Thorne!"

Samantha's eyes snapped open at the shout and her mouth went slack. Thorne stiffened, but he didn't turn from her.

"Lieutenant. You have a bad habit of showing up when

you're not wanted."

"Let her go."

The metal against her throat pressed harder until the tip pierced her skin. She gritted her teeth against the sharp pain and met Christian's gaze. How the bloody hell was he here?

A warm trickle ran down her chest and Christian drew his sword. "Stand down, Thorne."

Men began to pour from the trees with muskets pointed at the giants.

"The cannons we heard?" Thorne's lips pulled into a snarl.

"From my ships as we overtook yours. You've nowhere to run, Thorne. It's over."

Ships.

Samantha's heart soared.

Christian took another step toward them and Thorne lowered his sword. She lifted her fingers and pressed against the cut he left behind while she struggled to her feet.

"Drop your weapon."

Thorne stood rigid, his gaze never leaving Samantha. He lifted his arm, held his sword out at his side. But he didn't drop it. Something flashed in his eyes.

He wasn't going to give up.

Samantha took a step back.

"Not so fast, dear." His hand snaked out and closed around her shoulder. Before she could spin away, he yanked her around his front and swung his outstretched arm back in, resting the blade against her throat once more.

"If you want her to live, call off your men."

Christian came to a stop. After an agonizing second, he lifted his hand and his men halted their forward progress.

"We outnumber you four to one. Your ship is crippled. No matter what, this ends with you in chains."

Thorne tugged her against his chest. "I guess it all comes down to how much you want this pretty little piece of yours to live."

Forest-green eyes sparkled in the sunlight as Christian stared them down. A rustle came from behind and the pirate spun. Her crew still held their swords and edged closer.

"Stay back," Thorne warned. He twisted and began to edge away from the two groups of men. When they were clear, he backed up to the edge of the sinkhole.

Christian followed and the blade's pressure against her neck increased.

"I'll slice her throat right in front of you, boy. I mean it. Take your men and leave. Then maybe I'll let her go."

"She's innocent. Why shed her blood?"

"I told you, no one is innocent. Least of all her family."

Samantha glanced down at the crumbling edge of limestone they perched on. A pebble broke free and splashed into the water below. If she pushed hard enough . . .

Her eyes flew to Christian's, but he remained focused on Thorne. *Look at me.* She widened her eyes and tilted her head to the side. He frowned and took another step forward.

Blast.

She would have to make her move and hope he followed.

Closing her eyes, she took several deep breaths while sliding her foot forward to brace against.

One.

Two.

Three.

She slammed all her weight into Thorne.

Chapter Twenty-Five

CHAOS EXPLODED AROUND Christian as Red and Thorne tumbled over the bank and into the sinkhole.

The giants rushed his men with wild shouts, and gunshots drowned out all other noise.

He sprinted to the edge. Before he could start down the steep limestone, a flash of crimson stood out against the frothing water below.

Son of a . . .

He jumped.

With a splash, he landed hard and struggled to stay upright on the steep slope. He took a step toward the struggle and slipped. Damnation. He couldn't get closer, and even if he could, so much mud had been stirred up, it was impossible to see below the surface. A glint of steel emerged from the havoc, there and gone in an instant, and the water stilled.

After an agonizing second, Thorne lifted his head from the water and stood waist-deep, chest heaving. "Bloody wench." His father grasped his arm, where blood seeped through his fingers.

Heart racing, Christian leveled his blade at the pirate's neck and scanned the sinkhole. If the blood hadn't been hers, where was she?

Come on, Red.

His sword wavered and Thorne grinned.

Bubbles surfaced in the middle of the sinkhole, and a moment later, copper hair glistened in the sun.

Thank God.

The sounds of battle above them wound down and Christian pressed the point of his blade above his father's heart. "Captain Thorne, you're under arrest for high piracy."

Isaac poked his head over the edge. "Need any help down there?"

"Yes, help me tie up this criminal."

His friend climbed down and stepped behind Thorne, pushing him from the water. He pulled out a strap of leather, wrapping it around one of the pirate's wrists, then the other. Christian stood still, each beat of his heart reverberating down his arm and blade. His father's face had gone stony, the sporadic twitching of his lip the only hint of emotion.

Once Thorne's hands were securely bound, Christian lowered his sword, the weight suddenly unbearable. Isaac met his gaze for a brief moment before giving a subtle nod, then led the captain up the rocky bank. Once they disappeared from view, Red swam back. She stepped from the water and Christian tilted his face skyward to avoid staring at the wet fabric clinging to her body.

"How'd you find us?" Accusation dripped from each word.

He lowered his gaze enough to meet her flashing eyes. "I believe you meant to say thank you. You're welcome."

She wrung out her hair. "Of course I'm thankful. I just don't understand how."

He climbed the bank and turned to offer her a hand. "I had every ship in port being watched. Turns out I didn't need to. Only one woman I know would be foolish enough to barge through town in breeches. If you were trying to fool anyone into thinking you were a boy, you failed."

A faint blush crept across her cheeks. "We had watches set."

"And I have state-of-the-art looking glasses. Sent straight from Washington."

She frowned and glanced around them. The remaining giants were being tied up by his men and hers. "And what of us, Lieutenant? Are we under arrest as well?"

Her chest heaved and his gaze slid over wet cleavage. Damn her for making him want her.

He took a steadying breath. "For what? Treasure hunting? Hardly a crime, if you ask me."

At his words, she spun toward the sinkhole with wide eyes. "The treasure."

She took a step toward the bank and he reached out to catch her arm. "Don't you think you've wasted enough time searching for this treasure?"

Her eyes narrowed and she yanked her arm free. "We didn't come this far to turn back. Not when it's within grasp."

"And where might this fabled treasure lie?"

With a grin, she pointed out over the water. To a cave. If one could call the dark cavity a cave. Barely room enough for a head to fit through. He shuddered.

"You can't seriously think to go in there?"

One copper brow arched. "Afraid of the dark, Lieutenant?"

She had no idea.

Red didn't wait for his answer and climbed down the bank. "Griff, bring the supplies."

The old man picked up a rag-wrapped torch and handed it to her along with a little box. She pulled a bit of twine from her pocket and attached the box to the top of the torch.

When she stepped in the water, Christian shifted on his feet. Too many variables could go wrong.

"Red."

She twisted to face him. "Feel free to join me, Lieutenant. I'm feeling generous enough to share."

His gut twisted. "No thank you."

With a shrug, she began to wade out. "Your loss."

The cabin boy clambered down the bank and splashed into the water. "Can I go?"

She nodded. "We have to move fast. There's only a small window before the tide rises and the passage is underwater again."

Griff pursed his lips together. "Be careful."

The water reached Red's shoulders and she held the top of the torch out of the water. She swam to the steep wall of limestone and peered into the cave.

"Wish us luck."

He didn't miss the way she nibbled on her bottom lip.

Thorne glared at her from his spot at Isaac's side. His first officer nodded toward the cave as she ducked her head into the shadows. "They shouldn't go alone."

Clearly.

When Christian didn't move, Isaac met his gaze. "Should I go, Lieutenant?"

Damn it. He should let the officer go. Isaac would keep her safe. Still . . .

"No. Stay here with the prisoners."

Red and Tommy disappeared from view, and his stomach gave a little lurch. Now or never.

Christian unbuttoned his jacket and threw it to the ground. Before he could talk himself out of it, he scrambled down the bank and splashed into the water, sheathing his sword into his scabbard. When the water lapped against his chest, he turned back.

"If we're not back in a quarter hour, send someone after us."

Isaac nodded and Christian pushed off the bottom and kicked out to the crevice. "Red?"

Her name echoed back.

Tilting his head to the side, he slipped under the rocky overhang. The soft lap of water against the walls reverberated in his ears and his pulse began to pound. Shadows gave way to pitch black as he edged deeper into the cave. Treading water, he lifted a hand and brushed against the stone overhead. So little space.

Something sticky slid over his cheek and he jerked his face, smashing his nose into the low ceiling. "Damn it."

He clawed at the spiderweb in jerky movements, bobbing beneath the surface. When water filled his nose, he coughed and sputtered.

A hand closed on his arm and he jumped again, this time taking a blow to the forehead.

"Calm down, Lieutenant."

Red's smooth voice slid over him.

In the darkness, he fumbled for her hand. Her fingers closed around his and he took several deep breaths. With a tug, she kept moving.

Soon, even with his face pointing up, the rocks began to push him deeper into the water.

Tommy let out a groan. "You sure the treasure's this way?

"Red." Christian's voice came out strangled. "There's no more room. We need to turn back."

"I'm not turning back."

"You're going to get us drowned."

Silence fell around them, save for the drip of water. Something hard pressed into his chest and he clenched his jaw, trying to backpedal. His muscles refused to move.

"Hold this."

The torch.

She tried to pull her hand away but he couldn't bring himself to release it. The only thing tethering him to sanity right now was her touch. She lifted their hands and pushed the torch against his clenched fingers.

"Lieutenant."

"What are you going to do?" *Don't leave me.*

"Trust me."

"Pirates. Trust. Don't go hand in hand." His breaths came too fast.

"Are you—?"

"No." The word came out in a strangled gasp.

Water rippled against his face.

"You're scared."

Her voice echoed off his cheek and his insides tightened.

"It's alright to be scared, you know?" She squeezed his hand. "The first step to moving past it is admitting it."

If only it were that easy.

"Ever since I was a boy . . ." He paused when his voice cracked. "Small places have made me nervous."

"Then why on Earth did you come with me?"

Why on Earth, indeed.

"I couldn't very well let you go alone, with only a cabin boy for protection."

She sniffed. "How gallant."

With a yank, she pulled her hand free. His hand flailed underwater, but she slipped away.

"Damn it Red—"

"Wait here."

Before he could respond, water splashed and silence fell around him.

Shit. Clenching his eyes shut against the darkness, he began to count. It didn't help.

His heart slammed into his ribs while his stomach roiled. He swallowed forcibly. No need to feed his lunch to the fish—or whatever else lived in here.

A minute passed. Two.

What if she didn't come back?

Visions of treacherous seaweed and venomous snakes swirled through his mind. Alligators. God, if only he'd held her hand tighter. They could be on their way out of this hellhole.

"She'll come back." Tommy's voice wavered. "She's the best swimmer I know."

Christian couldn't answer. In situations like this, skill didn't matter.

Water bubbled and he went rigid, his fingers biting into the wood of the torch. She surfaced, sucking in a breath. A wave of pain radiated from where his teeth clenched together.

"You still there?"

He thrust his hand out. "Enough of this foolishness; we are leaving. Now."

She evaded his attempt to catch her.

"Nonsense. The tunnel opens up just a few feet ahead."

"Red, I mean it. This is a fool's errand. It's time to give it up."

Her heavy breaths filled the air. A few feet indeed.

"It's not as dark in there. Do you really want to turn around and try to find your way back in the dark?"

Yes. He could probably swim it in record time too. Back meant safety and sunshine and wide open spaces. His muscles fairly vibrated with the urge to get on the way.

"Now, Red."

She sighed. "Fine. Can I at least have the torch?"

Finally, some common sense. She could have whatever the hell she wanted if it meant getting out. He shoved it toward her voice and she took it. No sooner than it had left his grasp she disappeared.

"Son of a . . ." He made one last grab for her. "Damn it, Red."

His face bumped against the cool rocks and he curled his fingers into a fist.

"Fine. Go then." The hoarse shout reverberated in his ears.

Let her go. If she wanted to get in trouble, it was on her shoulders.

He pressed his lips together and turned toward the entrance. *Sunshine.* The word became a chant in his head.

A few feet later, he stopped. Who was he fooling? If he left her and something happened . . .

With a groan, he felt his way back to where the stone dipped below the water. He cautiously extended a leg and explored the underwater tunnel. At least it didn't get any smaller.

"Tommy, go back and let the men know we found a tunnel and possibly a cave. If the tide comes up, it'll be too dangerous for anyone to follow. Tell them to stand by."

Bracing his hands on either side of the walls, he took a steadying breath. And another.

Here goes nothing.

One last deep inhale and he pushed under.

He kept one hand on the rocks and kicked hard. More than a

few feet passed and he blindly surged forward. When his lungs began to burn, he slowed. Had he made a wrong turn? What a way to die.

And then, his hand broke the surface, blessed air cooling his fingertips. He pushed his face above the water and opened his eyes. A muted grey cut the darkness and he blinked as his sight adjusted.

"You came." She tread water just beyond his reach.

He wiped water from his eyes and craned his neck. The rocky ceiling sloped up, revealing a large cavern. His breath whooshed out as some of the built-up tension faded.

Space.

"Where's Tommy?" She swam toward the tunnel with furrowed brows.

"I sent him back."

The lines of worry eased and she turned to face him.

"Now what?" He spoke the question aloud.

"Now we find the treasure." She pointed ahead at the outline of a rocky ledge. The source of the dim light became clear. A tunnel.

Red kicked over and tossed the torch onto the dry ground. She got her hands on the edge and began to pull herself up as Christian followed. He stretched his feet down and his boots grazed the bottom. He could touch. Barely.

"Here, let me give you a boost." His fingers closed around a slender calf and she stilled. The wet fabric of her breeches clung to her like a second skin. With a swallow, he slid his hand down to the sole of her boot and she pushed up.

After she scrambled over the edge, he got a good handhold and lifted himself. When he stood, he had to duck to keep from hitting the low ceiling. Red unwrapped the torch and gave it a good shake.

"Should be dry enough." She shoved one end between her knees and opened the flint box. Water poured out. "Now, to see if we can get a spark."

After several tries, she dropped her hands. "No use."

Christian took the flint from her hand. "Let me try." A heavy tang filled his nose. "How much oil did you soak that thing in?"

She rubbed her finger over the rag at the tip. "Enough."

He held the flint next to the torch and began working it. Harder and harder, he struck it. If he was lucky, the friction would dry it out. Sure enough, a minute later, his efforts rewarded him with a shower of sparks.

The torch erupted into fire and Red nearly dropped it. Flames crackled and hissed while he shielded his eyes. Before he could lower his hand, a scream pierced the air.

He jumped and followed Red's gaze into the tunnel, angling his body between her and whatever danger lurked. His body blocked the light and he grabbed the torch and extended it into the darkness.

A gleaming skull grinned at him from its resting place against the wall.

"What? A pirate afraid of skeletons?"

She rubbed her hands down her arms and frowned. "I just wasn't expecting it, that's all."

He let out a chuckle and swept aside a curtain of cobwebs. "Shall I lead the way?"

Without answering, she yanked the torch back and strode forward. He had to hurry to keep up. "Careful, what if there's traps?"

She spun and stared at him. "Once again, your imagination is getting the best of you. That sort of thing only happens in novels."

He rubbed his jaw. "Still . . ." He examined the smooth walls as she continued on. If he were going to hide an invaluable treasure, he'd certainly—

He bumped into Red's back. "Now what?"

She pointed ahead. "It's like you spoke it into existence."

His wounded pride rushed back as the light flickered off a line stretched across their path. Well, at least it used to. Time had loosened the bonds and it sagged low.

He grinned. "Only in the novels, you say?"

She let out a huff and carefully stepped over it. He ran a finger over a rusted spear tip hidden in the wall. Morbid.

After clearing the trap, Red at least had the sense to move slower. They didn't go far when the tunnel opened into another cavern. A shaft of sunlight cut through the space and ended in a conspicuous glimmer.

Next to him, Red rubbed her eyes. "Please tell me I'm not seeing things."

He took the torch from her and strode out into the open, weaving his way between chests and barrels. When he flipped open a weathered lid, the firelight reflected off a thousand coins. He couldn't stop the little thrill that ran through him.

"You're not seeing things."

She stumbled forward and fell to her knees next to him, running her fingers over the coins. Her breath hitched.

Christian twisted in a slow circle. So many crates and chests. There had to be at least a hundred. Strings of pearls hung twisted among dusty cobwebs from a golden candelabra at his side. A wooden box ahead overflowed with tarnished silver goblets.

Read's fabled treasure.

"Red, this is . . ." There were no words. They'd stumbled onto the richest treasure in the world. One whose existence he'd scoffed at an hour prior.

She stood and wiped at her eyes.

"Are you alright?"

"We found it." She whispered the words to herself and took a step toward him. A grin broke free. "We found it!"

With a little whoop, she rushed toward him. Her enthusiasm must have been infectious, because when she threw her arms around his neck, he didn't try to dissuade her. And when her soft lips pressed against his, he wrapped his free hand behind her back and leaned into the kiss.

His body reacted instantly, humming with awareness as her

fingers tangled in his hair. Heat slipped through his veins, and the urge to claim her, to bend her over the nearest barrel, pulsed with each beat of his heart.

He backed into said barrel and laid the torch over the lid. With both hands free, he cupped her bottom and lifted her. She pressed her hips forward, grinding against his erection and he groaned. The thin fabric of her blouse pressed taut over her nipples and they brushed his chest.

"Red." Her name came out in a reverent sigh and he slowed the reckless pace of the kiss, twining his tongue around hers, sucking her lower lip into his mouth. And realization slammed into him.

He needed her. Same as he needed air to breathe.

Not a need that a brief coupling could sate. A need that had him wanting her like this every day for the rest of his life.

Forever.

He must have tensed because she tilted her head back a fraction, searching his eyes with hers. His mouth dropped to her neck, tracing the exposed line of her collarbone. With a heavy swallow, he ignored her little gasp and lowered her to the ground.

What was he thinking? He'd nearly taken her in the middle of a dark and dirty cave. Nearly laid his heart bare. The word *forever* still beat in tune to his pulse, hovered on the tip of his tongue.

The magic of finding the treasure. That's all it was. It couldn't be more. Not between him and Red. Not ever.

She let out a shaky laugh and untangled her hands, dropping her forehead to his shoulder.

"I didn't mean . . . I mean . . ." Shadows hid her face, but he'd put money on the blush creeping across her cheeks.

The thought of her being flushed drove his heart back into a wild rhythm and he took a deep breath. And another. They couldn't keep doing this. Meeting like this. He was liable to lose his mind.

"What's your plan?"

She cocked her head at the question.

"You've found your fabled treasure. Surely, this is the grandest thing you could hope for as a pirate. Why continue after this?"

She laughed again, the sound hollow against his throat, and gazed out into the room. "My parents died trying to find this."

Blood rushed to his head. Her parents. The ones his father had killed. How could he forget? He pulled away.

"Red, there's something I have to tell you."

Chapter Twenty-Six

S AMANTHA PRESSED A finger to Christian's lips.
"Later."

His breath rattled out and she forced herself to turn away. Before she kissed him again.

With tingling lips, she bent to unlatch a small chest. A cluster of jewels nestled inside, sparkling in the dim light. Her hand shook as she plucked one free and hefted its solid weight.

The corners of her eyes went damp as she imagined her parents and how much they'd wanted to find this. She'd done it. Somehow, against all odds, she was here.

A creak came from behind her and she turned to find Christian lifting the lid from a barrel. He blew a layer of dust away and picked up something tiny and round. She stood and leaned over. Buttons. Intricately painted porcelain buttons.

Another chest held glass bottles packed in sawdust. She popped the cork from one and the fragrant scent of jasmine drifted over her.

Christian pointed to a dozen casks stacked atop one another and she grinned. If it was rum, her crew would be in heaven.

A crate lay broken on the ground and he picked up a carved spinning top, its once-vibrant paint peeling away in flakes. "Looks like there's a treasure here for every age, every taste."

Warmth radiated through her body as they ventured deeper into the cavern. So many delights. Hers for the taking.

The crew would be able to buy whatever they wanted. Homes. Ships. Their families would never go hungry for the rest of their lives. And her uncle, perhaps he would retire.

She stumbled and Christian caught her elbow. If her uncle retired, that meant no more pirating. No more adventures. Her heart clenched, a dull pain radiating outward.

"Careful there."

Christian's voice snapped her back and she tugged her arm from his clasp. She ran a finger along the little cut on her side, scabbed over now. The euphoria of finding the treasure—of kissing Christian—had worn off, leaving a thousand aches behind.

She tripped again and this time, Christian swiveled her to face him. "What's wrong?"

"Everything hurts." Saying the words aloud unleashed a torrent of pain through her muscles and she sank onto the nearest crate. Turning her hand palm up, she opened and closed it, blinking at the sharp ache the movement brought.

Christian stepped behind her and set his hands on her shoulders. Long fingers pressed into her flesh and she let out a soft hiss.

"When's the last time you slept?"

Her eyes drifted shut as pain and pleasure twined together beneath his touch. "Two days ago. I think."

Silence fell around them as his hands moved down her back and up again. When he squeezed her upper arms, she let out a yelp and jumped up. Too much.

"You should get back to your ship. Rest. You overexerted yourself."

Back to the ship.

"Oh no."

He frowned. "What?"

She grabbed the torch from him and raced across the room, ignoring the burning in her calves. Darting through the corridor, she nearly forgot about the tripwire and jumped over it at the last moment. Christian's footsteps thundered behind her.

"Red, what's going on?"

She handed Christian the torch when he caught up and jumped into the water. As she splashed toward the wall, he let out a soft curse.

Groping along the slick rocks, she felt for the opening. A moment later, she banged her forehead against the stone and echoed Christian's curse. The water had risen. Significantly.

"Can we get out?"

She shook her head. Though she could swim far on one breath, it was too dangerous. Too dark. Too many unknowns. He blew out a breath and she paddled back to the ledge.

His hand clasped around hers, lifting her from the water with ease. "I had Tommy tell the men to stand by. Will your crew wait until the next low tide?"

She walked into the tunnel and stared at the skeleton. "Of course. But they will worry."

He lowered the torch to the dirt and twisted it, snuffing the flame. Darkness curled around them and she instinctively took a step closer to him, away from the bones.

"What'd you do that for?"

"We need to conserve it. No way it'll last another twelve hours."

Her eyes adjusted to the muted grey light and she blinked a few times. "Christian?"

He brushed his fingers across her shoulder, sending a little thrill up her spine. It would be so easy to turn into him. To kiss him again.

Instead, she stepped away, following the faint light. "We might not have to wait."

She hurried back to the big cavern. A single shaft of light came from overhead, where the wall met the ceiling and she pointed.

"It has to lead outside."

Christian frowned and navigated to the wall, weaving around crates and boxes until he stood below the spot.

"It's much too small to climb through. Barely bigger than the width of my arm."

Samantha joined him and peered up at the smidge of pale

blue sky. Pulling her lip between her teeth, she grabbed hold of a layer of limestone and boosted herself up. Wedging the toe of her boot into a crevice, she got herself a little higher.

"Find something that we can stick through the hole."

His eyes lit with understanding and he held up the torch. "Will this work?"

Of course.

"Tie your shirt to it."

She focused on getting up to the small opening and when she twisted to take the torch from him, the ray of light glanced off honed muscles. She snatched it and turned back to her task before her eyes could wander.

Taking a deep breath, she angled her face toward the opening and brought her fingers to her lips after propping the wood between her and the wall. When she whistled, the shrill sound echoed through the chamber. Another breath. Another whistle. One more.

They couldn't be too far from the sinkhole, and she willed Griff or any of the men to hear her signal.

Now to get the makeshift flag out in the open. She shoved the torch into the hole and wiggled it. With Christian's shirt, it filled the entire space. Darkness surrounded her as she forced it through, inch by inch. With one big push, it broke free and light splintered through the cavern once more.

If she could only get it a little higher. She shifted, stretching out to pull herself up.

The rock began to crumble beneath her fingertips and she scrambled for a new handhold.

"Careful." Christian's hands closed around her waist and she nearly let go at the jolt of energy his touch brought forth. He must have dragged a crate over.

Goosebumps tingled up her back and she scowled. Damn her body for reacting. She shook her braid over her shoulder and reached up for the torch once more. Her fingers brushed something soft. Something alive.

A long, thin, form materialized out of the shadows with a hiss, cool scales pressing against her skin. With a yelp, she yanked her hand back and lost her footing. Her arms flailed and one hand smacked Christian directly in the face.

"Oof!"

His grip tightened as she tumbled onto him. The momentum threw them backward and a loud crunch filled the air moments before they crashed to the ground.

She lay still, sprawled across his body. "Christian?"

Twisting, she tried to find his face, but her leg tangled with his. He closed his arms tighter around her waist. "Don't move."

His voice came out strangled and she froze, imagining the snake coiled on her belly. After a few tense seconds, she relaxed. No snake.

The rise and fall of his chest beneath her brought her senses into full force. Hot breath puffed against her neck and the beat of his heart thumped into her back. *Don't think about it. Don't . . .*

His bare skin fairly singed a hole through the damp fabric of her blouse. And then she felt it. She was not the only one affected by their close proximity.

Heat flooded through her body. Up to her cheeks. Right back down to coil at her core.

Two choices. Roll off him as gracefully as possible and pretend she hadn't noticed. Or . . .

She pressed her eyes closed and remembered how her movements had driven him wild in the sea. Unbidden, her hips clenched, brushing her bottom against his hard length.

"Red." His voice rumbled in her ear.

Again. A little more deliberate.

This time, he sucked in a sharp breath. "You'll drive me mad."

Madness certainly explained her actions. She shouldn't want this—want him. But she did. If only they could mend the rift between them, they . . . she bit her lip. No sense hoping for the future, not right now.

But the present? Her lips curved and she dropped her hand to his bare side, trailing her fingers across blazing skin.

He let loose a growl and rocked his hips against her. Before she could blink, his thumbs hooked into her blouse and peeled it up, baring her belly. Her rib cage. Until it bunched over her breasts, trembling in his hands, and the warmth at her core grew into a pressure between her legs.

When he gave one final jerk of fabric, a gasp caught in her throat. She arched her back, trying to press into his touch. Still, his hands hovered over her, just beyond reach. If he didn't touch her, she would die.

She pressed her bottom against him once more.

And blessedly, the touch she craved came. First, a feather-soft graze of his palms over her nipples. She whimpered, her breaths already ragged.

"Please."

His fingers closed over her and her head fell back against his shoulder. Every ache, every pain, dulled as her pulse thrummed. And when his teeth closed on the tender skin behind her ear, a happy sigh escaped her.

He moved beneath her, dragging his hands down her sides to rest at her hips. She writhed atop him, twisting her foot beneath a solid calf, and one of his palms crept over her breeches. He splayed it directly over her sex, pressed into her heat.

When she let out a soft moan, he rolled them over. Gold coins tinkled around them as he lowered his face. Full lips brushed hers, and she opened to him, their tongues colliding in a desperate dance.

"Lieutenant?"

The voice echoed around them and Christian froze.

"Are you down there?"

He caught her mouth with one last kiss and a muffled curse before jerking away and scrambling to his feet.

Samantha yanked her blouse back down as a cascade of dirt and pebbles rained down on them.

AFTER AN HOUR'S worth of men digging above, Samantha climbed out into blessed sunshine. When Christian came out behind her, the crew lowered ropes and one by one men rappelled down. Minutes later, a pile of treasure had already accumulated.

Griff led the first group of men to the ship and Christian gave orders to move the prisoners out. Each time she lowered her eyelids, it became a struggle to reopen them. She blinked, resisting the urge to wipe at her eyes.

When Christian started across the clearing toward Thorne and motioned from him to get up, she raised a hand.

"Not yet."

Christian cocked his head.

"I want him to watch."

He frowned and stepped closer. "Stoking his hatred can only cause more problems."

She glanced at the pirate captain, who glared at a crew member walking by, bent over the weight of the chest in his arms. "He deserves a taste of his own medicine."

Turning on her heel, she marched back to the opening, where boxes upon boxes continued to pile up. It would take them well into the night to shuttle it all to the ship. Some of the rotting wood had given out and several piles of coins lay strewn about the ground.

She bent and plucked one from the dirt at her feet, rubbing the warm weight of it between two fingers. Her gaze tracked over Christian's men as they led their prisoners one by one down the path back to the ships. His first officer strolled from giant to giant, checking the strength of bindings.

"Officer?"

Isaac twisted her way and lifted a blonde brow.

"I require your assistance."

After tightening a knot and giving orders for iron shackles to be placed on all prisoners as they boarded the ships, he strode over. "Yes, Captain?"

Christian folded his arms at his officer's address of her. Muscular, bare arms that bulged at his sides. She jerked her eyes away and smiled brightly at Isaac.

"Though your lieutenant has turned down my offer of sharing our spoils, I do believe it was out of formality. I'm in your debt, and would like to offer at the very least, a small reward."

Isaac's lips drew into a line. "I'm flattered, but we were only doing our duty, my lady. I must follow my lieutenant's orders."

She let out a soft laugh. "Tell me, Officer, how often the US government gives you men bonuses?"

A telling silence followed her pointed question.

"And do they pay you a fair salary?"

He let out a little cough. "Fair enough."

The coin flipped in the air, catching the sunlight with a golden shimmer. If he were anything like the lieutenant, he came from wealth. Most higher-ups in the military did. But lower-ranking men, they made little more than a farmer, if they were lucky.

"The men beneath you, how many provisions would even one of these provide for their families?"

He held her gaze. "Quite a bit."

Some of the nearby sailors had stopped what they were doing and watched with eager eyes. This stash held more wealth than her crew could spend in their lifetimes. If it weren't for these navy men, she'd be dead right now. The lieutenant could shove off.

She pointed to an open chest full of similar coins. "Take it. Share with those who need it."

"I can't." Isaac's jaw had gone rigid.

"Yes, you can." Clenching the gold in her palm, she turned to the sailor closest to her, a burly man with coal-colored hair, and tossed it to him. He caught it and stared at his hand.

"Could you use it, sir?"

He glanced at Christian, whose frown had returned, but

nodded. "Yes, ma'am. I've two boys at home, they've been needing new shoes for a while now."

"Keep it." She turned and grabbed the chest.

It didn't budge. Lord, she forgot how much gold weighed. With a heave, she got it to move a couple inches. Heat crept up her ears as the men watched her struggle with it.

A shadow fell over her. "What are you doing?"

"You hate pirates. So you stubbornly refuse to accept help or even payment from one. Don't you care what good this could do for them?" She spoke to the handle she tugged on, soft enough so only he could hear.

"Is that what you think? That I don't care for them?" He leaned in and placed a hand over hers, halting the minuscule movement she'd coaxed from the blasted chest. "Would you like to know how many of them died trying to rescue you, thinking you were the helpless esteemed Miss Warstein?"

A cold weight settled in her stomach. "No," she whispered, blinking back the memory of cannon fire.

"No?" He straightened. "When you're a captain, you don't get to pick and choose. You don't get to gloss over the dirty details, the hard reality of life at sea."

Tears stung her eyes. "I never said—"

"Don't ever insinuate I don't care for my men. Each loss I suffer cuts deeply."

"I'm sorry." And she was. Her temper had gotten the better of her and she'd shown just how naive she really was. Worse, the tentative camaraderie they'd enjoyed in the cave had slipped away like a handful of sand.

A muscle ticked in his jaw as he regarded her. "Isaac, take the chest. Split it however you see fit."

He turned and pointed to the man holding a sword at Thorne's back. "Bring him to the ship." Without a backward glance, he walked away and a thousand little fractures splintered across her heart as everything she'd let herself hope for earlier vanished.

"How amusing." Thorne stood and shifted his gaze between them. "The great lieutenant, taking charity from a pirate."

Christian stopped a few yards ahead of her. "Silence."

The word rang through the clearing, sharp with warning.

But Thorne chuckled. "I wonder if she would have offered it if she'd known who you are."

Isaac paused mid-lift of the chest and stared at her with wide eyes as Christian spun to face the pirate.

"Not. Another. Word."

The coldness in her belly turned to ice. "What are you talking about?"

Thorne turned his attention to her with gleaming eyes. "And what about you, Miss Warstein? Does your lover know your true identity?"

She blinked. "Of course he does."

His grin spread to reveal a flash of white teeth. "Or should I say, the identity of your uncle?"

Suddenly, she couldn't breathe. She tried to suck in air, but nothing happened.

No.

Anything but that.

"I thought not." The sailor at his back pushed him forward but the pirate kept his eyes locked on her. "Did the lieutenant tell you why he hates pirates so much?"

Somehow, her lungs drew air as she gave a curt nod. "His mother was killed by pirates."

"He left out the part that his mother was—"

Christian drew his sword and started across the clearing and Isaac dropped the chest. "Don't listen to him." The officer reached out as if to clap his hands over her ears, but she twisted from his reach.

"My wife."

It took a moment for the words to sink in. Christian slid to a stop and his face went pale as a ringing filled her ears. Thorne, his father?

Impossible.

But the look on his face said it all.

"Red." Her name tumbled from his lips in a strangled whisper.

She shook her head, slowly at first and backed away. "How?"

How could he have kept it from her? How long had he known? How could she have not recognized the similarities between the two men? Their hair color. The intense green of their eyes. The same damn nose and chin.

The little lines of pain in her chest exploded outward and she fell to her knees. His father murdered her parents.

Christian stepped toward her but Thorne's voice cut through the clearing. "Not so fast, son. Your pretty little piece here isn't any ordinary pirate."

She pressed her eyes closed.

"You're looking at Captain Remington's niece."

Her muscles tensed. But Christian didn't say anything. After several moments of tense silence, she opened her eyes to catch a glimpse of sodden boots twisting away. He left the clearing without so much as a word.

Spots filled her vision as her chest went tight. Her uncle. If she didn't get back to Savannah before the navy, he might very well face the noose. She pushed to leaden feet and stumbled down the path. "Christian!"

He turned and she stopped short. "You were right, Red. We are enemies. I was foolish to forget."

"Please." The brush blurred around her in a swirl of green. "My uncle."

He laughed, the cold sound extinguishing the day's heat. "Let me guess. You want amnesty for him as well? Tell me, what exactly do you have left to offer?"

The words cut through her.

"He's all the family I have."

His face twisted. "Family? How lucky you know of such a concept. Up until last week, I had no family. And look where I am now." He jabbed a finger back toward the clearing. "Don't cry to me about family when I'll be hanging my father by the end of the week." His voice broke and he turned away once more. "I'll give you and your uncle one week to disappear."

She caught her breath. "You know that's not possible."

"It's the only grace I'm willing to offer."

Those broad shoulders held a rigid stance, his breaths coming ragged. He was hurting. And damned her if she didn't want to reach out. Her own breath shuddered. He wouldn't accept any comfort from her. Not anymore.

"The favor."

He didn't move.

"You said you owed me a favor. This is what I want. Don't come after my uncle."

His fingers curled into fists. "I think we're even after today."

A tightness closed around her throat. "I'll talk to him. Tell him our pirating is over."

Silence pressed around her as he shook his head.

Fine. She swallowed back a strangled sob. "I'll never set foot on a ship again."

He turned, the movement slow and deliberate. "Do you mean it?"

She opened her mouth but couldn't bring herself to say it out loud. So, she pressed her eyes shut and nodded. A cicada buzzed overhead in the heavy silence as tears slipped down her cheeks.

"Alright, Miss Warstein. You have a deal."

Chapter Twenty-Seven

OPPRESSIVE HEAT BORE into the dark blue fabric of Christian's uniform jacket, his shirt clinging to his back as sweat dripped down his forehead. Funny how the sun seemed to know when a hanging was scheduled. It was determined to make everyone suffer, guilty and innocent alike.

Isaac stood next to him, blonde hair plastered to his neck. "A real scorcher today, isn't it?"

Christian merely grunted.

The noose hanging at the center of the square held every bit of his attention. It hung still, without even a breeze to set it swaying. A large crowd packed the area with people from every class milling together. He wouldn't have expected any less.

The infamous Captain Thorne, reaping his just reward. Ladies beat brightly colored fans in an eerie rhythm, the hurried movement playing with the corners of his vision. Some families had spread blankets and brought along baskets of refreshments. Children weaved among the onlookers, brandishing wooden swords.

"Lieutenant." A throaty voice brought his gaze down to a curvaceous brunette. Her dress had been laced so tight the mountainous globes of her breasts threatened to spill out. "We are in your debt because of your bravery. However can I repay you?"

Her eyes slanted and she ran them down to his feet and back up, pausing for a long moment below his waist. The insinuation couldn't have been more clear.

He clenched his teeth. "Being able to serve the wonderful citizens of Georgia is repayment enough."

She reached out and touched his forearm—a bold move indeed—and leaned in along with an overpowering wave of floral perfume. "I would be more than happy to serve you."

A cough lodged in his throat. While beautiful, she stirred nothing inside him. Not even a twitch. Because all week, someone else had dominated his thoughts. Someone who turned his blood hot as fire in the middle of the night when he lay awake in bed. Someone whose phantom lemon scent plagued him every day.

Someone off limits.

As if summoned by his thoughts, a flash of red hair glimmered across the square. He bowed to the lady still clinging to his arm. "If you'll excuse me, I've some final preparations to oversee."

Isaac followed him as he patrolled the edge of the square. He climbed the steps to the courthouse and scanned the crowd.

There.

She stood next to her uncle, dressed in a stunning blue day dress. Her hair twisted in a loose bun at her nape with curls cascading down one side. Unlike the other women, she held no fan, keeping her fists clenched at her side as she stared at the platform. Beneath her bonnet, the sun reflected off pale skin. Too pale. Her lips twisted and she rose two slender fingers to press against her temple.

She looked miserable.

"What are you going to do about her?"

He jerked his gaze to Isaac, who stared straight at Miss Warstein. "Nothing."

His friend snorted and turned to him. "Come now, you don't truly expect me to believe that?"

"Yes. I do. There can be nothing between us."

"You know I'm not sentimental, or even inclined toward believing in love, but I can't help but point out that there's something there. Besides, why not? Last I heard, she went clean."

Christian's throat grew thick. *Something there.* It was something he'd reflected on all week. Something he began to believe. Until he remembered what his father had done to her parents. Remembered her tears under the Florida sun. That he'd made her sacrifice her dreams.

He scowled. Never mind her dreams were the kind that would get her killed. She was far better off now. Safe. So he would take solace in her certain hatred, in knowing she was no longer risking her neck. It was the best he could hope for, even if it meant not being part of her life anymore.

The pressure in his throat increased and he coughed. He'd come to look forward to each time their paths crossed. The mere sight of her sent his pulse racing. Braver than half the men he knew, a damn good sailor, and more passion than he'd ever seen before. She was the perfect woman.

Almost.

A puffy cloud slid across the sun and he peered between two buildings, where the glimmer of the river caught his eye. This weekend, he would set sail once more. His fingers brushed the soft fabric of his badge of merit. Being back on the sea would set him back to rights. He had a job to do and needed to focus solely on it.

Bringing pirates to justice.

A bitter taste rose into his mouth. After spending days among Red's well-honed crew, after fighting at their side against Thorne's men, justice suddenly didn't seem so black and white. On the island, he'd heard fond stories of wives and children, sung along with them as they tried to keep spirits high in the face of uncertainty, witnessed the camaraderie between men so similar to those of his own crew. If he met those sailors out at sea, could he really put them behind bars? Sentence them to the noose?

He glanced at the jail, where his father would soon be led out. A monster. One born of grief and hatred. One he had no desire to become.

"Are you alright?"

Isaac's soft words punctured Christian's thoughts, and he turned back to him.

"You don't have to stay for the hanging, you know."

But he did. "If I leave, people will ask questions."

Questions that could lose him his job. He trusted his crew to keep quiet about Thorne's true identity, but showing weakness during the hanging of his greatest catch could make for some uncomfortable conversations. Ones he wasn't ready to have.

"Fine. But you're joining me at the tavern tonight for a well-deserved pint or three."

God knew, if he went home, he'd down a whole bottle. Perhaps more. A ghost of a smile played across his lips.

"Deal."

"And if you need to talk about your father—when you need to—you know I'm here."

His father. He ground his teeth together and pulled his hat off. Twisted it in his hands. And put it back on. Today, he'd lose his father for the second time. This time, for good.

Monster. He repeated the word in his head.

"Lieutenant, a word, if you please." Henry Warstein stood feet away and the hairs on Christian's neck lifted.

The very pirate he'd been tasked with hunting down. He would have never guessed. But all the signs were there. Wealthy. Warehouses full of goods. Never losing a ship to pirates. His gaze slid up the man's impeccable outfit. A true gentleman pirate.

It made one wonder how many more were hiding in plain sight.

Isaac raised a brow and shot Christian a look. But he waved his friend away. "I'll meet you near the platform in a few minutes."

Warstein—Remington—leaned against the white stone of the railing. "I'm glad you caught him."

Christian narrowed his eyes. "Did you know who he was?"

The man stared out over the crowd. "Fine day for a hanging, isn't it?"

"It's never a fine day for a hanging." He snapped his mouth

shut as a grey eyebrow lifted. "Answer my question, Remington."

"Thorne surprised us all. Thompson is a common name. I did not put his identity and you together until Samantha told me."

The mention of her name sent Christian's gaze on a quick hunt for her. Not by the platform anymore. The crowd pushed together even tighter as latecomers arrived. No blue dress in sight, however.

"I owe you my gratitude. If I had lost her . . ." The merchant cleared his throat. "She means the world to me."

Christian turned to him. "Will you truly stop? She gave me her word."

Warstein let out a sigh. "I suppose times are changing. If not you, there will always be another ambitious navy man or pirate with lofty goals keen to take me down. I'm getting old, and truth be told, all the action has begun to wear me out. I'm thinking of heading to New Orleans. Plenty of opportunities to be had there."

He pulled his hat off and fanned himself, running his free hand through grey hair. "Reckon we will have to arrange a meeting before then. Remington will fall to the mighty Lieutenant Thompson in a skirmish. Of course, his body will never be recovered."

Christian tugged one sleeve of his jacket. The thing about dishonesty was it had a habit of circling back, ready to strike when least expected.

"Too many witnesses. Too risky. Better for Remington to disappear without a trace."

"I suppose so. But everything in life carries risk, wouldn't you agree, Lieutenant?"

Warstein gave him a knowing look before turning to face the gallows. "You know, I wasn't always a pirate. My younger brother became a privateer during the war. When it finished and the privateering dried up, he couldn't resist the thrill. There was always something to chase. Spanish ships with their gold. British merchantmen laden with goods. He tried to get me to join him, but I was too busy building my shipping empire. He became the famed Remington."

Replacing his hat, he dropped his gaze.

"When he was killed, I started on the side, here and there, as a way to honor his memory. I inherited his crews, trained my own. One thing led to another, and . . ." He swept his hands out toward the water and shrugged. "Remington was resurrected."

"Why are you telling me this?"

"I made a mistake with Samantha."

Christian blinked.

"I gave her too much freedom. Told her she could choose her path in life. I shouldn't have taught her to sail. She's headstrong, just like her mother. I would have done her better by keeping her ashore and marrying her off."

A flash of heat prickled over Christian's skin as he tried to imagine her locked up at home. Wedded and bedded to some man who didn't deserve her spirit, who would probably try to snuff it out. "She doesn't seem the type to take well to that."

Never mind he'd practically thought the same thing minutes before, that keeping her off the sea would keep her safe.

Warstein gave a sad shake of his head. "I want her to be happy above all else. But now that she's tasted freedom, I fear she'll wither away like a bird with clipped wings. Being ashore will break her. I could have prevented that."

Something coiled in Christian's belly. Something that felt a lot like guilt.

I'll never set foot on a ship again.

He pressed his eyes closed. Warstein was right. He hadn't only taken her dreams from her—he'd broken her.

Lifting his hand, he squinted into the square again and frowned. Where was she? His heart began to pound a dull thud in his chest.

"You won't find her here. She never stays for the hangings."

The door opened behind them and Judge Williams strolled out. Christian's stomach roiled and fresh droplets of sweat beaded beneath his hat. Damn everyone's perceptions of him. He couldn't do this.

After nodding a greeting to the man who'd sentenced Thorne to death two days earlier, he turned and hurried down the steps. He didn't slow his pace until he ducked into an alleyway between two buildings. Ripping his hat free, he leaned his head against cool stone.

A thousand other things. His father could have chosen a thousand other professions. And their reunion would have been full of joy. What a cruel twist of fate.

His fist smashed into the wall, sending pain bursting up his arm. Again. And an anguished cry broke free. One that had been building since that day on his father's ship.

Spinning, he jogged toward the water before anyone could come investigate. He needed to get away from the square. Needed . . .

Red.

As much as he would regret it, he needed to see her. He'd examine what exactly that need meant later, preferably well into his cups.

For now, he lurched down the steep steps leading to the docks. Where else would a grounded pirate find refuge? Briny air filled his lungs as he strolled onto the thick wooden planks. He headed toward the end, where one of her uncle's merchantmen floated.

She stood at the bottom of the gangplank with one bare hand resting on the railing, her glove lying discarded at her feet. Her eyes were closed and a small smile played across her lips.

Listening to the vessel.

He'd gotten a chuckle out of it when one of her crew pointed it out that first night on her ship. But then he'd watched her face transform as she had taken the helm. He'd never seen anyone get so lost in the magic of sailing. It made him think back on his first days on the water as a lad, when each rise and fall of the ship held a new discovery.

And now, he'd taken that joy from her.

He stood still, the constant splash of water against the ship tempering his racing pulse. A dockhand pushed a cart laden with cotton bales past and mumbled an apology when he bumped into Christian. Still, he couldn't pull his gaze from her. He could watch her all day.

Forever.

The same thought he couldn't shake in the cave slammed into him and he took a step back. He loved her. The realization took the wind from him. He was in love with a pirate.

An ex-pirate. His heart gave a hopeful beat. Could it work? He curled his fingers into a fist. *No.*

Not after everything that had happened. Not after their family secrets had been revealed. Not after he'd so callously ruined her dreams.

Slender fingers clenched and Red's smile disappeared. He should turn around. Leave her be.

Instead, he started forward. He approached with quiet steps and stopped when the scent of lemons filled his nose. So close, he could touch her if he reached out. He clasped his hands behind his back.

"Miss Warstein."

Her eyes snapped open, blue and green hues swirling in the sunlight. They narrowed briefly and she spun and walked away.

Let her go.

He bent and picked up her glove, brushing away a speck of dirt from the white satin. She made it to the end of the dock and sat on a crate, crossing her arms and staring out over the water at the salt marshes of Hutchinson Island.

He glanced at the glove and back to her. Leaving it hanging on the railing would be wisest. A faint breeze pressed at him and he closed his hand around the soft fabric. Walk over. Drop it next to her. Retreat.

A sound plan.

When the glove rested on the crate next to her, he pivoted. Where to now? Planter's Tavern, a block from the waterfront, should be open. Isaac would find him there.

"Lieutenant?"

He froze, the soft whisper echoing in his head. His heart pounded against his ribs as he turned back.

"Are you . . . alright?"

He tensed at the repeat of Isaac's words from earlier. How could he answer that? His father was about to hang. At his hands.

She patted the spot next to her. "Join me?"

Alarm bells went off in his head. He should not have come out to the docks. Still, he couldn't bring himself to walk away. With a sigh, he stepped over and sat.

"You didn't know who he was until he called you up that first night on his ship."

A statement, not a question. God, he was not ready to have this conversation. Especially not with her.

"I didn't know."

She nodded. "You held yourself together well."

"I had no choice. I was there to save you—had to focus on trying to get us out of there."

Her bottom lip pulled between her teeth. "I'm sorry."

It could mean so many things. And suddenly, he had to know. "For?"

She twisted the glove between her fingers. "That my uncle sent you after me. If he hadn't, you might have never found out."

"Why did he send me after you? He was perfectly capable of retrieving you himself. In the end, it was his crew that saved the day."

Her hands stilled. "I don't know."

He stared at her for a long moment, but she didn't blink. Didn't flinch. She told the truth. Warstein had set something in motion. The question was, what?

"And you believe I would be better off not knowing what my father became?"

"Sometimes, things are better left unknown." Sea-colored eyes met his. "What good can come of the knowledge?"

The muscles in his chest constricted. "It's a reminder of what I could become."

"You're nothing like Thorne."

A cold laugh lodged in his chest. "How do you know?"

Pretty pink lips pressed together. "You're not. You . . ." She began to fidget with the glove once more. "You wanted to save me. Even though I was a pirate."

The hazy scene flashed before him, her curled naked against his side, staring at him from behind that blasted mask. Her soft words: *You can't save me.* His pulse thrummed anew.

A flush had spread across her cheeks and she dropped her gaze to her lap while the breeze tossed a curl over her forehead.

He reached out and tucked it back in place. "I would have, Red."

She sucked in a breath and pulled from his touch. "I think it might be best if you would stop calling me that."

Numbness tingled through his limbs. This was it, then.

Goodbye.

He pushed to his feet and stepped to the edge of the dock. Murky water swirled in angry eddies. Tide was going out.

A chorus of shouts came from the square and they both turned toward the shore. His father had probably been brought out. Not long now. He pressed his eyes shut.

Her fingers grazed his arm and he jumped at the contact.

"If it were my father, I don't think I could bear to stay, no matter what he had done."

He could barely manage a nod. "Let me take you home."

She inclined her head and he led her to the bank. At the top of the steps, she tugged his arm and pointed to a nearby wagon with two mules.

"They belong to my uncle's men."

Silence had fallen over the city and he hurried toward the vehicle. If they could get far enough, maybe they wouldn't hear the applause that would follow his father's death.

Son of a bitch.

A cold sweat broke out across his brow as he helped her up to the bench. When he took his seat next to her and took the reins, he caught her worried look.

"I'm a monster, aren't I?" The wagon lurched into motion and she grabbed his arm for balance. "I could have let him go."

"You were only doing your job."

He slapped the mules into a trot. "Would you have done it? Brought your father in?"

"I don't know. If he had done the things Thorne has . . ." She met his gaze. "I don't know."

He cleared his throat against the uncomfortable weight gathering there and his vision went blurry. If they kept talking about this, he was going to lose control. He needed to get her home and lose himself in a bottle.

The wagon bumped along the road as it opened into the countryside and he urged the team faster. Her grip on his forearm tightened as they reached a teeth-rattling speed and a few tendrils of warmth pierced through the coldness settled in his stomach.

"I don't t—think this wagon is meant to go so fast."

He glanced down where her fingers dug into him and pulled the reins back. The mules slowed to a walk and he blew out a breath. "My apologies."

The Warstein estate stretched out ahead, the big white house reflecting the sunlight. When he turned the team down the oak-lined drive, silence curled around them. He began to breathe in tune to the clip clop of hooves and the creak of harnesses.

Drawing to a stop, he jumped to the ground and held out his hand. Such a beautiful afternoon. Such a beautiful woman to help down. It could almost be a normal day.

He walked her to her steps and came to a stop.

She looked up at him. "What will you do now?"

He shrugged. "What I'm best at. I leave again tomorrow. Will probably stay out for a few months."

She pushed the toe of her slipper into the dirt, but her face stayed blank.

Ask me to stay.

He shook his head at the absurd thought. "And what of you, Miss Warstein? Will you be alright?"

Copper brows pushed together as hurt flashed through her eyes. Up here, away from the water, the green hues threatened to overtake the blue in them.

Her shoulders dropped. "I wanted to become a sailor my parents would have been proud of. To follow in their footsteps."

Her eyes glimmered and she twisted away. Climbed one step. "I thought finding the treasure would make me feel closer to them. But instead, I feel farther than ever before."

He touched her shoulder. "You need to steer your own course in life instead of trying to live up to other people's standards. You don't need to follow your family's legacy; you can make your own."

She sniffed and he reached out and gently turned her. Wet trails streamed down her cheeks and she pressed her eyes shut.

There was nothing he could say to lessen her hurt. So, he did the only thing he could think of. The step put her face nearly level to his and he skimmed his hands up and brushed away the tears with the pads of his thumbs. When her lashes lifted, he leaned in, hovering a hairsbreadth away from her lips.

Her breath puffed against his chin.

He closed the distance.

"Lieutenant!"

He jerked his head back as the shout echoed around them, followed by the thunder of hooves. Miss Warstein wiped at her face as Isaac pounded up the drive. The officer pulled his horse to a sudden stop and it tossed its head, sending bits of foam flying.

"It's Thorne. He escaped."

Chapter Twenty-Eight

S AMANTHA SAT ON the front veranda, stirring her lukewarm tea. Dusk's shadows stretched out across the grounds, bathing everything in muted purple tones. She'd stood on the steps for a long while after Christian borrowed a horse and tore off to town.

Some of his men had come by a long while after to search the property in case the pirate had revenge on his mind. The housekeeper had finally come out and shooed her inside, forcing her to bathe and eat a light supper. She stretched her legs, free from the confines of arduous skirts. At least no one had tried to stop her from dressing in her breeches and blouse.

She'd twisted her hair into a long braid and she unwound it, letting the damp waves fall to her waist. Her uncle's carriage rumbled into the drive and she stood. An extra horse followed, tied with a long lead. The one Christian had borrowed.

Her gaze flew to the forest between their properties. Had he returned home?

"Do I want to know why you're dressed like that?" Uncle Henry climbed the stairs.

"Ships aren't the only places one can wear breeches."

He sighed and crossed to the door.

"Any news?"

"Not a single sighting. It's as if he's disappeared."

"What happened?"

"The rope failed. And in the commotion afterward, a group of men disguised as onlookers in the front of the crowd swarmed the platform. By the time they were dispersed, Thorne was gone."

She shivered as an owl hooted in the distance. "Where do you think he went?"

Her uncle shrugged and opened the door. She frowned at his nonchalance.

Something was off.

"Did you have something to do with it?"

He paused and swiveled to face her. "Whatever would make you think that?"

"I know you have a history with him."

His eyes darkened. "Our history is a terrible one."

"So you had nothing to do with it?"

His hand tightened on the doorknob and her chest tightened.

"Why?" The word came out as a strangled whisper.

Uncle Henry stared out into the darkness. "I owed him."

Her mouth went dry. "Why help him? Why not let him hang?"

"It's good to have a powerful man in my debt."

She took a step back. "He killed my parents."

He pressed his eyes shut and when he reopened them, they were filled with anguish. "It's complicated. The score between myself and Thorne is settled, and that's what matters now. We won't have to worry about him or his men coming after us again."

A thread of unease crept through her. Everything her uncle did had a calculated reason behind it. She should know better than anyone else.

She set a hand on the door. "I think, in light of all that's happened, I deserve to know."

He stared at the door for a long moment. His shoulders slumped.

"Uncle?"

His hand curled into a fist. "Because Mrs. Thompson died on my watch."

Samantha reeled back a step and took a strangled breath as

Thorne's words echoed through her head. *"No one's innocent. Least of all her family."*

"You were the pirates who kidnapped her?" Her voice came out small.

"Heavens no, girl. Your father and I were part of the rescue operation. It went terribly wrong and she didn't make it."

A heaviness settled over her heart. And then, understanding hit her. "He blamed you for her death."

He turned with damp eyes. "It is my greatest regret. I've spent the last twenty-four years wondering what I could have done differently. Wondering if I could have changed the outcome." Tears sprung to her eyes as he lifted his arms and pulled her into a hug. "The world can be a terrible and cruel place, dear. My greatest wish was to keep the worst of it from you, to spare you from experiencing it firsthand. It seems I have failed."

"It wasn't your fault." She sniffed and smiled up at him. "Besides, I'm more resilient than you think, uncle."

"Indeed you are." He gave her a squeeze. "Also, I spoke with Lieutenant Thompson. We won't have to worry about the navy ever knowing my identity."

Wiping at her eyes, she stepped back. There was one more thing she needed to know.

"Why did you send the lieutenant after me?"

The lines of worry around his eyes eased. "Why do you think?" Though his face remained solemn, he gave her a halfhearted wink and strode into the house.

She stayed outside until the mosquitos buzzed in her ear. Her thoughts were a jumbled mess. Christian and his almost-kiss. Her uncle and Thorne. Her parents.

The dull throb lingering behind her brows pulsed. So much had happened today. Was it too much to hope that a good sleep would fix everything?

Inside, the halls were dark. The entire household had retired early. No, a light came from the crack in the study door. Though she wanted to press her uncle further, she wasn't sure her head could handle any more surprises.

So, Samantha climbed the stairs and locked the door behind her. Anna had left her nightgown draped on her bed. She began to unbutton her blouse but paused when her curtains flapped in the breeze. Her heart gave a little lurch before she remembered leaving the balcony doors open earlier when she changed.

Walking over, she began to close them. Before they clicked shut, she glanced across the field toward Christian's estate. A light twinkled on in a distant window and she caught her breath. He was home.

She pushed the doors open and walked out into the night. Leaning against the warm stone of the banister, she closed her eyes and sighed. Every time she closed them, she saw him.

Tomorrow, he'd sail away. Who knew when, if, their paths would cross again. She'd seen his look of resignation at the dock when she told him not to call her Red anymore.

Pain radiated through her chest, the sharp ache making her gasp. She pressed a hand there.

Steer your own course.

How? Living a life on shore was akin to asking a fish to survive on dry land. Easy for him to say. He would get on a ship and sail out of her life tomorrow. Would continue living his life. While she languished.

The blasted man had nearly kissed her. Her lips fairly burned at the memory of his breath on them.

A walking contradiction. That was what he was. Hot one minute, cold the next. Her heart beat a painful rhythm. If his first officer hadn't come, what would have happened? Would Christian have cut it off at a kiss and said goodbye? Or . . .

Samantha opened her eyes. Stared at the flickering light through the trees. She could still find out. A tingle ran though her limbs. It would be so easy to walk over, knock on his door. With a shaky laugh, she turned and stepped inside.

Nonsense.

She might never see him again. The thought sent a new ache spearing through her chest and she pressed her eyes shut. New Orleans might as well be on the other side of the world.

One more night. What she wouldn't do for the chance to sear one last memory in her mind of him. Of them. Her breath caught in her throat and she spun back to the railing.

Reckless.

She lifted a leg over it.

Reckless.

Eased her body along the wall.

Dropping to the ground, she hurried through the garden and slipped through a side gate. This time, she cut through the field, her boots pressing into damp earth, grass swishing around her knees. Darkness cloaked her and she blinked up at the black clouds covering the moon.

Lightning flashed far away and the soft rumble of thunder rolled over her. At the edge of the field, she paused at the road. His drive lay around the corner. A wild thrill raced through her as she jogged toward it.

She passed beneath a towering oak, heart hammering against her ribs. As she approached the house, instead of the urge to flee like last time, an invisible thread tugged her forward. At the bottom of the steps, she swallowed.

This was it. Her last chance to turn back. She took a step, then faltered. What if he turned her away? The door suddenly seemed impossibly far. Would a servant open it instead? Servants talked.

She groaned. Reckless indeed. She couldn't barge through his front door. Not without leaving her reputation in tatters. With a sigh, she retreated to the garden and sank onto a bench. Another roll of thunder. Closer this time. If she left now, she could beat the storm home.

She lifted her gaze to the lone window awash in light. His room. An ancient oak tree stretched its limbs toward the house, as if trying to push the walls down by brute strength. A shadow passed across the window and her heart caught.

If she climbed into the tree, would she be able to see him? One last look. Climb up. Climb down. Easy.

Pushing her hair over one shoulder, she approached the tree. One branch hung low and she swung up onto it. She had to reach high to get ahold of the next and her muscles screamed in protest as she slowly lifted herself up. One more branch and she sat level to his window.

Long clumps of Spanish moss and thick foliage blocked her view.

"Drat."

The thick limb stretched toward the wall and she edged forward. This deep in the tree, a whole colony of little ferns had sprouted along the length of the branch. Her fingers struggled to get a good grip on the damp wood. Still, nothing this mangy old tree threw her way would keep her from getting her glimpse of him.

She shoved a bundle of moss half her size out of the way and finally got a clear view.

Of the corner of his room.

Muttering a curse, she moved farther out on the branch. It sagged beneath her weight and she froze. If she went much farther, it may not support her. But she didn't have to.

Christian strode into view.

In nothing but a towel.

Her pulse slammed in her ears as he shook water from his hair before reaching up to slick it back. Muscles rippled across the flat planes of his stomach and she gulped. Any moment, he would drop the towel to get dressed for bed.

What had she been thinking?

Heat spiraled up and across her cheeks. Watching him felt wrong.

He moved to the bed and his hand went to the linen.

Oh God. She spun. And her hand shot out from beneath her. With a sharp cry, she toppled over the branch. Somehow, she got her fingertips to dig into the slick moss and jerked to a stop, dangling two stories above the ground.

"Who goes there?"

Blast it all.

She lifted one hand and tried to move away from his window, but slipped farther.

Footsteps sounded and a burst of light illuminated her as Christian leaned out the window with a lantern.

His eyes went wide. "Red?"

She looked down. Could she drop without breaking a leg? Doubtful. Still, it seemed a better option than facing him.

"What the hell are you doing here?"

She gritted her teeth. "Nothing."

He stared at her. "Nothing?"

"I was going to ask you something. I changed my mind."

"So you climbed my tree? What was wrong with the front door?"

The heat in her ears surely could start a fire. "I'm sorry to bother you. I'll be on my way."

With a grunt, she attempted a better handhold. As soon as she moved, an ominous crack came from the branch. She froze.

"Give me your hand."

"I'm fine."

"You're going to break your neck."

She bit her lip as the branch dipped lower. "Where have I heard that before?"

"Red." The word rang with authority. An order.

A fat raindrop splattered against her face. Another one. Her hand began to slip and she bit back a curse.

She reached out.

And the branch broke.

"Son of a—" Christian lunged forward and caught her hand.

A moment later, the heavy limb crashed to the ground. Her stomach hung somewhere around her throat as she swung against the wall. She blinked down at the broken branches scattered across the lawn. Christian grunted and began to pull her up. Once she got ahold of the windowsill, she heaved herself the rest of the way in.

When her feet hit the floor, she turned and strode toward the door.

"That's my changing room."

With a grimace, she spun. He stood between her and the main door. Droplets of water glistened in the lantern light on his chest and she went still, her eyes dropping to his bare feet. Heat began to flame anew and she took a step backward.

"Why are you here?" The words came out low. Dangerous.

"I needed to know."

He stepped toward her. "Know what?"

She blinked as rich sandalwood filled her lungs. The room lit in a flash of lightning and thunder shook the house. With a flinch, she swiveled away. The bed sprawled before her, gauzy layers of netting shifting in the breeze, and her throat went raw.

She slowly turned back to him as the heavy patter of rain filled the room. He stood still, dark hair framing his face. Was she brave enough to ask? Could she? His gaze fairly smoldered through her and she took a shaky breath.

Another flash of lightning. She closed her eyes. And as the thunder vibrated through her, she knew.

She loved him.

With every ounce of her heart, she had fallen for him. A man she couldn't have.

"I needed to know what you . . ." She took a breath and tensed as another soft footfall brought him closer. Opened her eyes to find him within reach.

"I think about you constantly."

Her chest constricted at his soft words. "You do?"

His lips twisted into a smile. "I think about how beautiful you are. How brave you are. But most of all, I think about all the things I want to do to you."

She tugged at her neckline as a flutter ran through her stomach. The night had come to an apex. What she chose to say, what she did, would steer the course for what would happen. She could continue blushing and ask to go home. Or . . .

Or she could make one last reckless decision.

"What sort of things?"

His eyes glinted in the lantern light. "First, I would undress you, get you out of that outfit that drives me mad with need."

Her breaths came faster as he stepped even closer and reached out. His knuckles brushed her hair.

"I'd touch you, in all the places I dream of."

The pressure gathered between her legs began to throb.

"Where?" Her voice had been reduced to a breathless whisper.

He stood still, shoulders heaving with each breath.

"Here."

His fingers dropped and grazed her breast, sending a thousand little bursts of fire shooting through her. She pressed into his touch but he moved his hand. Downward. It brushed against her belly, flitted around to her backside. All the while, he kept his contact feather-soft. Want and need collided within her until she couldn't think straight.

He leaned closer, his breath heating her neck. "And here."

When his palm pressed between her legs, a moan caught in her throat. He began to pull away, but she grabbed his hand and held it in place.

"Don't stop."

He let out a growl and tugged her against him, his fingers splayed against her sex.

With trembling fingers, she set her hands on his chest. Ran them down along solid muscles. Stopped at the fold of fabric holding his towel in place. Her thumb slipped beneath it, tangling in damp curls. He rocked his hips into her and she gasped at the bold contact of his erection.

She closed her hand around it, tugging against the towel until it came loose and fell to the floor.

"Red."

His lips crushed against hers.

Chapter Twenty-Nine

S AMANTHA TWINED HER arms around Christian's neck as he kissed her with an intensity rivaling the storm outside. He pressed against her so hard the momentum sent them backward. She fought to keep up with the greedy laps of his tongue as she bumped into the windowsill.

Mist from the heavy downpour clung to her while his hands rubbed up her side. He sucked on her bottom lip and tugged at the buttons of her blouse. She dropped one hand down his back until it rested on one carved buttock. God, he was all strength.

When she squeezed, he groaned and yanked hard, sending buttons clattering across the floor. His lips left hers as he pulled back and gazed at her bared breasts.

"Beautiful."

With a growl, he leaned them out the window and she clung to him once more. Rain pelted her face and ran in rivulets down her chest. He followed the watery trail with his mouth and her head fell back. His mouth closed hot and wet around one nipple and she cried out, the sound lost in the storm.

Branches clashed above them in the wind and the sky lit in flashes of white and blue. All that energy. Nothing compared to what raged inside her.

The hard length of him pressed between her parted legs as she wrapped them around his waist. With nothing but the fabric of her breeches between them, a wicked heat spread from the intimate contact. She craned her neck to the side, but her thigh obscured the view.

When Christian released one nipple and moved to the other, her hands began slipping on his slick skin. He tightened his grip, one palm coming to rest between her shoulders. She took advantage of the stability and slid a hand between their bodies. Soft velvet and solid steel brushed against her fingertips a moment later and she marveled at the contradictions.

With one thrust, he pushed himself fully into her hand. Closing around it, she moved up and down along the length. He wrenched his head away with a moan and pulled them back inside. His hands moved to her bottom, holding her tight against him as he spun to lean against the wall.

Samantha pressed her lips to his collarbone, grazing her teeth across his skin and he throbbed in her fingers. Leaning back, she glanced down. His hips rocked a slow rhythm as he slid himself back and forth in her grip. Her forehead dipped against his chest. Was it her imagination, or did he swell ever so slightly each time her hand reached the base?

What would he do if she kissed him there?

He bent to her ear. "What are you thinking?"

"On the beach . . ." She trailed off as he nibbled her earlobe. "What you did to me . . ."

A soft hum came in response.

"Can a woman do that to a man?"

He went still. "Yes."

"I'd like to."

His head fell back, bumping into the wall, and he stared at the ceiling. "I'm not sure I could bear it, Red."

But he dropped her to her feet, running his fingertips up and down her back. She copied the movement with her free hand and his eyes drifted shut. Her pulse began to hammer out an erratic tune as she tilted her head and kissed above one flat nipple.

The wild beat of his heart pulsed into her lips. She moved down in an ever-so-slow path, until she fell to her knees. Dark hair curled around her knuckles when she pushed her hand back, exposing as much of him as possible.

The heat at her core became a raging fire while she stared at him. A vein pulsed beneath her fingers, tawny skin stretched taut. She leaned closer and breathed in his musky scent, soap and sandalwood and something else all colliding in her nose. A carnal need to taste him filled her and she touched her lips to the rounded tip.

She planted a small kiss there. Brushed her mouth across smooth skin. Flicked her tongue out.

He groaned and gave a gentle rock into her caress.

"Is this good?"

"God, Red . . ." His breath came out in a shudder and his fingers closed around handfuls of her hair. "I . . . it's . . ."

Her lips curved against him.

Speechless was good.

She ran her tongue in a circle before tracing the little ridge encircling the head of his manhood. He quivered beneath her fisted palm and a heady thrill ran through her. When she licked harder, his hips left the wall.

"Christian." His name escaped her, reverberating back with each muffled syllable wrapped in husky need.

She opened her mouth, letting him slide a fraction inside and he growled, the low sound vibrating through him at the same time as a roll of thunder. The grip he held in her hair tightened, each tug sending little waves of pain entwined with pleasure right to her core.

Her teeth scraped across him as she let him in farther. Holding him like this, in her mouth, sent the space between her legs pulsing. She began to emulate the movement she wanted *there*. In and out, little wet noises punctuated the air.

How deep could she take him?

She opened wide and slowly, ever so slowly, slid forward. A strangled sound came from above her when his dark hairs tickled her nose.

"Dear God. I can't." He pulled her head away from him, loosing her contact on him in one slick motion. "Any more and

I'll lose control."

She pressed one last kiss to him and rested her forehead in the hollow between his thigh and manhood. "That sounds rather nice."

"I want to be inside you when that happens, love."

The word sent an ache through her as she lifted her gaze to meet the dark intensity of his. She nuzzled her nose into the coarse curls brushing her cheek and ran a single finger along his length, pausing when she encountered a sticky drop of moisture at the very end. He stumbled to the side and pulled her to her feet, capturing her mouth with his before she could protest.

His hands skimmed down her arms and he interlocked his fingers with hers. Pulling her arms back, he dropped his lips to her neck and began to suck. She tried to reach out to him, but he held her hands just beyond reach. Without being able to support her weight on him, her knees began to shake.

He pivoted so her back was to the bed and dropped his mouth to the valley between her breasts. The soft touch sent her back arching and her nails dug into his fingers.

"Christian. Please."

A wicked smile played across his lips as he touched them to one aching nipple. He licked. Blew a puff of air across it. She gasped out with a shiver as the already-hard point tightened further. He took a step into her, nudging her backward. Again. And again.

Until the bed bumped against her thighs.

He released her hands and swept the netting aside. A moment later, her blouse fluttered to the floor. Without wasting time, he unbuttoned the fall of her breeches and humid night air brushed across her damp skin.

The pants sagged open and his knuckles brushed into copper curls. An approving murmur rumbled through his throat as he flipped his hand and cupped her. When he pressed a finger into the swirling heat at her core, she grabbed at his shoulders.

"I can't tell you how many times I've dreamed of this." His

finger slid into a slick pool of wetness and he bent to her ear. "Feel how ready you are for me?"

Hot breath fell across her neck and her eyes drifted shut as a thousand prickles of sensation swept over her. If she could capture one feeling to commit to memory, that would be it. His finger slipped into her and she bit at the skin beneath his collarbone to keep from crying out. No. Definitely *that* feeling. Delicate and intense all at once while sending her pulse hammering.

He pulled free. Plunged back in. Caught her gasp with his mouth.

The solid weight of his chest pressed into her shoulders, followed by the conspicuous jab of his erection at her belly. Beneath his force, she sat on the bed. Soft linen tangled in her fingers as he deepened the kiss. His gentle pressure increased until she fell back into the plush sheets and he covered her body with his. Her mind began to unravel at her meager attempt to catalogue *this* feeling.

She lifted her hips and ground them against Christian's as he fumbled with the waistband of her breeches. He began to peel them down and she drew her legs up to help. They tangled around her boots and he let out a growl. Breaking the kiss, he stood. Warm lantern light washed over him and her breath caught at the sight of him standing between her legs. The flickering glow accentuated every muscle, the barely-there curve of his side where it met his hip. The proud display of everything that made him a man hanging in plain sight.

He tugged at her laces and tossed the boots aside with her breeches following seconds later. His gaze burned into her and she lifted one hand to cover herself.

"Don't." She stilled and he took her knees and spread her open to him. "Now this? I didn't dare let myself dream of this."

His palms moved down her thighs until he framed her sex between his hands. Muscles deep inside her clenched and released, as if they could beckon him to fully touch her. Both thumbs moved to part her and one settled on the spot where all the throbbing pressure had built up. This time, she did cry out.

He twisted in tiny circles, dipping into her wetness and drawing it up until the slippery friction brought her hips off the bed. She flung her hands over her head, grasping for something, anything, her fingers curling into a pillow. His lips pressed to the skin inside one knee and she jerked at the hot tingle it sent through her.

The speed of his finger increased and the spiraling sensation already building began to wind tighter. Her release. Now that she understood what it was, she urged it on, climbing higher and higher until she thrashed beneath his touch. Just when she began to teeter over the edge, his thumb disappeared.

"Christian!" His name came out on a strangled cry as she hooked her legs behind his to keep him from retreating.

He didn't move. Instead, his hands slid to her hips and he tugged her closer. Closer. Until her bottom reached the edge of the bed. The solid heft of his erection rested at the juncture of her thighs, her curls nesting around him. She arched from the sheets, scooting even closer and he let out a soft chuckle.

"Not so fast."

He began to slide himself up and down until her chest felt like it might explode. Each gentle caress sent her careening toward the release still hovering out of reach. And then he slipped down farther, his hands gripping her thighs as they quivered. Holding her open. He pressed *there*. At her opening.

She might die. Perhaps she already had.

He shifted on his feet and a blessed pressure began to fill her. Her legs tightened around his waist. Tried to pull him in deeper. The shadows in his eyes intensified as he gazed down at her. "This is so much better than anything I ever dreamed."

Samantha let out a whimper when he stopped his nearly imperceptible movement. Pulled himself free. Pushed back in. He repeated the motion until her hips bucked against him.

Her entire existence boiled down to this single moment.

They stared at each other, chests rising and falling in rapid unison. Christian's fingers dug into her hips, holding her steady. Her eyes began to drift shut.

No. She snapped them open. Not a chance she was missing this.

After one last withdrawal, the throbbing tip of him barely touching her, he slammed forward. The bed jerked with the force and she cried out at the fierce waves of feeling bursting through her as he stretched her fully.

His head fell back, dark hair cascading over his shoulders and his mouth went slack, lips parted in a moan that went straight to her core. The corded muscles in his arms trembled as he held her against him, grinding his hips in a slow circle as she adjusted to the intrusion.

"So wet. So tight. So good." The words tumbled from his mouth one after another, hardly recognizable in a reverent whisper.

She rocked into him, tilting her hips to allow him better access and he let out a soft curse. The movement seemed to unlock a tempest in him and he began thrusting with wild abandon. So much feeling. Had it been like this before? She couldn't remember. Couldn't think straight as her body fairly vibrated around him. Their grunts came out in sync with each deep bump against the heart of her sex.

In one abrupt movement, he lifted her into him. She let out a yelp as he climbed onto the bed without breaking contact or rhythm. Once his knees hit the mattress, he lifted one slender leg over his shoulder and tilted to the side. He leaned over her until she could hardly bear the stretch. At that exact moment, his finger settled over the throbbing little nub where all the energy in her body had centered.

The room began to spin as he worked the spot in rapid strokes while slowing the rest of his movements. Each deep plunge sent her careening toward her release. He dropped her leg and bent his lips to hers, murmuring nonsensical words. So close.

Her eyes fluttered shut and the rattle of rain on the shutters melded with the sounds of their joining.

This . . . this was heaven. His tongue pressed into her mouth at the same time his finger switched directions. And she leaped from that high-up ledge. One big shuddering breath and her world exploded.

He caught her screams as her legs went rigid and her back arched from the bed. Each surge of pleasure sent her muscles clamping around him, the delightful squeezes of pressure making her soar even higher. He continued his pace, holding her against him as the wild feelings began to subside and her body went limp. Feather-soft kisses covered her cheeks and neck.

"Samantha." Her name came out on a shaky breath as Christian slowed to a stop.

She opened her eyes and met his hooded gaze.

"Samantha."

Time went still as her chest constricted. *Samantha.* The way he said it, full of reverence, sent a burst of warmth blossoming around her heart.

God, she would never forget this moment.

His eyes closed. His head fell back.

Samantha felt him surge inside her, flaring within her swollen heat, a single moment before he went tense. His hoarse shout came at the same time a rumble of thunder rocked through them and his hips collided with hers in a heavy thrust. Her hands went to his backside, pulling him deeper as he trembled over her.

The slack lines around his mouth slowly transformed into a contented smile as the pulsing at her core subsided. A sheen of sweat glistened on his brow and she reached up to brush a damp curl away as the room lit in a flash of lightning. He bent and pressed his lips to her forehead in a tender kiss, his ragged breaths puffing around her face. One last thrust, one last moan, and he collapsed at her side.

SAMANTHA'S EYES CRACKED open and she blinked at the soft light of dawn. She'd overslept. With a frown, she began to roll over. The fresh scent of rain filled her lungs. Sandalwood. She went still. Breathed in again.

Did the scent linger from her dreams?

Bits and flashes came to her. Tan skin. Forest-green eyes. The mouth she dreamed of so often. Kissing her. Calling out her name.

Her real name.

Her heart began to thump as she shifted her legs. A swollen ache ran from her core as a ray of sunlight pierced the room, reflecting off yellow wallpaper.

Not her room.

Her lips curved as the full memory of last night flooded through her. It had all happened. Every delicious bit. She reached next to her, fingers settling on cool sheets, and jerked upright.

She was alone.

A chill ran through her as she took in Christian's room. A polished desk sat next to the window, the chair pushed beneath it just right. A few paintings on the wall. An armchair next to a spotless hearth. Every bit as immaculate as his cabin.

Even her clothes were folded in a neat pile on the end of the bed.

She reached forward and picked up her blouse, running her fingers over the torn buttonholes. The erratic beat of her heart began to slow. Where had he gone? Did he regret last night?

Her blood went cold.

He'd told her he would be setting sail. What if he'd left?

With a strangled breath, she began to yank the blouse on. She needed to get home before anyone realized where she was. The garment hung wide open and she forced back a laugh. If anyone saw her, she was doomed.

She swung her feet to the floor and grabbed her breeches and started toward Christian's dressing room. Hopefully she could make one of his shirts work. Before she made it two steps, the door creaked behind her.

Her heart seized and she spun, pressing the folded breeches between her legs.

"Now, this is a sight I could get used to."

Christian stood in the doorway, holding a tray with two steaming cups. He'd dressed, trousers stretched across his thighs and white shirt only half-buttoned. The bare expanse of his chest and the dark swath of hair sent her pulse skyrocketing.

She glanced down at her exposed breasts and heat burst across her cheeks. Her nipples hardened and she went even hotter.

Christian chuckled and crossed the room. He deposited the tray on the bed and reached out for her.

"Good morning, beautiful."

She searched his face, all her emotions at war within her.

He cupped her cheek. "What's wrong?"

"I—I thought you left."

His other arm snaked around her back and drew her against him. "Why would I leave?"

"Because . . ." She took a shallow breath. "Because of last night?"

Christian slipped his hands beneath her blouse and ran them up and down her back. "Last night was the single greatest night of my existence." The words came out soft against her ear and she shivered.

"You said you were going to sail today."

Christian nibbled her earlobe and she let out a soft gasp as all the heat from her blush seemed to refocus straight between her legs. "I have something to show you."

With a gentle tug, he guided her to his desk. A single sheet of parchment lay there with freshly inked lines of text scrawled out. A letter.

"Sit."

She did and couldn't help reading the first line.

I, Christian William Thompson, have come to the regrettable decision that I ought not retain my Commission in the navy.

Her brows pushed together. "What is this?"

"Keep reading."

A tingle began in the base of her neck, slowly spreading outward, and she took a deep breath before continuing.

I therefore tender my resignation which I request you will recommend for acceptance.

She jerked her head up. "You're resigning?"

"After the events of the last month, I realized I cannot continue this job with a clear conscience."

He picked up a white feathered quill and dipped the tip into his inkwell.

"I thought my calling in life was to mete justice out on the seas. To spend my life married to the ocean. But I made a mistake. I never made room in my plans for love." He cleared his throat. "I was wrong."

Her chest seized. What was he trying to say?

"I didn't lie last night when I told you I think about you constantly. It's not just my mind you fill. It's my heart. This morning, when I woke up and thought about my voyage, I couldn't bear the thought of leaving you."

He leaned over and scratched his signature across the bottom of the document before dropping the feather with a flourish.

Her heart caught in her throat and she turned to find him kneeling next to her.

"I've made a mess of things, and I hope you can forgive me. I should have never accepted your promise to stop sailing. It was a sacrifice you should have never been forced to make."

She drew in a ragged breath as the chasm in her heart threatened to reopen. "I don't regret it. I'd do anything—"

He brought a finger to her lips. "You should never be forced to choose between your happiness and your family."

Family.

Her chest tightened. "Your father. . ."

Christian dropped his head and pressed his eyes closed. "The things he did were terrible beyond belief. I understand if you hate me for it."

She shook her head and fumbled for his hand, wrapping her fingers around his. "No. I could never. What he did. . ." She took a steadying breath. "You had nothing to do with any of it. You are your own man. An admirable one at that."

His jaw trembled. "I do not deserve you."

A shaky laugh escaped her. "I could say the same."

"I think. . ." A faint smile played across his lips. "I think we need a new beginning."

A spark of hope ignited deep within her. Was it possible? Could they truly start anew?

"I love you, Samantha. If the last few weeks have taught me anything, it's that I cannot live without you." He squeezed her hand. "I cannot promise I'll be perfect. But I can promise to weather life's storms at your side. To give you the freedom to do the things that bring you happiness. To never stop loving you."

Samantha's lungs stopped working and the room swam around her. This couldn't be happening. Her eyes flitted to the bed. Had she fallen back asleep? He cleared his throat and she snapped her gaze back to him.

"Will you marry me?"

A dream. A wonderful and terrible dream, tempting her with her heart's greatest desires. Her vision swam as a roar filled her ears. *Breathe.* His other palm settled on her knee and she blinked down at it.

Not a dream.

Tears streamed down her cheeks and he lifted a thumb to one wet trail. "Say something."

She reached out through the blur and grasped his hand.

"I love you, Christian. So much it hurts." A sob broke free and he pulled her into his chest. "I didn't think you would ever . . . I mean, look at me. I'm—"

He pressed a finger to her lips. "Is that a yes?"

She managed a nod and he stood, lifting her into his arms with a grin. "Good. How about some breakfast before I show you just how much I love you?"

Epilogue

One month later
Savannah, GA

SAMANTHA SWALLOWED, HER feet rooted in place. Blue sky stretched overhead and clumps of Spanish moss draped from the branches shading the large crowd gathered in front of her. Heat prickled across her skin, a flush rising above her lace neckline.

"I now pronounce you man and wife."

The words echoed in her ears as the scene around her faded away until only one thing remained.

Christian stood there, clasping her hands in his with a crooked grin across his lips. His formal grey morning coat suited him—better than his navy uniform—and she'd spent the better part of the last half hour trying to keep her eyes above his waistline. Because white breeches clung to him like a second skin, showing every magnificently sculpted part of him.

His boots squeaked as he closed the distance between them and bent his lips to hers. He gave her an entirely appropriate quick kiss and began to pull away. She tightened her fingers around his.

Not so fast.

Samantha lifted onto tiptoes and tugged him back. He winked and drew one hand away to sweep his hat off. When their mouths met, he held the hat in front of them. A few onlookers let out whoops, and a few more released hearty "boos" at being denied the chance to witness. She grinned against the crush of Christian's lips.

His tongue swept inside her mouth and she stumbled into him, her knees weak.

He let out a soft growl. "Careful, Red. I'm a man, not a saint."

The pastor coughed behind them.

With a throaty giggle, Samantha broke the kiss. Christian placed one more on her forehead before swooping the hat back on and offering her his elbow. They passed through the throngs of people until they reached the street.

He stopped and turned to her. "Hello, wife."

"Hello, husband."

Husband and wife.

A warm blossom bloomed in her chest. She reached up and ran a finger across his lips. "Dare I ask why you're smiling like that?"

Bending, he plucked a violet sprig of salvia. "Can't a groom be happy on his wedding day?"

He tucked it into her neckline above the swell of one breast, the color a pretty contrast to the sapphire-blue taffeta gown and its white lace trim. She glanced up at the sun. Already so warm. Thank goodness for the short cap sleeves.

Setting one hand on Christian's arm, she frowned. "You must be sweltering."

He only grinned and nodded behind her. Isaac strode toward them, the bright gold buttons of his navy uniform glistening in the sun.

"Many congratulations." He bowed. "You look stunning, Mrs. Thompson."

She gave herself a little pinch. The morning had floated by like a dream, each part seeming too good to be true. *Mrs. Thompson.* She tested the word on her tongue. Christian gave her a little nudge and she started as Isaac chuckled.

"Thank you. I'm so glad you could make it before your voyage."

"Wouldn't have missed it for the world."

"What time do you leave?" Christian had tensed ever so slightly.

Isaac turned toward the river, a few blocks down. "We'll sail at noon. I'm sorry I'll miss the luncheon. If we don't make good time, someone's going to owe the governor of Tortuga a lot of money. And if Thorne returned to the Caribbean, chances are someone on that island will know."

Christian gave a tight nod. "Be safe."

When his friend walked away, Samantha squeezed his arm. "Are you alright?"

"It's hard. Knowing he's still out there. Knowing my best friend has been tasked with bringing him in." He shifted his hat. "Is it wrong to hope he doesn't catch him?"

She chewed on her cheek, trying to find the right words.

He drew her closer and set his hand over hers. "I'm sorry. Today is about us. We should be enjoying this to the fullest."

Her nose scrunched. "But your feelings matter too."

"Later." He pulled her hand free and lifted it to his lips. "You have the rest of my life to worry about me. For now, we have a wedding luncheon to go to."

He guided her across the street. She looked back with a frown. They walked toward the river. Away from the carriage.

When she stepped up off the street, her calf protested and she stumbled.

"Hold on." She drew to a stop and hitched her skirt up "I have a gift for you. I can't wait any longer."

His brows drew up. "My God, Red. Not here. I'll admit I cannot wait either, but let's not give the town something to gossip about."

A blush flamed across her cheeks. "Very funny."

Christian barked out a laugh as her boot became visible. "Should have known you weren't proper beneath those skirts."

She pulled a package free and rubbed her aching calf. "I needed somewhere to put this."

He took it from her and ran a finger over the embossed paper. "This day is already gift enough."

His finger slipped beneath the ribbon and tugged it free. Polished brass shone in the sunlight and his eyes widened. It had taken her a month to find a compass similar to the one he had lost, and another week for a jeweler to set the coin in the lid. The tarnished gold of the medallion glimmered beneath his fingertip.

"One from the cave."

Her pulse quickened as she remembered his body covering hers, the sound of coins tinkling in her ears.

"It's perfect." Warm lips pressed against hers.

She melted into the kiss, her heart beating a frantic tune. Pushing her hands beneath his jacket, she tugged his shirt free. With a groan, he pulled away and glanced around them.

"What was I saying about gossip?" He slipped the compass in his jacket pocket and his lopsided grin returned. "I have a surprise for you as well."

Eager anticipation danced across his face and she couldn't help but smile. "I don't need a gift."

"Trust me, you'll love it." He swiveled her around. "Close your eyes."

She did and he guided her up the street, made a turn. Another turn. They stopped.

"Keep them closed." A moment later, her feet swept out from beneath her and she cried out as he picked her up.

He began to climb down stairs. "Almost there."

When they reached the bottom, he set her down and covered her eyes with his hands. He led her a few more steps. Seagulls screeched and the breeze picked up.

The docks.

He dropped his hands.

She squinted in the bright sun. A sleek schooner floated in front of them. The planks on deck had been polished so smooth they gleamed. A pretty white stripe had been painted above the waterline and crisp white sails were reefed. A gorgeous vessel.

He wrapped an arm around her shoulder. "What do you think?"

"I don't understand."

"It's yours."

Tears welled in her eyes. "But I made a promise."

He pulled her into his embrace and pressed his lips to her forehead. "That promise was made to a lieutenant." Swiveling his head back and forth, he grinned anew. "And I don't see any lieutenants here."

She blinked up at him. "I could never see you as a pirate."

"Who said anything about pirating?" He wiped one tear away and kissed her again. "But adventuring . . . adventuring sounds like a grand idea."

Her heart jumped into her throat and she threw her arms around his neck. "Do you really mean it?"

He ran his hands down to her waist. "I meant what I said that morning in my room. I'll never ask you to sacrifice your happiness. Not for me. Not for anyone."

She pulled back and twisted toward the ship once more. The freshly painted nameplate caught her eyes and she let out a half laugh. *Red Siren.*

Christian noticed the direction of her stare and nuzzled into her hair. "I hope you don't mind her name. I'll never forget the day when a certain red siren swept in and brought me to my knees."

"Served you right for calling me a wench."

His teeth grazed her neck. "As long as you're my wench, I see no problem there."

She giggled and pulled away. "Can we go aboard?"

He swept his hand out. "After you."

With long steps, she raced up the gangplank. Once onboard, she ran her fingers over every surface she could touch. Smooth railings. Tightly woven ropes. Warm iron fastenings. Christian followed a few paces back.

At the helm, she gripped two spokes and let her eyes fall shut.

The river's gentle current pressed against the hull. She tested the wheel and her lips curved. A responsive rudder. A breeze pushed past them and the ship let out a soft sigh.

Christian's hands closed over hers and she lifted her lids. Warmth spread up her arms as he positioned himself behind her. "I never thought it would be possible. To find someone that shares my love of the sea."

She twisted to meet his sparkling green gaze. "And I didn't dare imagine I'd ever find a man who would let me."

He leaned down and caught her lips with his. "Good thing I found myself a lady of the sea."

The contact of his body pressing against her back sent a little thrill up her spine and she leaned her weight into him. They stood that way for a while, staring out over the water. A quiet current of energy ran through the ship and Samantha let out a happy sigh.

Adventuring. So many places they could go. Islands to explore, goods to barter. All with the man she loved at her side. For the first time, she could see her future clearly. Together, they would chart their own legacy.

Christian pulled his hands free. "Shall we go below?"

She followed him down the steps and stared at the carved doors leading to the captain's quarters. Each one had been engraved with a figure. The two were locked in battle, swords crossing over each door. A man in a cocked hat and a woman with wavy hair flowing behind her.

Reaching out, she ran a reverent finger over the man's face. "It's us. This ship holds our past."

He opened one door with a smile. "Not just our past. Today. Tomorrow. The rest of our lives."

Inside, the citrusy scent of wood oil filled her nose. A large desk was centered before the big windows with two chairs. Shelves stretched along a wall, one already full of shells. But most impressive of all, tucked into the other wall, a huge captain's bed, turned down with fresh linens. She smiled and strode to the desk, where a map was laid out.

Tracing her finger along the coastline, she met Christian's gaze. "Where to first?"

He joined her and inspected the map. Pointed to Bermuda. Tapped on Florida. Ran his palm over the Caribbean. Swept his hand away. A moment later, his fingers tangled in her laces and her dress began to loosen.

"First stop? The bed."